THE
SAMARITAN

Stephen Besecker

bancroft
press

Published by Bancroft Press ("Books that enlighten")
P.O. Box 65360, Baltimore, MD 21209
800-637-7377
410-764-1967 (fax)
www.bancroftpress.com

Jacket photography and design: Jeff Fisher/FCI Photography
Original cover concept: Kate Rawlings
Interior design: Tracy Copes, Daft Generation
Author photo: Michelle Zurowski

Printed in the United States of America

ISBN 978-1-61088-009-1 (cloth)
ISBN 978-1-61088-026-8 (paper)
LCCN 2011927127

First Edition

For my wife, Sue, who continually astounds me with her
unconditional love and support. I love you very much.

For my three children, Kevin, Alexandra, and Amy.
You inspire me every single day.

For my mother, Grace, and little sister, Annie, who were not
around to read this novel. I am humbled and haunted
by my memories of you both.

And for my father, Howard, who never stopped believing in me.
I love you, Dad.

Revenge is an act of passion; vengeance of justice.

Injuries are revenged; crimes are avenged.

— *Joseph Joubert*

There's nothing you can know that isn't known.

Nothing that you can see that isn't shown.

Nowhere you can be that isn't where

you're meant to be . . .

—*John Lennon and Paul McCartney*

PROLOGUE

Bronx (November)

L ike any experienced big-game hunter, the man shouldering the high-powered sniper's rifle ignored the elements and focused on opportunity. The temperature hovered near thirty degrees Fahrenheit. Around him, light intermittent flurries—the season's first traceable snow—fell, driven by gusts reaching fifteen miles per hour. At his back, the eastern horizon slowly brightened, ushering in a late November day.

The hunter wore black insulated boots, a black Gore-Tex hoodie, and thermal underwear underneath his dark blue jeans. He blended in perfectly with the flat, tarred roof of the Bronx building, and except for two eyeholes in the mask, known in military circles around the world as a balaclava, his face was completely covered, his composed expression hidden.

As he'd done for the past hour, the hunter kept his movement to a minimum. After weeks of exhausting reconnaissance, the first steps toward the inevitable shooting war in and around the five boroughs of New York City were about to be taken.

The sniper's rifle—a single shot M40A3 semiautomatic with a specially-made sound suppressor—rested comfortably against his right shoulder. He'd chosen a point of reference 324 yards from his perch. Pressing his eye to the Leupold scope, the hunter sighted a dented garbage can and once again calculated the wind's influence at this distance. Minimal. No problem. Control and discipline were his watchwords this morning. *Breathe slowly* was his mantra.

Just as he'd been taught, the hunter practiced patience, overcame emotion, and demanded calm. His resting pulse rate, which he'd monitored over the past three months, was a controlled sixty beats per minute. Steely eyes peered through the holes in his balaclava as his right index finger rested on the M40's trigger. Like the snowflakes passing through the scope's view, the seconds melted away. The time of reckoning was fast approaching.

The rifle's barrel rested on a bipod some sixty feet above 161st Street. Things were quiet in the middle-class neighborhood. That was about to change.

On the opposite side of the street, a brownstone door opened and closed. An olive-skinned, third-generation Italian-American man, his hair slicked back with a generous amount of gel, stepped into the cold morning air, his breath visible with every exhalation. The target rubbed his gloved hands together to keep warm.

The hunter shifted his weight just so. As he'd anticipated, his heart rate increased slightly as his index finger curled around the trigger.

The target, a man in his late twenties, wore a black leather jacket, designer jeans, and black Gucci shoes. He moved into the scope's kill zone.

Like dozens of mornings before, the man he intended to assassinate, a high-ranking member of a powerful New York City crime family, stood on the top step outside his home, his head turning left and right, observing the street.

The hunter now centered the crosshairs on the target's left eye, relaxed, slowly emptied his lungs, and gently squeezed the trigger. There was a metallic *click*, and a distinct *pop*, and a tongue of fire leapt from the end of the sound suppressor as the rifle bucked. Locked in the moment, the hunter felt and heard nothing; the results were all that mattered.

Three hundred twenty-three yards away, the target's head exploded as if a stick of dynamite had been placed inside an overripe cantaloupe. The .762-millimeter round tore through his handsome face, liquefying his brain and sending shards of skull rocketing against the wooden door that led into his brownstone. A fine pink mist quickly dissipated in the light snow. The man crumpled to the concrete steps, then slipped onto the sidewalk like a sack of sand, his body mostly hidden by a hedgerow.

A Honda Civic passed without pause, the driver oblivious to the murderer or the victim in his midst. An elderly woman wearing an oversized winter parka, taking her toy poodle for an early morning stroll, didn't see a thing. Neither did the two boys on their way to the Catholic elementary school.

With his head tipped back, the hunter's brown eyes moved away from the scope and quickly assessed the situation. Killing the target was supposed to mitigate the pain that began back in August, and it had to some degree, but the relief lasted only seconds. Now he felt no satisfaction whatsoever. Oddly enough, he experienced no emotion at all—and maybe that was for the best.

A car horn blared like an alarm clock. As if awakened from a dream, the hunter was suddenly conscious of the cold, the ache in his lower back, his heavy breathing, and the activity on the street below. An older teenage boy wearing a New York Giants jacket now stood over the headless corpse. Shrieking for help, the boy stumbled backwards over the dormant hedge.

"I'm sorry about that, kid," the hunter murmured. He calmly picked up the ejected shell near his boot, broke down the rifle, and stuffed the three sections into a tattered duffle bag. Before he headed for the fire escape at the back of the three-story building, he tossed a different shell casing near the brick parapet, peeled off his balaclava, and shoved it into his bag.

Two minutes later, the hunter was strolling west on Prospect Avenue, the cold morning breeze at his back.

PART 1
Before

CHAPTER 1

Manhattan, New York

Just as the private elevator carrying Emily Silverstone reached the sixteenth-floor penthouse suite, a thunderous explosion blew the apartment building's double glass doors and much of the brick and steel façade into the street-level lobby. Outside the Fifth Avenue building, where Jeremy Silverstone's black limousine had been idling in the frigid December night, pieces of charred steel, burning upholstery, and a single mangled axle smoldered in a deep, blackened crater.

And so a life had ended—or begun, depending upon one's point of view.

The insatiable New York media scrutinized the brilliant financier's violent death as only the media can. And though more than five years had now passed since the bomb had detonated outside one of Manhattan's most exclusive East Side properties, an air of skepticism still hung over a select group of irate investors, all of whom the victim had monetarily exploited before the limousine's explosion presumably ended his life.

As was exhaustively reported at the time, the dead man in question had been professionally assassinated at the direction of a bitter business associate, an irate client, or one of the many powerful political figures embarrassed by a very public scandal. After numerous investigations, conducted by no fewer than five state and federal agencies, the evidence left no doubt that the blast, which ripped apart the armor-plated limousine, had been intentional. And inside Washington's beltway, it was believed that Jeremy Silverstone's secrets had been permanently silenced.

The *New York Post* headline got it right: "SILVERSTONE GOES OUT WITH A BANG."

Privately, many breathed a heavy sigh of relief.

The recently elected New York State attorney general had promised a lengthy list of indictments against Silverstone and his associates as early as February. Painted as a monster who raided retirement accounts and mortgaged his clients' futures by purchasing subprime loans and other risky paper, Silverstone had become a political poison pill—a financial outcast.

Crumbling on a foundation of mud and straw, Silverstone's multi-billion-dollar empire was about to be decimated by a violent storm. His company hemorrhaged money from the very powerful investors who had trusted this new breed of Wall Street wizard. His unstable global firm would soon topple, taking with it a tidy percentage of fortunes from many of America's most prominent citizens: Hollywood celebrities, music icons, professional athletes, politicians, and business giants. No one was immune. Silverstone had not only laundered their money through an elaborate banking system with strong ties to the drug cartels in Mexico, Colombia, and the Dominican Republic, but he'd also made the unfortunate mistake of getting caught. Old money and squeaky-clean reputations were at stake.

And then the whispers about Silverstone's cooperation with the feds grew louder. Anonymous sources insisted he was about to roll over and implicate others. For some, that betrayal could not be tolerated.

The public's interest in the explosion waned, but as with most scandalous conspiracies, unresolved questions and theories lingered—even after five long years. Who paid to have Jeremy Silverstone killed? And why? What damning evidence did he hold?

Even the location of most of the missing $250 million was a mystery.

To those intimately familiar with Silverstone's life and gruesome death, an additional question—one more sinister in nature—would not fade away entirely: Did he really die that snowy December night in New York City?

Bahamas

Securing the monopod to the thirty-eight-foot fishing boat's port quarter, CIA field operative Kevin Easter removed his straw hat and tucked his long black hair behind his ears. He pressed his right eye to the viewfinder, focused the telephoto lens attached to the Nikon D2X, and surveyed the exotic landscape while recalling some of the more graphic details of Mr. Jeremy Silverstone's staged death.

A warm August breeze gently washed over the palm trees, grass huts, and miles of white sand. A multi-million-dollar Mediterranean-style home—expansive, modern, and very private—stood as a centerpiece to this portion of paradise. A wrought-iron fence ran along the property's perimeter—a perimeter kept secure by two sentries carrying MP7 assault rifles. Though Easter had no intention of breaching the security, he knew there were seventeen cameras, numerous motion detectors, and hundreds of pressure pads and thermo-activated sensors placed in and around the estate. The message to outsiders was loud and clear: You are not welcome here.

All of this information would be in his final report, the one he would hand-deliver to his employer within the next few days.

The background on Silverstone—a manila folder with the title *GREENBACK* and a red stripe indicating its top-secret classification, along with an encrypted CD—had been given to Easter by Jack Slattery, the deputy director for intelligence of the Central Intelligence Agency, six weeks earlier. From all indications, its classified contents neglected very little of the life and purported death of Silverstone, a financial, political, and social icon who'd lived and worked in New York City almost his entire life. Still, finding his latest subject had taken Easter nearly a month, even though a few key CIA analysts already suspected Jeremy Silverstone was indeed a fugitive, living under the radar south of the United States border. An innocent wire transfer—one a Bahamian bank manager had botched—set off an alarm inside the Agency. It had been their first solid starting point in five years.

Click, click, click, click, click. The high-speed shutter softly whirred. It was the second card of images Easter had shot since arriving at Andros, the Bahamas' largest island, one week earlier. Easter, who usually went by the nickname "Hatch," could sense the hunt's conclusion.

In his four years as a CIA field operative, there had been longer searches with more formidable quarry than Silverstone, but those had been political and military adversaries, all foreign and all labeled enemies of the United States. Up until six weeks ago, Hatch had never tracked an American citizen—a job typically left to the FBI.

Hatch was a man of extraordinary talents, with skills acquired from his grandfather, Low Dog, and honed in his youth on a Western New York Indian reservation. The Central Intelligence Agency not only furthered Hatch's education—both formal and nontraditional—but the clandestine organization also brought needed purpose and stability to his life.

What would eventually happen to this particular fugitive, once located, was of little concern to Hatch, but the fact that one of the world's best hunters of men was tracking Silverstone meant that his quarry, in faking his death and stealing nearly a quarter-billion dollars, had exploited the wrong people. A select few, with strong ties to the Thorn administration, wanted closure.

Sitting in a chaise lounge in the bright Bahamian sun 620 yards from Hatch's chartered fishing boat, Jeremy Silverstone was five years and 4,000 miles from his Manhattan life. The man considered legally dead back in the United States sipped something from a tall blue glass and read a hardcover thriller by Daniel Silva. Much thinner than in the dossier's three color photographs (head shots from his bankrupted company's last financial statement), Silverstone's sun-bleached hair was longer—nearly touching his shoulders. He looked refreshed and content with his change in venue. A multi-million-dollar estate on a private beach in the Bahamas could do that, Hatch thought, as could a pile of stolen money, servants, armed guards, two girlfriends, a new name, expensive toys, and a blank history.

But in today's world, it was nearly impossible to just disappear, especially for someone with expensive tastes and habits.

"Nice tan, Jeremy," Hatch said to himself. *Click, click, click, click.* "C'mon, how about a close-up of those dentures? Smile."

The evidence of Silverstone's fiery demise had included a few teeth, along with some hair, traces of blood, and fingernails scattered over snow-covered Fifth Avenue.

Click, click, click.

Turning toward the captain, Hatch cupped his hand to his mouth and shouted, "Take us in another fifty meters, Mr. Martinez! Then we'll call it a day."

Tipping his Miami Dolphins cap, the leathery-faced black man, a native of Andros Island, replied in British-accented English, "As you wish, Mr. Hatch, sir."

Hatch brought the Nikon camera around again. "Give me a quarter-billion-dollar smile, Jeremy. Come on." He turned the aperture ring, sharpened the frame, and drew in Silverstone's handsome face. "You are lookin' mighty fine." *Click, click, click, click.*

Nervously stroking his unshaven face, the captain looked down from the helm. "Ready to move on, Mr. Hatch?"

The CIA field operative peeked at his watch, then back to the man he'd come to depend upon these past few weeks. "How's the fishing around here, Captain?"

An errant gust swept Hatch's fine hair off his tanned face and revealed much of his lineage—soft features with brown oval eyes–and little about his life. He had a slight build, and his baby face, its walnut complexion darkened from his time on Andros, easily concealed the difficulties of his youth on the reservation, one from which he'd successfully distanced himself at Syracuse University. At twenty-five, Kevin Easter had already experienced more life than most people twice his age.

Removing his emerald green and white cap again, the captain dragged his thick fisherman's fingers through his dreadlocks and, for the first time since agreeing to chauffeur this American around Andros, seemed to relax. The grin was genuine. Huge. "I take you to the best of places, Mr. Hatch," he said, turning the boat away from the Silverstone estate and out into the Atlantic. "Blue marlin. It be the perfect fish for a good man like you."

Hatch felt the vibration as the twin Evinrudes throttled up. He looked back to see the private island shrink as they headed out to sea, and wondered, for some inexplicable reason, what would become of this now-resurrected financier who once resided in New York City as a king. Maybe a CIA colleague—whose job it was to take care of messy situations—would call on Jeremy in the very near future. Maybe Mr. Silverstone would be extradited back to the United States, arrested, and tried in a court of law.

"Jeremy," Hatch said quietly, "I suggest you read a little faster."

CHAPTER 2
Manhattan

Andrew Lloyd Webber's *Sunset Boulevard* had not only been a sensational climax to a perfect three-day weekend in New York City, but also a short-lived escape from the oppressive heat that had gripped most of the northeastern United States during the month of August.

With Kleenex in hand, Karen Easter blotted the corner of each eye, then tucked the damp tissue back into her purse while the cast members took their final bows. When the thunderous applause finally ended, the house lights came up, and the well-dressed audience began filing out of Radio City Music Hall. There were smiles, quiet words of praise, and even astonishment.

"Best show I've seen in years," a gruff male voice proclaimed to the woman at his elbow.

Dead center and six rows from the stage, Karen finally sat back in her thickly padded seat and turned to her older sister. "Patty, every single one of your people, God, they . . . they're all so incredibly gifted. They make me feel . . ." She searched for the appropriate words. "Awestruck. Envious. Puny. The show was wonderful. You're gonna hate me for saying this, but I'm so proud of you."

Patricia Durante exaggerated a grin. A rising Broadway director, she'd recently been named one of the Big Apple's top fifty "Faces to Watch." "Piece of cake, darlin'," she quipped in her best Marlene Dietrich. Getting to her feet, Patricia tipped her head forward, stretching her aching neck muscles. "Well, for better or worse, that's number 184 in the books."

Soon, most of the evening's audience had exited the theater; a few stayed, recognizing Patricia from Sunday's *New York Times* article. A frail-looking elderly lady, tense and apprehensive, asked for an autograph. Patricia put the woman at ease and signed a program. The spacious hall had grown quiet now, and six ushers congregated near a side exit, apparently waiting to lock up.

Karen stood up and smoothed out her snug black dress, which accentuated her thin frame. "You're like a movie star," she said quietly. "It's everything you've ever wanted. People actually stare at you. It's creepy—but cool, in some bizarre way."

"Flavor of the week, babe." Patricia snapped her fingers.

"God, you're never satisfied."

"I have a funny feeling you're about to find out differently," Patricia said with a trace of a smile. Clutching her purse in her right hand, she moved toward the aisle. "It's about time I let you in on a little secret of mine."

"You and your secrets," Karen said, laughing.

A timid stagehand nervously stuck his head through a gap in the curtain. "Ms. Durante, um, pardon me, ma'am," the young man said, his voice nasal and tentative. "What do you want me to do with the roses?"

Patricia turned back to look over her shoulder. "Same as always, Danny. Give them to tonight's MVP. You pick."

"Yes, ma'am." He slipped back through the heavy curtain.

"What was that all about?" Karen asked.

"Oh, just a very mysterious secret admirer," Patricia said, rolling her eyes. "I've gotten a dozen pink roses almost every Saturday night since June. The card never has any words—just a drawing of an arrow piercing a big multicolored heart."

"That's so sweet."

"My Cupid might want to take a few art classes."

"Should I even admit to being a little jealous?"

"They're a hybrid tea, fairly rare," said Patricia with a slight shrug, "or so I've been told by my smartass lead. They're actually very pretty."

"I'd kill for roses," Karen said, picking up her small purse. She followed Patricia up the aisle. "I can't tell you the last time Hatch surprised me with anything romantic. Maybe you can give him a little hint."

Patricia stopped, then pirouetted on her high heels. "Honey," she said, "tell me the last time me and Hatch spent ten lousy minutes together. Don't get me wrong, I love him to pieces, but your man is always traveling, and those photos of his . . . shit, they make me wonder if the world's coming apart."

Sighing heavily, Karen said, "Yeah, you're not the first to say that."

With Hatch's "jobs," a week could stretch easily into two or three. Though Karen was one of the few who knew her husband worked for the Central Intelligence Agency, tracking and photographing enemies of the United States, she rarely asked about his work, abiding by the rules set forth by Hatch's boss, Jack Slattery. Others—including her own family—thought Kevin was an independent photojournalist who, as of late, focused on the faces of poverty, and got paid handsomely for his effort.

Karen and Patricia stood in the brightly lit lobby.

"Okay, how about we grab a beer or two?" Patricia said. "Like old times. I know this little dive that's completely off the radar."

Karen's face brightened. "Only if you let me buy."

"Deal. And it's cheap, which is right up your alley."

"Me?" Karen said, spreading her hands. "You're the one still holding on to your First Communion money."

"Touché."

"What about the troupe?"

"The assistant director made it this far. Besides, there's something important we need to talk about before you leave tomorrow."

"Oh, right," Karen said, locking arms with her sister. "Your big secret."

Brooklyn

Although it was past midnight, the Brooklyn pavement and brick row houses retained much of the day's ninety-degree heat. Even at night, the Flatbush neighborhood was full of life. Some neighbors sat quietly on their front steps. Others exchanged gossip. Some debated the Yankees and the Giants over beers and soft drinks. There was even a hint of marijuana on the warm breeze. An opened fire hydrant sprayed out upon the mostly Italian neighborhood, a tradition their parents and generations before them considered a God-given right, a cool presence to even the most oppressive summers.

A few air conditioners hummed in the background. Occasionally a car, pickup truck, or customized SUV would stop in the street, its woofers and tweeters pushed to capacity. The stagnant air thrummed with some heavy musical beat. The driver, or maybe one of his companions, would have a spirited conversation with a group of teenagers gathered under a sodium vapor streetlight. Then they would speed off, evidently in search of a little Saturday night action.

Johnny Cercone, a Sicilian with deep roots in the cloistered neighborhood, tossed his empty Red Dog toward a garbage can about ten feet from the concrete stoop. The beer can bounced off the Rubbermaid, then slowly rolled into the small river that flowed toward a clogged grate. "C'mon, Vincent," he said, "do ya need a fuckin' nipple for that thing?"

Springing to his feet, Vincent Tagliafero downed the rest of his beer. At nineteen, Tagliafero had been given the opportunity to prove he was ready for a full-time position within the outfit of Anthony DiFilippo IV—his Uncle Tony— who ran one of New York's most powerful crime families. Tonight, he'd witness firsthand his older cousin, Johnny—already a veteran soldier at twenty-six—make a collection on behalf of their uncle.

"Yeah, yeah," said Tagliafero, "show me the magic, Johnny." He clapped his hands together.

"Jesus Christ, settle down or ya gonna hurt yourself."

Bronx

It was a topic Karen Easter and Patricia Durante had debated a thousand times during their lives. Even in their late twenties, the "grass is greener" issue never seemed out of bounds. Regardless of the occasion, the subject would eventually leach into their *tête-à-tête*—normal operating procedure for such competitive sisters. What had been a cancerous jealousy as teenagers had been reduced to a playful sibling rivalry thanks to Hatch's objective point of view: *You're both being assholes. Get over it!*

Karen's flippant remark about talent—or lack thereof—had caused a great rift in their relationship back in high school. Today, the sisters could joke about such enmity; today, they were best friends.

It was clear that Patricia had inherited their mother's artistic talent and father's big frame, while Karen possessed the physical beauty, athleticism, personality, patience, and poise. Karen was two years younger, four inches taller, thinner, and blonder than her twenty-eight-year-old sister. Her life, she felt, was mundane, working in a Charlottesville, Virginia advertising agency, but she had a way with men—including Hatch, a cute, funny, and bright pre-law student she'd met at a Syracuse University tailgate party.

Patricia's creativity transcended her lack of physical beauty, but she had a tendency to be curt and short-tempered, especially with actors. She insisted on perfection, constantly challenging those around her, and Patricia's colleagues respected her no-nonsense approach to their craft. She was an accomplished pianist, a progressive visionary, and one of New York City's young stars, even beyond the theater. *The New York Post* had run a glowing article highlighting Patricia Durante's accomplishments. And with her success came political influence, popularity, and an eclectic circle of friends, but her budding fame also brought new obstacles. Most eligible men seemed intimidated by Patricia's résumé. Her time-consuming work schedule and hard-charging personality were liabilities when it came to romantic relationships. Her last bungled date, which had been with a Wall Street hotshot back in the early spring, ended with a quick peck on the cheek, and not even a follow-up phone call.

It was at Rudy's Tavern that Patricia wanted Karen to hear her secret, and maybe get a glimpse of her newfound softer side.

Rudy's Tavern, located on East 188th Street in the heart of the Bronx, two blocks from Fordham University, was a quiet establishment, especially when the student population was home for the holidays or, as they were now, on summer vacation. It was also the perfect way to end the sisters' "girls-only" weekend.

Sitting on a wooden barstool in the mostly empty tavern, Karen Easter peered over her bottle of Corona and studied her reflection in the giant mirror again. *Wow, you look like shit,* she thought. *You need a romantic night with your husband and eight hours of uninterrupted sleep.* She always slept poorly when Hatch was on the road, something she didn't share with anyone—including her husband. *Thank God he's coming home this week.*

Patricia ordered her third beer of the evening and told the beefy bartender in the taut muscle shirt to throw a few ice cubes in a tall glass. "Hey, Bobby, rumor has it beer tastes better *cold*," she said, lightly elbowing her sister.

Looking around the small, poorly lit bar, Karen, who was still having a difficult time adjusting to her surroundings, whispered, "When you said 'little dive off the radar,' you sure did mean it."

There were eight round, wooden tables—all scarred, stained, and unoccupied—dark mahogany walls, and no noticeable décor, not even pictures or photographs. There wasn't a single waitress, and there hadn't even been a sign outside the place. The hardwood floor was covered by a generous layer of sawdust and peanut shells. Rudy's, a watering hole not on any tourist map, smelled like a combination of beer, sweat, cigarette smoke, and mildew, all masked by a hint of Pine-Sol.

"Bobby," Patricia said, "where's Pacino been hiding?"

The large man with the bushy red beard and bald head pushed a bottle of beer and a glass filled with ice in front of his regular customer. "Filming in Vegas. Another collaboration with George."

"Bush, Orwell, or Stephanopoulos?"

"Nice try, kiddo. Clooney."

An impish smile replaced Karen's puzzled expression, followed by a slow shake of her head. Leaning closer to Patricia's ear, she said, "Why would Al Pacino come to a dump like this?"

"Hey, don't let Bobby hear you say that. He'll take away my discount card."

The bartender cleared his throat. "I already did—and your little sister's officially on probation."

"Look around," Karen said, cupping her hand to her mouth. "It's after midnight on a Saturday in New York City, and we're it. How the heck does a place like this stay open? And why isn't there any air conditioning?"

"Bobby O'Rourke is old school," Patricia said, bringing the glass to her forehead. "He's cheap as hell. Ebenezer Scrooge with a big red beard."

"When it comes to coin, ladies, I'm tighter than bark on a tree."

Karen chuckled.

"Bobby makes his money when Fordham is back in session," Patricia said. "This place is usually mobbed with students from September through April. And he owns the building *and* the property. Urban legend has it that he won them both in a poker game."

"Fact," Bobby bellowed from the far end of the polished bar, the only surface that seemed even remotely clean. "Thirty-two years ago this Christmas. Had myself a full house."

"Poker?" Karen said, astonished.

"Beats workin' for a living." Bobby grinned, then began swapping out a keg.

"On Christmas?" Karen said. "O'Rourke? Would you be Irish Catholic?"

"Lapsed. My new wife is Jewish. You'd think it would free up my December twenty-fifth. No way."

"What number is the latest Mrs. O'Rourke?" Patricia asked, elbowing Karen again. "I may have missed one."

"Four," Bobby said with a shrug. "They love me, take my money, then leave me. What can I say? It's a modern-day tragedy. Like one of your plays, Patty."

Karen and Patricia traded bemused looks. "Just another way of grinding out a living in the naked city," Patricia said, laughing.

Leaning closer to her older sister again, Karen said, quietly, "He really owns this—"

"You should see my summer house in the Hamptons," said Bobby, his deep voice rising up from the floor like an active volcano.

Karen cupped both hands around Patricia's left ear. "God, he hears like Superman."

"Karen, you're in the Apple," Patricia said. "A college joint. Kids that age— even the smart ones—still love to party. An entrepreneur like my Bobby knows how to make money the old-fashioned way. Cash only. Isn't that right?"

"Look at you, handing out compliments," Bobby said, slowly shaking his head. "Is that the alcohol talking?"

"Is it a crime to be in a good mood?" Patricia asked.

"Must have been a blue moon out there last night," Karen said. "She's been like this all day."

"Ah-ha," Bobby said. "So it's still there."

Karen looked over at her sister. "It? What am I missing here?"

"The glow," Bobby said. "Big sis has been carrying the luminosity of love around—"

"Okay," Patricia said, gently cutting the big man off.

"Glow?" Karen said, scrutinizing her sister.

"The one Patty's boyfriend seems to have given her these past few months." Bobby tightened the coupling on the keg. "Is he coming in for the weekend again?"

Grinning, Karen turned her entire body to face Patricia, and said, "Bobby, did you say my big sister has a boyfriend?"

"And they're in serious love, these two. Obscene public displays of affection. Staring at each other dreamily, scaring the crap out of my paying customers. Flowers and boxes of expensive candy. Reminds me of Mr. Spock and his infamous mind meld." Bobby smirked.

"Okay, okay," Patricia said. "Can we please turn down the sarcasm?"

"Oh, damn it all to hell," Bobby said. "Was this supposed to be a secret?"

Patricia threw a damp napkin at the bartender. "He's stuck in traffic on the Cross Bronx Expressway. Something about an accident. I just got a text."

"Boyfriend?" Karen repeated, appearing incredulous, a trace of excitement in her tone.

"Yeah, that was my dirty little secret," Patricia said with a shrug. "I'm stupid in love, Karen. Bobby's right. He's perfect for me—if you can believe it. I'm no longer the ice princess. He's wonderful. A keeper."

"Oh ... my ... God," Karen said slowly, drawing the words out.

"Strike up the band," Bobby said. "This guy's a man's man. I seen it with my own eyes. These two kids are nuts for each other, and it ain't that superficial soul mate bullshit. The love bug bit your sister bad. Drew blood is my best guess. Hello wedding invitations."

"Easy," Patricia said. "She gets it, Bobby. How about some pretzels?"

The front door to Rudy's Tavern opened for the first time since Patricia and Karen arrived. Flipping a dirty bar towel over his shoulder, Bobby turned his head toward the entrance. His playful repartee disappeared and his body instantly went rigid.

Karen could almost feel the air escaping from the room. The tension hung like the missed beat of an instrumental or a botched line in a play. She saw fear radiating from Bobby's widening blue eyes, and beads of sweat appearing on the bartender's creased forehead. The two sisters remained still and quiet as they watched the two olive-skinned men through the mirror behind the bar. The floorboards creaked with their weight.

The older of the two patrons—he looked to be in his late twenties, Karen thought—wore designer jeans, a neatly pressed white shirt unbuttoned midway down the front to reveal his hairy chest, and black leather shoes. This new customer, his dark hair slicked back, slid in next to Karen.

The younger man, less attentive to his attire than was his associate, wore a dark blue T-shirt, faded Levi jeans, and black Nike cross-trainers. Chewing on gum like a hungry rat and constantly checking the front door with furtive glances, he appeared extremely anxious, even jumpy.

"Johnny, hey, what can I get you boys?" Bobby said, a slight tremor in his voice.

Elbows on the bar, Johnny Cercone remained expressionless. For what seemed an intolerable moment, he eyeballed his adversary like a gunslinger, as if waiting for Bobby to flinch.

Vincent Tagliafero shuffled his feet, temporarily easing his tension.

Karen could see everything in the mirror.

"Coke, lots of ice," Cercone finally answered, turning his head toward the women to his right. "Had myself a DUI that still needs fixin'. Nothin' for my idiot cousin who can't seem to stand still for even a goddamned second." Cercone gave Karen a lecherous grin. "Well, well, well, what do we got here? Bitches in the Bronx."

Karen reached for her Corona, brought the bottle to her lips, and took a sip. Patricia pressed her foot to Karen's ankle. Both women stared at each other through the reflection.

"Hey, girl," Cercone said with his best Joe Pesci impression, "I'm talkin' to you. Get off the wrong train or what? Look at you, all dressed up like some Midtown whore."

Patricia cleared her throat and said, "We went to the theater. I'm a regular here."

"At Rudy's?" Cercone snorted. "This shit-hole?"

Karen stiffened, and her right hand—the one holding the Corona—began to tremble.

Patricia said, "Me and Bobby—"

"Who the fuck gave you permission to talk, Miss Piggy?" Cercone bent back and eyed Patricia contemptuously. "Christ Almighty, would it really hurt to lose twenty pounds?"

"Thirty!" Tagliafero shouted from the door. "She's a hog in heels."

And again Patricia pressed her foot against Karen's ankle.

Cercone turned his attention back to Karen. "Theater?" Grabbing his crotch, he said, "The real attraction's in here, ladies. Wanna see? The greatest show on—"

Bobby slid a glass of Coke in front of Cercone, cutting off his rant.

"Asshole," Patricia said under her breath.

Ignoring the drink, Cercone remained focused on Karen. "You don't live around here, do ya, baby?"

Tagliafero moved directly behind Patricia.

After a long moment, Karen finally turned her body toward Cercone. A simple gold crucifix hung from the man's thick neck. He was handsome, lean, and self-assured—a product of the city streets, she suspected. And a bully. Hatch had once told her that the loud ones were usually the biggest wimps. Karen put her left hand on the bar.

Cercone's gaze moved to the gold wedding band and engagement ring, then back to Karen's face. "Do you really think I give a shit about your old man? Fucking ... stupid ... tourists. I should steal that thing, but the diamond ain't worth jack!"

"My sister's visiting me," Patricia said. "My boyfriend is on his way."

"Ahhh," Cercone said, letting the word draw out, glancing over at his cousin. "Looks like we got ourselves a good old-fashioned sister act, Vincent. Lucky us. Maybe we just won the friggin' New York State lottery."

Tagliafero chuckled, then covered his mouth, as if laughter broke some unwritten rule of intimidation.

"Put his Coke on my tab, Bobby," Patricia said.

Cercone ignored that and said, "You two sure as hell don't look alike. Your sister got all the good genes, Ugly Betty—or I bet you just eat too fuckin' much."

"On the house." Bobby put a bowl of pretzels in front of Cercone, whose attention instantly turned back to the real business at hand.

"You're late, Bobby," Cercone shouted. "Again! Uncle Tony wants his money. Fifteen large. That includes a late charge, plus interest, plus nuisance fee."

"My customers, Johnny. Please," said Bobby, spreading his hands. "Can we talk about this another time?"

Cercone shifted his gaze to Tagliafero and gave him a queer look that resembled a grimace. "See what I'm up against, Vincent?" He briefly spoke to his cousin in Italian. The younger man nodded. Cercone's face went rigid when he looked back at the bartender.

"You bet on the ponies, Bobby, and you lost yourself a nice chunk a change," Cercone said. "Now you expect my uncle to play banker? Are you fuckin' kiddin' me? You know we ain't handin' out *Monopoly* money."

"I understand," Bobby insisted, swallowing hard. "I'm good for it, Johnny. You know that."

"The boss ain't a very patient guy. He would like his money. Tonight!" Rolling the soft drink between his thumb and index finger, Cercone brought the cool, wet glass to his cheek. "You should get some air in this place, old man. I'm hot. And when I get hot, I get irritable."

Bobby O'Rourke's eyes darted between Cercone, Tagliafero, Patricia, and

Karen. Except for his right arm, his body went rigid again. In small concentric circles, he rubbed the polished bar top. "I need another week, Johnny. It's been bad–real bad. My regulars went to taverns with air conditioning or balconies. The economy sucks. You know that. And this goddamned heat is killing my business . . . but the students are coming—"

Cercone put the glass back on the bar. Karen continued to watch through the big mirror. Cercone caught the look and said, "How would you deal with this, Tourist Barbie?"

"I'd rather not get involved," Karen said in an anemic voice.

Leaning back, Patricia said to Johnny, "I'll pay Bobby's debt."

The corners of Cercone's mouth curled upward and formed a sardonic grin that looked painful. His eyes, though, clearly hadn't found anything amusing in her words. Cercone glanced at Bobby—who had abruptly stopped cleaning—took a step back, and walked behind the two women.

"I . . . I can probably have the money in a couple a days," Bobby stammered.

Cercone moved to Patricia's right, nearly pressed his lips to her ear, and said, "Honey, I don't like you or your snobby attitude," whispering loud enough for everyone to hear. "You act like your shit don't stink. For Christ's sake, that was the second time you interrupted me. You're making me look like a douche bag. Ain't that right, Vincent?"

Tagliafero nodded dutifully.

From the small of his back, Cercone revealed a pistol—a Smith & Wesson Model 64—and laid it beside Patricia's Corona. The handle and trigger were wrapped in black electrical tape. "Beer muscles, lady. That's the only explanation I got for you. We wouldn't be having this conversation if you wasn't drinkin' that warm piss Bobby serves."

Part of it was the alcohol affecting her sister's judgment, Karen thought, but the other part was Patricia's strong will—a personality trait that not only fueled her successful career but also had a history of getting her in trouble.

"Your uncle wants his fifteen thousand bucks, and I have it," Patricia said, her voice steady, firm. "Does he really care who pays? What's the big deal?"

"Big deal?" Cercone repeated, cocking his head.

"This isn't our problem, Patty," Karen said, sensing her sister had crossed a very thin line with this dangerous man.

"You should listen to your good-looking sister, *Patty*," Cercone said. "New York can be a very dangerous place. Truly, *Patty*. People get hurt all the time in this city, *Patty*. Read the papers." He glanced over at Tagliafero. "And this is why Uncle Tony pays me so much. Jesus, there's always bullshit when money and broads—"

Snatching the Smith & Wesson from the bar top, Patricia pressed the barrel firmly against Cercone's cheek. Cercone went silent. Vincent Tagliafero's shaky hand clumsily reached for his Glock 9mm. Bobby stumbled backwards into the cash register, three shot glasses fell onto the wooden floor, and Karen emitted an adolescent squeak, then covered her mouth with her hand.

"Don't even think about it, Vincent," Patricia said to Tagliafero through clenched teeth. "Put it on the ground. Now!"

"What should I do, Johnny?" Tagliafero asked his cousin in a shaky voice.

"Be cool, Vincent. Listen to the broad."

Karen found herself frozen, uncomprehending. The impulse to scream or cry was overwhelming, but she remained mute.

Cercone recovered some of his machismo. "Oh . . . baby, how I love a naughty girl. Fuck me, Freddy on the freeway, you're getting more attractive by the minute. You wanna kill me or spank me?"

No one smiled.

Tagliafero removed the pistol from the small of his back, crouched, and laid his weapon on the sawdust-covered floor.

"Patty, please . . . put the gun down," Bobby pleaded in a tremulous voice that sounded like an old woman's. "Listen to me. This ain't good. Think this through. This is just business. Happens all the time. Tony D's a reasonable man. I'll have the money in his hands when the banks open. I swear to God, Johnny. Everyone just . . . just calm down."

Cercone took an exaggerated pull from his glass. The ice tinkled. He acted like the loaded gun—the one pressed to his face—was of no consequence. "Maybe you should listen to the Irishman and your sister, *Patty*. This ain't no Hollywood chick flick."

"We should leave," Karen said in a shaky voice.

"Is my money good or not?" Patricia asked.

Cercone considered the question. "What do you think, Vincent? Can this broad's cash cover Bobby's overdue bill?"

"Sure!" said Tagliafero. "Absolutely."

"Wrong!" yelled Cercone. Everyone, including Patricia, jumped. Her hand and index finger reflexively tightened on the trigger. "No! Bobby owes Uncle Tony, not some fancy bitch from the burbs—"

Like a trapdoor spider ambushing its next meal, Johnny Cercone's right arm came up and slapped Patricia's hand to the side. The pistol discharged into the ceiling with a loud crack. Karen screamed, then covered her ears.

Cercone threw Patricia to the floor, wrenched the pistol from her hand, and then kicked her solidly in the right knee, tearing her anterior cruciate ligament. Curling into the fetal position, she, too, began to scream. Cercone, his reddening face filled with rage, now had the gun and the advantage. "Fucking nosy bitch," he said, breathing hard.

Bobby turned toward the mirror and reached for something next to the cash register. Karen came around the barstool to help her sister.

Wide-eyed and close to hyperventilating, nineteen-year-old Vincent Tagliafero looked to his mentor—his *caporegime*—for guidance, but Cercone continued to wildly kick Patricia, seemingly unaware of Bobby's movement. Tagliafero crouched, then shouted, "Johnny! The dude's got a piece!"

Bobby O'Rourke's head snapped around to face Tagliafero, a confused expression fixed about his open mouth. In his hand, he held a black object.

"Stop it!" Karen yelled, shoving Cercone. "Please!"

Cercone raised his Smith & Wesson, but before he could slam it down upon Patricia, the sound of five successive, evenly-spaced cracks filled the room. Unopened bottles of Jack Daniel's and Seagram's 7 exploded to Bobby's right, sending shards of glass and half a dozen quarts of liquor onto the floor. Centered on the mirror was a dark red pattern, a lumpy mess, shape-shifting as it slid toward the counter.

Bobby, with a small, dark hole drilled directly above his right eye, let the black telephone slip from his hand. The pigtail cord went slack. His crow's feet deepened as his face took on a look of shock, and he exhaled for the last time in a rough gurgle. Crumpling to the floor in what seemed like slow motion, the bartender was dead before his body landed amidst his shattered inventory.

Cercone bellowed at his cousin, "You stupid fuck! What did you do?"

Tagliafero's entire body shook. His pistol thumped harmlessly to the wood floor and he studied his trembling hand as if it were some foreign object attached to his wrist. What Cercone had yelled didn't seem to register.

"Oh, mother of God," Tagliafero muttered, gasping amid the coppery smell of blood and gunpowder.

Karen Easter lay crumpled beneath the bar.

Tagliafero dropped to both knees as if in prayer. "I . . . oh, shit, lady, I . . . I thought Bobby had . . . Oh, Jesus, Mary, and Joseph."

Cercone shoved aside his blathering cousin, knelt beside Karen, and spoke softly. "Hey, lady, you okay?" he said. His hostility had been replaced with a hint of fear.

Patricia rolled over. The pain in her knee made a fierce return, and she grimaced. "Is she hurt? Tell me she's okay!"

Tagliafero got back to his feet. Like a blind man, he shuffled about the small room in a lazy circle and muttered, "Mistake. It was a . . . a mistake. I . . . I'm sorry. Sorry. Really. Horrible mistake."

Cercone pressed two fingers to Karen's throat, searching for a pulse. A large pool of blood began to spread into the cracks of the old floor. It soaked through long blond hair and into the sawdust.

Panic replaced Patricia's physical agony. She looked at her little sister and then turned to Cercone. "Is she alive?!" she screamed.

Cercone slowly shook his head. He glared at Tagliafero, yet his tone remained remarkably calm. "Pick up your gun, Vincent. We're leaving."

"I wanna go home," Tagliafero said, on the verge of tears.

"No! You can't do that!" Patricia shouted at Cercone. "Call nine-one-one! Please! Help her!"

Tagliafero backed away from the mess he'd created. Cercone repeated his instructions in the same composed voice. This time, the younger man did as he was told.

"Vincent, I want you to grab the bills from the cash register," Cercone continued, "and their purses."

"Don't do this," Patricia begged in a tremulous voice. "Please."

In an almost dreamlike trance, Vincent walked behind the bar and stuffed the bills into his pants pockets. He grabbed the two small purses and returned to Tagliafero's side.

Both men stared down at Patricia Durante. Cercone sighed.

Patricia clutched her dead sister's hand. "Karen . . . wake up."

"I'm sorry," Cercone said in a hushed whisper.

Patricia looked slightly upward and found herself at the deadly end of the Smith & Wesson, but there was no time to close her eyes, let alone avoid her destiny.

CHAPTER 3

Langley, Virginia / Miami, Florida

For the past three days, Jack Slattery, the CIA's deputy director for intelligence, had been dreading this phone call. Seven years as the DDI, and he'd never dealt with a crisis quite like this. He felt grossly unprepared.

"Thank you, Molly," Slattery said to his secretary through the phone's intercom. "Put him through." Clearing his throat, he found his seat, stood up, then sat down again. The red light on his phone blinked as the call was forwarded to his secure line on Langley's seventh floor. He finally snatched up the receiver. "Kevin, are you back in the States?"

"And a very good morning to you, Jack," Kevin "Hatch" Easter said over a boarding announcement that resonated throughout the airport terminal. "Yep, I'm in Miami, waiting for my connection to Dulles. Wanna buy me lunch?"

Slattery got to his feet and stepped to the bulletproof window. "Something happened while you—"

"I got you some really cool photos of Greenback," Hatch said. He set his heavy backpack, filled with expensive photographic equipment, on a bench near the food court. "Your friends are gonna love them. And I did a little fishing on your dime. Caught myself a marlin. Thing was a monster. I'm actually still dressed like a tourist . . ."

John "Jack" Slattery, a stout, retired Marine, dragged his fingers through his gray crew cut. Recruited by the CIA in 1975, he'd worked at the U.S. embassy in the old Soviet Union and, while there, quietly thwarted an assassination attempt on the American ambassador. Returning to the United States in the early eighties, he'd climbed through the CIA's ranks and was presently the number-two man at the Agency.

Intelligent, complex, independent, fiercely private, and seemingly always in control of his emotions, Slattery didn't have a political agenda. He had very few friends outside the Central Intelligence Agency. The job defined him. He had little free time or outside interests, save his wife of nearly forty years.

Hatch rambled on about his angler's proficiency while Slattery unbuttoned the top button of his heavily starched dress shirt. Tugging frantically at his tie, he scribbled Easter's whereabouts on a lined legal pad and buzzed Molly.

"...and because you're such a skeptical guy," Hatch said, "I took about a dozen shots of my prized fish. Even named it after you. Jack—has a nice ring to it. I'll e-mail you a few copies. It'd probably make a great Christmas card, but I'm not sure Karen would appreciate—"

Slattery tapped his Baldwin pen on the Jeremy Silverstone dossier. "Hatch, I really need you to listen to me." The DDI's tone was firm, level, and yet strangely sympathetic. "You're not coming to Langley. Not yet."

"Wow... Man, did you just call me Hatch?"

"There's been a change in plans."

"What kind of trouble am I in now?"

The young redheaded secretary stepped back into Slattery's corner office, took the note from his outstretched hand, and rushed out the door.

"C'mon, Jack, what's going on? Is it that crap in Berlin? It wasn't my fault. I told you that. The milk truck came out of—"

"Karen was murdered in the Bronx this past weekend. So was Patricia Durante." Slattery paused. "I'm so sorry, son."

"What?" Hatch said, barely above a whisper.

"One of our Miami-based field agents will assist you. She's on her way to the airport. Her name is—"

"How... Jack, what happened?" Hatch slid to the floor next to the bench, his legs no longer able to sustain his weight.

Slattery reached for the New York Police Department's preliminary homicide report detailing the murders of Karen Easter, Patricia Durante, and Robert O'Rourke. Gray Taylor, a veteran CIA field operative who lived in Manhattan, had faxed the information to the DDI. Taylor had gotten the report from a homicide detective, a friend and reliable contact in the New York City Police Department. "We got word on Monday," Slattery said. "Robbery. The cops got lucky and ID'd Patricia from the media guide to her play. She was on the cover with the lead. The program was on the bar. Purses, cell phones, wallets–all their identification was taken by the shooters."

Hatch said nothing.

"I even sent two of my people to the Bahamas, hoping they could locate you."

Hatch looked around the busy US Airways concourse. For the first time in many years, he noticed the faces of his fellow travelers—excited children with their parents; businessmen and women buried in laptops, cell phones, i-Pads, BlackBerrys, magazines, or books; a teenage Asian couple holding hands, laughing;

a baby asleep in a stroller. *How very odd*, he thought. So many people, yet the airport was absolutely silent—like a muted television program. And then an icy spike sent a violent tremor through his entire body, awakening every nerve ending.

"Kevin!" Slattery shouted a third time.

Hatch closed his eyes, then leaned his head against the steel bench. It was cool to the touch. He tried desperately to steady his thoughts. Instead, he was a little boy again, running recklessly with his older brother, Steven, through the planted fields in and around the Cattaraugus Indian Reservation. *Knee-high on the Fourth of July*. Acres and acres of corn. A brutally hot day. The summer his parents were killed. Steven was eleven years old at the time of their deaths. Hatch, nine and inconsolable, was told he'd be living with his grandfather—an ageless mystic who frightened the hell out of him.

Indistinct words shattered the memory. The US Airways concourse exploded to life, and one recognizable voice rose above the others.

"Kevin Easter!" Slattery shouted into his phone.

"I'm here. I, yeah . . . I'm fine," he said in a voice that no longer resembled his own.

"You're not fine. That's why I'm sending Siming Lo Zhang to assist you."

"No witnesses, Jack?" Hatch asked, ignoring his boss. "On a Saturday night in New York City?"

"Rudy's Tavern is a college hangout, and most of the students are home for the summer, so it's conceivable. And the neighborhood is allegedly quiet."

"You expect me to believe that?"

"The detectives in charge of the investigation—"

"Jack, you didn't answer my question!"

"We'll discuss this when you get back."

Gritting his teeth, his jaw muscles flexing, Hatch said evenly, "I want your opinion, Jack, not our nuclear launch codes."

"Not on the phone," Slattery said, tossing his pen on the Greenback file, "and definitely not until you've had a chance to digest all of this. You need to calm down."

"I am calm."

"It's pointless to argue, Kevin. You're not thinking straight."

"Is there anything you're not telling me?"

"I've been promised an update by five o'clock."

Hatch visualized the gruesome scene at Rudy's Tavern: black-and-white images, like his photography. *Crack, crack, crack, crack, crack.* Five shots from a Glock 9mm. Karen and the bartender were both mortally wounded, yet three bullets had gone wild. Not a professional. A second gun, with .38 Special ammo, had been used to kill Patricia—a headshot at point-blank range. Yet another .38 slug had been retrieved from the wooden ceiling. Seven total shots, three dead bodies. *Two killers?*

An additional boarding announcement pulled Hatch from his reverie. The intense mental pain he'd so ably ignored for the past few moments burst into his consciousness like a cluster bomb. An agonizing ache, like the one he'd experienced at age nine, reappeared. This new round of grief, like a wild animal, had begun to bite.

"To answer your question," Slattery said, "no, I'm not holding any information back. And I don't have an opinion because I don't have all the details."

"Jack, it's—"

"We'll worry about the investigation later. If you want to make your sister-in-law's funeral, you need to sit tight and wait for Siming."

"When is it?"

"This afternoon. I can put you on a private plane to New Jersey. A Mr. Taylor will pick you up at Newark Airport."

"Where can I find Siming?"

"Stay right where you are," Slattery said. "She's coming to you."

CHAPTER 4

Manhattan

Anthony DiFilippo IV was not happy.

The disaster at Rudy's Tavern on Saturday night had grown legs, and they were very ugly legs. The murders of three people—two innocent women and one of his best gambling customers—had disgraced his organization, and embarrassment was something he would not tolerate. Worse yet, the deaths brought unwanted attention to his vast empire.

A fourth-generation Italian American, Anthony DiFilippo, who quietly controlled New York's largest and most sophisticated crime family, didn't flaunt his station in life like many of his arrogant predecessors. Instead, he insulated himself through Ivy League attorneys on retainer, loyal family members, and childhood friends he could trust. He was seldom seen in public and had never been interviewed by the media; not even a simple *no comment* had passed his lips. Surveillance teams from the FBI and local law enforcement agencies like the mob division had found it very difficult to even record the old man. Privacy was DiFilippo's prime directive. Without secrecy, most of his businesses would hemorrhage like a bullet-riddled body.

At sixty-three, Anthony DiFilippo IV, or Tony D as he was called, was revered by his own people, respected by his enemies, and loathed by those trying to put him in prison. In a business environment that practiced violence, the don, who had graduated from Harvard University with a philosophy degree, preached pacifism. Rarely did his people kill the competition, as in the bad old days of Capone, Lucchese, Gotti, or Bugsy Malone. Good communication, Tony D stressed with his crew, could outgun most arsenals, and murdering a loyal patron like Bobby O'Rourke was bad for business, both now and in the future.

Word had gotten out: The owner of Rudy's Tavern had been fatally shot in the head over a lousy fifteen grand. Like any company predicated on making money, the bottom line meant everything. A dead customer usually led to an uncollectible debt.

Now, the reclusive don sat alone in the back room of the Ravenite Social Club, a men's-only establishment located on Mulberry Street in Little Italy. He sipped an iced tea. The air conditioner, welded fast to the only window in the small room, sputtered and coughed. Replacing the old unit wasn't even a consideration, although a reliable handyman had already repaired it twice this brutally hot summer. The ceaseless noise prevented an eavesdropper from overhearing private conversations.

One fat candle under a red ornamental glass sat in the middle of Tony D's round table. The weak glow kept his face hidden in shadow.

Folding his hands on the tablecloth, Tony D said, "Bring him in, Marco."

The husky bodyguard with thinning dark hair and acne scars wore a green polyester shirt, black slacks, jackboots, and a shouldered pistol. A gold cross hung around his fleshy neck. He shuffled across the room, opened the door, and gestured with his head.

A moment later, Johnny Cercone, six inches shorter and two decades younger than Marco, stepped into the Ravenite meeting room. Marco wordlessly pointed to the table where the don sat.

Squinting as his eyes adjusted to the room's dimness, Cercone came to the table where Tony D had conducted most of his business affairs—both as a *caporegime* and don—for the past eighteen years. Like a loyal subject, the younger man stood obediently before his boss. "Thank you for seeing me."

"Have a seat, Johnny." Tony D's voice rumbled like an earthquake. "Something to drink, perhaps?"

"No, sir. I'm good." Cercone sat down in the wooden chair directly across from his uncle.

The don wore a tweed Hugo Boss sports jacket over a white Fendi dress shirt and dark blue Versace tie. Though he sat in the semi-dark, his tiny beetle-like eyes were hidden behind a pair of Ray-Ban sunglasses. He had thick, professionally-styled white hair, bleached teeth, and a handsome, tanned face that gave Tony D a grandfatherly charm. Still, his grave expression was anything but comforting.

"Johnny," Tony D began, regret in his voice, "this issue in the Bronx—"

"Vincent thought Bobby had a gun, and the next thing I knew—"

From the far side of the room, Marco cringed at the interruption.

Tony D had put up his right hand like a traffic cop. The details of the incident were no longer up for debate. The confidential police report was tucked in the don's inside jacket pocket.

Intentionally absent from the report were a couple of key facts. An eyewitness had seen two men walking briskly away from Rudy's Tavern around the time of the murders, but most problematic were Cercone's fingerprints, recovered from the throat of one of the dead women—Karen Easter. These omitted details had cost Tony D a great deal of money and, more importantly, future favors.

The Mafia don hated owing anything to anybody. Debt was a sign of weakness.

The old man picked up a linen napkin and politely dabbed the corner of his mouth. "Johnny, if you were in my position, what would you do?"

Cercone considered his answer for a moment, then said, "I don't know."

Tony D exhaled. "That's too bad."

"Vincent wasn't ready, Uncle Tony," Cercone said, lifting his head to make eye contact with the don. "I should have known. I should have handled this Bobby thing by myself, or maybe I should have brought Woody along for the collection."

Tony D removed his sunglasses and laid them beside a crystal pepper shaker. For the first time in the past few days, he knew the decision he was about to make was the right one. He smiled, albeit briefly. "You're right, Johnny. You should have known Vincent wasn't equipped, mentally." A pause. "He's your responsibility—still is. You're his *capo*. He looks up to you."

"He's an immature little fuck!"

"Please . . . don't curse. It demonstrates ignorance."

Cercone pursed his lips. "Sorry."

"I'm afraid this problem is also my problem, Johnny," said Tony D. "And it's not going away any time soon. Am I making myself clear?"

"I'm not sure." Cercone glanced over at Marco as if he could clarify some part of the conversation, but the bodyguard was solely focused on cleaning his fingernails with a salad fork.

Tony D pushed his iced tea aside and quietly said, "Friends of mine are taking a lot of heat because of this unpleasant incident at Rudy's. The police—good, hard-working people—are sticking their necks out on this case. They helped me, which means they helped *you*, Johnny. They continue to support the family during this very difficult time."

Cercone opened his mouth to speak.

"Let me finish," the don said.

"Sorry."

"To show these friends how grateful I am for their cooperation, I need to reciprocate in kind. *Quid pro quo.* Do you understand?"

"Uncle Tony—"

"Do you understand?" Tony D repeated.

"Yes, sir," Cercone said dutifully. "I'll do anything to make things right. You know that."

"Of course."

Cercone sat up a little straighter. "Just give me the orders, and it's done."

"My homicide detective friend needs the shooter."

Cercone, his face suddenly a mask of panic, shot out of his chair. He pounded his chest. "You want me to confess?"

Marco, as if by magic, now hovered over the don. The big man clutched the gold plated dinner fork like an ice-pick and said, smoothly, "Back away, Johnny." His whisper came across as a menacing growl.

Tony D patted the bodyguard on the forearm. "Easy, my friend."

Marco returned to his chair near the door, yet the fork remained gripped in his big hand. He stared at Cercone like a rabid dog with every intention of attacking at a moment's notice.

"Confess? Johnny, no, no, absolutely not," the don said. "You're much too valuable to the organization. You're my godson. My sister's only boy. I could never allow such a thing."

Cercone's anxious expression morphed into puzzlement. He found his seat. "Who, then?"

CHAPTER 5

Northern New Jersey

The Christian Mass that celebrated the life and death of Patricia Durante had nearly concluded by the time the CIA's private jet touched down at Newark Airport. On the flight, Kevin Easter had shaved and changed into a white dress shirt, dark blue tie, and black pants. Numbed by Jack Slattery's revelation, he'd spent most of the remaining flight staring at the cloud formations outside the Cessna's oval window.

Siming Lo Zhang, the petite Chinese-American CIA field operative who'd accompanied Easter on the three-hour flight from Miami to New Jersey, respected his privacy. She interrupted his troubled thoughts only to offer a soft drink and to notify him that they would be landing in fifteen minutes.

At 2:10 p.m., the small jet taxied to a VIP arrival area near the US Airways terminal. The engines went silent, the cabin door opened, and the steps unfolded to the tarmac. Hatch was greeted with a blast of hot and humid air.

"Your ride is waiting for you beside that hangar," Siming said, pointing.

Raising his hands to shield his eyes, Hatch peered into the brightness and saw the rear end of a black SUV. "Thanks."

"I pray you find comfort in the very near future, Mr. Easter."

"I appreciate that."

Hatch slipped on a pair of designer sunglasses and tucked his long hair behind each ear. He slung his backpack over his shoulder, then stepped into the heat, walking down the eight steps and across the concrete.

The Cadillac Escalade idled near a four-story airplane hangar. When Hatch got to within ten feet of the SUV, the driver stepped out of the idling vehicle and moved around to the tailgate. The big man, built like an NFL linebacker, had a chiseled face, grim expression, and short blond hair.

"You must be Taylor!" Hatch shouted over the shrill whine of jet engines spooling up.

The big man offered a quick nod. "We're about thirty minutes from the cemetery. Toss your bags in the back."

Hatch did as he was told. A moment later, he slid into the Cadillac's passenger seat and pulled the shoulder harness across his body. Gray Taylor stomped on the accelerator and pointed the SUV toward the airport exit. A Newark Airport security guard waved them through.

———————

For the first five minutes of their trip, the two men said nothing. WFAN, a sports radio station out of Manhattan, played softly in the background. Hatch noted the simple gold wedding band on Taylor's left hand.

The Escalade merged with light traffic on the Garden State Parkway and headed north toward Parsippany, New Jersey.

"You work for Jack?" asked Hatch.

"Yes."

"You live around here?"

"In New York."

Unlike Siming Lo Zhang, Taylor appeared indifferent to his distress. Hatch briefly studied him: a loner in a lonely business, he suspected. Taylor—tanned and fit, probably in his early thirties—was dressed in a black Armani suit and polished shoes. An ugly L-shaped scar streaked across his forehead, but rather than disfigure his face, it added character.

"I didn't catch your first name," Hatch said.

"Gray."

"Friends call me Hatch."

"I know."

Hatch wasn't stunned or upset that Taylor knew his nickname, but the man's admission still came as a bit of a surprise.

"I'm sorry to hear about your wife and sister-in-law," Taylor said a couple of minutes later. The clipped words of sympathy seemed to come with great difficulty, as if he'd rehearsed a foreign language. The big man then fell silent and focused on the highway, both hands on the steering wheel.

"Thanks," Hatch said, turning to look out his window.

Cliché though it seemed, Low Dog had taught Hatch that the eyes of every living creature were a gateway to the soul. If Grandfather's premise was correct, Taylor had experienced a great deal of life and death, yet there was something deeper—something enigmatic—about this quiet individual that was not easy to read.

Hatch cleared his throat, then said, "You don't seem like the chaperone type—"

"I was available, Mr. Easter."

"Hatch."

"Right. Sorry."

"Jack's known about the murders for a few days," Hatch said, tapping his knuckle against the passenger side window. "Which means you must have been contacted at least two days ago."

"He called me this morning."

"Am I considered a threat?"

Taylor briefly shifted his eyes to his passenger. "Jack asked for my help—"

"What sort of help?"

"I actually like your style," Taylor said, and there was a hint of a smile. "You scrape away all the bullshit, which is a rare quality nowadays, especially in our business."

"Since it's fairly obvious that you read my file, or Jack gave you a history lesson, you know I work alone."

"Correct."

"Okay," Hatch said, exhaling. "Given that you consider me a bottom-line guy, what's your deal? Why are you here? I know how to rent a car. I can even read road maps. Higher education."

"You're a valuable CIA asset, and you're considered dangerous," Taylor answered without pause or emotion. "You know how Jack loves to protect the Agency's rep. Consider me an insurance adjuster, or something comparable."

"He seriously thinks I'm gonna do something stupid?"

"You're badly wounded, and you have a tendency to leap before you look. You're young—"

"And reckless?" Hatch said. "Is that in my file, too?"

"Not in those exact words, but yes."

"Since you're obviously an expert on me, Taylor, you know I've never killed anybody," said Hatch. "I leave the wet work to Jack's darker minions."

"I've seen many of your photographs over the last few years," Taylor said. "You're talented. I especially like your night-vision shots."

Gray Taylor's comment meant at least one thing, Hatch thought. This man driving the Cadillac Escalade was a CIA assassin—a professional killer. Some of Hatch's photos had been forwarded to Taylor over his time with the Agency, and his presence here meant that Jack had brought in the first team to oversee their damaged field agent.

"I'm not looking to get even with the person who killed my wife," Hatch said, clearly annoyed. "Christ, I'm not a threat to anybody."

"Murder has a way of changing things, especially when it happens to someone we love. Take it from an expert on the subject."

Take it from an expert on the subject. Hatch thought about this statement as the SUV moved past a slow-moving tractor-trailer. "A fucking babysitter," Hatch muttered under his breath.

"Believe me, I have better things to do."

The Cadillac exited the Parkway and took the ramp to 280 North. The view grew more rural as Hatch stared out the window. "How much longer?"

"According to the GPS, nine minutes. I'll get you there on time."

"Maybe that's what I'm afraid of."

They rode in silence for a few more uneventful miles. Then, Taylor reached behind his seat and grabbed a short stack of newspapers. He tossed them onto Hatch's lap. "Thought you might want to see how this is playing out around here. The media loves this one."

Hatch picked up the Monday edition of *The New York Post*. The headline read, "THREE BUTCHERED IN THE BRONX."

B. J. Butera was the author of the two-page article. It focused on Patricia Durante's meteoric career in the entertainment industry and how her tragic death had touched her diverse—and politically connected—circle of friends.

After Hatch read the four-day-old copy, he turned to Tuesday's edition, which carried a follow-up story on page three. B. J. Butera again. Another piece—on page eleven—took on a nastier tone, with local cops and detectives obviously getting pressure from the community and elected officials about their lack of progress. Even the mayor had weighed in. Still no suspects. People demanded a quick resolution; they wanted the killer identified and brought to justice.

A Fordham University spokesman insisted that their college continued to be a safe haven in the big city. Incoming freshmen and returning students had nothing to worry about. Security in and around the campus had been beefed up.

Rudy's Tavern, according to Robert O'Rourke's widow, would not reopen.

Hatch tossed the newspapers into the backseat. "Yep, a real sensitive bunch you got around here," he said, shaking his head in disgust.

"This is an appealing story, even by New York standards," Taylor said. "Patricia Durante was on the fast track, a rising star in more than a few crowds. Your sister-in-law was very popular."

"Apparently."

"Trust me, the cemetery is going to resemble a traveling circus, minus the animals." Taylor pointed to his BlackBerry, which sat on the center console. "A contact of mine in the New York Police Department told me that the media went overboard at the funeral. They moved to Woodlawn Cemetery in a caravan."

Hatch closed his eyes, slowly shook his head, and said, "Another all-time low for journalistic integrity." *And my Karen is only a footnote*, he thought. The newspaper articles, the media frenzy, and Gray Taylor's presence added color to his nightmare.

Hatch's memory moved back to the first time he'd set eyes on Karen Durante. It had been a crisp fall day in upstate New York, and many of the Syracuse students had been tailgating outside the Carrier Dome before the big football game against Penn State. Hatch and his lacrosse buddies were in a competitive match of beer pong. Karen and her small group of very personable friends—sitting in nearby lawn chairs, drinking bottles of Budweiser—teased the raucous jocks, especially after a missed shot. When two of the more adventurous girls insisted they could beat any of the guys in a doubles match, the challenge was quickly accepted. Hatch and his senior teammate—a mammoth goalie from a farm community north of Albany—took on Karen and a tall brunette, who turned out to be the graduated star center from last year's varsity basketball team.

The first game wasn't even close. Neither were the rematches—all eight of them. Hatch and his partner had to sit down before they fell down. From the opening kickoff of the game through the final gun, Hatch's Carrier Dome end zone seat remained empty, as did Karen's, nearer the thirty-yard line. Instead, the two remained in the parking lot, enjoying the warm sun and breezy conversation.

As the fans poured out of the stadium three hours after kickoff, Karen Durante did something that still brought a smile to Hatch's lips, even after four years. She lightly kissed him on the cheek, then said, "My father's a racist, but I have a funny feeling you might change his mind."

It had been a bold statement, Hatch thought, one that suggested this new friendship might very well turn into something more—something special. And Karen had been right about that.

Gray Taylor's black SUV moved from the residential street to Woodlawn's gravel roads. Loose stones clinked in the wheel wells. The vehicle passed under a towering wrought-iron archway that opened to a rolling landscape filled with mature trees, memorials, and monuments for the deceased.

"Karen's mom is buried here," Hatch said, leaning closer to the dashboard.

"I know," Taylor said. The CIA dossier had covered that and plenty more, including Hatch's youth on an impoverished Indian reservation in Western New York, and even his efforts to distance himself from his heritage after his marriage to Karen. As a gift to his new bride, Kevin Easter had secretly taken classes to convert to Catholicism, which hadn't sat very well with his own family.

Taylor was also well aware of Hatch's estranged relationship with his father-in-law, whose mind had not in fact been changed. The severity of the estrangement between Dr. Homer Durante and Kevin Easter had not been clarified in the dossier, but it was obvious that Karen had been the center of both men's lives. And Hatch had ultimately won the tug-of-war.

Bathed in the bright sunshine of a hot August afternoon, ancient oak trees lined many of the gravel roads, and a sea of headstones followed the gentle contour of the land. The grass was brown and withered from a long, rainless summer, and this section of the cemetery was relatively quiet and serene. There wasn't a soul in sight, and even the birds appeared to have taken refuge from the heat.

The blast of an automobile's horn ended the tranquil moment. Taylor glanced at the rearview mirror and frowned.

Looking back between the captain's chairs, Hatch said, "Bring in the clowns."

The driver's side window of the Cadillac glided down. Taylor waved an ABC news van past. The female driver, taking advantage of Taylor's courtesy, sped by the slower-moving vehicle, producing a long cloud of dust in her wake as she traveled up the gradual slope and dropped out of sight.

"Seriously, what could they possibly want?" Hatch said, disgusted.

"Despair and tragedy sell," Taylor said. "And those idiots are the tip of the proverbial iceberg."

Taylor abided by Woodlawn's five-miles-per-hour speed limit. The dust had begun to dissipate about the time they reached the crest of the hill, which overlooked the northern end of the cemetery with its chestnut trees, weeping willows, and Dutch elms.

Hatch's breathing suddenly became rapid and labored. "I don't think I'm ready for this," he said, staring at the crowd. "Shit, look at them."

Taylor pulled the SUV onto a patch of hard packed dirt. The circus had indeed come to Parsippany, New Jersey.

From behind the Escalade's tinted glass, about two hundred feet from Patricia Durante's casket, Kevin Easter and Gray Taylor watched the brief ceremony unfold. Biting down on his lower lip, Hatch gathered himself.

A Roman Catholic priest dressed in a white surplice with a green tippet draped around his neck stood over the oak casket. In his right hand, he held a clear vessel of holy water. Sprinkling the water onto the coffin, he blessed Patricia's remains with the sign of the cross and delivered her soul into the righteous arms of the Almighty.

Family members and friends huddled around their spiritual guide. Head slowly bobbing up and down, as if struggling with some unseen weight, Dr. Homer Durante stood alone in front. For some reason, he'd already removed his tie. Fifty feet from the burial site, five New Jersey State Troopers held back at least fifteen members of the media. A few photographers with telephoto lenses hid among the gravestones.

One by one, the mourners paid their last respects. Some touched the coffin, while one left a single pink and white rose on the perfectly polished hood.

"Cajun Moon," Hatch said, barely above a whisper.

"What?"

"The roses. They're fairly rare. Or maybe they're Moonstone. Both are a hybrid tea. My grandfather grows about thirty varieties back on the rez. Cajun Moon is one of his favorites." The priest stepped away from the coffin. "That's it for me, Taylor," Hatch said. "Get me out of here."

"We can wait for everyone to leave—"

"I've seen enough," Hatch snapped.

Taylor was in no position to protest. His orders were to safely transport Kevin Easter to Patricia Durante's burial, then put him on the next available flight to Charlottesville, Virginia.

"New York City is too close," Jack Slattery had said to Taylor during their last telephone conversation. "Kevin needs to go home and grieve."

Taylor turned the SUV around. "Airport?"

"I have a better idea."

CHAPTER 6

Bronx

There was no way of getting around it. Whatever path he selected, Johnny Cercone was convinced he was going to hell. Raised Catholic by his God-fearing mother, and an altar boy through grade school, he'd learned from an early age that there were always consequences to life's choices.

If he disobeyed Tony D's wishes and let his younger cousin just slip away, the air of uncertainty would forever follow Johnny. Even with his life threatened, was Vincent mentally equipped to leave New York City and start a new life? At nineteen, was he too young and immature to understand how things really worked in their world? Those associated with the Family, captained by Anthony DiFilippo IV or even his successor, would never forget the contract on Vincent Tagliafero's head or, more importantly, the man given the responsibility for fulfilling that contract.

Do I have the guts to lie to my uncle? Johnny asked himself again. *The man who watched over me as a kid after Dad died? The man who pays my mother a weekly allowance so she never has to work? How can I ever deny a request from my godfather?*

"Finish this thing by Sunday night," the don had ordered.

It was early Friday morning, and Johnny Cercone had a very hard decision to make.

Smoking a Marlboro, Vincent Tagliafero leaned on the lamppost at the corner of Westchester Avenue and East 172nd Street, one block east of Crotona Park, trying his best to look like a hard ass. Johnny Cercone pulled his late-model Corvette to the curb. Tagliafero flicked his cigarette onto the sidewalk and climbed into the car.

"Shit, Johnny, it's three in the goddamned morning," Tagliafero complained as Cercone drove away.

"Thank your skinny ass it ain't February," Cercone said tersely. "If you don't like the hours, fill out an application at 7-Eleven."

"What's with you?"

Cercone turned right onto the Bruckner Expressway. Traffic was light. Trash and overgrown weeds littered the median. They passed burnt-out husks that had once been cars, a dilapidated auto parts company, and empty warehouses. A few homeless people staked a claim to the dumpster outside a fast-food joint. Pedestrians were scarce. Steel bars or mesh covered nearly every unbroken window in the neighborhood.

"Hey, when the boss tells me to jump," Cercone said, jerking the steering wheel to the right, "I fuckin' fly to the moon. And the old man wants this lowlife prick handled tonight. Another collection." He paused. "Here's some words to live by, Vincent: Do as I say *and* as I do. Got it, shit-for-brains?"

"You mind if I turn down the air?" Tagliafero said, reaching for the dashboard.

"Yeah, I do mind!" Johnny shouted. "Keep your sticky little fingers off the leather upholstery. Christ, you're like a goddamned kid. Are you even listening to me?"

"Man . . . seriously, what's your problem?"

"Just keep your eye on the ball, Vincent."

"You sound like my—"

"Don't these people got any self-respect?" said Cercone, turning his attention to the rows of cardboard boxes filled with homeless people.

"I say we ship the bastards to Canada or New Mexico."

"You mean Mexico."

Tagliafero thinned his eyes. "Yeah, right. I was just tryin' to be funny."

"Of course you were." Cercone made a quick right, and the Corvette's rear end fishtailed on the oily street.

"Where we goin'?"

"Hunts Point Market. Our delinquent boy sells fruit for a living." Cercone glanced over at his little cousin. "Got your piece?"

Tagliafero folded back his windbreaker and patted the Glock 9mm tucked in his shoulder harness.

Cercone turned left onto Longfellow. Every streetlight had been broken along the brick-covered boulevard. The industrial neighborhood was quiet.

"Hey, Johnny, did you talk to Uncle Tony about our . . . my problem?"

"Yeah," Cercone said with a what-the-hell shrug.

"What'd he say?"

"He said you're a stupid fuck. You made a mistake—a big mistake, but it's nothing we can't handle. You're family."

"Uncle Tony cursed?"

"No, you asshole, he didn't use those exact words," Cercone said, righteous indignation in his tone, "but you get the idea."

"Yeah, yeah, right."

"And he said I should whack you," Cercone said, his expression grave.

The blood drained from Tagliafero's olive complexion. "You playin' with me, Johnny?"

"Whack you over the head with a goddamned two-by-four, you idiot," said Cercone. "Knock some sense into that monkey skull of yours."

Tagliafero manufactured a smile. "Yeah, real funny."

"C'mon, I need you to focus for once in your miserable life," Cercone said. "We're almost there. You fuck this one up, Vincent, and we'll both be working for tips at Zimmerman's car wash."

"Jesus," Tagliafero said, swallowing hard. "For how long?"

There wasn't a hint of humor in Johnny Cercone's voice when he replied, "Until death do us part."

CHAPTER 7

Hackensack

Kevin Easter took a long pull from his third Miller Lite and rested the bottle on the pitted mahogany table. This New Jersey sports bar, the End Zone, was in sight of Route 80 and a few miles west of the George Washington Bridge that led into the northern tip of Manhattan. The old gin mill had two pool tables, a dartboard, a broken foosball table, five antiquated video games, and eight television sets bolted to five different walls; none were flat-screen. Sports memorabilia—jerseys, signed photographs—on the walls dated back at least twenty years. The End Zone had obviously seen better days.

The soothing effect of the alcohol had already begun to cloud Hatch's judgment. Picking up the bottle, he studied the label, then said quietly, "It's been almost a year."

The wooden chair groaned as Gray Taylor shifted his weight. "For what?"

"Since I've had a drop of alcohol."

"Maybe you should stop."

"I don't have trouble with booze, if that's what you're thinking."

"I read your file, remember?" said Taylor. "And even if you did have a problem, I'm not here to judge."

Hatch chuckled, and then said, "What kind of babysitter are you?"

"Seriously, do you ever stop talking?" Taylor said, slowly shaking his head.

"My people," Hatch said, seemingly ignoring Taylor, "at least my father's half, the Indian half, have a history with booze—"

"Can we please move on to something else?" Taylor said, reaching for his club soda. "You're starting to bore me."

"*My people*," Hatch repeated. "Did I really say that?"

"Yep."

"Shit, I must be screwed up."

"You sound like a racist."

Hatch rested his elbows on the table, leaned forward, and said, "I'm a realist,

Taylor. Look it up on the Internet under *drunks* and *firewater*. I bet you'll find a photo of an Indian like me."

"Maybe you've had enough firewater for one day."

For most of an hour, Taylor had listened to Hatch talk through a shroud of self-pity. Karen on their wedding day. Karen's sarcastic sense of humor. Karen's love for comic books, summer blockbusters, and NHL hockey. The funny birthmark on Karen's right buttock that looked something like a crow in flight. Karen's trip to visit Patricia in New York had been his idea, Hatch said regretfully.

The sports bar, Taylor noticed, momentarily shifting his gaze, had become increasingly crowded with working-class men. U2's "Beautiful Day" played on the jukebox, followed by "Hold Me, Thrill Me, Kiss Me, Kill Me." Taylor looked at his watch.

"You got an appointment?" Hatch asked, pushing his beer to the side.

"Nope."

"Married?"

"Uh, yeah."

"Children?"

"I'm not a big fan of small talk, Hatch, especially when it's about me," Taylor said. "I didn't think you were one for bullshit either, but booze is an equal-opportunity offender."

"Fair enough," Hatch said, finishing off his beer. "Why don't you call the little lady—tell her you'll be missing supper?"

"You really think you're in shape to hop a flight?"

"The way I see it," Hatch said, "Jack thinks I need an escort while I'm relatively close to the scene of the crime. You happen to be that lucky fella."

"I can see where this is going," Taylor murmured, clearly annoyed.

"I just decided I'm staying the night," Hatch said. "Time to find me a great steak house and an expensive hotel."

"Better yet, maybe I should *ask* my wife to set up the guest room. I'll buy you that steak, and then you can stay with us tonight."

"I'd rather not inconvenience you ... or Mrs. Taylor."

"Trust me, Hatch, we're way beyond that." Taylor got to his feet, fished the SUV's keys from his pants pocket, and headed for the door.

"What if I run?"

"Then I'll shoot you," Taylor said over his shoulder.

And of the few men who overheard Taylor's comment, not a one smiled.

CHAPTER 8

Brooklyn

Homicide detective Katherine Montroy rolled over in her bed and stared at the illuminated clock on the nightstand. Four-twenty in the morning. The phone rang a third time.

"Go . . . a . . . way!" She wrapped a pillow around her head and mumbled something unintelligible.

"It's definitely not for me, Kat," came the voice of the sleepy woman on the other side of the bed. Pulling a silk sheet over her slender, naked body, Montroy's partner of six months curled into a tight ball.

Montroy groaned. The phone kept on ringing. She'd been promoted to the homicide division two years earlier, and these intrusions into her private life were the only part of the job she could do without.

Montroy reached over and lifted the phone. "This better not be a joke," she said groggily.

"Sorry to wake you, Detective," dispatcher Byron Davis said, sounding anything but remorseful.

"What is it, Davis?"

"We found a body at Hunts Point—near the Terminal Market. Caucasian, male, late teens—"

"What about Nicholas Benedetti or Philips? Aren't they on tonight?"

"Nick's at another homicide near—"

"Okay, okay, give me the address," Montroy said, her feet hitting the plush carpet. "Yeah, I think I know the place. Tell the officer in charge I'll be there in thirty."

———————————

Less than a minute later, Katherine Montroy leaned on the bathroom sink, staring at her mirrored reflection. Even as a child, she was never considered pretty or cute. Her large frame and round face wouldn't allow it. Today, at age twenty-nine, it would be a stretch to label Montroy attractive, or even handsome. At nearly six feet, she had a big body with short, auburn, almost mannish hair that accentuated her clear, pale complexion, brown eyes, hawkish nose, and thin lips. Still, what Montroy lacked in physical appearance, a quality not helped by her simple taste in clothing, she made up for with her gregarious personality. She was the queen of practical jokes, and had "cop sense," a gift she was just beginning to understand and use. And since embracing the fact that she was gay—a revelation that struck her like a hammer to her head during her sophomore year at Cornell University—Katherine really liked the person she saw in the mirror.

The men of the Twenty-Eighth Precinct pretty much had no choice but to enjoy their colleague's company. Witty, engaging, a team player, Katherine Montroy was one of the brightest homicide detectives the South Bronx had. To improve her skills, all she needed was more field experience.

The early-morning phone call promised to give her just that.

Detective Montroy arrived at the abandoned Best-Way Produce Company building a half an hour later. She was wearing a white golf shirt, designer jeans, and canvas walking shoes. There was now a hint of dawn on the eastern horizon, and the local meteorologists had predicted another scorcher, even with morning showers in the forecast. A small group of dockworkers had gathered outside the yellow crime scene tape that separated them from the victim. A snack truck was cashing in on the unexpected entertainment.

Parking her Ford Taurus on the street, Montroy tucked her badge in her elastic waistband and got out of the vehicle. She waded through a crowd of curious bystanders and ducked under the crime scene tape.

A young patrolman approached. Looking no more than twenty-two, he was a tall, skinny pretty boy with short blond hair and light blue eyes. "Detective Montroy?" he said tentatively, glancing at her identification.

"Afraid so. Wow, this whole place smells like an overturned outhouse at a Dead concert."

"Officer Peter Pearsall." They shook hands. "Ma'am, I'm afraid it gets worse near the water."

Half-expecting the young cop to click his heels together and demonstrate his best Nazi storm trooper salute, Montroy said, gesturing ahead, "So, who's our friend in the cowboy boots? That better not be Kenny Chesney. God, I love his music."

Officer Pearsall chuckled, then read from his notepad. "Vincent Tagliafero," he said. "Age nineteen. Home address is Prospect Avenue in the Bronx."

Montroy listened, but her eyes wandered to the body, which was covered by a green plastic tarp weighted down at the corners with broken bricks.

"One round to the face. Must have been a heavy-duty caliber," said Pearsall. "The back of his skull is gone. Probably in the water. Or maybe a rat ran off with—"

"You learned his identity how?"

"The driver's license in his wallet."

"Excellent detective work." Montroy winked. "And, wait a second, now you're gonna tell me Mr. Tagliafero's money is missing?"

"No, ma'am," Pearsall said, shaking his head. "He was carrying twenty-six dollars—all singles. His credit cards were there, too."

"Huh." Montroy glanced around the crime scene. "You find any of this odd, Peter?"

"Well, since you asked . . . yeah. Looks like a mob hit. Italian name. Gold cross, diamond pinky ring—they're all still on the vic."

"You're stereotyping, Officer. This isn't a movie of the week."

"Sorry, ma'am." Pearsall averted his gaze like a scolded child.

Folding back the plastic tarp, Montroy looked at the body. A collective gasp rose from some of the spectators as they got their first glimpse of the corpse. The man lay on his side, blood and brain matter spilt on the cracked pavement. "But you might be on the right track, Peter," she said, narrowing her eyes.

Montroy crouched. Officer Pearsall did the same, although he looked uncomfortable. Pearsall's hands clenched and unclenched. Most of his breakfast was already in the East River.

"Your first ride at the rodeo?" Montroy said under her breath, in an attempt not to embarrass the young officer.

Pearsall nodded. "That obvious?"

"Don't sweat it," Montroy said. "We've all been there."

Pearsall wiped his brow of perspiration but said nothing.

"Mr. Tagliafero was shot in the face at point-blank range. The goddamned face," Montroy repeated firmly. "If it's a hit, another family most likely isn't involved. There's a time-honored code among these principled gentlemen. Maybe this is a gang thing."

"Tagliafero had two handguns."

"Go on."

"A Smith & Wesson Model 64," Pearsall said. He pointed to the small of Tagliafero's back. "And then there's the Glock 9mm near his feet. He must have been holding that one when he got—"

"Any idea who called the cops?"

"Dispatch radioed me," Pearsall said. "I can ask Davis."

"I'd appreciate that."

"Yes, ma'am. My pleasure."

"Average citizens don't like to get involved with shit like this nowadays," Montroy said, drawing a breath. "I'll bet you lunch that the call came from a pay phone or cloned cell—but it never hurts to try. Where's your partner this glorious morning?"

"He called in sick."

"Ah, Peter, look at all the fun he's missing."

Chuckling, Officer Pearsall said, "Yeah, I wouldn't miss it for the world."

Montroy pinched the bridge of her nose and grimaced. "Jesus on horseback, it really does stink around here."

"The place is crawling with huge rats, and they're bold," said Pearsall. "It's a good thing I got here when I did. A big one, God, it was the size of a cocker spaniel, was sitting on Tagliafero's hip—"

"Dr. Espinoza!" Montroy shouted to the medical examiner in exaggerated Puerto Rican-accented English. "Welcome to a side of life very few New Yorkers have the pleasure to experience. We're truly blessed, you and me."

Officer Pearsall followed Detective Montroy's gaze. Carrying an oversized silver briefcase, the short, balding medical examiner pushed his steel-rimmed bifocals up the bridge of his nose and then waddled toward the deceased.

"My, my, the lovely and talented *Señorita* Katherine."

"The one and only," Montroy said, smiling.

"God must be looking down on my wretched soul." Espinoza took a cursory glance around the crime scene. Whispering, he said, "I was expecting that asshole, Philips. Please tell me the little bastard died of a heart attack and I missed the obituary."

"Matty isn't such a bad guy," Montroy said. "He's old school."

"Katherine, you'd find redeeming qualities in Osama bin Laden."

"I'd marry Osama for his money, but the cave and the beard would have to go." Montroy quickly introduced the two men.

Dwayne Espinoza shook Pearsall's hand. "You new, Officer?"

"I've been with the Twenty-Eighth for almost two months."

Snorting, Espinoza asked, "Did you touch anything?"

"Only to remove the victim's wallet. And I used gloves."

"Please tell me you were careful."

"Yes, sir," Pearsall said, standing a little straighter. "I didn't linger in the grid, and one of the techies put my shoeprint on file."

"I bet he read that in some procedural book," Espinoza said.

"Peter," Montroy said, "it's time to let this very important man go about his work before the rain starts. Maybe you and I can scrounge up some coffee."

"Black, lots of sugar," Espinoza said. "I've got another dead client in the Bronx, probably with that jerk Benedetti. I'll be quick here." Tipping his head forward, he looked over his glasses. "You sure you secured the area, Officer?"

"Yes, sir," Pearsall repeated. "I was the only one near the body before Detective Montroy arrived."

"I don't need some hard-ass wannabe from the DA's office calling me incompetent in front of a jury," Espinoza said. "Believe me, I may be a little guy and a little flabby around the midsection, but I carry a big fucking bat. And I want my pension—every stinkin' penny of it."

"Dwayne, I'm sure Peter did just fine. Look at him—one part Starsky, one part Hutch, two parts Dudley Do-Right."

"By the book," Officer Pearsall said.

Espinoza shook his head but smiled nonetheless. "Yeah, that's what I was afraid of. Hey, Pete, don't forget my coffee."

CHAPTER 9

Manhattan

Kevin Easter rested his chin on the marble railing of the private balcony and stared at the busy city street seven stories below. Last night's alcohol had temporarily eased his pain, but the hangover was an unpleasant reminder. Yellow taxicabs filled West 72nd Street and Central Park West. The light rain did little to impede their progress. A sea of black umbrellas sheltered their owners from the elements as they marched along the wet sidewalks and across intersections. Even before dawn could peek into Manhattan's famous concrete canyons, the city had come to life.

And, Hatch noted, the pace seemed to quicken as the darkness receded.

The sliding glass door opened and closed behind Hatch. A dark-haired woman stepped to the railing and followed her guest's gaze to the street below. Hatch's head slowly rotated to the right. He pushed the wet hair from his face and said, "You must be Terri."

"And you're Kevin."

"Sorry about last night," said Hatch, "rolling in late, missing dinner, drinking most of your red wine."

Patting Hatch on the shoulder with a small, delicate hand, Terri Taylor said, "I'd rather blame my husband, if you don't mind. I've had my eye on this cute summer dress in Greenwich Village, and this is my big chance."

"Glad I could help."

"Would you like to be alone?"

"No, not really."

"I love the rain," Terri said, sniffing the air and turning her face into the breeze. "I know it's a cliché, but everything *does* smell cleaner, fresher, especially in a big city like New York."

"Yeah."

"And I know this is gonna come across as weird, but I've always liked the sound of the traffic moving over wet pavement. I was one of those kids who rarely missed an opportunity to jump in a puddle."

"It poured about an hour ago," said Hatch.

"Some of the walls in the Dakota are eighteen inches thick," Terri said. "I didn't hear a damn thing."

"One of the paths in Central Park turned into a river, and the joggers never missed a beat."

"New Yorkers have a much-deserved reputation for adapting to just about anything that's thrown their way. I think it's always been that way." She smiled. "You've been out here all that time, Kevin?"

"Closer to four hours," he said. "And my friends call me Hatch."

"Hatch it is."

"This place, your home—it's unbelievable."

"One of my favorite buildings in the city," Terri said, looking over at her guest. She stroked a marble gargoyle. "The Dakota has a very old soul."

"Does Yoko Ono really live here?"

"Yep, and she's actually pretty cool," said Terri. "We've been to a few of her parties—a really diverse bunch. Mick Jagger's supermodel girlfriend got completely drunk at Yoko's annual Christmas gathering last year and hit on Gray most of the night. His head was swollen for a month, although he'd be the last to admit it."

"Gray seems like a private guy."

"We both are. And between you and me, I hate to shop, especially for clothes." Terri paused a beat, then let out a long breath. "I'm sorry for your loss, Hatch. I can't imagine how you feel, or if there's any appropriate thing to say. Losing Gray would, wow . . . I don't know what I'd do."

"It's probably a good thing your husband's been chauffeuring me around."

"Why's that?"

"I might have driven a rental into the Hudson River by now." Turning toward Terri, Hatch grinned. "You were supposed to laugh."

"Slow on the uptake. Sorry. I haven't had my first cup of coffee yet."

Hatch shrugged. "It wasn't all that funny."

"If there's anything we can ever do to help, please don't hesitate."

Hatch looked over at Terri and pinched a smile. "Thanks." He saw an eye-catching woman in her mid-thirties, maybe a few years older than Gray. She was tall and thin—a dancer's body came to mind—and her dark, curly, shoulder-length hair was parted to one side. Terri had large green eyes, tanned skin, and a cluster of freckles on her nose. She was barefoot, wearing a tight pair of Levi blue jeans with a hole in one knee and a cream-colored blouse, open at the neck. Hatch could see her beauty was God-given and not purchased on Fifth Avenue or in a physician's office.

"You could have used one of the spare bedrooms," Terri said.

"Gray would have had to carry me."

"There's always next time."

There won't be a next time. The lines deepened about Hatch's mouth. "I really have no idea how to deal with all of this . . ." His voice trailed off and he pursed his lips.

"Time and faith," Terri said, lightly touching Hatch's hand. "Trust me."

"Easier said than done."

"I've never been one for handing out personal advice, so I'm not gonna start now." Terri smiled. "The 'time and faith' thing came from a book my dad gave me about three years ago. *Why Bad Things Happen to Good People*. It's in our study if you're interested." She paused for a long moment, then said, "It helped save Gray's life."

As Hatch reflected on Terri's words, Gray Taylor stepped onto the balcony. "Your version of a shower, Kevin?"

"I need fresh air. And it's Hatch. Only Jack and my brother call me Kevin. Didn't we go over this last night?"

Taylor slipped an arm around his wife's thin waist. He pulled her close and kissed her full on the lips. "Did I snore?"

"Are clowns creepy? Is Elvis dead? Am I buying a new dress in the Village?" Terri winked at Hatch.

"I'll take that as a big affirmative," Taylor said, kissing her again.

"Too much Merlot makes my husband snore," Terri said, whispering loud enough for both men to hear. "His party-animal days are over."

"She talks more than you," Taylor said to Hatch, gesturing to his wife. "Imagine that."

"It's actually nice to know that Gray can still let his hair down," Terri said, reaching for the sliding glass door. "Breakfast?"

"All I need is hot tea," Hatch said.

"Scrambled eggs and coffee would be terrific," Taylor said. "I'll make the toast."

Terri closed the door, giving both men privacy.

"Damn, look at you, old man," Hatch said, chuckling. "Where'd you meet her?"

"We'll leave that for another day."

"You sure as hell don't like to talk about your personal—"

"Jack called," Taylor said. He leaned against the railing.

Hatch turned his attention to Central Park and beyond. "What's on his mind?" His humor had disappeared like the puddles in Central Park.

"You know Jack. He's like a shadow."

"What did you tell him?"

"The truth," said Taylor. "We got drunk, you felt sorry for yourself and finally passed out on the couch. And you're still here."

"You could have stretched it."

"What's the point? We're talking about Jack Slattery."

"It's really none of his business."

"Sure it is. You're one of his boys, Hatch. And he's worried . . ."

". . . that I might do something stupid," Hatch said, finishing Taylor's thought. He turned his body to face the taller man. "I'm quitting, Gray. I'm done. Out. I really don't care what Jack thinks. I don't care what anyone thinks. No offense."

"You know what they say about people making rash decisions after a—"

"I don't give a fuck what these goddamned experts think or how time heals all wounds—"

"Cops in the Bronx may have identified Karen's shooter," said Taylor.

Hatch's eyes narrowed, darkened, and then focused on Taylor. "What?"

"A detective from the Twenty-Eighth Precinct may have found the guy who killed your wife, Patricia, and the bartender."

"Jack told you this?" Hatch's tone was low, conciliatory.

Nodding, Taylor said, "He's obviously keeping a very close eye on this one."

"Do they have this guy in custody?"

"Not exactly."

"Don't play games with me, Gray."

"They found his body in the Bronx, behind an abandoned building at Hunts Point near the Terminal Market—it's a produce distribution center on the East River. Nineteen-year-old kid. He was carrying a Glock 9mm and a Smith & Wesson Model 64. Ballistics confirmed that both guns fired the bullets that killed Karen, Patricia Durante, *and* Robert O'Rourke. The vic had been shot in the face at close range."

"When did all this happen?"

"Very early this morning. Nine-one-one received an anonymous call. A cop found the body."

As Hatch listened to Taylor's account, he wasn't exactly sure how to feel. Something primal had awakened in him over the past twenty-four hours; his emotions were flying around in about a hundred different directions. He squeezed the bridge of his nose in a desperate attempt to stave off another punishing headache, or something worse.

"No way, Gray," Hatch said, shaking his head. "A little too convenient for my taste."

"I'm only telling you what Jack told me. This investigation—the Twenty-Eighth Precinct guys are calling it 'The Three Tenors' because of Patricia's Broadway connections—is politically charged. You read the papers."

"Take a look around," said Hatch. "This city is huge. How many homicides do you have each day? Two? Five? Twenty? They find this teenager a few hours ago, and ballistics suddenly has matches for the Rudy's Tavern murders? No, I'm not buying it. And neither are you. I can tell."

"Or maybe finding the killer was a real lucky break, Hatch—lucky for you, even luckier for the New York cops who were on the hot seat."

"We're taught and trained never to believe in coincidences."

"I'm saying it's a possibility."

"Try again."

"Look," Taylor said, exhaling audibly, "before we pass judgment—"

"The pressure on some of these cops has to be enormous," Hatch said, a little too loudly. "The media's been fueling the fire for almost five days. You've been hammering home that point since I landed. 'Politically charged'—your words. The mayor and a bunch of his brethren are feeling it from all angles, and then you have the DDI of the friggin' CIA asking hard questions. The cops find their man with both weapons. Presto, the problem vanishes. No way!"

After a long minute, Taylor said, "Okay, the dead teenager's guns matched the bullets at Rudy's Tavern. Ballistics is a whole different ballgame. Now you're talking a larger conspiracy with a number of players. That's when you lose me."

"Maybe this nineteen year old is a patsy, a kid who had nothing to do with the murders. Maybe the guns were planted. Maybe the cops set him up."

"Pressure is one thing," Taylor said, "but something like this leads to prison if any of them got caught. Hatch, this kid was murdered."

"Which means he's not talking, right?" Hatch tapped his lip with his index finger, then said, "Darts at a dartboard. That's what we're doing here."

"To pull this off, somebody still needed to locate the murder weapons—the Glock and Smith & Wesson," Taylor said. "And as you so beautifully pointed out a few minutes ago, this is a massive city. More than six million people. Somebody high on the food chain would have had to know where the guns were."

Hatch nodded.

"If the cops fixed the investigation to protect somebody or to lower the heat, who would admit it?" Taylor said. "Nobody. Cops are an exclusive club. They're like us, Hatch. Cloistered. We protect each other. If that doesn't work, we eat our own. It's all about survival."

Reaching for the sliding glass door, Hatch said, "It's hard to bury the truth."

"Depends how deep you're willing to dig." Taylor paused. "Did you bring a shovel?"

CHAPTER 10

Bronx

From the rear seat of the green BMW 740L, hidden behind the bulletproof windows that doubled as tinted glass, Anthony DiFilippo IV watched the South Bronx come into view as his car passed over the 145th Street Bridge from Manhattan. Lunch had been at Constantine's, a semi-private Italian restaurant in Little Italy. As he'd done for the past eight years, the owner, Constantine DiBello, had served Tony D and his guests personally.

The rumble of the steel bridge beneath the wheels of the luxury car had a reassuring appeal to the don, as did the presence of Marco, his chauffeur and bodyguard, behind the wheel. Johnny Cercone, a passenger in the BMW, sat quietly.

In Tony D, sight of the bridge triggered memories of a simpler life. As a young boy, the skyscrapers had enchanted him. But Manhattan, only a few miles from the two-bedroom Bronx apartment of his youth, had been as foreign as France back then. The ever-familiar flat black roofs of the Bronx's commercial district projected a grim image to outsiders, but one man's garbage is indeed another man's treasure, the don thought. The same theory applied to those residing in Manhattan's shadow. If given the chance to relive their childhoods, none of his close buddies would ever exchange life on Coney Island Avenue for a penthouse overlooking Central Park. Their relationships were too meaningful, their lives forever interconnected.

Thousands of two-story structures, most of them duplexes, lined the city streets in neat rows. Returning to the Bronx should have brought a wave of nostalgia and security to Tony D, yet those comforting sentiments had eluded him for most of the week. Something was wrong. As with the early signs of an impacted tooth, he was aware of a problem that needed to be taken care of.

The BMW moved off the 145th Street Bridge and turned right on Grand Boulevard, where traffic came to a standstill.

"What now, Tony?" Marco said, tapping the steering wheel impatiently.

"I'm in no hurry."

Cercone glanced over at his uncle. The old man stared off into space.

"A detective friend of mine called me a couple of hours ago," Tony D finally said, as the car turned left on East 138th Street. Marco leaned on the horn to scare off some kids playing stickball. "This detective thanked me, Johnny!" the don said, clearly annoyed.

Cercone swallowed hard.

Tony D shook a manicured finger in the air. He coughed—gruff and guttural—pulled a linen handkerchief from his jacket pocket, and covered his mouth. "Not once did my friend express condolences. Not once. Nothing. Instead, only a lousy 'thank you.' Your cousin takes a bullet in the head, dies because of his lapse in judgment, and my detective friend probably gets a medal. Respect is in short supply in today's world."

"It's not like the good old days, Uncle Tony."

"Good old days?" the don spat. "We conveniently forget how bad it was back then. So much death when conversation would have been enough to solve differences."

"Fat Paulie might help—"

"I don't like what's happening, Johnny. Something's wrong. You should have staged it like a robbery, not a hit."

Cercone turned his body to face his uncle. "What do you mean something's wrong?"

Rarely did the don express his personal thoughts, let alone his premonitions. He was a Harvard-educated man, and also street-savvy—one who made decisions based on facts and a great deal of thought, like a master chess player.

But like a tsunami silently approaching a tranquil coastline, subtle signs of danger had begun to appear along the shore of Tony D's mind. Gentle waves of trepidation rolled into his consciousness and pushed aside six years of relative peace. The incoming tempest would soon appear, Tony D understood, but he didn't know where it was coming from. Or why. Last night, in a dream, an enormous crow had pecked at his face, aiming for his eyes and throat. Tony D had awakened with a start. He'd found swallowing difficult ever since.

"I have a bad feeling, Johnny," he said quietly.

"Because of the cops?"

"No. They're small potatoes. I believe one of our competitors is about to make a power play."

Cercone leaned closer to the old man. "Who?"

"That's what I want you to find out. Go into Brooklyn, Queens, and Staten Island. Nose around, ask a few questions, but be discreet. See what the other families are thinking. I want you to look into Tapia's operation. The man is unstable. He can't be trusted."

Tony D was referring to a *capo* in the rival Genovese family. Tommy "Bull" Tapia was known to have his sights set on the highest position in their outfit. For nearly a year, rumors had circulated about an impending coup. The life of Frank DeVincenzsa, the godfather of the Genovese crime family, had been drained like an old car battery.

"Okay, okay . . . good," Johnny Cercone said, suddenly excited, clapping his hands together. The BMW rounded another corner. "Now we're getting somewhere. I'll take Woody and a few of the—"

Tony D's finger came within an inch of his godson's face. "Tell nobody."

Cercone fell back into the plush seat. "Yes, sir."

"This stays between me and you—that includes Mr. Biasucci and Paulie."

"Yes, sir," Cercone repeated.

"You'll do this after we bury Vincent." Tony D's raspy voice had a trace of sadness. "Your mother is going to need you."

Bronx

Sitting in her cramped office, Detective Katherine Montroy sipped her split pea Cup-a-Soup and flipped through the medical examiner's field report on Vincent Tagliafero's murder. It didn't tell her anything she didn't already know. The actual autopsy was scheduled for early Monday morning. A few minutes before one o'clock now, and it was the first time since the early-morning call that she'd found a quiet moment. She still carried the stench of the Hunts Point Market.

The glass door swung open, and the sounds of a busy squad room swept in like a winter gust. "Knock, knock," the little man said in a nasally voice, sticking his head into Montroy's cluttered workplace.

Her eyes never left the report. "Out damn'd spot! Out, I say!"

"No can do, Lady Macbeth." Detective Matthew Philips took a seat on a rusted metal chair beside the potted plant he'd given his colleague last Christmas. He ran his thumb over the large variegated leaves, cleaning off a thin layer of dust. "Poor thing."

"You're on the wrong side of the door, Matty."

"Huh?"

"I'm attempting to enjoy my lunch." Montroy thinned her eyes, which should have sent a clear message, but Philips simply ignored it—an attribute he'd perfected over the years. Although Montroy respected Philips and could even categorize him as a close friend, she hated when he did this. He knew that lunch and dinner were clearly out of bounds. Everyone in the precinct was aware of this unwritten rule.

But still, Philips's anxious smile greeted Montroy's glacier-like expression. Stalemate.

Montroy sat back in her chair, clasped her fingers behind her head, exhaled deeply, and said, "Okay, you win. What's on your mind, Matty?"

If people were animals, Philips would have been a turtle minus the shell. He was thin, short, and frail, maybe a hundred and forty pounds after a big meal. His face had a sickly yellow tinge, and his greasy hair—what hair he still had—failed to cover an expanding bald spot. His teeth and fingers were permanently nicotine-stained by a smoking habit he blamed on seventeen years as an NYPD homicide detective.

Philips cleared his throat. "Um . . . did you get the preliminary on that Bronx murder?"

"Honey, which one might that be? We've had eight in the past two weeks. Charles Bronson's ghost must be filming another dreadful sequel to *Death Wish*."

Philips grabbed a cigarette, then tapped it on the wooden armrest.

"Don't even think about it," she said resolutely. "See that sign? It was put there, right in the middle of *my* desk, specifically for people like *you*, long before the great state of New York got their act together." Montroy slid the paperweight closer to her guest. *NO SMOKING!*

"We're the millennium's new lepers, Kat."

To colleagues, peers, uniformed cops, and just about anyone who worked with him, Matthew Philips was a royal pain in the ass, but his record for closing homicide cases was remarkable, even compared to Katherine Montroy's. Nobody could accuse Philips of not being meticulous, methodical, and professional. He was also steady and dependable, and he rarely rocked the boat.

"Is there a point to this invasion of my privacy?" Montroy asked, reaching for her soup.

"The kid in the Bronx, behind the old Best-Way Produce Company building."

"What about him?"

"He's Tony D's nephew."

"Yes, I believe that was brought to my attention," Montroy said, rolling her eyes. "Looks like a gang hit, a little payback probably. Some of the boys are calling the case 'Forrest Gump' because the vic wasn't all that bright."

"I was just wondering if they found the slug."

"It's probably in the East River, along with a big chunk of the boy's skull. An ugly exit wound." She paused. "Why you so interested in this one, Matty? Come to Momma. What's going on?"

Offering her a nicotine-stained grin, Philips said, "Thought we might have a connection between your stiff and the one I found in Claremont Park a few hours ago. My guy took a .45 to the melon. Surprise, surprise, he's allegedly a soldier in the Genovese family."

"I never said anything about a .45 wasting Mr. Gump. You're fishing, Matthew. For the record, my stiff's name is Vincent Tagliafero."

"Yeah, that's what I heard." Philips slowly stroked his unlit Lucky Strike. "Must be new to the organization."

"Occupational hazard," said Montroy with a slight shrug. "Maybe the kid should have finished high school and got a real job."

"Yeah, and I'm entering the Miss America pageant next month."

"I don't know what caliber bullet killed DiFilippo's nephew," Montroy said. "But we did find a Glock at the scene. Tagliafero had it out. He also had a Smith & Wesson tucked in his pants. Our vic was loaded for bear."

"Peter Pearsall filled in a few of the blanks for me. Nice kid."

"No secrets around here," Montroy said, dipping her spoon into her Cup-a-Soup. "Maybe before Monday's autopsy Dr. Espinoza can give you an educated guess about the bullet."

"Whatever." Philips slipped out of the chair. He pulled open the glass door, and the sounds from the Twenty-Eighth Precinct filled the small office again. He hesitated, then turned back to face his colleague. The unlit cigarette now dangled from the corner of his mouth. "What if I told you ballistics has a match between Tagliafero's handguns and the slugs left behind at Rudy's Tavern?"

"The Three Tenors?" said Montroy, sitting a little straighter. "I'd call you a goddamned liar, because even if there was a match . . ." Her voice trailed off. "Hey, what genius made the connection so fast?"

Philips grinned wolfishly.

"Why wasn't I told?" Jumping to her feet, Montroy splashed green soup across her desk, and then yelled, "Hey, hey . . . oh, no you don't!"

"Maybe you should read your e-mail, Kat. Espinoza copied you."

The glass door closed between the two detectives.

"Damn you, Matty," Montroy murmured, reaching for the keyboard.

CHAPTER 11

Bronx

Placed at the base of the marble altar, Vincent Tagliafero's polished teak casket was nearly buried in a mound of flowers. The Catholic Mass was emotionally driven, extravagantly orchestrated, and filled with embellishments and lies about Vincent's nineteen years on the planet. Nobody mentioned his criminal background, violent history, or possible involvement in three deaths at Rudy's Tavern. The elderly priest—a close friend of Anthony DiFilippo IV—praised a young man he'd never met. It was as if the congregation was paying homage to a complete stranger. By the time the Mass was over, most parishioners would have believed Vincent was one step away from becoming a Franciscan monk.

St. Andrew's Church, at the corner of Gerard Avenue and East 168th in the Bronx, was packed with mourners. Older family members—seasoned veterans of such ceremonies—dominated the front pews. Out of loyalty, peers, associates, and even some past enemies made an appearance at either the wake or the funeral.

A few curious citizens and members of the media were stationed across the street from St. Andrew's, hoping for a brief glimpse of the elusive man who allegedly controlled much of the New York City underworld.

Twenty-seven-year-old B. J. Butera, reporter for *The New York Post*, had written four pieces on the Rudy's Tavern triple homicide. He stood on the curb, hands in the pockets of his Dockers, watching the procession of sullen people make their way to their vehicles.

Over the past few days, the connection between the don's nephew and the brutal triple slaying had brought unwanted notoriety to Tony D and his organization. And now there were whispers of revenge on the streets. This had been a violent attack, but unlike most contract killings, nobody seemed to know who'd given the order.

And why did it appear as if the cops had lost interest? Because Tagliafero had been implicated, and was now dead, the heat generated from the "Three Tenors" case had dissipated, and much of the New York media had promptly moved on to other inflammatory stories. A mother in Harlem, for example, had traded her newborn for crack.

Watching Anthony DiFilippo and his wife Mara slip into the back of an expensive BMW, Butera tugged on his blond goatee and considered the facts. The bullet that had torn through Tagliafero's face had turned attention away from Tony D's Italian rivals. Out of respect, Sicilians rarely mutilated a target, because an open casket helped bring closure. So the Tagliafero ("Forrest Gump") contract killing pointed to other equally ruthless adversaries. A gang perhaps? The Serbs? Maybe the Russians? Retaliation, in any case, was almost a certainty. Then again, maybe the kid had been involved in something dirty on the side.

But why in hell was Tagliafero carrying both Rudy's Tavern murder weapons? Could he really have been that stupid? Those who knew the don's nephew gave a resounding "yes." "Dumb as a stump," one DiFilippo associate had told B. J. a day earlier.

"You'd think he'd toss the damn things in the Hudson," B. J. said out loud. That being said, what genius in the police department had the brains and wherewithal to match Tagliafero's handguns with the slugs taken from the triple murder at Rudy's so quickly? If this Einstein (who must have been tipped off) had waited just a day or two, would anyone have been suspicious? The answer was probably no.

When the last car in the funeral procession pulled away from St. Andrew's and the curiosity seekers dispersed, Butera whistled for a cab. "Mr. Einstein, you moved way too fast," he said.

A cab came to a stop. Butera slid into the backseat and pulled the door closed. "The *Post*," he said. "I'm in a hurry."

"Like I've never heard that one before," said the Asian cabby under his breath.

CHAPTER 12

Charlottesville, Virginia

In stark contrast to Vincent Tagliafero's funeral, no more than twenty people attended Karen Easter's hillside service. It was held in a private cemetery a few miles north of Charlottesville, Virginia. Partly out of contempt for his father-in-law, partly out of selfishness, but mostly out of self-pity, Hatch had given Dr. Durante one day's notice, after he'd found the mental strength to make the funeral arrangements. The telephone conversation between the two men had lasted less than thirty seconds. The closest they'd come to each other today was about ten feet, and that happened to be right at this moment, as both stood at opposite ends of Karen's casket.

The Blue Ridge Mountains, partially covered by a blanket of low-lying clouds, filled the western sky this morning. Like most of the eastern United States, the grass was brown and withered, scorched from the brutal August heat and dry from lack of rain. The gentle breeze that played with Hatch's hair promised cooler temperatures ahead. A storm was coming.

A hint of fresh dirt drifted up from the grave. Sprinkling holy water on the coffin, a young Jesuit priest recited another verse of Scripture, then said, "Karen's spirit has been delivered into God's loving hands. Together she is watching over us . . ."

Hatch's mind drifted back to last week. The Jeremy Silverstone op had taken place in a world that no longer concerned him. *What's the point of it—of any of it?*

The priest glanced over at two cemetery workers. Both men quickly went to work, one guiding the coffin, the other manually turning a steel crank—one badly in need of lubrication—attached to twin straps draped around the casket. With each squeaky revolution, Karen's body moved closer to its permanent resting place.

Only then did Hatch notice the single pink and white rose on the hood of the casket. He took a few steps forward, as if drawn by some preternatural force, but the rose, it turned out, was not a Cajun Moon hybrid tea like the one he'd seen at Patricia's graveside ceremony in northern New Jersey.

A moment later, the priest turned around to face the small gathering. "Food and refreshments will be served at the home of Ida and Larry Scott," he said. "Everyone is welcome." He provided the address.

Terri Taylor leaned against her husband and whispered, "Is Dr. Durante a complete ass or what? The guy wouldn't even acknowledge Hatch."

Behind dark sunglasses, Gray Taylor showed no reaction. His arms remained folded across his wide chest. Jack Slattery smirked, albeit briefly. The coffin slowly dropped into the earth. The coffin disappeared into the cement crypt.

A large black crow appeared to watch the ritual from a gnarled sycamore tree's lowest branch. As if suddenly incensed, the crow screeched loudly, then took wing. Slattery was the only one who watched the bird fly off.

Hatch felt like part of his soul had been lowered into the ground alongside his dead wife. His grief was palpable, a blackness determined to extinguish his purpose—his love for life. This final goodbye was unimaginable, impossible. Karen had been his future—his reason for breathing. They'd planned on starting a family next year. *How can it be over so quickly?* he thought. *Where do I go from here?*.

Hatch's mind flashed to the night before he'd left for Andros Island to locate Jeremy Silverstone. He and Karen had been at a drive-in theater. Halfway through the latest Jennifer Aniston romantic comedy, Karen wondered aloud about some buttered popcorn, and Hatch volunteered to go—all of Ms. Aniston's films seemed pretty much the same.

When he got back to the Nissan SUV, holding a jumbo box of buttered popcorn and two Diet Cokes, Hatch found Karen in the backseat, a thin multicolored blanket—Buchanan plaid—pulled up to her neck, a mischievous expression on her reddening face. "Care to join me, Little Crow?" she'd purred, using his Native American name.

Conflicted by both deep sorrow and brief contentment, Hatch nevertheless smiled at the memory of making love to his wife that night—the last time. A moment later, all he could do was drop his head, turn, and walk away from the grave.

Gray and Terri Taylor, along with Jack Slattery, moved to their shared rental car without saying a word.

Soon thereafter, as Terri closed her car door and turned from the front seat to face the DDI, she said, "Okay, what's Dr. Durante's problem?"

"She's never been one for subtlety, Jack," Taylor said, dialing up the air conditioning.

"I seem to recall that distinctive attribute."

Terri's elbow hung over the seat. "You must know something."

"Terri," Slattery said at length, "it's who Kevin is that offends Dr. Durante."

"Because he works for CIA?" said Terri.

"He doesn't know anything about that part of Kevin's life," Slattery said. "I expect nobody at the service has a clue he works for me, except for the people in this car."

"Please don't tell me this has anything to do with the color of Hatch's skin."

"And his heritage," Slattery said. "Kevin's a minority, and his family doesn't come from money. Two strikes."

"The doctor should be ashamed," Taylor said under his breath.

"So let me get this straight," Terri said, her face darkening. "Back in college, Karen Durante falls in love with a cute guy who happens to be Seneca Indian, and Daddy Durante doesn't approve?"

"Pretty much," Slattery said.

"You have got to be kidding me," Terri said.

"He stopped paying Karen's tuition. And that was before they even considered marriage."

"Ignorant and short-sighted," Terri said through clenched teeth. "Shit!"

"We live in a very confused world, Terri." Slattery paused. "Maybe you'd like to come back and help us change—"

"We never even made it out of the cemetery," said Taylor, laughing quietly.

"I told you," Terri said, briefly turning to her husband. "Sorry, Jack, but my answer is still no, no, and absolutely not."

"Can you help me out here, Gray?"

"Boss, if you pick a fight with Mrs. Taylor, you're not going to win," Taylor said. "Ever. Take it from a punch-drunk boxer like me. If she doesn't want to come back to the Agency, there's no way I can change her mind."

"The man knows where his bread is buttered." Terri gave her husband a quick peck on the cheek. "And he's well-trained."

"At least I can tell Director Walsh I tried," Slattery said, looking out the window.

"The director," Taylor said. "The big dog. Now I'm impressed, Ter."

"Look, I appreciate the offer, Jack. Really, I do. But I've moved on," said Terri. "It's tiring jetting off to lands unknown. And I could never be a desk jockey at Langley. I'd go crazy staring at intelligence reports all day long."

"I'm sure we can find you something interesting," Slattery said.

"I like New York," she said a little too forcefully, as if trying to convince herself. "I like my new life."

Gray Taylor made eye contact with the DDI in the rearview mirror, then said, "The more you push, the more she'll push back. I'll bet that's in her file."

"Hey," Terri said, playfully hitting her husband, "stop giving away my secrets."

"It's an open invitation, Terri, but you already know that," said Slattery.

"This girl is a free bird," she said. "And this free bird wants a baby while her biological clock is still keeping time."

Taylor turned his head and stared at his wife. The rental drifted into the gravel. "Baby?"

Nearly everyone from Karen's ceremony ended up at Ida and Larry Scott's suburban home. It was a catered affair with finger food, a variety of salads, cold cuts, desserts, and plenty of alcohol. Hatch appeared robotic as he patiently made his way through the people, thanking each of them for their support. He even laughed after someone recalled a story about Karen—something about sneaking backstage and meeting Green Day at a concert at the University of Virginia last April.

Hatch's suit jacket hung on a doorknob in the kitchen.

Terri stood between her husband and Jack Slattery in the great room. The room was tastefully decorated, bright, airy, and noisy. Sipping her bottled water, she briefly studied each person. Dr. Homer Durante was a no-show. Small groups of three and four huddled together, deep in conversation; a few children maneuvered around the adults.

Terri nudged her old boss with her elbow. "Tell me about Hatch."

Gray Taylor, holding his Molson, looked over at Jack. "She still knows how to keep a secret."

"Anything in particular?" asked Slattery.

"What's his family like? What drove him to CIA? How was life on an Indian—"

"One question at a time, Ter," said Taylor.

"Believe it or not," Slattery said, "Kevin's mother was your typical Irish Catholic girl, born and raised in a blue-collar South Buffalo neighborhood. His dad was a full-blooded Seneca Indian, and a very vocal tribe leader, from what I've learned over the years. His parents met as teenagers on the Cattaraugus River while fly-fishing; both died in a hit-and-run when Kevin was eight . . . or nine. I've forgotten the exact age."

"Hatch was nine," Taylor said.

"That's horrible," Terri said, briefly looking over at her husband. "Did they catch the guy?"

"The driver was a she," Slattery said. "And she was drunk, according to reports and transcripts I've read. The whole thing turned into a political hot potato."

"Why?" Terri asked.

"The woman was a very wealthy mother of three," Slattery said. "She was white. Her family was connected to some powerful individuals in Western New York. The husband hired a big-time Manhattan firm to handle the case. The defense team convinced a jury a larger conspiracy was afoot—that Kevin's father's life was in danger because of his position in the tribe, specifically because of the casinos, which were taking root back then. Maybe they were run off the road by someone who had more to lose or gain. The driver walked away without so much as an apology. In the end, the district attorney couldn't even prove she was behind the wheel of the vehicle that killed Hatch's parents. Three of the four witnesses, all of whom saw this very drunk woman leave a local bar, recanted their initial stories."

"That's unbelievable," Terri said, shaking her head.

"Money is the great equalizer," Slattery said.

"Who raised Hatch?" Terri asked.

"His paternal grandfather, Low Dog—a terrific man, one of a kind. A loving, supportive father figure, and very, very smart. He's a shaman for the Senecas."

"The medicine man?" Terri said, narrowing her eyes.

"Exactly," Slattery said. "From what I know, his power on the reservation is absolute and rarely contested. Low Dog and the Seneca chief oversee the entire tribal community."

Glancing up at her husband again, Terri said, "That is so cool."

"Sounds like a dictatorship," Taylor murmured.

"Depends on who you ask," Slattery said. "The people at the top obviously appreciate their system."

"While the little guy gets squeezed . . . again," Taylor said, shaking his head.

"You're not being fair, Gray," Terri said. "What government is perfect?"

"The Senecas," Slattery said, "like most Native American reservations, are considered a sovereign nation with their own set of rules and laws, so the United States government has limited jurisdiction on their lands."

"A country within a country," Taylor said to his wife. He took a sip of his bottled beer.

Slattery cleared his throat. "Terri, even back when Kevin was a lowly recruit for CIA, getting indoctrinated at the Farm, his work ethic stood out from the rest. If someone beat him in a shooting drill, Kevin stayed late at the range. He's driven."

"Sounds like someone I know," Terri said, glancing at her husband.

"Before bringing Kevin to my side of the building, I personally interviewed him," Slattery said. "I'd seen all his tests—most grades were at the top of his class—and I'd talked with his instructors, but I wanted to know what motivated a guy like Kevin Easter. Yes, we recruited him, but why was he such an enthusiastic candidate?"

"I suppose you're gonna say that Hatch's answers are classified," Terri said.

Shaking his head, Slattery said, "I've taken you this far."

"Wow," Terri said, "you'll do anything for me to come back."

"Kevin said he wanted to be considered an American," said Slattery, "not just a Native American. Being employed by the United States government, specifically working for CIA, made him feel he was contributing to the good of the country. By finding and photographing enemies of the United States, Kevin Easter was saving lives, making our nation a safer place—making a difference. Growing up on an Indian reservation was like living in a foreign nation, he told me. He liked being part of a group working toward a common goal, like with his high school and college lacrosse teams."

"But he works alone, Jack," Taylor said.

"And so do you, Gray. But you both understand it's a collective effort."

Taylor nodded, looked over at his wife, but said nothing.

Terri cleared her throat. "Any siblings?"

"A brother," Jack said. "Steven. Retired Marine. Two years older than Kevin. They're pretty close. Steven owns a security firm that protects Middle East refineries. Spends a lot of time in Saudi, but I really don't know that much about him."

"Ah, so Big Brother does have its limitations," said Terri, grinning.

"We just don't have much of an interest in Steven Easter."

"Is he—" Terri began.

"Look who's here," Gray Taylor said.

Hatch kissed Terri lightly on the cheek. "Thanks for coming."

"We're only a phone call away," said Terri. "A spare bedroom is yours. Take advantage of it. Please. We'll track down John Lennon's spirit."

Taylor shook hands with the younger man. "We'd love to have you back."

Hatch turned his attention to the DDI. They shook hands. "You didn't have—"

"I wouldn't be here if I didn't want to be," Slattery said firmly.

"You still worried about me, Jack?"

The second-most powerful man at the CIA raised one eyebrow. "Should I be?"

———

Gray Taylor and Kevin Easter stood in the corner of the great room, quietly sipping their drinks. Others spoke quietly in small groups. Slattery had stepped out to make a phone call. Terri was using the bathroom.

Hatch finally broke the silence. "I feel like I owe these people."

"You don't," Taylor said decisively, laying a hand on the shorter man's shoulder. "There's no agenda here, Hatch. No payback. They're your friends."

"I didn't know you studied philosophy at West Point." Hatch smiled.

"Jack taught me about this stuff a few years ago."

"Care to share?"

"Maybe some other time," Taylor said.

"Can I have a word with you, Kevin?" Slattery asked, having snaked his way through the room.

"With or without my babysitter?" Hatch said, jerking a thumb toward Taylor. "It's up to you."

"The big guy seems okay to me," Hatch said, glancing sideways at Taylor.

"This is probably the wrong time," Slattery said, his voice all business, "but I think I need to address an issue with you face to face. I have a flight to Chicago this evening, and I'm not sure when I'll have another chance to explain a few things."

Hatch shuffled his feet. Taylor set his napkin and beer on the walnut bookcase near his shoulder.

"Look," Slattery said, "I know that neither one of you is satisfied with the investigation in New York. This Vincent Tagliafero kid is killed around three in the morning. NYPD receives an anonymous tip within an hour. He's murdered behind an abandoned warehouse at the Hunts Point Market in the Bronx—not what I call a popular tourist attraction. Without a Good Samaritan picking up the phone, Tagliafero would have been lying on that trash heap for a week . . . or longer. So who's fooling who?"

"The rats would have had their way with him," Taylor said.

"For what it's worth," Slattery said, "whoever murdered Tagliafero wanted him to be found—wanted him to be fingered for the three murders at Rudy's Tavern. Rigor mortis hadn't even set in. His wallet was left behind for an easy ID. The shooter apparently didn't take any of the guy's gold jewelry. The ballistics report is a whole separate issue—a shaky one at that. Tagliafero's guns were immediately identified as the weapons used in the murders. That crime took place thirty blocks away and almost a week earlier."

"Did ballistics really have a match that morning?" Hatch said.

"Yes and no," Slattery said. His tone was flat, yet appeasing.

Taylor's expression darkened. "Meaning?"

"Yes, there was a ballistics test that put Tagliafero's weapons at Rudy's Tavern," Slattery said. "But I've received contradictory reports—one verbal, the other written—as to when that analysis took place. One source tells me it was the morning they found the body, which is what I passed along to Gray when you spent the night at his place. A second written report tells me it was the following Monday, which points to somebody trying to cover his or her tracks."

Taylor and Hatch traded looks.

"Regardless, Tagliafero's Glock and his Smith & Wesson were positively identified as the weapons used to kill Robert O'Rourke, Patricia Durante, and Karen." Slattery sighed. "Did Tagliafero pull both triggers? We may never know."

"Jack," Hatch said, "the dude happens to be carrying both murder weapons? C'mon, he's gotta be a patsy."

"So who was bright enough to match Tagliafero's gun with the murders that quickly?" asked Taylor.

"According to the information I received, her name is Katherine Montroy," Slattery said. "But I've got nothing in writing to confirm that. Ms. Montroy is a homicide detective who works out of the Twenty-Eighth in the Bronx. Her partner is Detective Matthew Philips."

"Somebody helped them," Taylor said.

Hatch jiggled the ice in his tall glass. "Somebody intimate with both crimes."

"Or maybe this Detective Montroy just got lucky," Slattery said.

"Don't get me started," Hatch said under his breath. "I've had this conversation with Gray."

"Any dirt on this woman?" Taylor asked. "Or Philips?"

"None," Slattery said. "But who really knows nowadays?"

"Two guns, two shooters," Hatch said after a moment of reflection.

"The investigation is ongoing," Slattery said, spreading his hands.

"So the cops in New York have a few issues to contend with," Hatch said. "Starting with, who killed Tagliafero and why?"

"What about Tagliafero's buddies?" Taylor said. "That's a logical starting point. Was he with somebody at Rudy's?"

"An early report suggests he didn't have many friends," said Slattery, but before he could finish his thought, Ida Scott emerged through the crowd.

"Hatch, um . . . I'm really sorry to bother you," she said, biting her lower lip, clearly apprehensive.

"No problem, Ida. What's up?"

Glancing over her shoulder twice, she said, "Your brother just arrived."

The color immediately drained from Hatch's face. "Steven is here?"

CHAPTER 13

Bronx

D etective Matthew Philips, alone in his office and enjoying the solitude, removed his wire-rimmed glasses and rubbed his irritated eyes with both palms. The source of the inflammation dangled between his chapped lips. The overflowing ashtray in the corner of his desk—he refused to smoke outside with the rest of the geese—was a constant reminder of his noxious habit, as was a smoker's cough growing progressively worse with the August heat wave.

The office was stuck in a time warp, circa 1970. Kojak would have been proud.

A can of Planters Salted Peanuts in hand, Katherine Montroy exploded through the open door, fell back onto the soiled, pastel-colored couch, and grinned at her colleague—a little payback for Philips's deliberate interruptions during her meals these past few weeks.

"Holy cow, it totally stinks in here." Montroy pinched her nose and said, in a nasally tone, "Is that dirty underwear I smell? Or did you forget to wash your feet again?"

Philips slipped on his glasses. "Kat, can you *please* give it a rest, for one lousy minute?" He sounded as pathetic as he looked. "I'm beggin' ya."

"Oh, honey, what's eating my little buddy?"

"I haven't been sleeping, not that you care."

Montroy cupped a hand to her mouth and whispered, loudly, "Is it your prostate?"

"Is anything private around this dump? God!"

"You should get laid, Matty. It's a great cure-all. Works for me."

"Whatever." Philips waved his hand dismissively.

"An orgasm a day keeps the doctor away."

Philips let out a long sigh, got up from his chair, crossed the room, and shut the door. "Since you're here, I've got to talk to you about Rudy's Tavern and Vincent Tagliafero."

"I'd rather chat about your sex life—or lack thereof." Montroy grinned again, then popped a few peanuts into her mouth. "Okay, okay, what gives?"

"It's Tagliafero's connection to Anthony DiFilippo's organization. The mob division took over both cases. I just found out. We're out. Done. Sent to the bench."

Montroy choked on a peanut. "You can't be serious."

"As my bleeding ulcer," Philips said, settling back into his leather chair again.

"But . . . the kid didn't even work for his uncle. I made a few inquiries last night."

"That makes two of us."

"So why are the mob guys taking over our case?!" Montroy shouted.

"Because Tagliafero is Anthony DiFilippo's nephew, Kat. He's family."

"Big fucking deal."

"Kat, as far as I'm concerned, Tony D's justice is swifter and more humane than ours. We all know there's gonna be some payback from the don's team. Things could turn messy."

"You mean bloody."

Philips shrugged. "It's not our problem anymore."

"But what about our second-shooter theory?" Montroy said, sliding to the front of the couch. "You can't really believe this dumb-ass Tagliafero acted alone. C'mon, Matty."

"We've been over this," Philips said, clearly annoyed. "Tagliafero was a loose cannon, a loner—a punk who dabbled in the white powder, which is a no-no in DiFilippo's world. Tony D likes smart soldiers, and his nephew didn't fit the profile. One of my informed sources brought me up to speed last night—told me the kid had a hellish temper, flew off the handle when Tony D offered him a job stocking shelves in his plumbing business. For all we know, Tagliafero burst into Rudy's Tavern, a gun in each hand like Jesse James, looking for a quick score."

"Then who the Christ shot little Vinny in the face, Matthew?"

"Maybe it was a drug deal gone bad. Could be anything."

"Yeah," Montroy said, pursing her lips. "Sure. Whatever."

"As of fifteen minutes ago, it's all the mob division's problem." Philips clasped his hands behind his balding head.

"I'm sick of this bullshit," Montroy said under her breath, springing from the couch.

"Hey, where ya going?" Philips called out.

"To chew a little ass," Montroy shouted back over her shoulder. She slammed the office door behind her.

CHAPTER 14

Charlottesville

"Hey, you okay?" Gray Taylor asked, reaching out to steady Kevin Easter.

Hatch's apprehensive gaze moved to the open door at the far end of the great room. "Steven?"

Ida Scott nodded. "I'll go get him."

"Oh man . . . he wasn't supposed to get back to the States until next week," Hatch said quietly. "Jesus, I thought he was somewhere in Kuwait. I never called him . . ."

Jack Slattery and Taylor traded troubled looks.

"Low Dog doesn't even know about . . ." Hatch's words trailed off.

At that point, Terri Taylor, having snaked her way through the crowded room, finally reached her destination. "Hatch, there's this guy in the foyer," she said, pursing her lips as if to stifle a smile, "and he looks a lot like you."

Hatch, nervously tugging at his chin, said, "Yeah, that would be my big brother."

Except for the neatly cut black hair, the attractive man escorted by Mrs. Scott clearly resembled Kevin Easter, even down to the crooked smile. He had brown, almond-shaped eyes that appeared to twinkle, and a dark, clear complexion. Of average height, and maybe a few pounds heavier than Hatch, Steven Easter wore a white T-shirt that accentuated his taut, muscular body. His faded 501 Levi jeans and cowboy boots were from a bygone era.

"How'd he know to come here?" Taylor said under his breath.

"I have a neighbor watching my house," said Hatch. "Maybe she told him."

"Hey," Slattery said, squeezing Hatch's arm, "it's going be fine. Easy."

Hatch drew in a slow breath and looked at the DDI. "Jack, I wanted to be the one to tell Steven and my grandfather. But not like this."

"I'm sure your brother will understand," Slattery said.

The mourners stepped aside as Hatch met Steven Easter in the middle of the room. Their postures, height, and facial expressions were almost indistinguishable.

They stared at each other for a very long moment.

Finally, Hatch lowered his head and began to sob.

Steven stepped forward, wrapped his arms around his little brother, and held him tight. "I'm here, Little Crow."

———————————

Ten minutes later, Hatch pulled the upstairs bedroom door closed. The room belonged to Lindsay, the Scotts' seven-year-old daughter, who had a vast collection of stuffed animals. The walls were painted yellow, but nearly every square inch was covered by Disney posters.

"You look healthy again," Hatch said, his voice apprehensive, nervous.

Steven rotated his right shoulder like a baseball player warming up. "Yep, I heal quickly. Good genes from Dad's side of the family, I guess. The bullet broke my collarbone, but missed all the important stuff."

"You always were lucky."

"I'm being more careful now. Even changed the way I move around the Mideast." Steven sat on the bed, which was covered with a thick comforter and a dozen animal bears. He grabbed a small teddy bear, its brown fur rubbed away from excessive use.

"It wasn't supposed to be this way," Hatch said softly, pacing now.

"Evidently."

"I'm sorry."

"Shit, man, look at how I'm dressed." Steven manufactured a smile.

"I thought you were coming back to the U.S. next week."

"I was in Al Jahrah five days ago, Kev. Coming to Charlottesville wasn't even on my radar."

Hatch stopped. He looked squarely at his brother. "Did Jack call you?"

Shaking his head, Steven said, "We'd never spoken until a few minutes ago."

"Who then? Nobody would have known where you were . . ."

Steven stared, but gave no response.

"Who called you?" Hatch pressed, this time with a hint of anger.

Steven laid the bear on the pillow and pulled an envelope from his back pocket. He handed it to his brother. "Maybe you should start with this."

"What is it?"

"I'm still trying to make sense of everything myself, little brother. Read it."

Hatch took the wrinkled, dog-eared envelope from Steven's outstretched fingers and recognized the address. It was handwritten in neat script he knew belonged to Karen. The envelope was addressed to Mr. Steven Easter on the

Cattaraugus Indian Reservation, specifically Low Dog's home at 717 Elk Road. There was a postmark from Syracuse, New York, dated March 15—four years ago.

"Why would Karen send—?"

"Aren't you supposed to be the patient one? For Christ's sake, read the damn thing."

The letter was long. The first paragraph mentioned some of Karen's business courses at Syracuse University—one marketing class she really liked—the record snow that year, and Hatch, and how he'd *really* proposed during their ski trip to Montreal's Mont Tremblant.

On their second day in Canada, Hatch had taken her dog-sledding, deep into a forest of evergreens, most of the branches heavy with a foot of new snow. In a secluded valley, six miles north of their resort, the dogs came to a stop in front of a picturesque log cabin overlooking a frozen lake. A gorgeous fire was burning in the hearth, and there was champagne on ice.

Hatch silently read the note:

Steven, I can't imagine what your brother paid to pull this off, but the ambiance was perfect for a gal like me. Later that evening, after we started on our second bottle of champagne, Hatch told me he'd been recruited by the Central Intelligence Agency earlier in the semester. He was going to accept their offer. Your brother was so excited. Then he explained a few things about his youth, like how the Seneca tribe had given him the name Little Crow as an infant. He talked about hunting his first deer with Low Dog, and how that unpleasant experience turned into a blessing. He talked and I listened, Steven. It was if Hatch needed to confess everything, which, looking back, was exactly the point. Once the history lesson was over, a diamond engagement ring appeared in Hatch's hand as if by magic. He said to me: "If I'm privileged enough to be your husband, I wanted you to know my past as well as my future."

And he looked like a little boy who'd lost his parents in the mall. I can't really describe his expression. Then he asked: "Will you be my wife, Karen Durante?" There was real fear in his eyes, Steven, something I'd never seen before or since. He nervously chewed his lower lip, and his outstretched hand—the one holding this beautiful ring—shook. And, of course, I said yes. Then I jumped into his arms, where I've always felt so safe.

The rest was a personal note from Karen to Steven.

Hatch loves you very much, Steven. I've heard all the stories about how you watched over your little brother, especially when you were kids, and when he was afraid of Low Dog. That's a very special bond I will help keep intact. You're officially the first person to be invited to our wedding this fall.

Can you believe this is really happening? Hatch makes me feel so incredibly happy. It's like a beautiful prince picking me (ME!) to be his wife. We'll be visiting at spring break to tell Low Dog. Thank you for being so supportive.

I'm sorry (and embarrassed) that my father can't overcome his prejudice. It would be a wonderful gift for him to see the love in Hatch's heart, to see how genuinely happy I've become. Your brother makes me feel like anything is possible, Steven. I'm a very lucky girl. The Seneca are a fascinating people, and my new family.

It will be a great honor and privilege to be your sister-in-law.

Love,

Karen (soon to be Mrs. Little Crow)

"That's my girl," Hatch said quietly. As he folded the note, a single tear ran down his cheek. He made no attempt to brush it aside.

Her presence in the bedroom was suddenly as real as it was imagined. He could almost hear her words in his ear, almost smell the jasmine-scented perfume she'd wear on special occasions, like in that cabin in the Canadian woods. For the first time in many days, Hatch thought that maybe, just maybe, he could make it through this hellish ordeal. He slipped the letter into the envelope and handed it back to Steven.

"I brought it for you," Steven said, pushing it back. "Keep it."

"It helps more than you can imagine, brother."

"You told Karen your tribal name," Steven said, a corner of his mouth turning upward. "That's when I knew you two were for real."

"We had no secrets."

"Yeah," Steven said, choking up a little, his voice hitching. "I . . . we're all gonna miss her. I'm so sorry, Hatch."

"If you didn't know about what happened in New York City, then what made you bring the letter? Why now?"

"I don't have an answer. I don't know."

"Who told you about Rudy's?"

"Nobody. I learned about Karen from the woman watching your house."

"Steven, you never answered my question," Hatch said. "Why'd you come to Charlottesville in the first place?"

Steven Easter took a moment to contemplate his answer. "Low Dog," he said in a tone that sounded somewhat perplexed. "He insisted."

"Grandfather?" Hatch asked, equally puzzled. "I haven't told him yet."

"You still don't get it, do you, Little Crow? He just knew."

"Knew what?"

Steven lifted his eyes to meet Hatch's. "That you were in trouble."

"When did he tell you that?"

"It was Saturday afternoon in the States," said Steven. "Ten days ago. He called my office from the reservation's community center, and left a message with my secretary."

"The night Karen and Patty were killed," Hatch said softly, turning toward the window. "I was in the Bahamas hunting for Jeremy Silverstone—"

"Patricia?" Steven cocked his head. "She . . . she was with Karen?"

Hatch nodded. "They were together." He filled his lungs and then told his brother everything.

"Oh my God," Steven said to himself, covering his mouth.

"If you thought I was in trouble," Hatch said, "why didn't you call?"

"I tried! Jesus, Hatch, your fucking answering machine wasn't on. Same with your damn cell. I left at least six voice messages."

Hatch had been back in Charlottesville for only a few days. He and Karen didn't own an answering machine. And since Slattery had dropped the bomb in the Miami airport, he'd found no reason to retrieve any voice messages.

"I almost called Karen's dad—the miserable bastard—thinking he could help me out," said Steven.

"Would have been a really bad idea," Hatch said, "especially with Patty gone, too. He probably wouldn't have talked to you. I expect he's blaming me for everything."

The room fell silent as Hatch withdrew for a moment.

"Why didn't I see that?" Steven asked, putting his head in his hands. "I thought Patty must have left with her dad before I got here."

"Dr. Durante took off right from the cemetery. We never spoke."

Steven squeezed his eyes tight. "I want all the details," he said. "Confidential. Whatever. I need to know everything."

Hatch sat beside his brother on the bed and told all.

Kevin Easter and Jack Slattery were greeted by the day's heat and humidity when they stepped onto the Scotts' wraparound porch around four o'clock. They strolled down the bricked sidewalk toward the driveway. A very large African-American man, wearing a neatly tailored gray suit, guided the DDI into the idling limousine.

"Where's he been hiding?" Hatch said, gesturing with his chin toward the driver.

"Ezell arrived about ten minutes ago," said Slattery. "He's taking me back home so I can pack. I can't miss my flight to Chicago tonight."

"Must be nice to be so important." Hatch forced a smile.

"The traveling gets old, regardless of the accommodations."

"Don't I know it."

The rear door shut and the window glided down. "Kevin, take as much time as you need. You're on a paid leave of absence."

"I'm not going back to Langley, Jack. I've had enough. I'm tired. I'm—"

"We'll talk."

"My decision is final," Hatch said a little too harshly. "I have my photography—"

"You're making a decision based on emotion. That's rarely a good idea. I believe you already had this conversation with Gray."

"I don't care what it's based on, Jack. I'm done. It's over for me."

"Son, you're blaming yourself for Karen's murder. It's a natural response. If you were a nine-to-five husband, living a quiet life here in the Blue Ridge Mountains, maybe she'd never have gone to New York City. Maybe you would have gone with Karen, protected her. That's what you're thinking."

Hatch remained quiet, though his body had begun to stiffen.

"None of this is your fault," Slattery said. "Every single day wonderful people die tragically, and most of the time there's little we can do about it. We all shoulder regrets. Take it from me."

Hatch wanted to scream—tell his boss to get lost, go to hell, and leave him alone.

"The world can be a very cruel place," Slattery said. "Of all people—and you're one of my very best and brightest—you've experienced plenty, and at a very young age. But don't ever lose sight of the good. It's what we're dedicating our lives to protect."

"Is that advice?"

"A statement of fact," said Slattery firmly. "Pick up the phone next week and ask Gray about good and evil. Take a break. Go back to the reservation. Talk with Low Dog, and really listen to the old man. Take time to think and reflect, and I promise you'll stay with us. CIA is your home. You need us as much as we need you."

Hatch stepped away from the limo. "Have a safe trip, Mr. Slattery."

"Be very careful, Kevin. Think."

"What does that mean?"

"You know exactly what I mean." The window glided up, leaving Hatch alone with his thoughts.

CHAPTER 15

Bronx

Tiny ripples of trepidation rolled into Anthony DiFilippo's consciousness. The storm's ferocity, though still hidden beneath the horizon of his mind, intensified with each passing night. Waves of uncertainty spilled into his dreams. An invisible enemy was fast approaching. The don sensed its presence. All the king's horses and all the king's men were ready to wage war, to die with honor—to die for a noble cause. A dark-skinned warrior—was he the enemy?

Bathed in a thin layer of sweat, Tony D awoke with a start. The recurring nightmare—its images more defined each passing night—had won out again. His cotton pajamas were damp, just as they'd been the night before, and the night before that. He rolled over in his bed and squinted at the digital clock perched on the dresser. Two fifty-two in the morning.

A noble cause. A dark-skinned warrior.

Though they may have mattered to the magnificent kings of ancient times, noble causes counted for little or nothing in the don's hard world. As a younger man, he sought respect, wealth, and power through intimidation. Now it was all about survival. *Perhaps the world is changing too fast,* Tony D thought. Johnny had learned nothing new about Tommy Tapia's rumored coup against Frank DeVincenzsa. In fact, the streets were quiet, although his people were still searching for Vincent's killer—a man they'd never find.

Perhaps he'd inadvertently made a deal with the devil; maybe his motives—the bigger picture—had somehow been exposed to his enemies. But how?

The stout, barrel-chested man let his bare feet hit the hardwood floor. His right hand blindly searched for the glass of water on the bedside table, but he backhanded it, spilling its contents. "Stupid." The darkness amplified his gravelly voice, and he coughed. The pain shot through his body like electricity.

Mara DiFilippo stirred and opened her eyes. Getting to one elbow, she focused on the silhouette of her husband of thirty-six years. "Another bad dream?" she said quietly, reaching for his hand.

Tony D fell back into bed. "Yeah. I'm exhausted."

Mara pushed her husband's thick hair off his forehead. "You're scared, Anthony," she said. "Your cough needs to be checked out. It's getting worse."

A brief hesitation was followed by a simple shrug. "I get it every summer. Allergies. It's fine."

"Something is bothering you."

"I'll handle it," Tony D said. He reached out and touched Mara's cheek.

"We should run off to Italy before one of us ends up in a wheelchair or loses our marbles."

"My God, you're beautiful," Tony D said quietly. "Even after all these years, your skin is still so soft. Like it was back in high school."

"You're not listening, Anthony. Maybe it's time to get out. Maybe we—"

"And do what?" Tony D barked, turning his body to face his wife. "Move to one of those swanky retirement communities in Florida? New York is our home, Mara. This is my life."

"Our life."

"I'm making a difference, remember? This city needs me. We talked about this years ago. Without my position in the community, I'm just another Italian slob from the Bronx—"

"That's not true!" Mara sat up and turned on her reading lamp. Her intelligent blue eyes adjusted to the brightness before she spoke again. "I don't like what's happening to you, Anthony. You talk in your sleep about storms, kings, and noble causes. You look like shit."

"Please don't curse."

"Save the lectures for your people! I'm your wife."

Cocking his head, Tony D raised his hand. "Yes, you are."

"Anthony, if you're scared, I'm scared."

Unlike most men in powerful positions, Tony D shared nearly everything with his handsome, gray-haired wife. Through all the turbulence outside their home—family members and friends being murdered, indicted, even imprisoned; accusatory newspaper articles and television reports about her husband—their personal life remained surprisingly peaceful. They not only loved each other, but also shared a healthy respect built on friendship and trust.

"What my eyes can't see," Tony D said, pointing to his chest, "my heart tells me. Something's not right."

"Is it Vincent?"

For all of their trust, Tony D could ill afford for his wife to know the facts behind their nephew's death. It was one of the very few things in his life he would not share with her. And he was thankful she'd never insist on the details. Giving the order to have Vincent murdered would be an unforgivable sin from Mara's point of view, and their marriage would certainly suffer if she were ever to learn that Johnny had pulled the trigger. But sacrifices like Vincent were required to maintain the peace. The greater good.

Stuffing a pillow behind his head, the don said, "It's handled."

Mara knew well enough when to push ahead, retreat, or drop a subject entirely. "Would you like some tea?"

"Only if you join me."

Mara slipped her arm around Tony D's waist and pulled him close. "I'm your best friend, Anthony," she whispered in his ear. "You're not alone."

You're wrong, my love, Tony D thought. *I'm very much alone.*

CHAPTER 16

Manhattan

Gray Taylor kissed his wife goodnight, pulled the heavy wooden door of his private study closed, tugged on the desk lamp's small silver chain, and leaned back in his high-back leather chair. Antique toys he'd collected from all over the world surrounded him, perched on bookcases he'd made specifically for his collection. Here in the semi-dark, with his diverse arrangement of playthings from simpler eras, Taylor felt most comfortable.

After picking up his office phone, Taylor punched in the seven-zero-three exchange and dialed, listening to the first ring, then the second. He glanced at his watch. Three twenty-six in the morning.

Before the phone rang a third time, a pleasant male voice answered, "Thanks for returning my call, Gray."

"The airline cancelled our flight," said Taylor. "Terri and I rented a car and drove back to New York."

"Sorry to hear that," Jack Slattery said. Then he got to the point: "Your opinion on Kevin?"

"Can you be a little more specific?"

"Will he recover?"

"In the words of the immortal Stephen King, you pretty much have two options in this world: Get busy living or get busy dying," said Taylor. "He'll pull through, Jack. A little time and space is what he needs."

"Will he come back and work for me?"

That particular question had gnawed at Gray Taylor nearly the entire drive back to Manhattan—six long hours. He'd even discussed the matter with Terri, who was unusually evasive with her answers.

"I have no reason to believe he won't," Taylor said.

"He told me otherwise."

"Jack, that's your conventional short-term emotional response. I've been there."

"Kevin Easter is unique in a number of ways."

"Meaning?"

"For starters, he doesn't have an ego," said Slattery. "In our line of work, that's typically a prerequisite. Second, he means what he says. Third, the kid doesn't lie."

"Jack, his wife and sister-in-law were murdered. Come on, what did you expect? For Hatch to show up at your office on Monday morning with a big goofy smile on his face? Let him work things out."

"Therein lies the problem, Gray. I'm afraid of the way he may choose to do that."

Taylor got to his feet, bumping his knee on the desk. "You lost me, Jack."

"No, I pretty much doubt that."

Taylor stayed quiet.

"Let me ask you another question, Gray."

"Okay," Taylor said slowly, letting the word draw out.

"Do you think he's stable?"

"Jack, would you be if some asshole shot and killed your wife? Of course he's a little screwed up, but that's normal. He'll snap out of it. You did after your daughter's death. I did."

"He's deeply wounded. Karen was everything to him. Wounded men carrying deadly weapons—ones they're trained to use—concern me." Slattery stopped for a moment. "Look at your life."

Taylor now understood why his input had become so vital to Slattery. Why bother with the many psychiatrists, psychologists, and sociologists on-staff inside the Behavioral Science Division when he could talk to a veteran of revenge?

"Hatch's situation is different," Taylor finally said.

"Don't be so quick to judge. You were deceived, Gray. Your life was damaged, almost irreparably. You and Terri came under attack. You still haven't forgiven yourself."

"It's different," Taylor repeated with a sharp edge of irritation.

"He thinks like you."

"I wouldn't know. We just met. Jack, why are you pushing?"

"From my point of view, there's one unaccounted-for shooter out there," said Slattery. "And probably a cover-up. You and Kevin seem to agree with my assessment of the situation there in New York: two guns, two killers, too many pieces of the puzzle too easily falling into place."

"The case is ongoing—your words, not mine," Taylor said. "And cutting to the chase, Hatch is a far better man than I'll ever be. That part of the equation I do understand."

Slattery's words were clipped yet passionate. "Kevin Easter could turn out to be a very dangerous man and thus a major liability to the Agency."

"Meaning?"

"Tell me he's not capable of conducting his own investigation, Gray. He's a tracker—one of the very best in the world. Damn near brilliant. His success rate is beyond remarkable. He's not satisfied with the results in New York. And he's pissed off."

"Jack," Taylor said vehemently, "Hatch is not the type you're alluding to."

"Gray, you just admitted to not knowing this man."

"You're twisting my words."

"With the right motivation, anyone can cross the line," Slattery said. "You know that."

"Don't you think you're getting ahead of yourself?"

"In our world, that's impossible."

Gray Taylor drew the blinds. From seven stories above, he peered down at Central Park West. The Manhattan streets were relatively busy, even at this time of night. "So what do you want me to do about it?"

Charlottesville

The night of Karen's funeral had been a lesson in futility for Kevin Easter. During the course of the last eight hours, he'd replaced his Pepsi with Coors and, soon after, Jack Daniels right out of the bottle.

Steven Easter woke to hear retching from the upstairs bathroom. He got up slowly from the couch, letting the thin blanket slip to the carpet. He grabbed his BlackBerry from beside the TV remote and brought it close to his face. It was 3:48 a.m. "Shit," he murmured, dragging his fingers through his black hair. He'd only been asleep for an hour.

The retching got louder. Yawning, Steven plodded upstairs in his boxers. He leaned into the bathroom and flipped on the wall switch.

"Turn it off, Goddamnit!" Hatch's indignant voice echoed as if in a cave. Kneeling over the toilet, embracing the bowl, he vomited again, and then cleaned his face with a sloppy backhanded swipe. "You're blinding me, Steven! Leave me alone."

Steven grabbed a white cotton towel near the sink and handed it to Hatch. "Here."

Hatch, his face puffy and pale, squinted up at his older brother through narrowed, bloodshot eyes. He ripped the hand towel from Steven's hand and shouted, "I don't need your help!"

"Yeah, I can tell." Steven flicked off the light switch and headed back to the couch.

Soon, the toilet flushed again. Just as the antique grandfather clock gonged four times, Hatch appeared in the dark family room. Disoriented, he staggered, using the furniture and walls for balance. He still wore his clothes from the funeral, and he reeked of beer, bourbon, body odor, and vomit. Hatch fell back heavily into a La-Z-Boy recliner. "I'm sorry," he said in raspy whisper that sounded like an old man in the last stages of esophageal cancer.

"Karen would be disappointed in you, Little Crow."

"I know." Lowering his head, Hatch began to cry in deep, wet heaves.

CHAPTER 17

Manhattan

The faces hired to deliver the news had become more popular than the stories they were paid to report. Woodward, Bernstein, and Walter Cronkite were pioneers who walked that very fine line some thirty years ago. Matt Lauer, Katie Couric, Brian Williams, and Wolf Blitzer were now bigger celebrities than most of the people they interviewed. With the advent of cable TV, satellite radio, the Internet, and the accompanying sensationalistic journalism, the world had quickly changed.

B. J. Butera, like many in his generation, aspired to become a household name, with all the rewards to follow. Because his uncle had been a political reporter at *The New York Post* for nearly twenty years, and well-liked by his colleagues long before a heart attack took his life, getting an interview with the right people—specifically with the *Post*'s editor in chief, Howard Stapleton—hadn't been much of a problem for B. J., resulting in internships his sophomore and junior years at Fordham University, then full-time work on graduation. The path of least resistance had always been his.

Now, five years after getting his first job as an unpaid copy editor, he was a crime beat reporter, sitting at his small steel desk in the *Post*'s large, brightly-lit newsroom.

B. J. tapped a number two pencil against his perfect teeth. Today's deadline had passed four hours ago. It was almost four-thirty Sunday morning. The expansive room, with its hundreds of cubicles, was quiet, a rarity in the era of the twenty-four-seven news cycle.

Perhaps it was the thrill of authoring a front-page, above-the-fold story that kept him at work, or maybe he had nowhere better to go. Jennifer, his girlfriend of three years, had dumped him earlier in the month, but tying the Rudy's Tavern murders to Vincent Tagliafero—and to Anthony DiFilippo IV's family—before the competition had been a strong consolation, a great ride, and a nice spike in sales. The mob still sold papers.

B. J., just two years removed from writing fluff pieces in the *Post*'s Lifestyle section, had stood at the pinnacle of his profession—albeit briefly—and that orgasmic sensation only whetted his appetite for more accolades, although the investigative aspect of his job could be more work than he was normally accustomed to. Still, the praise and backslapping from colleagues was like reliving his glory-filled high school basketball days.

His blue eyes gazed down at the Harlem address he'd just written on the lined legal pad—another very interesting tip from a reliable source who happened to work at Merrill Lynch. But placing a sizeable wager on the winning horse was always the tricky part.

B. J.'s cell phone vibrated on the desk again. Checking the LCD display, he smiled after reading the incoming text message: *Soon it will be time to keep an eye on that 145th Street warehouse. Property was officially purchased by an off-shore company with ties to LLW. Perhaps a nice bottle of Scotch for my troubles?*

Make it a case of Scotch . . . if this pans out, B. J. responded. "Looks like Mr. Lawrence Luther Wright is expanding his drug empire."

Brooklyn

The distribution of cocaine in the five boroughs of New York offered great opportunity and wealth to those willing to dance with the devil. Lawrence Luther Wright, a product of Manhattan's Hell's Kitchen, sold the white powder, and variations thereof, to a growing spectrum of customers, one that reminded him of Reverend Jesse Jackson's Rainbow Coalition. In the eyes of many—friends, enemies, law enforcement officials, media, and admirers alike—the reticent black man, in his white Georgio Baroni suit and matching Gucci shoes, had deposed Satan a few years ago, at least in the Tri-State area.

Lawrence Luther studied the vacant warehouse and considered the possibilities from the comfort of his air-conditioned Mercedes 500LS. A thin smile showcased the drug dealer's movie-star appeal.

The brick five-story building on Harlem's 145th Street was perfect for his diverse empire. Soon, New York City's largest distributor of cocaine would enter the world of manufacturing—meth, for example. More control meant greater profit margins, which led to bigger vacation homes, faster cars, more expensive toys, younger women, and heightened security. One needn't be a Rhodes scholar to understand that particular business model, Lawrence Luther thought, although a fine college education surely didn't hurt.

"Do you have the time, Su Lyn?" Lawrence Luther asked his driver in a baritone voice. "I left my watch at home."

The Chinese woman, a retired kick boxer who'd relocated from Los Angeles, wore a patch over a missing eye. She glanced at the dash of the Mercedes. "Four twenty-two, Mr. Wright."

"One more stop and we'll call it a night. Head to the Brooklyn Bridge. Please don't speed. I want to take in the neighborhood."

"Yes, sir, Mr. Wright." She pulled away from the curb.

"How many MP5s we talking about?" He was referring to the new order of assault rifles coming in from the West Coast.

Glancing in the rearview mirror, Su Lyn said, "Two hundred."

Lawrence Luther breathed in deeply as the urban landscape moved past his tinted window. "Not a bad start," he said, rubbing his hands together. "But there's still room for aggressive expansion if we put the right people in the right places."

CHAPTER 18

Charlottesville

They were three miles into the evening run, but neither man appeared the least bit fatigued. Competitive by nature, they gradually increased the pace while subtly monitoring each other's progress.

Wearing a green T-shirt, baggy gym shorts, and Converse sneakers, Gray Taylor had a gait that was long and graceful. Kevin Easter wore bright red, tight-fitting Lycra shorts, a sleeveless white shirt, Reebok running shoes, and a yellow bandana. Although his stride was compact, the methodical nature of each step revealed a veteran runner who could probably finish a full marathon in less than three hours.

The two of them headed west toward the Blue Ridge Mountains on a horse path that passed through Hatch's two-acre property. The sun's orange glow washed over Virginia's rolling hills in a desperate attempt to suspend another hot August evening, but as with every day before it, the majestic mountains were the first to silently extinguish the light.

At the four-mile marker, Taylor said, "So, how far do you . . . normally go?"

It was the first time either man had spoken in nearly thirty minutes. One corner of Hatch's mouth turned upward. "You tired, old man?"

"Hey, just thinking . . . about your safety." Taylor's breathing had become labored. "It's getting . . . dark."

"This is Virginia, not the Big Apple," Hatch said. "No gangbangers around here."

"The trail is full of holes. I can't afford to . . . to break an ankle. Jack would—"

"I suggest you keep your eyes wide open. Or maybe you should quit while you're ahead. Hate for you to have to call in sick."

The dirt path made a gradual bend and opened to a breathtaking view of the valley. Long expanses of white picket fences followed the contour of the land, and sprawling estates with large homes and gigantic barns dotted the countryside. Horses grazed on the parched grasses. A herd of Holsteins, at a leisurely pace, headed home for the night. Sheep—too many to count—stood motionless beneath a cluster of sycamore trees. The water level on a twenty-acre lake was down at least three feet from a normal summer. The scent of burning brush and cow manure was bitingly present.

Pointing to a set of stables in the distance, Hatch said, "That's the halfway point—about ten miles round trip. You can turn around here or follow me." The younger man didn't wait for a response, but instead picked up the pace.

"Shit," Taylor said through gritted teeth. "I'll drop dead of a heart attack before I give up."

Close to ninety minutes later, Gray Taylor came to a stop in the middle of Hatch's side yard, drenched with sweat, his stomach cramped. The grass was completely burned out and brown, withered from the lack of rain. A spotlight from the eave of the house was trained on Hatch, who sat in a white Adirondack chair under a chestnut tree. Smirking, Hatch slapped at mosquitoes and casually sipped a red Gatorade, a second plastic bottle near his feet.

Taylor fell to his knees, trying to catch his breath. "No problem."

"You are one stubborn dude," Hatch said, shaking his head. His smirk turned to a grin. "The hose is by the door if you want to cool down."

Taylor finally straightened up, his back making an audible pop. He walked gingerly toward the house, then let the cold water from the hose run over his head and neck, groaning from time to time. A few minutes later, he sat down on the hard ground and snatched a Gatorade from Hatch's outstretched hand. "Thanks."

"It was closer to eleven miles," Hatch said with a good-natured shrug.

"I figured," Taylor said, taking a hearty pull from the plastic bottle. "Where's Steven?"

"The store. Hope you like steaks on the grill. He's the master."

"I'm not on PETA's mailing list, if that answers your question."

Hatch untied his running shoes. "Yep, you don't strike me as a liberal, vegetarian, tree-hugger type."

"You might be surprised," said Taylor. "I voted for President Thorn. I actually lived on a commune as a kid, and Terri joined Greenpeace last year, probably just to piss me off. I never know with her."

"Can I ask you a question, Gray?"

Chuckling softly, Taylor said, "Yes, Jack sent me. I'm not the drop-in type, either."

"What are you gonna tell him?"

"That you're doing pretty well, even after a week."

"I was on a two-day bender," Hatch said. "Thank the gods Steven stuck around. Without his help, I might have flushed myself down the toilet."

"Maybe I'll forget to mention that part." Taylor gave a small, enigmatic smile.

"Jack could have just called me."

"Hatch, you still won't answer your damn phone."

"I've been busy with my photography."

Taylor took another swig of Gatorade, then said, "Maybe it's time you—"

"You're done playing babysitter, Gray. I can handle myself."

Taylor raised both hands defensively. "Hey, hey . . . easy," he said. "Truth be told, Jack wants your pictures from your trip to Andros Island. And if you have a preliminary report on Silverstone, all the better. That's the number-one reason I'm here."

"Jeremy Silverstone," Hatch said quietly, a hint of regret in his voice. "Man, that op seems like a million years ago."

"Jack's itching to tie this one up. I think he's feeling pressure."

"From the director?"

"It goes higher—right up to some folks in Thorn's administration. And it's complicated."

"So," Hatch said, letting the word draw out, "will *you* be the lucky contestant to visit Mr. Silverstone?"

"Who's to say?" Taylor said, frowning. "That's why they pay Jack the big bucks."

"Enough said on that topic."

"Roger that."

"Any other reason you're here, Gray?" Hatch asked, climbing easily to his feet. "It can't all be about the *GREENBACK* file or my mental health. That much I've already figured out."

Taylor seemed to ponder his answer, rubbing his stubbly chin. "Look, they want you back," he said. "Jack's obviously leading the charge. Apparently you have more than a few admirers at the Agency."

"I'm flattered."

Taylor sighed, opened his mouth as if to continue with some explanation, then fell silent instead.

"What?" Hatch said. "Jesus, just say it, Gray. I'm not wearing a wire."

"Here's the big surprise behind door number three," Taylor said, turning to face Hatch. "Jack thinks we should work together. A partnership. It's an arrangement I've never tried before, but, hell, I'd be willing to give it a shot."

"I'm not listening," Hatch said, plugging both ears like a pigheaded child.

Taylor climbed to his feet, then headed toward the house. "Maybe when you grow up, we can revisit the issue."

Hatch caught up to Taylor, grabbed his thick forearm, and spun him around. "You read my file, Gray. I don't—won't—kill people. I know what you do for Jack and—"

"Who said you needed to start now? Christ almighty, you assume a lot."

"And you're lousy at subliminal messages," Hatch said. "For the record—and let me make this crystal fucking clear—I have no intention of heading to New York City, or anywhere else, to find this second shooter. Maybe that Tagliafero kid did act alone."

"What about working with me?" asked Taylor. "Do you even have an opinion on that?"

Hatch contemplated his answer for a long moment. "Look, I seriously appreciate Jack's offer, but I'm not coming back to CIA. And I'm flattered that a guy like you would be willing to work with an asshole like me, but that part of my life is in my rearview mirror. I'm out. I'm done—"

"Okay, I get it," Taylor said, waving his arms.

"Once I hand over my *GREENBACK* report, and all the other shit I've borrowed or stolen from the Agency over the years, I'll expect only Christmas cards from you guys, maybe a phone call on my birthday. Hell, send me a gift if it makes you feel better. And please tell Jack to call off the dogs. I've identified at least two of his people watching me here. It's embarrassing to think that he doesn't trust me."

Headlights suddenly swept across Hatch's property. Steven was back from the store.

Gray Taylor looked at Kevin Easter for a long second but said nothing.

Around midnight, Taylor and Hatch stood in an open field behind the house. Each smoked an Arturo Fuente, Cuban cigars Taylor had smuggled from Montreal on his last op. Four years separated the two men. Physically, they had little in common, and in personality, they couldn't be more different. Kevin Easter was outgoing and funny, while Gray Taylor exuded quiet confidence—a stillness. They maintained different lifestyles.

Still, they enjoyed each other's company, and the more they talked, the more they realized that their view of the world was very similar: Evil existed, and good men were responsible for beating it back, even at great expense and sacrifice. Honorable men and women needed to be at the tip of the spear to protect freedom and democracy.

Although it was Hatch's job only to locate and photograph enemies of the United States, he clearly understood that his work led to the deaths of some of his subjects. That degree of separation was enough for him. Men like Gray Taylor finished what Hatch started, and as long as their work made the United States a safer, better place, Hatch could accept his role, knowing it was for the greater good.

Taylor pointed to the southern horizon. "Look at Scorpius."

Hatch followed Gray's finger. "I got it."

"See the bright red star in the middle?"

"Yep."

"That's Antares. It's Scorpius's heart," said Taylor. "Legend has it that Tiamat created Scorpius to kill the sun god, Marduk."

"Who the hell are Tiamat and Marduk?"

"Beats me." Taylor took another long drag from the fat cigar and blew smoke upward. "But I do know that Scorpius represents death, darkness, and evil."

"Gray," Hatch said, thinning his eyes, "is there a moral to this nutty story?"

Puffing out his cheeks, Taylor considered the question. "I was in South Africa last year, and this elderly priestess pointed at me and shouted that I was Scorpius. Her people scattered in all directions, like antelope on the plains catching the scent of a dangerous predator. That's pretty much it."

"Terrific." Hatch paused. "It's probably best if you keep that one to yourself."

"You're the first, and probably last, person to hear that story." Taylor smiled.

"So you're originally from New York?"

"Terri and I lived in Maryland up until three years ago," said Taylor. "We needed a fresh start."

"Yeah, but an apartment in the Dakota? I don't need to be a financial whiz—"

"Terri's family has money," Taylor said. "And I'll leave it at that for now, if you don't mind."

"That's the second time you've avoided bringing up your past," Hatch said, smirking. "I'm beginning to see a trend here."

A cool eastern breeze fanned the cigars' embers. From the screened-in porch, Steven Easter, sitting in a rocking chair, stared at the two orange points of dancing light. "Boys, I'm calling it a night," he called out, cupping his hand to his mouth.

"Thanks for dinner, Steven," Taylor said. "You grill a mean piece of meat."

"Come hunting with me on the Cattaraugus Indian reservation, Gray, and we'll have fresh venison on a spit," Steven said. "It's fantastic."

"Call me when you get back to the States," said Taylor.

"What time's your flight?" Hatch asked his brother.

"Nine-fifty."

"I'll be up early," Hatch said.

Like the smoke from the cigars, the conversation between Kevin Easter and Gray Taylor drifted. They touched on the National Football League, Western New York winters, life in Midtown Manhattan, weapons, politics—specifically the Thorn administration's view on homeland security—and working for Jack.

And then a few quiet moments passed before Hatch said, "Gray, do you believe in God?"

Taylor wanted to say, "Terri's presence in my life is absolute proof positive of a higher power." Instead, he said simply, "Yes."

"Jack gave me the impression that, once upon a time, you dealt with an incident like mine. Something about good and evil, a gunslinger and portals, searching for some faraway dark tower—"

"Jesus, are you on drugs?" asked Taylor, shaking his head.

Hatch laughed. "Just wanted to see if you were still listening."

Taylor blew on the lit end of his cigar, and his hard expression glowed in a surreal light. "My past and your situation are different animals—if that's what you're getting at. There's really not much to say."

"And how did you fix your . . . situation?"

"I killed them. Five people, including a good friend. Or someone I thought was a good friend."

Even in shadow, Hatch could see the transformation in Taylor's attitude and body language. "Did it make the pain go away?"

"Yes, but we're talking only a few minutes," Taylor said, kicking the hard dirt. "Revenge is like crack cocaine, Little Crow. At the very most, it's only a short-term fix."

Little Crow, Hatch thought. He looked over at the bigger man.

"I actually felt incredibly alive for that moment," Taylor went on, "but after the adrenaline bled off, when I snapped back into reality, and most of us do, my issues were still there, bigger and uglier than before. Then I was introduced to guilt—always a lovely addition to the emotional family. An alcoholic probably feels the same after a bender."

"But you survived it."

"Jack threw me a lifeline, and I grabbed hold."

The curtain from the spare upstairs bedroom fell back into place.

Heads tipped back, both men looked up at the vast night sky. To the east, a shooting star shot across the heavens, then burned up in the atmosphere. A hearty male laugh carried across the lake.

"Do *you* believe in God, Hatch?"

"Low Dog would consider it a stain on our family name if I thought otherwise," said Hatch, "but his interpretation of God isn't necessarily the same as mine."

"I'd love to meet your grandfather. He sounds interesting."

"He's Yoda with good hair."

"Since you apparently believe in a higher power, then you certainly must believe in heaven and an afterlife," Taylor said, flicking the stub of his cigar into the dirt.

"I think there's far more than this planet," Hatch said with a shrug, "and we're all connected, in this world and the next. Does that answer your question?"

"Then tell Karen how you feel," Taylor said, turning back for the house.

"What if I said I'm afraid she's not listening?"

"Faith," Taylor said from the darkness. "You should give it a try."

PART 2
After

CHAPTER 19

Manhattan

Anthony DiFilippo IV's expression revealed only what he chose to show the world, and that was enough for those in his company, but one didn't need a Ph.D. in psychology to recognize his disgust.

Johnny Cercone, his favorite nephew, had been assassinated—shot in the head—early this very November morning, while standing on his front stoop. And there were no witnesses. Nobody saw or heard a thing.

The executioner's identity and objective puzzled the don and his three high-ranking associates, who'd been summoned on short notice. Grief for Tony D's dead godson would have to wait.

Though it was near freezing outside, the air conditioner at the Ravenite Social Club rattled, clanked, and sputtered. Tony D's small dark eyes remained fixed on the men nervously shuffling about the dimly lit room.

Pushing his half-eaten rigatoni aside, Tony D folded his hands on the linen tablecloth and cleared his throat. A nervous waiter, his brow wet with perspiration, promptly picked up the plate and left the private room, pulling the door closed behind him.

Tony D waved a hand at the three men he'd summoned an hour earlier. "Please," he said, gesturing to the wooden chairs. "Make yourselves comfortable."

His underboss and the two *capos* took seats at the round table. They respectfully said nothing. Tony D moved the flower centerpiece to the side, then tapped a soup spoon against the tablecloth like a perfectly timed metronome.

Underboss Paulie Franco, the eldest of the three, balled his hands into tight fists. He was Tony D's age, with an anger bolstered by a dip in the shallow gene pool, but three busted marriages and three stints in federal prison had tempered his hostile disposition over the past two decades. Franco was no longer a lighted stick of dynamite, but he could still lay down the lumber when necessary.

"Fat Paulie," a nickname from childhood, fit him like the proverbial glove. His right eye, damaged in a fight sometime during his early days as an enforcer, twitched constantly, another wrinkle to his scary urban legend. He certainly didn't resemble the pretty-boy wise guy Hollywood continued to miscast in their gangster films. If not for his boyhood friendship with the don, Paulie, no doubt, would have been destined to a life in his uncle's roofing business in Queens. Instead, he was the second-most important man in the DiFilippo crime family, and known for getting things done with or without violence.

At twenty-eight, Donald Biasucci was Tony D's youngest and most feared captain, now that Johnny had been murdered. But nobody who associated with the tall man ever referred to him as Donald, Donny, or Don. Because of one particularly large physical attribute—about which Biasucci loved to remind the ladies—he was known as Woody. A few of the newer soldiers in the outfit actually addressed him as Mr. Wood.

Woody dressed sharply, usually in a black sports jacket, and had an insatiable appetite for all makes and models of women. His dark complexion, day-old stubble, cleft chin, lean body, and striking blue eyes helped him fulfill that desire. Using a small black comb, he obsessively attended to his hair like his movie idol, James Dean.

Woody's loyalty to Tony D had never been questioned, and his tight relationship with Johnny Cercone only inflamed the need for swift retaliation. *Blood for blood* had been his rallying cry since the moment he heard about Johnny. Patience was not Biasucci's strongest virtue.

Louis "Lady Luck" Ciambella was in his early fifties, but he looked closer to sixty-five. His nickname came from his incredibly good fortune with the ponies, dogs, and any animal with a pulse, which included pit bull terriers in Harlem. The man rarely lost, because he cheated. Fixing horse races was his specialty, but Ciambella had recently drifted back into boxing. A young white fighter, Felix DuBois, was making some interesting waves down in Louisiana.

Unlike Woody and Fat Paulie, Louis Ciambella was not one hundred-percent Sicilian and would never have the opportunity to become a "made man"—an important step for the underworld's inner circle. His hair, typically pulled back in a ponytail, was gray, thin, and oily, and his facial features were fleshy and pockmarked, though not as pronounced as those of the other three men sitting in the Ravenite's private room.

What he did have was a gregarious and charming personality, and he was always the first with a new joke or the latest street gossip. Spreading rumors and innuendo, the don promised his *caporegime* on a number of occasions, would eventually catch up with him.

Three months after Vincent Tagliafero had been murdered behind the abandoned Best-Way Produce Company building, these three men had yet to identify the shooter, nor had the police made any progress, although the case was still open. Now that Johnny was dead, only the don knew the truth, and he would make sure it stayed that way forever.

Today's meeting was about Johnny. The nature of the attack on Cercone suggested that a rival family had not committed his murder. So who had shot him this morning?

As he drew in a long, slow breath, the iciness in Tony D's eyes melted. "Gentlemen, I want the truth," he said with an urgent edge. The three associates appeared to sit up a little straighter. "Was Johnny involved in something diametrically opposed to my personal beliefs? Might he have had something on the side that I didn't know about?" The second question was directed toward Woody.

Woody swallowed hard. "No, sir, Tony. Johnny wasn't involved with drugs. Nothin' on the side, neither. He knew how much you hated dope."

Woody's answer wasn't completely truthful. He and Cercone had been using coke recreationally for years.

Because of their ruthless approach to distribution, the gangs had pretty much taken control of the narcotics trade. It was an ugly and violent business anyway, as Tony D constantly reminded his people. But Cercone's desire to grow the business into the world of prescription and illegal street drugs was well documented among his peers and some enemies.

At the top of their short list of suspects, Fat Paulie's crew had placed the name of Lawrence Luther Wright. Competing families respected the sanctity of one's turf, but Mr. Wright and his people didn't give a shit about tradition.

"Anything else?" asked Tony D, sighing regretfully. The air conditioner clanked to a stop. The tapping of the spoon stayed constant. The tension in the room climbed.

Woody shook his head. "No, sir."

"Was my godson sleeping with the wrong girl perhaps? A married woman? Hanging out with a bad crowd?"

"No, sir," Woody said again. "He has . . . had a girlfriend in Brooklyn. A nice—"

"Tony, c'mon, Johnny's pecker was like a land cruise missile, armed and ready to fire at a moment's notice," said Ciambella, spreading his hands. "And the kid was never satisfied. He was almost as bad as Woody, for Christ's sake."

Woody gave his fellow *capo* a hard glance.

"Truth is, Tony, we ain't got nothin' yet," said Fat Paulie.

Tony D placed the spoon near the centerpiece and folded his hands on the white linen tablecloth. "Anyone in the neighborhood see something they didn't want to tell the police?"

"We've made a few inquiries," Woody said. "So far, we got us a big fat zip.

Some widower in the neighborhood called nine-one-one, but the old man never actually saw the body or a shooter. The teenager who found Johnny puked up his Cheerios."

Ciambella said, "Tony, a single bullet through Johnny's head—"

Tony D's fist crashed onto the table, and the spoon fell to the tiled floor. Fat Paulie and Ciambella flinched. "You're not telling me anything I haven't heard, gentlemen! Even the radio news is reporting this much!" the don shouted, his voice breaking. He coughed in a deep, guttural croak. "I know Johnny was shot, but I seem to be missing the details as to who did this and why. Now, I'll ask you again: Who did this to my godson?" He coughed again, wiped his mouth with a napkin, then rubbed his throat.

The don rarely lost his temper. Although Anthony DiFilippo was the head of a powerful crime family, he preferred to be perceived as the CEO of a large company rather than as a crook.

"Boss, the shooter used a rifle, not a pistol," said Fat Paulie.

"Nobody heard it," Ciambella added. "We think this guy used a silencer."

"Probably took the shot from a window," Fat Paulie said. "Or maybe the roof."

Tony D turned his full attention to his underboss, Paulie Franco. "Sniper? Some guy carries a rifle into Johnny's quiet little neighborhood, shoots him in the head, and nobody sees anything? Nobody hears a thing?" He pursed his lips into a tight line. "No, I won't accept that. Seven in the morning. School's in session. There are elderly people on that block. Old men get up early to use the bathroom or walk the dog. They see a lot."

"I've been told there ain't nothin' left of Johnny's head," Fat Paulie said, drumming his fingers on the table. "We're talkin' large caliber here. Cop-killer bullets."

Woody and Ciambella went rigid.

A high-powered rifle suggests a professional, Tony D thought. A gangbanger would have undoubtedly used an assault weapon, hosing down the neighborhood to leave a lasting impression. This was no message sent by punks attempting to claim some unspecified turf. *No, Johnny's murder was intended to . . . to do what? Frighten me? Insult me? Get even for something?* The onus likely was on a rival family. *Can that be? Tommy Tapia, perhaps?* It was only three months ago that Johnny had been asking questions about Tapia's future in the Genovese family.

"Me and some of the boys think that maybe it's the same guy who whacked Vincent," Woody said.

"Stick with the facts," Tony D said evenly. "Leave the speculating to the media and nuts on the web."

"Why wait three months between hits?" Ciambella said to Woody. "They ain't connected, you idiot."

Sipping his glass of ice water, Tony D let the cool liquid momentarily lubricate his sore throat. He pointed to his two captains. "Go to Johnny's neighborhood and start asking the hard questions," he said. "Talk to everybody: hot dog vendors, garbage men, kids playing stickball. Wave some money in front of these people if it helps open their mouths." He turned his attention to his oldest friend. "Paulie, do you have the name of the detective who's leading the investigation?"

"There's two," the underboss said, nodding. "Katherine Montroy was the first detective called to the scene. When Ms. Montroy identified Johnny, she brought in a second guy, her partner, Matthew Philips. The chief at the Twenty-Eighth don't want to screw this one up."

"Can't say I blame him." Tony D blew his nose into a white handkerchief. "Maybe I should speak with these two detectives."

"It can't hurt," Fat Paulie said.

"Okay," Tony D said after a moment of thought. "Paulie, you get me an appointment with one or both of these hotshot detectives. I'd like it to be tomorrow. Tell them I would very much appreciate a little of their time. I promise not to waste any of it."

"I'll make it happen, boss," Fat Paulie said dutifully.

The don's eyes shifted to the *capos*. "Gentlemen, I want updates every two hours. Get the word out to our people and their friends—anyone with ears, eyes, and half a brain. Fifty large for information leading to Johnny's killer. If that doesn't work, I'll double it. I want this handled fast."

Before the storm hits me broadside.

CHAPTER 20

Manhattan

Christmas lights from popular department stores reflected off the wet pavement in Manhattan. West 72nd Street was quiet and pretty much devoid of privately owned automobiles on this Thanksgiving night. Yellow cabs ruled the roads.

Gray Taylor, who'd spent the last thirteen days in and around Andros Island monitoring Jeremy Silverstone's mundane routines, took a leisurely stroll with his wife around their neighborhood. They stopped at the Friends of the Night People homeless shelter and marveled at the beautiful, colorful mural painted on the front side of the brick building. According to a small plaque mounted on the wall, it was a rendition of the Pilgrims' first Thanksgiving dinner with the Indian natives near Plymouth Rock, Massachusetts.

"Is it racist to say this reminds me of Hatch?" Terri said, taking her husband's elbow.

"When did you become politically correct?"

"You know, it's his first holiday without Karen. Have you spoken with him lately?"

"About a month ago," Taylor said, tucking his scarf into his leather jacket. "He actually called me, but we really didn't have much to say. Since he resigned, he's not cleared to hear the interesting stuff. And you know me and small talk."

"Maybe you two should have joined my fantasy football league," said Terri, grinning. They began to walk down the sidewalk again. "How's he doing?"

An impetuous cabby leaned on the horn, and two more drivers added to the noise.

"Good," Taylor said.

"Is he still living back on the reservation?"

"Yes."

"With his grandfather?"

"That's what Jack told me."

"Jesus, you can be such an ass sometimes," Terri said, coming to a stop at the next crosswalk. "We're not discussing Israeli military secrets here, Gray. I like Hatch. I'm actually interested in his well-being. An honest opinion of the situation might be nice."

"We've talked about this, Ter. There's nothing new. Hatch dumped Jack, sold his Charlottesville house, and moved back in with Low Dog. End of story. What more do you want me to say?"

"Is Jack still keeping an eye on him?"

The light turned red, and they both crossed over to Central Park West.

"Surveillance ended about six weeks ago," Taylor said.

"Do you think that was a good idea?"

"Two CIA shrinks ran three follow-up debriefings. In their eyes—and they're supposedly the experts—Hatch is on the right track. He's not a threat to himself or others, if that's what you're really asking."

"Babe, you still didn't answer my question," Terri said, a trace of frustration in her tone. "I'm asking for *your* expert analysis."

"Look," Taylor said, letting out a long breath, "the kid threw himself into his photography just like he told us he would. He hasn't done anything stupid or even visited New York City since he stayed with us in August. The Cattaraugus Indian Reservation doesn't have Internet access. From what I know, Hatch shut himself off from the rest of the world, and he's content. The last time I looked, that wasn't a crime."

Terri thinned her eyes. "And nobody has seen or talked to Hatch in how many weeks?" she said, incredulous.

"Ter, I really wouldn't know. I just got back home. Remember? I have other things—important things—on my mind, if you know what I mean. Hatch's life isn't at the top of my To Do list."

"Testy."

"If you're so damn interested, take a few minutes out of your busy social life and call him," said Taylor. "You can leave a message at the recreation center."

Terri Taylor looked over at her husband. "Nobody has seen or talked to him in how many weeks?"

Bronx

It was late Thanksgiving night. The Century Club, a quiet Bronx pub near Yankee Stadium typically frequented by wise guys, was open, and business was unusually brisk. Cecil Schultz, the bartender, had made that proud declaration more than once over the past few hours. Johnny Cercone's murder had put a damper on the long weekend, but the fifty-thousand-dollar reward had quickly turned some mourners into cheap imitations of Dog the Bounty Hunter. Mob members and informants with bad tempers, deadly weapons, and a lust for quick money now patrolled the five boroughs of New York, as well as Long Island.

Even so, as of tonight, not a single solid lead had surfaced, which Fat Paulie found remarkable. He'd even commented to a few patrons at the bar that Johnny's murder felt strangely like Vincent's death, because nobody knew a thing. It was as if a ghost was responsible for both deaths.

Not even the calming effects of six shots of Jack Daniels could make him forget why he was drinking in the first place. Who called for Johnny's hit, and for what purpose? Had the sniper been hired for that one job, or was this murder only the beginning?

A secret—especially one of this magnitude—has a price, Fat Paulie thought, although, for some strange reason, he'd stopped believing his own words after the fourth shot of bourbon whiskey.

Even Cecil, a cadaverously thin German-American of nearly eighty, with thinning white hair and a bulbous red nose, wanted in on the action. He bombarded Paulie with theories, questions, and potential suspects.

"You want another, Paulie?" Cecil asked, leaning on the cash register, a toothpick sliding from the left corner of his mouth to the right.

Fat Paulie glanced at his Rolex. It was 11:23 p.m. "I'm good." Reaching into his pants pocket, he removed a thick wad of money and said, "The wife won't fall asleep until I get home. She's weird like that now—always frettin' about me, especially . . ." Paulie's words trailed off as he peeled two one hundred-dollar bills from his roll and slid the money across the bar. "Have yourself a nice holiday, Cecil, and don't be quittin' your job lookin' for Johnny's killer. Let us professionals handle it."

"Professionals?" a male voice—squeaky and shrill—called out from the far end of the bar. "What a joke."

"Ah, go fuck yourself, Wayne." There was a slight titter of amusement in Paulie's words.

Hunched over a glass of beer, Wayne Rambus, a recently divorced insurance salesman, said, "Paulie, twenty bucks says nobody finds this guy, especially you and Tony's collection of misfits. Another twenty says this thing ain't over—not by a long shot. I can see it in your eyes, old man. A pro blew Johnny's brains all over his front door. Pros keep their mouths shut, and this guy ain't talkin'."

"Shit, Wayne, if you had any money," Fat Paulie said, chuckling, "I'd take both bets. The shooter is probably drinking a Mai Tai in Mexico. He's not coming back.

It's the guy who paid him I'm after."

Cecil poured Rambus another draft and slid the glass down the bar without spilling a drop. "Mind your own business, Wayne."

"Ah, I was just pokin' fun at the fat man," said Rambus. "I remember Paulie when he was a skinny drink a water. We was kids, growin' up with Tony in the Bronx . . ."

Fat Paulie patted Rambus's bony shoulder on the way to the door. "I'll take both bets."

"I'm good for it."

"Of course you are. Hey, Wayne, send my love to your mom. She's a great lady. Best chocolate chip cookies in New York."

"Moving in with her is only temporary," Wayne said a little too forcefully, and a few patrons laughed out loud. "The wife cleaned my clock."

After glad-handing a few patrons, Fat Paulie stepped into the cold night air and took in a deep, refreshing breath. "God, I love this city," he murmured. He shivered briefly, as if icy water had been injected into his bloodstream, then pulled up the lapel of his trench coat and stumbled toward the Lincoln Town Car.

As was usually the case, his vehicle was in a handicapped-parking area, close to the building. Light flurries passed through the sodium vapor streetlights. The car idled quietly, its windshield wipers slapping the moisture aside.

The ever-vigilant Paulie Franco shifted his gaze, surveying the quiet Bronx neighborhood, seeing nothing that concerned him. He opened the passenger door and slid his thick body inside. "Mikey, it's colder than a witch's tit out there," he said to the man paid handsomely to protect his life. "What, no talk radio tonight?"

The baldheaded driver, Michael Testa, didn't respond.

Fat Paulie looked to his left, and the effects of the bourbon vanished like smoke on a windy beach, his affable mood turning sour. "No fuckin' respect!" he said, shaking his head in disgust. Didn't Mikey understand who he was protecting?

"Hey, hey, you warm pile of dog crap!" Fat Paulie shouted. "C'mon, I'd like to get home before midnight or the old lady might turn into a pumpkin." Reaching over, he grabbed hold of Testa's shoulder, and then pulled his hand back, as if he'd touched something red hot. "Oh, Jesus."

Michael Testa, like an unsteady Christmas tree, toppled over, his head thumping into the window. Paulie quickly reached for the door handle.

"If the dome light comes on, you die," the man's calm voice said from the backseat. The hunter leaned forward and pressed the silenced automatic Smith & Wesson against Franco's left ear. "If you don't let go of the handle right now, you die. If you reach for your piece, you die. If you scream or call out, you die. If you have a bad attitude, fart too loudly, or shit your pants, you die. Do you get the idea?"

Eyes wide, Fat Paulie swallowed hard, then nodded very quickly. "Yeah." He folded his hands on his lap.

"Tinted windows can be a bitch."

"Do you have any fuckin' idea who I am?" Fat Paulie asked.

"Bang!" the hunter shouted, and Paulie let out a yelp that strangely enough sounded like a dog in pain. A wet spot appeared on the front of the fat man's Dockers. "Don't make promises you can't keep, Mr. Franco."

"Promises? What . . . what are ya talkin' about?"

"The shooter is probably drinking a Mai Tai in Mexico," the hunter said, repeating Fat Paulie's words from inside the Century Club. "He's not coming back."

"Jesus Christ!"

"Would you like to try again?"

CHAPTER 21

Manhattan

Gray Taylor grabbed his telephone—it was on the kitchen table, between Friday's edition of *The New York Post* and his bowl of Life cereal. Although the phone was encrypted with an STU-6 device, designed to scramble incoming and outgoing signals, something made him stop before he punched in the numbers. "Shit," he murmured.

Instead of making the call, Taylor flipped open his Dell laptop, then pointed and clicked his way to the *Post's* website. He glanced at the microwave's digital clock—6:38 a.m.—then muted the television mounted to the wall near the Krups coffee maker.

On a typical business day, Jack Slattery's commute from his Maryland home to Langley took about forty minutes. If the boss had left his house by half past six, as he normally did—Taylor knew this from experience—he suspected the DDI would either be on the Georgetown Pike, Capital Beltway, or Route 66. The day after Thanksgiving meant traffic would almost certainly be light. Many businesses and government agencies were closed for the long holiday weekend.

Taylor hesitated. He needed a few moments to gather more facts, then arrange his thoughts. It was out of character for him to sound an alarm for no good reason, but Terri's seed of concern about Hatch had begun to take root in his mind.

Light jacket draped over her shoulder, Terri swept into the kitchen and gave her husband a peck on the cheek. "I still feel bloated from all that turkey," she said. "Nothing an hour run through Central Park can't cure."

"Show-off," Taylor said, lightly patting her backside.

The heavy apartment door swung closed, and Gray Taylor, white towel draped around his sweaty neck, focused his attention on B. J. Butera's front-page article in *The New York Post*: "CAPO TAKES NAPO."

Caporegime Johnny Cercone, according to the story, had been shot dead early Wednesday morning. It wasn't the tasteless headline that troubled Taylor, or the deplorable manner in which the newspaper displayed Cercone's corpse. Even the details didn't concern Taylor—not at first. It was the inserted picture of Anthony DiFilippo IV that had Taylor reliving a past problem he felt had never been truly resolved.

Taylor read the story a second time. Reputed mob boss Tony D was both Johnny Cercone's employer and his uncle, and if Butera's piece was even half true, Taylor thought, the Harvard-educated DiFilippo was, without a doubt, a force to be reckoned with—intelligent, respected, wealthy, and connected. Violence, however, was something the don tried to discourage, according to Butera's piece.

Taylor's interest in the lives of Johnny Cercone and Anthony DiFilippo might have waned if not for the morning news programs.

"Fat Paulie" Franco, underboss to Anthony DiFilippo, had been shot dead late Thursday night, according to the local NBC affiliate. Franco's driver, Michael Testa, had miraculously escaped with only a concussion. He was taken to Sloan-Kettering hospital for tests, then released. NYPD detectives were investigating the crime. They had no suspects. "Is there a connection between these heinous crimes?" the overly enthusiastic anchorwoman asked her morning audience.

"Lady," Taylor said under his breath, "of course there's a goddamned connection."

"A car fire on the George Washington apparently has the bridge looking like a Wal-Mart parking lot," the blond anchorwoman continued in her same sassy voice. "Traffic is next."

On the ABC affiliate, Detective Katherine Montroy, in reference to Johnny Cercone's murder, talked about a "professional hit" by a "very talented marksman."

Taylor scribbled Montroy's name on a lined legal pad. Jack had mentioned her a few days after Karen's funeral. She and her partner had allegedly identified Vincent Tagliafero's weapons as the ones used to kill Karen Easter, Patricia Durante, and the owner of Rudy's Tavern.

When the ABC television piece was over, Taylor opened to the *Post*'s website: "UNDERBOSS PAUL 'FAT PAULIE' FRANCO SHOT DEAD."

Detective Katherine Montroy was again quoted. Matthew Philips, a second homicide detective at the Twenty-Eighth Precinct, had refused to comment.

Taylor's antennae twitched as he added more names to his growing list. DiFilippo and Cercone were both related to Vincent Tagliafero—the man who allegedly killed Hatch's wife and sister-in-law. Cercone reported to Paulie Franco. Both men had been murdered within forty-eight hours of one another. Taylor had been trained by experienced CIA personnel never to believe in coincidence.

Katherine Montroy and Matthew Philips had originally been assigned to the Rudy's Tavern murders. A second shooter—if one existed at all—had never been identified.

Searching the *Post*'s archives, Taylor revisited a Vincent Tagliafero article written by B. J. Butera back in August. The mob division guys had taken over the cases shortly after Tagliafero's Glock and Smith & Wesson Model 64 were matched with the slugs used to kill Robert O'Rourke, Karen Easter, and Patricia Durante. Nothing was ever mentioned about a second gunman at Rudy's that night.

Two dead Mafia guys with connections to Tagliafero, thought Taylor. *One of them a cousin to the deceased.* He shook his head.

Gray Taylor finally reached for the phone again. Instead of punching in Jack Slattery's number, though, he tried a four-three-four exchange—Charlottesville, Virginia. It took only a moment to find out that Kevin Easter's cell was no longer in service. And if Hatch had gotten a new phone with a Western New York number, Taylor didn't have it. He left a quick message for Hatch with a young girl at the Cattaraugus Indian Reservation's recreation center, just as he'd suggested to Terri. The girl couldn't make any promises that Hatch would get it.

Gray Taylor fell heavily back into his chair. "Now what?"

Rockville, Maryland

"Slattery," the DDI answered in a gruff voice. He circled the name Jeremy Silverstone on a lined legal pad.

"Jack. It's Gray. You alone?"

Slattery was in the backseat of a government-issued limousine, one perk the bean counters on Capitol Hill couldn't wrestle away from his office. Cradling the phone to his ear, the DDI laid his leather-bound binder on the seat's upholstery and said, "Yes, I can talk, if that's what you're asking." There was thick, bulletproof glass between him and the driver, giving Slattery privacy.

"Are you heading into the office?"

"Yes." Slattery glanced through the window, identifying landmarks. "I'm about ten miles away."

"Is this line secure?"

"Is it snowing in New York?" Slattery was asking if there was a serious problem.

"The weatherman is calling for heavy rain, but who really knows?"

"Give me twenty minutes. I'll call you back."

Manhattan / Langley

Gray Taylor snatched up the phone after the first ring. "Jack, have you spoken to Hatch lately?"

Jesus, Slattery thought. Kevin Easter wasn't a topic he'd even considered since Taylor had initiated this conversation thirty minutes earlier. In fact, he hadn't thought about Hatch for nearly a week. The Silverstone op, which had turned from a simple sanction to a complicated extraction, had been his top focus. Taylor's surveillance of the fugitive's estate was still being discussed internally.

Slattery closed the *GREENBACK* file. "Not in over a month. Why?"

"Has anyone?"

"From this office?" Slattery asked, knitting his brow. There was a trace of concern in his voice. He peeled off his suit jacket, tossed it over a high-back chair, and began circling the large antique desk like a great white shark.

Taylor pressed. "Jack, has *anyone* talked to Hatch?"

Slattery paused, then said, "What's on your mind, Gray?"

For the next fifteen minutes, Taylor defended his own self-described ludicrous assumptions. He ended with, "Please tell me I've got an overactive imagination."

"I'll need time to read those articles from the New York papers," Slattery said, "and I'll get copies of Johnny Cercone's and Paulie Franco's homicide reports. Gray, I want you to pack an overnight bag."

"What about *GREENBACK*? I'm scheduled to leave in two days."

"Mr. Silverstone can wait," Slattery said, his tone uncharacteristically on edge. "Have you ever been to the Cattaraugus Indian Reservation?"

"No, sir."

"So, you've never spoken to Hatch's grandfather, Low Dog?"

"No, sir," Taylor repeated, "but you've told me a little about him."

"You'll like him," Slattery said, scribbling another note. "He's . . . grounded, but complicated, if that makes any sense. Old school."

"Sounds a lot like you."

"When's the last time you talked to Kevin?"

"About a week before Halloween."

"What was his attitude?"

Searching for the right word, Taylor said, "Short, like he was in a big hurry to get off the phone. He called me—from that rec area they have on the reservation."

Slattery stopped pacing. "On your cell or at home?"

"Home," Taylor said after a moment. "Why?"

"You're sure he made the call?"

"Yes, sir," Taylor said, getting to his feet, understanding where this line of questioning was headed. And then the question Terri had asked him the night before, just after they'd crossed over to Central Park West, came back to him: "And nobody has seen or talked to Hatch in how many weeks?" In truth, she had asked twice.

"I'll get back to you within the hour." Slattery terminated the call.

"Jesus," Taylor said.

Brooklyn

The hunter walked east on Tremont, a busy tree-lined street, then turned left on Southern Boulevard and headed north toward the Bronx Zoo. The light flurries of the past few days had been pushed out and over the Atlantic Ocean by a high-pressure system, leaving New York City with a gloriously clear day and temperatures predicted to hit fifty. Still, at 7:22 a.m., it was closer to freezing.

The leather bomber jacket, scuffed at the elbows, nearly covered a cream-colored scarf folded neatly across his chest and neck. His leather gloves were the same color as his black Nike cross trainers and wool driver's cap. Shouldered beneath his left arm was a Walther PPK—used to end Paulie Franco's life—minus the serial number, which had been filed clean a month earlier. Electrical tape covered the pistol's handle. He carried this morning's edition of *The New York Post* under his arm and a laptop in his backpack. His wallet contained American Express and Visa credit cards, a driver's license, and seventy-two bucks in cash. All the credentials identified him as Robert Mahany of 2530 Bainbridge Avenue. Bainbridge Avenue was a middle-class Bronx neighborhood not far from Fordham University.

Although it was relatively early in the morning, pedestrian and automotive traffic had begun to swell. It was Black Friday. Retail stores braced for the first wave of post-Thanksgiving shoppers.

None of this concerned the hunter. Holidays had no meaning to him this year—since August, every day resembled the last. Instead of turkey, he'd eaten cold canned soup. Instead of football games, lively discussions about politics, big business, fishing, and tabloid celebrities—all family traditions—he'd prepared himself for war, physically, emotionally, and spiritually.

Passing under the gothic gates of the Bronx Zoo, the hunter made himself comfortable on a wooden park bench about fifteen feet from a hot dog vendor, an elderly black man who was busy putting out for display his collection of condiments, assorted bags of chips, and cans of soft drinks. Within minutes, the smell of Italian sausages wafted through the air.

Thursday's edition of the *Post* reported the Johnny Cercone murder on the front page. It included an outdated and unflattering mug shot of the young *caporegime*. A second photograph, this one in black and white, was graphic, sensational—perfectly placed to sell newspapers and support Internet advertisers. Taken from above the crime scene, undoubtedly by an amateur, Cercone's contorted body was shown lying on the concrete steps near a hedge, leaving no doubt that most of his head was gone. NYPD crime scene tape cordoned off the area.

Anthony DiFilippo IV, owner of a wholesale plumbing company and a reputed Mafia don known for being publicity-shy, now found himself in the unenviable limelight—his grainy colored photograph had been positioned to the left of his dead nephew's picture.

The *New York Post*'s headline read, "CAPO TAKES NAPO." The two-inch letters were printed across the photo of Johnny's body, which held the caption, "Tony D seeks revenge for murdered godson?"

Two articles reported the same story from basically the same perspective. Johnny Cercone, nephew of Anthony DiFilippo IV, was shot dead soon after he left his Bronx brownstone early Wednesday morning. A shell casing was reportedly found on a rooftop down the street from Cercone's home.

B. J. Butera, reporter for the *Post*, had written the more complete article. Throughout his front-page story, he quoted "unnamed sources" with a wide range of theories:

"Johnny probably flexed the wrong muscle, if ya know what I mean."

"Johnny maybe had some dealings outside the family."

"Some rival has his eyes on Tony D's empire. That's why they took Johnny out."

"The DiFilippo family is getting into the drug trade, and the competition ain't happy about it. Killing Johnny was a stern message to the don and his associates."

There was even speculation that Cercone's flamboyance and history of wild parties with the ladies, which usually included his pal Donald "Woody" Biasucci, had bruised a fragile ego.

Some of the local gangs got some ink. The E-Street Boys, the Ñetas, Akrho Pinoy, and the Latin Kings, a Chicano gang known for trafficking in marijuana, found themselves under the media microscope. A Puerto Rican crew dealing PCP, meth, LSD, and various prescription narcotics was also mentioned. The used-weapons trade, controlled by a nameless bunch of hooligans in Queens, suddenly gained notoriety.

Lawrence Luther Wright, who had ties to Manhattan's high-society cocaine clientele, was also discussed. He was quoted. "Speculation is the mother of all evil," he said. "I've never met Mr. Cercone, although I have great respect for his Uncle Anthony. My heart and prayers go out . . ."

The hunter knew this was the deadly world that the DiFilippo family had built, manipulated, and dominated for over a decade. And now, according to the *Post*'s B. J. Butera, the fragile peace might have been violated. The reporter had raised a few interesting questions in his cleverly worded article. One stood above the rest: Was this the beginning of the end for Anthony DiFilippo IV?

Cercone's "assassination" had created the aftershocks the hunter had sought. The print media's interpretation of the events had, in fact, given him a wider variety of targets. The E-Street Boys, Akrho Pinoy, Lawrence Luther Wright, and others would soon be pushed into open warfare, victims of collateral damage for a cause they had no idea existed.

On the *Post*'s second page, Butera co-authored a shorter piece. Homicide detective Katherine Montroy was quoted in the article: "Nothing to report; it's too early in the investigation; neighbors are being interviewed; no suspects yet." Routine. Detective Montroy, nevertheless, used the phrase "professional hit."

"Professional hit," the hunter said, glancing over at the hotdog vendor. After a brief moment, he neatly folded the newspaper and placed it on the bench. He slid his Apple computer out from the backpack and placed it on his knees, hitting the power switch. He picked up a wireless signal from a nearby tower and googled *The New York Post*.

Once he was on the newspaper's website, the most recent news articles became available.

UNDERBOSS PAUL "FAT PAULIE" FRANCO SHOT DEAD
by B. J. Butera

Early this morning, Paulie Franco, underboss for reputed mobster Tony D, was found dead in his parked car outside the Century Club in the Bronx.

Franco, age sixty-two, purportedly the second most powerful man in the Anthony DiFilippo crime family and childhood friend of the don, was shot once in the head soon after leaving the Willis Avenue tavern.

There were no witnesses at the Century Club, known for its colorful patrons, although one regular, Wayne Rambus, said, "Paulie seemed really nervous, and I'm pretty sure he drank about twelve shots of Jack before leaving the bar that night."

Found unconscious in the late-model Lincoln sedan was Michael Testa . . .

"Consider yourself very lucky, Mr. Testa," the hunter said, scrolling down.

The newspaper article continued: "Johnny Cercone, DiFilippo's nephew, was shot dead outside his Bronx home on Wednesday morning."

The hunter closed his laptop. "A very good start," he said.

Manhattan

Gray Taylor grabbed the telephone in his personal study as soon as it rang. Fifty-two minutes had passed since his last conversation with Jack Slattery. "Hello." His gaze swept over an antique Fisher-Price toy—a wooden bumblebee—that Terri had purchased from a private dealer in Bangor, Maine.

"The situation is definitely worth taking a closer look at," Slattery said.

"What do you have?"

"It's only my opinion, and I haven't shared it with anyone, but I think Kevin called you at home for a reason, Gray—I think he wanted to know where you were."

"For a guy who has a rep for sticking with the facts, you just jumped the shark, Boss. That's quite a stretch." *Unfortunately*, he thought, *I feel the same.*

"Call it a hunch," Slattery said. "You're heading to Western New York today. Find out what our mutual friend is doing. I have an agent collecting information on both homicides—just in case this thing goes south."

Taylor's face darkened. "So the clock is ticking?"

"Gray, this thing *could* be a time bomb if . . ." Slattery's words trailed off.

For Taylor, the idea of Hatch running around the five boroughs of New York killing people had seemed oppressively surreal and utterly ridiculous just a few hours ago, but now he could sense Slattery's trepidation.

"According to the report I'm reading, the shooter was about 325 yards from the target," Slattery said. "He was on top of a three-story building. Cercone was struck in the left orbital socket, and it damn near exploded his head."

A perfect shot, Taylor knew from his training at Quantico. "Three hundred and twenty-five yards?"

"And it was snowing lightly. Winds were gusting upwards of fifteen miles per hour that morning," said Slattery. "But the slug that killed Cercone didn't match the shell casing CSI personnel found on the roof; not by a long-shot. That round came from a Vietnam era weapon. An M16, 5.56 millimeter. A very lame attempt to throw off investigators—probably a joke, for reasons I can't even begin to speculate. Detectives also found one of those bogus shells at Paulie Franco's murder scene. And Franco was killed by a small-caliber handgun. Still waiting on ballistics for that one."

"Witnesses?"

"No, but NYPD recovered the slug in Cercone's front door." Slattery picked up the faxed report from his desk. "Standard NATO sniper round. Subsonic ammo. The sniper probably had an AWS version, which accounts for the lack of witnesses."

"British Special Air Service likes to use them," Taylor said quietly. "A sound-suppressed barrel. This sure doesn't feel like your routine Mafia hit."

"My thoughts exactly."

"Street gangs and drug dealers prefer good old-fashioned assault rifles. They're noisy, and they rarely miss their target."

"Unless one of those groups paid for some outside help."

"But why, Jack? Don't these bad guys thrive on notoriety? Don't they throw some weight around just to show the competition who's in charge? Most of them are bullies masquerading as businessmen. Am I right?"

"I'm not a student of New York City gangs or the Mafia life," Slattery said. "That's something the FBI and the local cops—specifically the mob division—will have a better handle on. As for the drug dealers, they certainly have the money to pay for a guy of this gunman's caliber—*if* they knew where to look."

"Jack," Taylor said, exhaling, "I need your honest opinion on something."

"I'm pretty sure I know what you're asking."

"Could Hatch make a shot like the one that killed Johnny Cercone?" It was a question Taylor had been contemplating since Jack had explained the degree of difficulty—weather conditions, distance.

"He scored in the top one percent at the Farm."

"I remember that from his file."

"But he'd need a good bit of practice to get back to that level."

"Time is something Hatch had a lot of back on the reservation," Taylor said. "But why would he make it so obvious to us? Why kill Cercone with a world-class shot?"

"At first, I thought maybe he didn't want to get his hands dirty," Slattery said, "but Paulie Franco's murder was up close and personal. So to answer your question, I don't have a clue."

"Does he think Cercone and Franco were at Rudy's Tavern that night?"

"It doesn't really make a difference, Gray. Only that they were targeted, then murdered. And DiFilippo's crime family is vast. Lots of targets to choose from."

"Do you think Hatch is done?" asked Taylor, leaning back in his chair. "Is he satisfied? Now that Cercone and Paulie Franco are out of—"

"Watch yourself, Gray. You can accuse a man of a crime, but now we need to prove his guilt. Finding Kevin Easter is obviously our priority."

"Is he satisfied, Jack?" Taylor repeated, this time in a tone that had taken on a sharp edge.

"Would you be?"

"Not until I finished the job, which means eliminating everyone associated with my wife's death." Taylor cleared his throat. "I would get more than my pound of flesh. But that's me."

"Like I told you back in August, Kevin thinks like you, Gray."

"I'll drive to Buffalo," Taylor said. "It'll take me about seven hours. Most airlines wouldn't care for the gear I'll be bringing."

"Think Terri would be interested in tagging along?"

"Is this your way to get her back in the game?"

"If what I think is happening in New York City turns out to be true," said Slattery, "I want both of you to eyeball the situation on the Cattaraugus Indian Reservation. On this project, two heads are better than one. Gray, we need to be absolutely perfect across the board on this one."

"And if she has other plans?"

"Tell Mrs. Taylor it's a favor I intend to repay with interest."

CHAPTER 22

Bronx

D etective Matthew Philips's Ford Taurus raced down East 233rd Street in the Bronx, made a tight right on Webster Avenue, slowed, and then drove under a giant wrought iron archway. Leaves skidded in front of the car. Curved steel bars were inscribed with the name "Woodlawn Cemetery" atop two stone pillars, one to each side of the gravel road.

Philips was behind the wheel, an unlit cigarette clamped between his yellow teeth. "Christ on a rented polo pony, Kat, I hate places like this," he said, grimacing. "They scare the crap outta me."

Sitting in the passenger seat, Detective Katherine Montroy was equally anxious. "Yep, I'm having a ball over here," she said, rolling her eyes. "Cemeteries, dentists, and puppets bring out the little girl in me."

"Thank God it's the middle of the friggin' day."

The Taurus rolled past a sea of graves. A diverse cross-section of dead New Yorkers—some more than a century old—lay below a vast collection of headstones of different shapes, sizes, and colors. Tall deciduous trees, now dormant for the winter, cast shadows over many of the graves.

As the white Taurus rolled over a small rise, Montroy pointed. "Shit, there he is."

"I'll be damned," Philips said under his breath. "No way I thought this would happen, especially with Fat Paulie's murder—"

"Slow down, Goddamnit!"

Head bowed and hat in hand, Anthony DiFilippo stood before an elaborate monument, the sun directly overhead. About thirty feet from the don, a black limousine idled, exhaust trailing. A well-built man in a charcoal-colored overcoat, dark sunglasses, and black gloves stood like a pit bull sentry next to the vehicle. He followed the Ford's progress with keen interest.

Philips parked the car next to the limo.

"I'm guessing this part of Woodlawn holds a few of Mr. DiFilippo's colleagues and relatives," Philips said, turning the ignition key. The engine fell silent. "He's been involved with the underworld since he was a teenager."

"And I thought my childhood in Scranton was fucked up."

"Even when he was away at Harvard, the old bastard stayed in close contact with the action, or so the story goes."

"A man with a dream," Montroy said sarcastically. "A real visionary."

Tony D's head remained bowed as he paid his respects to Vincent Tagliafero. Because of the dry summer, grass had never had a chance to grow on the gravesite.

"Damn, he looks so old," Montroy said, leaning over the dashboard.

"The guy's about to bury his second nephew in the past three months, Kat. That's stress. And then Fat Paulie—arguably the don's closest buddy—gets himself killed last night. The guy called me from the Century Club to set up this meeting— probably an hour or so before he was gunned down." Gesturing to a pile of fresh dirt not ten feet from Tagliafero's headstone, he said, "Johnny's funeral is Monday morning."

"Wanna hear something crazy, Matty?"

"Probably not."

"I actually feel sorry for Mr. DiFilippo."

"He may look like a harmless old man, with his legitimate plumbing company, and he may even play the role to perfection," Philips said, "but Anthony DiFilippo's a dangerous motherfucker. Never forget that, Kat. And he's smart. I don't think he's ever been arrested."

"A speeding ticket twelve years ago," Montroy said. "I checked."

Tony D made the sign of the cross, set the black fedora back on his head, then turned toward the parked cars. He smiled warmly at his two guests.

"You ready for this, partner?" said Philips.

"Ready as kidney stones on Christmas morning."

The two detectives got out of the Taurus and moved around to the front bumper. Tony D's bodyguard, a brutish man with a graying goatee and apparently no sense of humor, said, "Mr. DiFilippo thought you guys would be more comfortable in *his* vehicle."

Hands deep in his coat pockets, Tony D said, "I can assure you, Ms. Montroy, Marco doesn't bite—at least not that I know of."

"Kat . . . when's the last time you had a tetanus shot?" Philips whispered.

"I can't believe you talked me into this," Montroy muttered.

Tony D climbed into the limousine.

Instead of searching Montroy and Philips, Marco ran a metal wand over their bodies.

"Hey, buddy, you steal that thing from LaGuardia?" Philips said, lightly elbowing his partner.

"Kennedy," the driver said without the slightest trace of emotion.

"We're cops, y'know," Philips said.

"Like I care," Marco said, offering a smile that appeared painful.

When the two detectives climbed into the limousine, they found Tony D sitting comfortably in the backseat, legs crossed, facing forward. His cashmere overcoat was unbuttoned, the black fedora balanced on his thigh. Montroy sat directly across from the don.

Philips fell in next to his colleague. "Hi-def?" he said in a shaky voice, gesturing to the flat-screen TV with his chin.

"I wouldn't know," Tony D said. "We usually drive something far less conspicuous."

When the door closed, Tony D folded his hands. "Detective Montroy, Detective Philips," he said in a raspy voice, "I appreciate you meeting with me, especially on such short notice. I know your time is valuable—"

"Is there something we can help you with, Mr. DiFilippo?" Montroy asked, a trace of irritation in her tone.

Tony D shifted his gaze to outside the tinted window. "I've been told you two are investigating Johnny's murder. Is there any truth to this?"

"Yes, sir, we're in charge," Philips said. "Same goes for Paulie Franco's murder."

"But that's gonna change," Montroy said. "Our mob division is taking over, just like they did with Forrest Gump . . . ah, I mean, the Vincent Tagliafero case."

"That's not going to happen," Tony D said with the confidence of a mystic.

Philips narrowed his eyes. "How can you be so sure?"

"You're just going to have to take my word for it, Detective Philips," Tony D said. He stared holes into the little man. "Maybe it's because of the way those people handled—or didn't handle—Vincent's murder investigation. I haven't seen any progress in finding my nephew's killer, even after three months."

"Sir," Montroy said, "the case is still open. I'm sure—"

Tony D patiently raised his right hand. "Makes me wonder if the New York Police Department gave up on this one. Makes me wonder if it's because Vincent's a family member—just another cold case in a big room filled with cold case files."

Montroy and Philips traded looks.

"For now, we're handling both the Cercone and Franco murder investigations," Montroy said. "I try not to worry about things I can't control."

"Has there been any progress?" The don let out a long and disconcerting breath. He looked to Philips for an answer.

"Sir," Montroy said, "we can't discuss investigations while—"

Tony D's deep cough interrupted her statement. Grimacing, he pulled a white handkerchief from his overcoat and covered his mouth. His whole body convulsed in a desperate attempt to mitigate the pain.

The episode subsided. Tony D relaxed again. He blew his nose, and then shoved the handkerchief back into his coat pocket. "I apologize."

Marco tapped on the window with his knuckles: "You okay, Boss?"

Nodding, the don waved him off. "I'm fine."

Both detectives glanced at one another again.

Tony D unwrapped a throat lozenge and laid it on his tongue. "My doctor tells me it's a chest cold. My paranoid wife thinks it's cancer. Perhaps it's a little of both."

Montroy said, "We were told you *may* have information—"

"Ms. Montroy, I'm fairly certain Paulie said no such thing when he contacted Detective Philips last night. Their conversation was very brief, according to my old friend. But Paulie isn't here to debate this issue, so I have nothing to support my position."

"Sir, I'm sorry for your loss," said Philips.

"I appreciate that," Tony D said quietly. "Paulie was a very loyal friend."

"So, how do you suppose the owner of a plumbing company can help us?" Montroy asked. She crossed her arms over her chest.

"Easy, Kat," said Philips, reaching over and gently patting his partner's leg.

"During an investigation, especially a murder investigation," Montroy said, seemingly ignoring Philips, "we can't—"

"I know all about such rules and regulations," Tony D said, smoothly interrupting her. "Sadly, I'm a student of your world." A renewed strength now carried in his words. "But, as the old saying goes, for every rule there is an exception. Am I not right?"

"Um . . . it depends on the case," Philips said.

Tony D crooked his thumb and pointed his index finger at Matthew Philips like a gun, and the cop flinched. "That, Detective, is exactly the answer I was looking for," he said. "It all depends on the case. A problem, unfortunately, the three of us share."

"The three of us?" Montroy said, thinning her eyes. "Sir, this really has nothing to do with you."

"Ms. Montroy, you can't honestly believe that," the don said, setting his fedora on the seat. "These murders have *everything* to do with me. From what I've learned, you're both very astute and very good at your jobs, so you know this is an attack on my organization *and* me."

Montroy continued: "I meant we can't share—"

"These murders . . . they're not a good thing," Tony D said, his intelligent blue eyes shifting between the two detectives. "You both understand what happens when the first domino is pushed over."

These murders are not a good thing? Montroy thought. *Not a good thing?* No, this was a very bad thing, a terrible thing. Two malicious attacks had taken place these past two days, and she and Matty both assumed it was the beginning of something bigger. As a sign of strength, the DiFilippo family was now obligated to strike back with force. It was the law of the jungle. The dominos Anthony DiFilippo referred to were already in motion.

"Maybe," Tony D said, "we could, for a brief period, become partners."

"Partners?" Philips said, incredulous, spreading his hands.

Tony D coughed, then grimaced. "Exactly. Please, hear me out."

Pressing the Bose headphones to his ears, the hunter sat cross-legged on the cold cement floor next to his hi-tech recording equipment and focused primarily on Anthony DiFilippo's gravelly voice. The don's cough had gotten worse over the past five weeks, he noted. Four hundred feet from the private meeting, hidden in a marble crypt lighted only with a small Coleman lantern, he listened to the conversation between the Mafia don and the two New York City homicide detectives.

Directly behind the hunter, their discussion was being recorded to a CD. He would later filter out the static or crosstalk that might have occurred via interference from a local cell phone, BlackBerry, or some other wireless device. Even a police scanner or ham radio operator could momentarily scramble the dialogue on which he was eavesdropping.

Still, that had happened only a few times during the course of nearly 294 recorded hours of Anthony DiFilippo's conversations. The transmitter placed underneath the black fedora's hatband—one of three he'd planted—had, to date, worked flawlessly.

"Tony wants partners," the hunter mused. The mob division was officially cut out of the loop, which was something Tony D had handled early in the day, and now there was a deal on the table—good guys allied with the bad guys. *Well, well, well.*

This could only mean one thing: The war would draw still more combatants.

Tony DiFilippo coughed again, then grimaced. "My associates and their contacts outnumber the police assigned to your cases a good twenty or thirty to one." He reached into a small refrigerator, removed a bottle of Perrier, and offered one to each of his guests. They both declined. "You know I'm right."

"Excuse my fucking French, Mr. DiFilippo," said Montroy, "but aren't you one of the highest-ranking Mafia figures in the northeastern United States?"

"There's really no need to curse," Tony D said.

"You probably haven't even set foot in your bullshit plumbing business for years," Montroy continued, ignoring the don. "Do you even know how to use a pipe wrench?"

For the first time since August, the hunter found his sense of humor. He laughed quietly, and would have paid handsomely to see DiFilippo's expression. All he heard was silence.

Tony D shifted his gaze between the two detectives, and then slowly placed the cap on the bottled water. Pursing his lips, he appeared saddened or pained by her response. He then rested the Perrier in a cup holder near his elbow and said, "Must we play games, Ms. Montroy?"

"Is that what we're doing?" Montroy glanced over at her partner.

"Kat," Philips said angrily, letting out a long breath. "Easy."

"I was hoping my position in the community could be an advantage instead of a liability," Tony D went on. "Have I misjudged the situation? Have I misjudged *you*, Detective?"

"We're here, sir," Philips said. "And we're listening."

The hunter thought: All this time secretly listening to the don, and yet the old man had never discussed his "position in the community." Even behind closed doors, Tony D rarely flexed his muscles. He was a great communicator in that he listened. As with most corporate moguls, his day consisted of solving various problems and heading off potential trouble spots. The framework of his empire never came up.

Johnny Cercone, the don's most trusted *capo*, had been an exception to that rule. As of late, almost everything important had moved through his nephew; even Fat Paulie Franco wasn't privileged to hear the don's long-term vision or business model. It was mostly through Cercone that orders and ideas had been implemented. Now Tony D's most trustworthy intermediary was lying in an eighteen-thousand-dollar casket at the Triamante Funeral Home.

"Sir," Montroy said firmly, "your position in the community is well documented—"

"Please," the don said, "let's not lose focus here."

Closing his eyes, the hunter could almost feel the tension climb in the limo.

"Look, Mr. DiFilippo," Philips said evenly, "I'm no genius, and it's clear that you have some of *our* people in *your* pocket. Your comment on the mob division pretty much puts a fork in their credibility. Why not ask them for help?"

Ironically, as the hunter was well aware, one of the two Twenty-Eighth Precinct detectives sitting in Tony D's limousine was also on the don's payroll. Identifying the dirty cop was proving to be a difficult task, as Cercone had been the key intermediary. By requesting a partnership of sorts and bringing both detectives into this clandestine meeting, it appeared as if the don was attempting to recruit both individuals assigned to the murders, not just the one he paid. He was, the hunter had learned quickly, a cagy businessman and negotiator.

Regarding Philips's query, Tony D said, "Because you two are smarter than all of them put together."

"We're flattered," Montroy said tonelessly. "Nonetheless, my gut tells me that recent promotions of certain individuals in and out of the mob division didn't come at a very good time for you—isn't that right, Mr. DiFilippo?"

"I've always appreciated bright people, Ms. Montroy. Well played."

"Sir, how can we help you?" Philips slid forward on his seat. "How can you help us?"

Tony D shifted his weight, then said, "My people have been looking under rocks for almost two days, and nobody has a clue what's happening. The streets are too quiet."

"Could one of your enemies have hired outside help?" asked Montroy.

"For what purpose?" Tony D said with a shrug.

"To confuse your people," Montroy said. "You're preoccupied with the murders of Cercone and Franco. Could that be what this is all about? Take a step back for a moment. Who really benefits from their deaths?"

"These men were important people in my life," the don said. "I loved them."

Yes, you did, the hunter thought. *And that's the point of this little exercise.*

Cocking her head, Montroy said, "So you consider these attacks personal?"

The don pondered the question for a long moment, then nodded. "I do."

"That's interesting," Philips murmured, glancing over at his partner. "Why?"

"Call it a hunch," Tony D said. "Like a storm out at sea you can't see yet."

"Which one of your associates in the neighboring New York boroughs would benefit the most if your organization stumbled? Are things really that good, Mr. DiFilippo? Your piece of the pie is getting smaller," said Montroy.

Tony D nodded just so, and the right corner of his mouth turned upward, briefly. "But it's still big enough to make a nice living."

"Fifteen years ago, the gangs were uneducated, disorganized punks with knives," Montroy said, her words coming forth like bullets. "Like it or not, these miscreants are legitimate players in your world, especially when it comes to the drug trade. Some are flush with money, smart, and protected by fancy lawyers and imaginative financial advisors, but you already know this."

"Drugs are a dirty business I don't participate in," Tony D said firmly.

"You, your soldiers, and their buddies spend all their time looking for this sniper," Philips said, "and in the meantime, the competition is working something bigger. Could that be it?"

"A shell game, perchance?" Montroy said.

"So you're telling me you think another family is behind this?" Tony D said.

"One of a few theories," Philips said.

"I'm having a difficult time believing that one," Tony D said. "My friends in Queens, Brooklyn, and Staten Island, even Long Island and Jersey, have bent over backwards denying any involvement in the murders. And I believe them. We have mutually beneficial partnerships. Some have been helping me find this shooter. They all insist that business is good. Nobody wants war. War is messy. It's not cost-effective." He coughed again.

"Don't dismiss or eliminate anyone," Montroy said. "It's critically important to stick with the facts. We're talking about a gunman who waited on a rooftop, in the cold, more than 320 yards from Johnny's stoop."

"The round nearly decapitated your nephew. Our experts tell us it was a perfect shot."

"So I've been told," the don said quietly.

"Leaving us with one very interesting theory," Philips said. "An outside pro was specifically hired to assassinate Cercone. Maybe the same guy took out Paulie Franco. We're still not totally convinced the two are connected."

"But if they are connected, why is this happening?" Montroy leveled that hard question directly at Anthony DiFilippo. "Did you maybe rattle the cages of the wrong competitor?"

"A distance of almost three football fields . . . in light snow," Tony D said, as if in a dream, glancing out the car window again. "And it was windy that morning."

"And not a single witness," Philips said. "Nobody heard the shot."

"Yes, a sound suppressor," Tony D said. "I've read the preliminary report."

Philips and Montroy traded looks again.

"To answer your question, Ms. Montroy," said Tony D, "I have no reason to believe I've angered anyone to this degree. Nothing's changed in the past few years—at least, not that I know of. And nobody in my organization is about to lead a coup d'état. My ear is always to the ground. It has to be."

"I hadn't realized how competitive plumbers could get," Montroy said, smiling.

Tony D laughed. "Well played again, Ms. Montroy. Like any successful businessman, I can't come across as vulnerable. If there's blood in the water, you can bet the piranhas are moving in for the kill."

"Then it's just a matter of being patient," Philips said. "Somebody will talk."

"Patience," Tony D muttered, shaking his head. "Not this time. No. I need to be proactive. All of my top people could be targets. I could be a target!"

"Which brings us to this place and time, Mr. DiFilippo," said Montroy. "You believe these murders are just the beginning. Correct?"

Tony D leaned back in the plush leather seat. Nodding, he said, "I do."

"You're concerned that things may spiral out of control?" Philips said. "Your words."

"That's right," the don said.

"So you propose we pool our information," Philips said.

"Quid pro quo, Detective Philips. You scratch my back and I'll—"

"And if we identify this shooter or the guy who paid for his services?" Montroy asked. "What then?"

"We'll get them off the street," Tony D said. "One way or another."

"What does that mean?" Montroy looked briefly at her partner, then back to the don.

Tony D leaned forward in his seat, smiled ruefully, and said, "I thought we weren't playing games."

CHAPTER 23

Bronx

Donald "Woody" Biasucci, the youngest *caporegime* in the DiFilippo crime family, tried to keep his frustration in check, but fatigue was catching up to him like age on a supermodel. Rivulets of sweat ran down the small of his back, and his dark blue dress shirt was damp. Perspiration beaded on his forehead. He was afraid his anger would erupt before he had the opportunity to ejaculate.

The twenty-eight-year-old man, with his lean, hard body, pounded his flaccid penis into the blond teenage girl's midsection. Her adolescence had been extinguished by years of drug abuse and domineering men. Stoned, her doll-like expression fixed with a moronic grin, she appeared indifferent, even as her thin frame took the brunt of Woody's violent thrusts.

The teenager's red leather skirt was unzipped to expose her emaciated body. Yellowish bruises and dozens of ugly needle marks dotted the insides of both elbows. Tiny nipples pressed against her tight halter-top. Her ripped panties lay on the matted carpet near the desk. Her legs folded back from the edge of the double bed, she didn't seem to recognize that a man was attempting to have intercourse with her. With each hard push, tiny puffs of air escaped from her parted mouth. Woody grunted like an agitated silverback gorilla.

"Shit," Woody said. He stepped back from the hooker. "Jesus fucking Christ! Can you at least act like you're getting into it?"

Woody blamed Johnny's murder, Fat Paulie's murder, the don's grim attitude these past few days, the organization's failure to retaliate, the cocaine coursing through his bloodstream, this afternoon's funeral, Monday's wake for Paulie, the weather, and just about everything else he could conjure up for his limp penis.

"You're an asshole, Johnny!" he shouted to the dark motel room.

"Johnny?" the prostitute said weakly in a voice resembling that of a small child just awakened from an afternoon nap. She turned her head from side to side. "I thought Johnny was dead."

"Shut your mouth!"

Looking down for another excuse, Woody blamed the Armani slacks bunched at his ankles. His temperamental equipment needed more room to maneuver—that had to be it. He quickly kicked off his shoes, then tossed his pants over the wooden chair. Grinning wolfishly at the young blond, he said, "Come here, girly."

Woody's little friend came to life.

But three quick raps on the motel room's outer door interrupted the session before it could begin again. Woody slipped the nine-millimeter Beretta semi-automatic from his shoulder harness and moved to the left of the window.

The young prostitute lay on the bed, unmoving, limp, used up. She closed her eyes and seemed instantly to fall asleep, breathing heavily through her mouth.

Two more knocks. "Mister? Hey . . . hey, you in there?" the Asian-accented voice asked in a hushed whisper. "If you own that black 'Vette, you might want to take a look out here. Some kids are screwin' with your ride, my man. Yeah, I think, yeah, they're tryin' to steal it."

Woody could hear footsteps move away, followed by knocking on the next door. The man was relaying his message to another guest in the motel. With his finger, the young *capo* slid the colorless curtain to the side and peered into the parking lot of the Sunset Inn Motel, located in one of Brooklyn's seedier neighborhoods.

Woody spied his Corvette parked along the busy city street. His left hand clenched into a tight fist. His right hand held the pistol.

Two black teenagers, both dressed like hip-hop artists, stood next to his shiny car. One of the boys was trying to jimmy the driver's-side door with a piece of steel the size and shape of a ruler.

"Little fucks!" he shouted, tossing his handgun on the bed next to the sleeping girl. Quickly pulling on his pants, he slipped his feet into his Bruno Magli shoes and picked up the Beretta again. "No-good motherfuckers!" He snapped back the deadbolt and turned the doorknob. Like Wyatt Earp making his grand entrance into a Wild West saloon, Woody yanked open the door, then realized this could be the last day of his life.

The black twin holes of a shotgun's sawed-off barrels were about an inch from Woody's wide eyes. The Beretta, like his penis, had become an impotent weapon.

The teenage girl sat up and giggled. "Hey . . . are you Johnny?"

"Put the gun on the floor," the hunter said firmly. "Right now."

Woody swallowed hard. The shotgun's handler, rigid as steel, had brown eyes that were cold—almost lifeless. This guy, he suspected, was not some common thief who'd bumbled into the wrong motel room. The man holding the weapon was of average height, and wore an older bomber jacket, faded jeans, gloves, black running shoes, and a balaclava over his face.

Woody crouched and carefully placed his weapon on the green carpet. "Easy with that thing."

"Arms way up," the hunter said. "I won't ask twice."

Woody slowly complied.

The two teenage boys drove away in the Corvette.

This had all been carefully planned, Woody knew. The punks who'd just taken his car had been a clever diversion, and they probably hadn't even known their part. Then a new reality set in: *Is this the fucking guy who whacked Johnny and Fat Paulie?* "Hey, listen, take . . . take it easy, my brother," Woody said, his voice quavering.

"I'm not your brother," the hunter said, pressing the barrel of the shotgun into Biasucci's left eye.

"Look . . . I meant—"

"Inside."

Woody took two giant steps backwards. "We need to talk about this."

"Get dressed and leave," the hunter said to the stoned girl. In his hand was a folded fifty-dollar bill. "Go back to Ronkonkoma, Paula. Your parents and little brother are worried sick about you. That's enough for a cab ride home. Don't disappoint me."

The blond teenager now sat on the edge of the bed, and for a brief moment, her eyes lost that dull, apathetic glaze. She quickly gathered her torn underwear, red pumps, and thin winter jacket, then passed by the two men, but not before snatching the money from the hunter's fingers. "Thank you," she said quietly, then slipped into the daylight.

"Man, you are fuckin' with the wrong—"

"Sit down, Mr. Biasucci."

"I ain't movin' a goddamned inch until you tell me what this is all about."

The hunter clubbed Woody in the head with the shotgun's heavy stock, and the dazed *capo* fell back onto the bed. "We'll see about that . . . brother."

"Fuck!"

"Yes, we do have a few things to talk about."

Swiping the blood flowing into his eyes, Woody said, "Man, why are you doing this?" A two-inch gash had been opened at his hairline.

"Because Johnny Cercone and Vincent Tagliafero killed Karen Easter, Patricia Durante, and Bobby O'Rourke," the hunter said. "I want you to hear their names."

"You . . . you're . . . hey, what're you talkin' about?"

"Repeat them."

"Huh?" Woody again wiped away the blood pouring into his left eye. He grabbed the pillow and pushed it against his head wound.

"The innocent people Tagliafero and Cercone killed back in August," the hunter said. "Tell me their names."

"Um . . . Bobby O'Rourke, Easter—"

"Don't forget their first names." The hunter placed the shotgun's barrel against Biasucci's crotch. "Think very, very carefully before you speak, Donald, or I'll start with the anatomy you're evidently very fond of."

"Oh, God—"

"Names!" The hunter pushed the shotgun against Woody's groin. "I want to hear them from you. Now!"

"Bob . . . Bobby O'Rourke, Karen—"

"Karen Easter!" the hunter snapped. "I'll help you with that one."

"Jesus . . . you killed—"

"Fat Paulie Franco also screwed up the names, Mr. Biasucci. But he was very helpful in identifying your brethren at Rudy's back in August. Nice of him."

"What?"

"The names!"

"Patricia . . . Durante. She was the third."

"Was Vincent Tagliafero the only shooter at Rudy's Tavern?"

Swallowing hard, nodding hurriedly, Woody said, "Yeah, yeah, that's what Johnny told me. Jesus, man, that's the truth, so help me God."

"And Johnny never told you he killed one of the women?"

"No. No!" Woody exclaimed. "It was Vincent. He fucked it up. Seriously."

"Were there any others involved that night?"

"You mean, like, besides Vincent and Johnny?"

"That's exactly what I'm asking," the hunter said.

"There was nobody else there!" Woody shouted. "That little shit Vincent got stupid when they was making a collection. It was Vincent's first—and last—job for the boss. Johnny said one of the ladies at Rudy's got hold of his piece, and that's when the shooting started. Vincent went Rambo 'cause he thought Bobby had a gun."

The hunter's eyes seemed to moisten. "You sure?"

"Yeah, that's what Johnny told me a few weeks after it went down."

"Is Anthony DiFilippo looking for me?"

"Shit, man, the whole damn world has an APB out for you," said Woody, turning the pillow over and placing the clean side against his brow. "Tony D set things in motion. There's fifty large on your ass. It's gonna double after the funeral because nobody's talkin'. People think you're some kinda ghost."

The hunter said nothing.

"But what the fuck does Vincent's meltdown have to do with . . ?" Woody's words trailed off.

The hunter flinched as if he were about to be struck.

"Holy shit," Woody said, dumbfounded. "You knew them girls, didn't you?"

"Did DiFilippo have anything to do with Vincent Tagliafero's death?"

"Huh?" Woody's face seemed to crumple. "One of our own? Are you nuts?"

The hunter pressed the gun into Biasucci's midsection. "That, I suspect, depends on your point of view."

"Hey, that . . . that's not how things work! Vincent was family."

"Then who killed Tagliafero?"

"We . . . we still don't know," said Woody. "Could have been anyone. Some think it was you."

"Were the cops told where to find Tagliafero's body?"

"An anonymous call is what I heard, but we had nothin' to do with it."

"And Tagliafero just so happened to have both murder weapons on him?"

"The kid was a total idiot," said Woody. "Everybody knew it. Johnny ordered Vincent to toss 'em into the river. Apparently the little prick didn't listen, which was pretty much par for the course for him. Between me and you, Vincent got what he deserved."

"And what do you suppose Tagliafero was doing at the Hunts Point Market the night he was murdered?"

"Maybe he was shaking down a drug dealer, or maybe he was trying to rip somebody else off." Woody paused, then slowly shook his head. "Jesus, you . . . you're getting even because Vincent killed—"

"Which cops are on DiFilippo's payroll, Mr. Biasucci? Give me a few names and we're done here."

"The old man . . . he don't tell me stuff like that. Only Johnny knew who to pay."

"Yeah, that's what Fat Paulie said."

"Look," Woody said, slowly raising his hands toward the ceiling. More blood flowed down his cheek. "I . . . I told you everything, man, and I had nothin' to do with what happened at Rudy's. You understand that, right?"

A siren wailed faintly in the distance.

"I'm a slow learner," the hunter said, pointing the shotgun at Biasucci's head.

"No . . . no, you can't do this!" Woody stammered.

Thirty seconds later, the hunter was finished in the hotel room. He removed his balaclava, slid his silenced pistol back into his shoulder rig, the rifle under his jacket, and slowly opened the door leading to the parking lot. The sirens were a few blocks away.

Stepping back into the cool morning air, the hunter, taking full measure of the situation, failed to notice the curtain in the neighboring hotel room suddenly closing.

CHAPTER 24

Manhattan

A little before two o'clock in the morning on the Saturday after Thanksgiving, Lawrence Luther Wright and two of his bodyguards stepped from the warmth of a black Mercedes Benz into the cold Harlem sleet. Dressed stylishly, the dapper drug lord had just returned from another night of clubbing in Manhattan. But Lawrence Luther's management style dictated that he attend to nearly every detail of his expanding empire. He'd arrived early for a progress report.

Wearing a long army jacket and jackboots, a tall African-American man stood dutifully inside the doorway of Mr. Wright's latest acquisition. The property had been purchased through Merrill Lynch by one of his offshore land management companies. It was a five-story warehouse on 145th Street, a neighborhood that had yet to experience urban renewal, and a perfect location for Lawrence Luther's growing needs. In less than a month, the entire third floor had been transformed into the largest and most sophisticated cocaine distribution center and illegal pharmaceutical laboratory in all of New York City. Twenty-seven employees, including three full-time chemists, had been hired to work in the new facility.

The stern-faced sentry tipped his hat to the boss. "Evening, Mr. Wright," he said, obediently opening the building's front door for the three men. Su Lyn, the ex-kick boxer-turned-personal driver, remained inside the car.

"Stay warm, Quentin," Lawrence Luther said to the sentry. "Could be a long winter."

"Mind over matter, sir. The U.S. Rangers taught me well."

Lawrence Luther Wright considered himself to be thirty-three years old. He was also under the impression his birthday was May 19. Both were nothing more than educated guesses. An elderly aunt and a crippled uncle, the latter since killed in a Harlem convenience store robbery, had raised him from an early age. His birth parents, drug addicts from Biloxi, Mississippi, were also dead; he'd never known them. Even Lawrence Luther's birth certificate had been forged to circumvent the adoption process.

Education, his Aunt Teresa had preached, was the only way out of this multi-generational nightmare, and she'd been right. While other kids his age played stickball and basketball, experimented with drugs, and joined gangs, Lawrence Luther hit the books. Even in middle school, he'd studied more than three hours a night on a diverse range of subjects. His formal education ended with a law degree from Manhattan College and a separate graduate degree in Christian Studies.

It was only after a three-year stay in a prestigious Wall Street financial institution that Lawrence Luther's real training in life began. Returning to the old neighborhood had turned into a financial windfall.

Even without two bodyguards at his side—both with advanced military backgrounds and both carrying MAC-10 assault weapons under their long jackets—Lawrence Luther's presence was daunting. A collection of Versace, Zegna, Bugatchi, and David Eden suits were tailor-made for his tall, athletic body, and his weight rarely fluctuated by more than two pounds. His full beard blended nicely with his dark complexion, and his shaved head reflected off the sodium vapor streetlights this cold morning. He wore large diamonds in both earlobes, and four gold rings—two on each hand—encrusted with jewels on his long, manicured fingers, as well as thick gold chains around his neck. Some envious observers claimed he sported enough bling to pay down Mexico's national debt. And the haughty Lawrence Luther had a stride so pure, it was unadulterated theater.

In and around Harlem, Lawrence Luther rivaled the popularity of Mike Tyson during his peak, though he quietly idolized educated men—leaders, like Colin Powell, Malcolm X, and Martin Luther King. He was especially admired around the holidays because of his gifts: frozen turkeys, bags of potatoes, fresh Italian bread, and canned fruits and vegetables. And he was a man of God, a practicing minister at the newly-renovated Our Lady of Sorrows, a Harlem church his Aunt Teresa attended daily.

Under Aunt Teresa's tutelage, Lawrence Luther had memorized much of the Bible before beginning grade school, and he was known to recite scripture verbatim, whatever the occasion.

Lawrence Luther and his two associates stepped onto the ground floor of the warehouse, waiting under a single bulb attached to a black cord. The warehouse was damp and cold. Water from a broken pipe dripped from the ceiling and pooled on the cracked concrete. Graffiti, garbage, and other debris littered the long, murky room. The air was stale, yet a smile formed on Lawrence Luther's lips. What was once the building of a furniture manufacturer had now become the perfect location for his expanding enterprise.

Standing silently in front of a large fire door painted candy-apple red, Lawrence Luther and his bodyguards waited. Somebody on the other side manipulated the newly installed electronic locks. A faint buzzer sounded, steel grated against steel, and the door swung open slowly.

A diminutive man wearing a white lab coat and a blue surgical cap quickly ushered them in. He was the only Caucasian employee in the operation. "I . . . I'm so sorry, Mr. Wright," said the man, who resembled Jerry Lewis's nutty professor. "Sir, I . . . yeah, I wasn't expecting you for another hour. But that's perfectly okay, really, we . . . we're still ready with our presentation."

Lawrence Luther stepped past his chief chemist, who had a doctorate in pharmacology from the University at Buffalo, but said nothing. His two associates didn't even acknowledge the frightened little man. Already, the atmosphere of the condemned building had changed dramatically. It was warmer and brighter, and the rank smell of decay was gone. Muted voices could be heard from above. Music was playing—some hip-hop artist.

With the touch of a keypad, the reinforced bolt slid back into place, and the chemist said, "Sir, yes, yes . . . we've increased meth production nearly eighteen percent this week alone. That's way ahead of our . . . your schedule. We . . . we're running at about seventy-five percent capacity and should be able to begin to fill orders within—"

A cell phone chirped and interrupted the chemist's progress report. One bodyguard stiffened. Lawrence Luther looked to the second man, who had long dreadlocks, a goatee, and a nasty expression made nastier by the cell's annoying cry.

It chirped again.

Jamar Hightower retrieved his phone from his inside coat pocket, stared at the number on the LCD display, shrugged, and answered. "Who is this?" His voice was deep and harsh and meant to intimidate. Within a moment, the lines about his brown eyes deepened. "Huh?" Another pause. Jamar shuffled his feet. "You jerkin' with me, white meat? Because if you are . . ."

Pushing his thick rimless glasses up his nose, the chemist swallowed back his trepidation as he watched Jamar's attitude turn from frustration to irritation to anger.

"You threatening me?" Jamar shouted, glancing over at his boss. "Five minutes for what? Huh?" Another pause. "I will fuckin' bust you up if I ever find your punk ass."

Shaking his head slowly, Lawrence Luther thinned his eyes.

"No, no, no . . . it don't work that way," Jamar said through clenched teeth. "You need to identify yourself and state your business before the big man takes your call; everything comes through me. Everything!" Another pause. "You can't be demanding no audience with . . ."

Lawrence Luther watched, quietly.

Jamar listened for another short moment, and then yelled, "You little fuck! I couldn't give two shits if you saw us get out the Mercedes . . ."

The chemist grimaced. The second bodyguard reached under his coat, as if to verify that his weapons were still close at hand. Extending his arm palm up, Lawrence Luther said, "'I am the vine, you are the branches.' John, chapter fifteen, verse five. Let me chat with your friend, Jamar."

Another steel door opened and all four men stepped into another lighted hallway.

Jamar frowned and reluctantly handed over his cell. "White trash with a death wish, Boss."

"Can I help you?" Lawrence Luther's voice sounded like a bullhorn cutting through a thick Louisiana fog. He listened for about twenty seconds, his expression locked in neutral, then said, "And why would I possibly believe such a thing?"

"I suspect you're the type of guy who needs a little convincing," the hunter said, his voice lacking any emotion. "Give me a second." He set his phone on an empty oil drum, picked up a small plastic box the size of a pack of cigarettes, and lengthened the antenna. Stepping to the left of the window in a warehouse almost directly across the street, he said, "Fire in the hole, Mr. Wright."

The hunter then pressed the transmitter's small green button.

"If you're trying to scare—"

A thunderous roar rocked the desolate Harlem neighborhood as a giant fireball turned Lawrence Luther's new Mercedes into what seemed like hundreds of pieces of burning shrapnel. Chunks of the mangled automobile, now flaming projectiles, clattered to the wet pavement and continued to burn in dozens of mini-campfires. One lone tire rolled into the darkness, out of sight. Glass from neighboring buildings blew inward.

The sentry, who'd been standing outside the double doors, along with Su Lyn, who'd been sitting in the car, became two more casualties of this war.

Lawrence Luther braced himself against the cinderblock wall. Jamar Hightower and his colleague drew their weapons. The chemist slid to the floor and quivered in the corner, pulling his knees to his chest.

Across the street, on the second floor of another vacant building, the hunter picked up his cell and said, "Did you have full coverage on your Mercedes, Mr. Wright?"

Lawrence Luther's neutral expression had been replaced with one of fury. "When I find you—"

"Three minutes, Mr. Wright. It's time enough to clear the building of personnel, but not your expensive equipment or arsenal. I suspect that most of those people don't deserve to die—not tonight. Their blood is on your hands; their lives are *your* responsibility."

"What are you talking about?" Lawrence Luther asked the man on the cell phone.

"Your facility will be gone in two minutes and forty-six, forty-five, forty-four, forty-three . . ."

Lawrence Luther's hand, the one holding the cell phone, dropped to his side. "Jamar, get everyone out of the building!" he yelled. "Now! Move it!"

The chemist, scrambling to his feet, now clawed at the steel fire door, trying to free himself, having momentarily forgotten about the electronic keypad.

Jamar and his companion raced up the dimly lit staircase to the third floor. With his pistol at his side, Jamar hollered, "Out! Everyone out of the building! Hurry! Leave your stuff!"

Nearly twenty of Lawrence Luther's employees had already begun to seek refuge, and now a stream of cheap labor that packaged the cocaine, mostly black teenage girls with terror etched on their faces, scrambled down the wooden steps with nothing more than the clothes on their backs.

The chemist finally opened the heavy red door, stumbled through a short hallway, and stepped into the cold, rainy night. He squealed like a small child. The gruesome remains of the armed sentry, with his long overcoat still ablaze and his face melted down to the skull, lay at the bottom of the steps. Grimacing and gasping for air, the chemist stepped around the man, ran recklessly into the darkness, and vomited on the sidewalk.

Lawrence Luther walked past Quentin's mangled body, then gazed at the carnage in the road. He was reminded of the dead financier, Jeremy Silverstone, who'd been incinerated about five years ago while sitting in his limousine. Though wrath threatened to consume Lawrence Luther, he forced himself to remain calm. His employees, along with scores of people in his neighborhood, looked to him for leadership. Reputations were built in times of crisis.

"Get away from the building!" Lawrence Luther shouted, waving them back. "There may be a bomb."

Employees scurried about like a frightened herd of animals, running down the street in both directions. Some screamed. Some whimpered. Everyone, including Jamar, the second bodyguard, and the chemist, distanced himself from the brick structure.

Lawrence Luther Wright pushed his hands into his wool overcoat and calmly strolled away from the charred and distorted metal that had once been his Mercedes Benz. Placing a bomb under his car was one thing, but circumventing an elaborate alarm system and armed men was something altogether different. He was beginning to fear this brazen caller.

From a broken window directly across the street from Lawrence Luther's latest real-estate acquisition, the hunter looked at the results of his handiwork. The C-4 plastique that had once been attached to the Mercedes's fuel tank had left a three-foot crater in the pavement. The hunter studied the remarkably calm black man, with his arrogant expression and cocksure stride.

"You clearly don't believe me, Mr. Wright," he said to himself.

About ninety feet from his five-story brick structure, Lawrence Luther turned his back to the cold sleet driven in from the northwest. His intelligent eyes assessed the situation. A few seconds passed before he brought the cell phone back to his ear. "I think you're bluffing."

"Ten, nine, eight, seven . . ." the hunter said. "Maybe you should brace yourself, Mr. Wright. This one is gonna leave a mark. Three, two, one . . ."

Lawrence Luther brought his forearm up to protect his face as the top floor of the vacated warehouse blew outward in a deafening explosion. The intense heat from the blast melted both the steel framing along the windows and the tar roof. The hunter's second message of the early morning had thirty times the force of his first, the result of separate packages of C-4 placed below the roofline of the building, and now detonating simultaneously. Giant flames escaped into the night, and an orange glow illuminated the wet city streets. Debris from inside the structure rained down, joining the burning wreckage that had once been the black Benz.

The fireball momentarily illuminated the hunter's face, and he could feel the heat through the broken window. But exposure was of no concern just yet. Lawrence Luther's employees stared not at him, but at the inferno engulfing the structure they'd occupied precious minutes earlier. Some, mouths agape, watched the conflagration from a safe distance.

The shockwave had knocked Lawrence Luther onto his back.

Satisfied with his work, the hunter shoved the transmitter into his leather bomber jacket and shouldered his silenced automatic pistol. He grabbed hold of the MP7 assault weapon that leaned against the splintered windowpane and shoved it into his duffle. If Wright or any of his key personnel had sense, they would quickly call in soldiers, secure a wide perimeter, and begin a search of the nearby buildings.

Heading at a brisk pace for the staircase at the rear of the building, the hunter put the cell phone to his ear and said, "Mr. Wright?"

Lawrence Luther slowly got to his feet, momentarily stumbled like a drunk, then stood erect. The seat of his Bugatchi suit had a long tear in it, and he was bleeding from his chin. Soaked, but apparently unaffected by the wetness, the ash, or the wound, he watched his new business burn. Over two million dollars'-worth of cocaine and chemicals to produce high-grade methamphetamine, and nearly two hundred thousand dollars in cash were completely gone. Expensive pharmaceutical equipment, an assortment of weapons, including one hundred sixty MP5 assault rifles and two rocket-propelled grenade launchers, and a failed surveillance system were all ablaze or destroyed.

But more than material loss, Lawrence Luther's authority had been threatened. He was no longer bulletproof, as so many peers, competitors, law enforcement officials, and customers once thought.

"'So have no fear of them,' Lawrence Luther said quietly, "for nothing is covered up that will not be uncovered.'" *Matthew, chapter ten, verse twenty-six.*

There would be another day to embrace his anger. Retaliation was only a whispered secret away. In a few short hours, individuals living in New York City would talk, and Lawrence Luther's friends would be there, listening to the gossip. If that approach failed to uncover this enemy, inquiries would be made to associates who had come to rely on him and his product.

"Are we having fun yet, Mr. Wright?" the hunter asked, a suggestion of satisfaction in his voice.

Lawrence Luther looked at the cell phone in his right hand. The red *low battery* light flashed at him like an evil eye. He brought the phone to his ear and said, "What's this about?"

"I was beginning to think you'd become a casualty of war."

Casualty of war? "Is there a point to this?"

"I'm a Nancy Reagan disciple. Just say no to drugs."

The first fire engine rolled into an area now resembling the aftermath of a suicide bombing. Black smoke billowed from the ruins and climbed into the gray sky. Small fires smoldered throughout the neighborhood. The search would have to wait—the suspicious explosion set off enough unanswerable questions for the fire inspectors, detectives, and CSI personnel assigned to this case without civilians brandishing automatic weapons.

"Seems we have a problem, you and me," Lawrence Luther said.

Jamar and the second bodyguard joined their boss, taking up positions to his right and left, then quickly escorted him down the street and around the corner of his building.

"Problem?" the hunter said, chuckling. "Not anymore."

"What the fuck does that mean?"

"That's for Johnny and Fat Paulie. Have a good one."

The line went dead. "Sweet mother of the baby Jesus," Lawrence Luther mused, pulling free of his bodyguards. "Is Tony D picking a fight with me?"

CHAPTER 25

Brooklyn

Brian McGowan was in a warehouse in a dangerous section of Harlem. Two uniformed policemen guarded the only usable staircase remaining in the brick building, which three other cops watched from the street. It was only a quarter after eight on a Saturday morning, yet crowds of curious folks from nearby neighborhoods pressed up against the yellow crime scene tape. Lawrence Luther Wright's Mercedes Benz—or what was left of it—was particularly appealing to the onlookers.

McGowan was standing on the third floor of a charred building that, until last night, had housed a very sophisticated laboratory for designer drugs and crack cocaine. He was considered a specialist in his field of arson, but McGowan didn't need his five years of experience, including an up close and personal view of roadside bombings during his eighteen-month hitch in Iraq, to figure this incident out. Though multiple explosions and giant fireballs had consumed this state-of-the-art facility, a great deal of evidence had been left behind.

Residue from the cocaine and melted pharmaceutical equipment were everywhere, alongside cheap furniture turned to kindling. Smashed beakers, high-tech scales, and an industrial oven lay next to a pile of unusable desks and lockers. Scattered items were strewn across the blackened room, including six Compaq personal computers, a Sub-Zero refrigerator, purses, and clothing.

McGowan had been told that burnt money littered an adjoining office, along with a serious cache of new weapons. The guns and cash were not his concern, the fire chief had informed McGowan. His job was identifying the source of the fire. Period. It was simply a matter of cause and effect: Like a blood splatter expert, study the patterns left behind, work backwards, and find the origin, maybe even the accelerant.

The huge room smelled like an extinguished wildfire. Traces of cocaine and an assortment of chemicals mingled with the burnt embers and insulation. Half of the roof was missing. Water had dripped in from the rainy night, creating large puddles on the floor.

Brian McGowan wore the traditional firefighter's attire: a black turnout with an orange reflective strip that passed across his chest and forearms, along with black rubber boots that reached nearly to his knees. Across the back of his rubber coat, large fluorescent letters read "ARSON INVESTIGATOR." Missing from the front of his yellow helmet was the unit and badge number. That was because arson specialist McGowan was no longer a Greater New York City civil servant. He was an independent consultant, known for his proficiency and quick results.

McGowan's pike pole, which resembled a fisherman's harpoon, rested against charred sheetrock with a framed photograph of Frank Sinatra still in place. Ol' Blue Eyes was unscathed. Preoccupied with something near his right boot, McGowan crouched, gently nudged the object with his gloved hand, found a brick of clay-like material nearby, and then shook his head in amazement. Not often was the source of arson so easily recognizable. He pulled a walkie-talkie from his long coat and said, "Hey, Alex, I need the bomb squad."

"Come again, Brian?" Officer Alexandra Sahlen said from outside the building. She sat in a retrofitted van filled with high-tech surveillance equipment.

"I'm only taking an educated guess," said McGowan, "but it looks like five or six bombs were planted along the roofline. C-4. One of the little fellas didn't go boom."

"That was fast."

Picking up the silvery steel object—it was a little wider than a pencil—from the wet floor, McGowan said, "One of the detonators, which should have been jammed into the plastique, found its way all the way down to the third floor." He glanced up. "I also have a small block of the C-4. From the looks of it, I think it's high-grade material. Tell Demeris and the boys not to rush—no need to run over an innocent civilian on a lovely day like this."

"Roger that," Alex said, laughing quietly. "I'll call it in."

Most people didn't understand how safe the Silly Putty-like material could be. Burn C-4, manipulate it, even hit it with a hammer, and the stuff wouldn't explode. The all-important detonators were the key to a successful job, and sometime during last night's chaos, one of them had separated from this surviving package of C-4.

"Yep, caught ourselves a break," McGowan said to a uniformed cop who stood dutifully near the front windows.

"Looks like you're as good as advertised," the elderly black policeman replied.

The cop seemed to be having a difficult time making eye contact. It was a reaction McGowan had come to expect. "A little luck doesn't hurt," McGowan said.

Forty minutes later, Brian McGowan had seen enough at the building. The C-4 plastique was being transported from the warehouse district of East Harlem to a containment facility in the Bronx. Samples and photographs of the crime scene were being taken, and early assessments were being discussed with the fire chief and the homicide detective, a sarcastic guy named Nicholas Benedetti, who typically worked Manhattan. Detective Benedetti had been assigned to investigate the two fatalities.

At street level, McGowan walked through the heavy double doors and past the spot where the dead man had been found. Stepping over a pile of burnt timber, he inhaled deeply, filling his lungs with the cold morning air. The angry, low-lying clouds were gunmetal gray, yet local meteorologists were calling for a partly sunny day with above-average temperatures.

McGowan removed his protective fireman's helmet and let his thick, curly red hair tumble to his shoulders. He was Irish Catholic, but he hadn't seen the inside of a church since his wedding day four years earlier. With his slim physical presence, creamy complexion, freckles, dark brown eyes, and chiseled face, McGowan had once been considered a handsome man, and a great catch for some fortunate lady. That distinction, along with his beautiful wife, had left him two years ago, the result of carelessly entering into a backdraft.

The grisly scene behind McGowan reminded him of that day.

Confined to a room, a backdraft acts like a living, breathing animal, seeking flammable materials in hopes of strengthening. Combustible objects may fuel its intensity, but the fire's real nourishment comes from oxygen. Trapped inside a restricted space like an office or bathroom, it begins to starve. The fire desperately searches for alternatives, pulling life-sustaining oxygen from beneath doors, small cracks along windows, even ductwork. In spite of that, the danger of being extinguished forces the fire into a patient mode—like a hunter waiting for its prey to pass. Slowing its pace of consumption, it waits for either deliverance or ruination.

At the time of his own near-fatal accident, Brian McGowan was a twenty-five-year-old New York City fireman from the Eighty-Second Precinct. That snowy February morning, he was at the wrong door, behind which this particular backdraft was desperate to escape. First, he was hurled violently across the hallway, then sent crashing into the wall, the explosion ripping off McGowan's oxygen mask and melting the right side of his face—his nose, cheek, neck, and ear. The plastic surgeons considered it a minor miracle their patient's right eye hadn't been severely damaged.

The nightmares, though not as frequent of late, still disturbed McGowan's sleep. They always began the same way: turning the doorknob with his gloved hand, thinking the room had already been checked. Cool air rushes past his neck, and then the explosion as this searing force of nature smashes directly into McGowan's face like a sledgehammer. Ripping the door off its hinges, the fire acts like a wild beast finally let off a constricting chain. The conflagration sweeps through the three-story apartment building with no regard for any life but its own.

After six skin grafts, a broken marriage, and two years of dissecting his shredded life with the help of a therapist, McGowan had ironically found solace in the midst of the same voracious creature that nearly killed him. Instead of burying his grief, McGowan decided it was best to confront his emotions head on.

"Heard ya found a detonator, Brian," a raspy male voice called out.

Brought back to the present, McGowan moved his helmet from his right hand to his left, leaned the pike pole up against the brick building, and smiled at Nick Benedetti. The homicide detective, with his bushy mustache and curly black hair, looked to be in his early forties. He wore a rumpled sports jacket, tan trousers, and soot-covered hiking boots.

"Yep. I can't identify it yet, but I will," said McGowan. "Give me a day or two, Nick."

"That fast?"

"Detonators typically have a distinct signature, and this one doesn't seem to be homemade." He tossed it to Benedetti. "Take a look."

The detective, at least four inches shorter than McGowan, turned the silver piece of polished steel over in his hand. It was about three inches long, with two trailing wires. "I'll be damned."

"Maybe I can trace it back to the manufacturer. That would be a great start."

"Which will probably lead us to that infamous needle in a haystack," said Benedetti, clapping McGowan on the back. "Or maybe not."

Jerking a thumb to the corpse under the yellow tarpaulin, McGowan said, "I'm guessing that's why you were brought in."

"According to a couple of folks who walked by the building over the past few weeks, this poor bastard guarded the front door. He took the explosion face-first when the car blew," Benedetti said, handing back the detonator. "If the good Lord decides my time is up, I'd rather take a bullet in the back of the head." The cop paused for a moment, pursed his lips, and said, "Hey, seriously, that came out all wrong. Sorry."

"I'm not that sensitive, Nick." Tipping his head back to look up at the building, McGowan said, "You're thinkin' the Mercedes went first, then the building? Am I on the right track?"

"If it had been the other way around, the doorman and driver of the Benz probably would have survived, but a whole bunch of workers might have been killed or hurt," said Benedetti. "That seems like a reasonable explanation. I saw all the ladies' purses on the third floor. The CSI people said it must have been quite the operation."

"So we got ourselves a bomber with a conscience?"

"Brian, let's not get all carried away. Two people aren't breathing, remember."

"So what do you think happened?"

Benedetti came closer to McGowan as if to expose a sensitive secret. He said, quietly, "We're dealing with a pro. Not a doubt in my mind. As for a damn motive? You know what they say on TV."

"Nick, I'm one of the few people in the United States of America who doesn't own a television, so I have no idea what you're talking about."

"Stay tuned," Benedetti said, grinning. "Don't touch that dial."

"You're saying a competitor's behind this?"

"If so, they have access to high-grade explosives and remote detonators," said Benedetti. "You have the evidence, my man. Makes me wonder if we're dealing with an outside professional brought in to shut down Lawrence Luther Wright's expansion plans."

"Huh," McGowan said, glancing at the debris.

"And our guy was talented enough to circumvent some pretty intense security."

McGowan whistled. "With Mr. Wright shut down," he said, "who benefits the most?"

"That, my friend, is the multimillion-dollar question. Lawrence Luther is one of the biggest dogs in the kennel, but there's always a few mutts itching to lead the pack."

McGowan headed for his car. "Good luck playing dogcatcher," he said.

Five minutes later, McGowan was packing the last of his equipment into the trunk of his battered Volvo sedan.

"Yo, Brian!" a male voice yelled from across the street.

McGowan smiled before turning toward the familiar voice. "B. J. friggin' Butera! Yeah, I thought maybe I'd hear from you on this one," he said. "Death, murder, mayhem, hot chicks, and free beer—right up your alley."

"Did you say free beer?" said B. J., cupping his hand to his mouth. The reporter slipped under the yellow crime scene tape and crossed the wet pavement. "Looks like you've been playing with matches again."

"Only the aftermath," McGowan said in a flat, unaffected monotone.

The New York Post reporter B. J. Butera wore a New York Yankees cap and a dark green ski parka, his laminated press credential hanging around his neck. He shook McGowan's hand.

"You're as ugly as ever," B. J. said, lightly punching McGowan in the shoulder.

Even a year ago, that "ugly" crack would have led to a few missing teeth, or a crying jag in some dark room. But hundreds of hours of therapy with an expensive shrink, all paid for by the NYFD, made the remark at least tolerable.

"I'll take that as a compliment," McGowan said, smirking. "Good to see you again."

"How ya been?"

"One day at a time, brother."

"A little bird told me you moved back." That bird, a fireman friend, had passed along that particular information about a month ago.

"More business here in the Apple," McGowan said with a shrug. "I have some decent contacts in the department, mostly because of my old man. Your articles didn't hurt my rep, either."

"Sorry to hear about you and Joyce."

"Good women are hard to hold on to, B. J. It wasn't her fault."

"Dating?"

"C'mon, Butera, don't patronize me with this touchy-feely bullshit. It makes you sound phony, and me feel like some loser."

"Sorry. Bad habits. I'm playing journalist," said B. J. "We're mostly pathetic, remember." A pause. "So, ya getting laid much? Sorry, sorry. Just trying to be funny."

McGowan removed the pike pole from his trunk, showed it to Butera, smiled, then said, in Cuban-accented English, "Say hello to my little friend."

B. J. Butera and Brian McGowan were both products of quiet Brooklyn neighborhoods, and although they'd attended different Catholic high schools— walking distance from their respective homes—they'd competed against each other in basketball and baseball right through their senior year. The competition led to healthy respect and, strangely enough, a friendship of sorts.

McGowan received a basketball scholarship to St. John's University, broke his ankle his freshman year, quit college, and joined the Army; one tour of duty in Iraq was enough. His father, a decorated, retired NYC firefighter, and his brother, a smoke-eater on the West Coast who jumped out of planes for a living, had always been important role models. Whether he liked it or not, putting out fires was in McGowan's blood.

Breston James Butera, Jr. graduated from Fordham, leaving the university with a degree in journalism after five years of serious partying. His deep roots in the New York community, quick wit, and disarming personality made a good impression on his colleagues at the *Post*. After his internship, his period as a full-time reporter for the Lifestyle section, and a very brief stint covering the local sports scene, he'd been elevated to a crime reporter.

B. J. knew all about the backdraft that had killed a significant piece of his friend's soul more than two years earlier. He'd written a series of articles about McGowan's ordeal, even wept in a snowy hospital parking lot after his first visit to the burn treatment center in Queens.

"Nobody should endure such pain," he'd written. "And surely not someone who has given so much of himself to others over the years. Even as a kid growing up in Brooklyn, Brian had a reputation for helping out the little guy, standing up to bullies, painting a neighbor's porch for nothing more than a cold lemonade and a pat on the back. Everyone loves and admires Brian McGowan, and I'm no exception. I feel fortunate to call him my friend."

The poignant and moving series facilitated B. J.'s career at the *Post*, but after McGowan moved to Philadelphia last year, their paths hadn't crossed. Only one phone call, initiated by B. J., had taken place since then, and the conversation had been limited to a few awkward minutes.

"Let me buy you lunch," McGowan said, closing the Volvo's door.

"It's nine-thirty in the morning," B. J. said, looking at his watch. "And shouldn't it be my treat?"

"Lunch. Breakfast," McGowan said over his shoulder. "What's the difference? You interested?"

"Why? Hey, hey, hey, do you have something for me?" he said, gesturing with his chin toward the warehouse.

McGowan fingered the detonator in his pocket. "I believe I owe you, Butera."

"You owe me?" asked B.J. "After all those years of me kicking your ass on hardwood, I thought it was the other way around."

"Bro, you were absolutely the worst point guard in the history of New York City high school basketball."

"No way! Billy Thompson has that title."

"Look," McGowan said, "as far as I'm concerned, it's a little payback for all those embarrassing articles you wrote about me."

"Just doin' my job, big man. That means using you to get ahead in the world."

"Shit, B. J., you made me into a local goddamned superhero, and I probably wouldn't have this consulting gig if it weren't for you," said McGowan. "So yeah, I owe you lunch . . . or breakfast, or a few beers."

"I'll take cold hard cash if it makes you feel any better."

With weathered fingers, McGowan dragged his thick red hair back over his head, revealing the scarring along his neck and ear. "There's something you might want to see," he said quietly.

CHAPTER 26

Bronx

An intimate service for immediate family and close friends was scheduled to begin at exactly 1:30 Saturday afternoon. Roland Triamante, the proprietor of the Triamante Funeral Home, would offer a brief prayer, followed by a final goodbye from the deceased's loved ones. While the survivors made their way to their designated vehicles, Mr. Triamante and his two sons would have time to ready the casket. Then they could deliver Johnny Cercone's remains to their intended two o'clock appointment at St. Andrew's, three miles from the funeral home. Vincent Tagliafero had followed the same path back in August.

Wearing a perfectly tailored, freshly dry-cleaned suit and polished shoes that most military drill sergeants would have been proud of, Triamante was anything but happy about how the day's schedule was playing out. Punctuality in his profession was an absolute prerequisite, and a trait he continually stressed to his sons, who were only a few years away from taking over the family business. Arms at his sides, the funeral director stood at the back of the crowded viewing area, which looked more like a florist's showroom. Six rows of wooden folding chairs, five to a row, all faced the beautiful cherry casket. Every seat was filled with grieving relatives and friends. Usually, the closer to the front they sat, the more emotional the loved ones would be.

A tall and frail second-generation Italian American with hooded brown eyes and acne scars, Triamante wrung his hands, glanced at his watch for the fourth time in the last minute, then sighed heavily. One forty-five. Traffic was always an issue to contend with in New York, even on a Saturday afternoon with a police escort. He'd yet to give the final prayer. The tearful parade hadn't begun, and some of the more expensive flower arrangements needed to be loaded into a private van and delivered to St. Andrew's before the casket arrived.

For the first time in forty-six years, Triamante feared that one of his clients would be late for his own funeral. Unfortunately, like Johnny's friends and relatives, he was but a helpless bystander to the deceased's final piece of history. Anthony

DiFilippo IV, the man paying for this extravagant service, was a loyal and frequent customer, and he insisted they wait. No other patron, Triamante knew, wielded such power. And so they waited. For what? He didn't dare ask or even venture a guess.

But Tony D knew. Sitting in the middle of the front row, the don ignored his catatonic sister-in-law, Johnny's mother, and his wife, Mara. He stared at the closed casket, his mind drifting to another subject: Woody had still not arrived, nor had he answered his cell phone. And this was very troubling.

A young portly man with short nappy hair emerged through the back door and positioned himself beside Triamante. He searched the crowded room, evidently found who he was looking for, then grimaced. The message he carried was not a good one.

The man walked to the front of the mourners and whispered into Tony D's ear. After digesting the news, the don relayed a succinct reply.

A moment later, the messenger pulled Roland Triamante to the side and said, "Mr. DiFilippo says it's okay to start."

Brooklyn

Dr. Dwayne Espinoza, a veteran New York City medical examiner, slipped a small plastic bag over the deceased's right hand. The bag, secured by a rubber band around the wrist, helped preserve crucial evidence on the dead man's fingers—specifically, debris under his nails.

The crime scene investigators had already placed, in the corners of the room, twin seven-foot tripods with large spotlights. The lighting helped enhance the investigation, but it also brought out the worst in the room: cigarette burns and discoloration on the coffee table and TV, nicotine stains on the ceiling, soiled water marks on the green carpet, and peeling gray paint on the chipped cinderblock.

One particularly witty client of the Sunset Inn Motel had written a cute slogan on the wall above the toilet: "EAT ME! TASTES GREAT! LESS FILLING!"

Two sheets, the second one even dingier than the first, lay on the double bed. A ripped and frayed blanket was balled up beside the corpse.

Three investigators examined Room 124, while outside the door, a morbidly obese man was being questioned by Detective Matthew Philips. The dead man lay on his back, a shocked expression distorting his once attractive face. There was a dime-sized hole between his eyes and dried blood on his mustache, cheek, and forehead. A large section of his brain and skull had splattered on the wooden headboard. The bed sheets and mattress soaked up much of the fluid.

"*Señor* Espinoza," said Detective Katherine Montroy cheerfully as she stepped into the room. She took another sip of her Dunkin' Donuts coffee and set the Styrofoam cup beside a cheap plastic lamp near the bed. "People are gonna start gossiping, seeing me and you in a swanky place like this."

Espinoza snapped a rubber band around the dead man's left wrist, let the arm flop to the bed, then turned to look at Montroy. "Good afternoon, *mi amor.*"

"Grrr, I live for French-speaking Puerto Rican men, especially married ones. Stop. Stop it, Dwayne. I'm swooning. Somebody catch me."

"I'll be with you in a minute, Kat," Philips said, sticking his head into the room.

"Take your time, Matthew."

When Philips was gone, Espinoza whispered, "That son of a bitch is driving me nuts."

"Everybody drives you nuts," Montroy said. "Haven't you figured that out yet?"

"Something isn't right about Philips," Espinoza said, glancing back at the open door. "He's creepy, and he never kisses my ass. What's with that?"

"Dwayne, next to Matty's black soul is a heart of gold. Or maybe he's a practicing serial killer."

Espinoza shook his head in mock disgust.

"Okay, okay," Montroy said, clapping her hands together, "enough of me—what gives?"

Gesturing in Philips's direction, Espinoza said, "Ask the hanging judge. He's the one who requested . . . um, insisted on your presence. I thought this one looked fairly cut and dried, but no, your friend over there gets all Gestapo. Guys like Philips are taking all the fun out of my job."

"Is Matty talkin' to Jabba the Hut?" Montroy asked. She took a quick sip of her coffee.

"Your *Star Wars* obsession is showing again, Katherine."

The cameraman, taking still photographs of the crime scene, laughed. "I'll be adding a few pics of Jabba to my personal collection, Kat," he said. "I'll e-mail you a couple."

"Not my type," Montroy said, a thin smile appearing on her red lips.

"He's the owner of this five-star resort," Espinoza said, stripping off a latex glove. "Maybe Philips is asking him out on a date."

"Did Jabba find our vic?"

"The maid, if you can believe this dump actually has one." Espinoza wrinkled his nose. "It smells like cat piss in the bathroom."

"Among other unmentionable bodily fluids," Montroy said, grimacing. "Wouldn't it be more pleasant to have sex in a compost pile?"

"The maid is waiting in the office," Espinoza said. "She's an elderly Jamaican woman, probably an illegal. She's shook up."

"Wouldn't you be?"

Shrugging, Espinoza said, "Doubtful. Twenty-two years in the biz and I'm almost impervious to things like this. Nothing surprises me. 'Been there, done that' is my motto." He snapped his silver medical evidence kit closed and stood up. "I'm outta here."

"Does our vic have a name?" Montroy asked, looking over at the body.

"Don. Donald something," Espinoza said, shrugging his bony shoulders.

"What's the rush?"

"I hate the neighborhood, Kat, and have you noticed how weekends are getting progressively worse around New York? I'm afraid someone might actually steal my car. All the damn nuts come out to play—lunatics with guns and knives and illegal drugs and Louisville Slugger bats—"

"Holy . . . shit," Montroy said, letting the words draw out. She bent at the waist to take a closer look at the dead man on the bed.

"What is it?" Espinoza asked, suddenly anxious.

"Now I know why Matty called me."

Espinoza dropped his heavy case to the filthy carpet and stood next to Montroy. "You know this guy, Katherine?"

"Woody Biasucci—another one of Anthony DiFilippo's *capos*."

"Are you telling me that our dead vic worked for Fat Paulie Franco?"

"Yep."

"The same Paulie Franco who's lying in my freezer and scheduled to have an autopsy Monday morning?"

"The one and only."

Espinoza reached for his physical evidence kit and set it on the bed beside the corpse. "God Almighty," he said, "this is the kinda mess that kills a career."

An occupation in law enforcement or forensics was injected with rocket fuel or shattered into pieces because of high-profile corpses. The O.J. Simpson case was a shining example. Another mob hit would bring unwanted attention not only to Anthony DiFilippo, but also to the people who'd spent so much money, time, and energy trying to put the mob boss behind bars. Because of Biasucci's relationship with Tony D, reputations in a case like this potentially hung in the balance.

"Katherine, I need to recheck my work," Espinoza said, turning serious. "I sure as shit can't afford to screw the pooch on something that could potentially turn into a nightmare for the D.A." He paused, then added, "And me."

"I hear ya," Montroy said. Stepping around the bed, she had a brief word with the young cameraman. He nodded, then began photographing the wall and the bloody headboard.

Philips entered the room, apparently finished with the owner. "Local prostitutes bring their johns to Disneyland here, then take them on a short ride; most rooms are booked for thirty or sixty minutes." He looked around. "Please don't touch anything, Kat. You might catch some disease. I ain't kidding."

"I know why you called me."

"Let's get some air."

Both detectives stepped into the cold afternoon. The sun peeked through a gap in the swiftly moving cumulus clouds. An overzealous cop had partitioned off a large area of the parking lot with crime scene tape. Behind it, a few dozen curious people watched the investigation, chatting amongst themselves.

Philips slipped an unfiltered Camel between his cracked lips, and then struck a match.

"You should quit," Montroy said.

Philips lit up and took a deep, satisfying drag. "What, and miss out on lung cancer?"

"You're never funny when you're nervous, Matty."

"Yeah, that's Donald Biasucci, which I'm sure you already figured out."

"You think Mr. DiFilippo knows yet?"

"My gut says yes. The man has eyes and ears everywhere." Philips explosively exhaled cigarette smoke from his mouth and nose. "I can promise you one thing, Kat: Our Mafia friend is gonna have a cow over this one. He has to push back, and it ain't gonna be pretty when he does. First his nephew, then Fat Paulie, now Woody. That's two captains and the underboss. His organization is definitely under attack."

"Now what?"

Philips pulled a clear plastic bag from his coat pocket. "Look familiar?"

"Another 5.56 casing from an M16? Jesus, is there a point to this?"

"Nice calling card," Philips said. "I found it standing up on the nightstand."

"Maybe this thing *is* spiraling out of control," she said, remembering Tony D's words.

"For the time being, we're detaining as many guests as we can find. Most are still in their rooms. Others are being held in the motel's registration area. Probably about ten that I know of."

"God, I hate my job on days like this," Montroy said, gesturing to the parking lot.

A white van with NBC's multi-colored peacock painted on both sides slowly carved a path through a swarm of curious bystanders. The driver leaned on the horn. A small satellite, used for live broadcasts, was attached to the van's roof.

Some of the more emboldened bystanders kicked the tires as the vehicle crunched over the gravel, taking up prime real estate near the crime scene tape.

Philips frowned. "Fuck me, Freda on a Friday. Who the hell tipped them off?"

"It's more a question of what took them so long," Montroy said.

Espinoza, still wearing his second pair of latex examination gloves, joined the two detectives outside the stuffy room. "Those vultures were probably at Cercone's funeral," he said. "It has to be over by now."

"Quite a day," Philips said as he watched an attractive blond reporter appease the growing crowd by shouting questions and sticking a microphone in their faces.

"Stupid moths to a flame," Montroy said. People were pushing each other now.

The allure of Andy Warhol's fifteen minutes of fame had a humbling effect on even the most demonstrative groups. The NBC cameraman snapped on a bright light and began filming the bystanders, all of whom seemed eager to get their faces on the local television news.

"Don't bad things come in threes, Kat?" Philips asked hesitantly. "Is it over?"

"Something tells me this is gonna get way worse," Montroy said.

Espinoza sighed heavily. "Terrific," he said quietly, stepping back into the room to continue with his work.

Philips sucked on his cigarette. "Now what?"

CHAPTER 27

Western New York

E arly Saturday afternoon, a new sports car raced down Old Lake Shore Road, a scenic byway running parallel to Lake Erie's rocky coastline. It was a clear, crisp, and calm November day, and the Porsche 911 Carrera S, with its 355-horsepower engine, handled like a dream, particularly on the severe curves. Looking to the northwest, Terri Taylor could barely make out the Canadian coast, with its multi-million-dollar mansions on the Point Abino and Sherkston beaches. To the south, Lake Erie's rolling surface blended seamlessly with the horizon.

Erie, the shallowest of the five Great Lakes, was known for its lake-effect snowstorms that pounded Buffalo and Western New York. Winter was not yet official, but it wasn't uncommon this time of year to have freak blizzards born of the cold Canadian air rushing over the warm lake. Today, though, weather was not an issue for Gray and Terri Taylor as they drew nearer the Cattaraugus Indian Reservation.

"Is this the best you can do?" Terri shouted as the Porsche hugged the pavement around another curve. Smiling shamelessly, she turned up the volume on Ani DiFranco's *Red Letter Year* and sang along with the hard-edged, socially conscious folk rock.

Unlike the many wives who might insist their spouses ease up on the accelerator, Terri loved speed. Her entire life was about faster, bigger, and best. Her soccer career had ended with an NCAA Division 1AA championship at Stanford thirteen years earlier, and as a senior, Terri Holden, an All-American striker, scored the winning goal over Florida State—then promptly hung up her spikes, having nothing more to accomplish in the sport. The CIA recruited the political science major soon after, recognizing her particular gift for languages. Terri's talent for thinking on her feet during a crisis situation was an added bonus to her handlers, specifically Jack Slattery.

"It's not going to work, Ter," said Taylor. "I'm already fifteen over the speed limit. Driving off a cliff into Lake Erie doesn't appeal to me."

"Chicken Little." She turned to the lake rushing by her window. "We close?"

"I'm guessing less than twenty minutes . . . but we need gas. Can you lower the volume to a low roar?"

Smiling coyly, Terri ejected the CD. "I still can't believe Hatch ditched his phone. That should be illegal in our country."

"A lot of things on the Seneca's land may surprise us."

"What do you mean?"

"It's a sovereign nation," he said. "Native Americans have their own rules and laws. To be honest with you, I'm not sure what to expect . . . or how we'll be greeted."

Terri considered this for a moment, then asked, "What if Hatch isn't there?"

"Then Jack could have a real problem back in New York."

"Does that mean it turns into your problem?"

"One step at a time, babe."

Gray Taylor's BlackBerry vibrated on the middle console. Terri picked it up and checked the LCD display. "Speak of the devil—it's your boss."

"Why don't you put him on speaker?"

Pressing the *send* button, Terri laid the phone on her lap and said, "Hi, Jack. You're on speaker, so easy with the colorful language. I'm a lady, remember?"

"Is Gray right there, Terri?" Slattery was evidently in a foul mood.

"Trying to keep the car on the road, Boss," said Taylor, downshifting into third gear.

"Have you made contact?"

"We should be on the reservation around two-thirty."

"We've had another incident in New York," Slattery said, calling from his Langley office. "Donald Biasucci, an Anthony DiFilippo captain, was found dead in a hotel room."

Taylor's hands turned a creamy white as he squeezed the steering wheel.

"Johnny Cercone's funeral is over," Slattery said. "I suspect that Mr. DiFilippo knows Biasucci is missing the service, but I'm not sure if he's been told that the young man was murdered—not that it matters at this very moment."

Gray and Terri Taylor traded looks.

Slattery explained the details of the shooting, or as much as he'd learned so far. "A week ago, I wouldn't have believed this was possible, but now—"

"It still doesn't mean Hatch is involved," Taylor said. "We've been over this, Jack. There could be another plausible explanation."

"Maybe, but it sure doesn't look good," Slattery said, sounding anything but confident. "Whatever you learn, call me ASAP. I need to brief the director, which tells you both just how critical this situation has become."

A few minutes later, Gray and Terri Taylor passed through the quiet town of Irving, located on the border of the Cattaraugus Indian Reservation. Taylor pulled the black Porsche into Jan's Smoke Shop, a truck stop that peddled cheap wooden furniture, groceries, imitation flowers, alcohol, lottery tickets, jewelry, T-shirts, tobacco products, fireworks, refreshments, fresh sandwiches, soft drinks, and a host of tribal knicknacks. It also doubled as a tourist information center both for Niagara Falls and for a number of casinos owned by the Seneca Nation of Indians.

Terri glanced at the sale items lined up on the walk. "Holy cow, talk about covering all your bases. And the prices are ridiculously low."

"Native Americans don't collect or pay state or federal taxes," Taylor said, parking the car next to one of thirty gasoline pumps.

A pimply-faced teenage boy, his long black hair braided and hanging over one shoulder, shuffled over to the Porsche's open window without any sense of urgency. "Nice car, dude."

"Thanks," Taylor said. "Fill it up with the good stuff, please."

"We only take cash."

"Not a problem."

The Native American teenager went to work at a leisurely pace. Gray and Terri Taylor sat in silence while the kid washed the windows and filled up the Porsche. "That'll be forty-seven bucks," he said when finished.

Handing the attendant fifty dollars, Taylor said, "Keep the change."

"Hey, thanks, man." The teenager's face and attitude brightened considerably.

Taylor turned the key, and the Porsche's engine rumbled to life. "You live nearby?"

"Yeah." The teenager pointed to a mud-covered Schwinn. "I ride that rust-bucket to work."

"Maybe you can help us out."

The teenager peered into the open window, but didn't touch the car. "What's up?"

"I'm looking for Kevin Easter."

Suspicion crept into the boy's brown eyes. Shuffling his feet, he shrugged nervously. "Ah, nope . . . never heard of him. Sorry."

Terri leaned over her husband. "His friends call him Hatch."

"I worked with him when he lived in Virginia," Taylor said, embellishing his relationship.

"Yeah, Hatch . . . why didn't you say so?" said the teenager. "Shit, nobody calls him Kevin around here . . ." An impatient customer, behind the wheel of a very long Winnebago camper, tapped his horn three times. Turning his head, the teenager appeared ready to strike back verbally, but instead, he cursed under his breath, then said, "Dude, I gotta go."

Taylor looked in his rearview mirror and saw an elderly gentleman behind the wheel of the vehicle. "Somebody important?"

"The chief." The teenager's words were clipped, tense. "Um, yeah, he owns this place—and just about everything else around here. I need to take care of him."

Terri peered over the seat. "Don't those beasts go for about a quarter mil?"

"Try five hundred grand with all the extras," the teenager said, raising his index finger for the driver to see. "It's totally loaded."

"Apparently he's in a big hurry," Taylor said, shifting into first gear.

"Why don't you pull ahead, let me fix him up, and I'll give you those directions when I'm finished? Hatch lives with his grandfather up on Old Elk Road. It's not far."

"Thanks." Taylor drove the Porsche into a parking spot right outside the busy store as the teenager attended to his boss. "It appears as if the chief holds the purse strings around this place."

"Wow, you must work for the CIA, *dude*," Terri said, chuckling.

The teenager ran over. "Ah, hey, he wants to talk to you guys."

"The chief?" said Taylor, cocking his head. "Is there a problem?"

"Um . . . well, ya better ask him. And don't mention the tip, okay?"

"What's his name?" Taylor shouted over his shoulder.

"Chief Daniel Blackburn," said a deeper, authoritative voice. "Jake tells me you're looking for Kevin Easter."

Resting his elbows on the Porsche, Chief Blackburn leaned into the open window and eyed both occupants. He was a tall and lean man with a full head of white hair that fell to his charcoal-colored sports jacket. The chief's long face, with its dark complexion and liver spots, offered nothing pleasant or inviting. A man in the twilight of his life, he seemed to have perfected the art of intimidation.

Taylor's hard gaze moved from the chief's hooded brown eyes down to his arms—the same arms now touching his expensive sports car.

"We were hoping to surprise Hatch," said Terri, leaning over her husband.

"Oh, really?" Blackburn said, drawing out the words, his intense stare directed to Gray Taylor's indecipherable expression.

"Like we told the gas attendant," Terri said, "we—"

"Jake," the chief said. "The boy's name is Jake, and he's my nephew."

"Sir," Terri snapped crisply, "did we offend you in some way?"

A crooked smile formed on Blackburn's lips as the corners of his mouth turned upward, revealing two rows of capped teeth. "Oh, a lady who doesn't mess around," he said in a tone laced with sarcasm. "I like that."

"Can you please get your hands off my car?" Taylor said coolly.

"All we want is Hatch's address," Terri said.

"Look, seems like we got off on the wrong foot," Blackburn said, lifting his arms. "My apologies—my fault. As the chief and president for the entire Seneca Indian tribe, it's my job to watch over my people, and I take my job seriously—some say too seriously."

"Apology accepted," Taylor said, although his cold blue eyes implied otherwise. "Gray Taylor. This is my wife, Terri."

"Let me be the first to welcome you to the Cattaraugus Indian Reservation."

"Are we close to Hatch's place?" asked Terri.

"Less than two miles," Blackburn said, pointing down the road. The directions to the house on Old Elk followed. "Low Dog owns the cabin. That's where you'll find your friend . . . if he's still around."

"When's the last time you saw him?" Terri asked.

"Let me think," Blackburn said, narrowing his eyes and tapping his lower lip with his middle finger. "Ah, probably a couple months back is my best guess. From what I understand, this tragedy with his wife has Hatch keeping pretty much to himself." He turned and yelled, "Jake, hey, has Kevin Easter been around?"

"Not recently. He stopped at the store back in September," said Jake. "A couple of us were laughing about it because Hatch came in three times in one week to buy ammo. We even kidded him about it. He said something about target practice."

Purchasing lots of ammo, Taylor thought. *Practice. Top one percent at the Farm.*

"Come to think of it," Blackburn said, snapping his fingers, "the last time I saw Hatch and Low Dog together was the night before Steven flew back to the Middle East—close to two months ago. Big brother works for some security company over there."

"We appreciate your help," Terri said.

"Look, Mr. Taylor," the chief said, "I'm sorry if I came across as inhospitable, but we're, well . . . very, very protective around these parts, especially since Hatch had those two big guys following him. Those city boys stuck out like feathers on a frog, and they made a number of my people real nervous."

Taylor knew the chief was talking about the CIA field personnel assigned to keep Hatch on a short leash. Though the men were meant to blend in during that three-month period of time, it was nearly impossible in a small homogeneous community like the Indian reservation.

"Thanks," Taylor said, shifting into reverse.

"Rumor has it the FBI thought Hatch was gonna do something stupid, like maybe head back to New York City and settle the score," Blackburn said with an odd little titter. "But why the damn government cared so much about a photographer—one who wouldn't harm a fly—is anyone's guess. I was under the impression the cops back in the Big Apple found the killer, and this lowlife coward was shot dead. Is that true?"

"That's what I've heard." Taylor's tone was stern, level.

"Employees of the United States should have bigger fish to fry, Mr. Taylor. Sticking their noses in other people's business isn't right. I have the same problem here, especially with my casinos."

"Thank you for the directions," Terri said.

"My pleasure," Blackburn said, with a smile that looked disingenuous.

The Porsche pulled back and onto the road. Checking his rearview mirror, Taylor dragged the seatbelt across his body and sighed.

"Trouble?" Terri asked.

Gray Taylor shook his head. "The world is full of assholes."

After turning onto the gravel road, the Porsche passed a green and white metal sign that read "CATTARAUGUS INDIAN RESERVATION." Three rusted bullet holes in the sign gave newcomers an ominous first impression. Taylor cracked his window, and the car instantly took on a campfire smell. A chainsaw whined in the distance.

"Reminds me of my year in Appalachia," Terri said.

Driveways overgrown with brush led to a collection of prefab trailers set up on cinderblocks, railroad ties, bricks, or flat rocks. All of the homes were at least fifty feet from the road, and the wooded lots appeared sizable. Yet, nearly every structure was in desperate need of repair. A number of roofs were haphazardly patched with tarpaper, thick plastic, or tarpaulin. Shutters were missing, and broken windows were boarded up.

"Makes you wonder if Chief Blackburn shares the wealth," Taylor said.

Nestled in the old-growth forest and parked around the trailers and dilapidated homes were rusted carcasses of trucks, automobiles, snowmobiles, and lawnmowers. Discarded toilets, broken appliances, rotting furniture, and piles of trash polluted a place that once must have been picturesque, if not beautiful.

An emaciated black dog with matted fur slept on a shredded couch near an overturned outhouse. Lifting his head, the mutt surveyed the source of the disturbance—the Porsche, slowly moving past, stones clinking against the wheel wells. The dog yawned, then stretched out.

The Porsche passed two teenagers—one boy, one girl—holding hands and laughing. "Young love," Terri said, smiling. The two kids scrutinized the expensive car and the white passengers.

"Seven-One-Seven Old Elk Road," Taylor said, pointing to the mailbox. "We're here."

"That's Hatch's Pathfinder," Terri said, gesturing to the SUV in the driveway.

"Still doesn't mean he's around." Taylor gave his wife's hand a reassuring squeeze, then checked his Glock in his shoulder rig. "You okay?"

"What if he's really in New York killing people?" said Terri. "The whole thing is nuts."

"Ter, you have a tendency to waste your time worrying about stuff you can't control."

"Maybe you should heed your own advice, Mr. Taylor." Smiling ruefully and patting her husband's hand, Terri said, "I can see it in your eyes, Gray. It's been there all day. You think Hatch is—"

"Babe, looks like we're about to find out."

Low Dog's home stood apart from most of the residences they'd driven past. The two-story log cabin appeared to have been recently remodeled, brandishing new windows and skylights, and the property wasn't littered with debris—in fact, the landscape was scenic, with brick walking paths and gardens, now dormant until next spring.

The Porsche came to a stop behind Hatch's dark blue Nissan. Taylor turned the key, and the engine went silent. "Ready?"

Nodding, Terri narrowed her eyes and said, "Sounds like someone's chopping wood."

Getting out of the car, they followed a red brick sidewalk to the back of the cabin. A man, his back to the Taylors, placed an eighteen-inch log on a wide stump and, with an easy stroke, split the cherry wood with an axe. Two pieces of firewood joined small piles to the left and right of the stump. The man wore a dark green hooded sweatshirt pulled over his head, faded jeans, Sorrel work boots, and tan gloves. He reached for another log, hesitated, then appeared to sniff the air.

The woodcutter slowly shook his head, chuckled to himself, then said, "Are you spying on me, Terri?" Kevin Easter pushed back his hoodie and turned around, a huge grin on his boyish face. He removed iPod earphones from both ears and let the trailing wires hang limply. "And you brought along the old white guy."

"Yeah . . . well, we happened to be in the area," Terri said, trying to suppress her own relieved smile. She went to Hatch and embraced him. "You have no idea how good it is to see you."

"In the area?" Hatch said, eyebrows edging together.

"Could be a wee bit of an exaggeration," Terri said, stepping back next to her husband. I'd say something about your fall foliage bringing us to Western New York, but it looks like we missed it by a month or so."

"I know how Jack thinks," Hatch said. "It's good to see you, too, Terri. Even you, Gray." Removing his right glove, Hatch shook Gray Taylor's outstretched hand. "You look fit. Been running lately? Did you maybe drop in for a rematch?"

"I've been married to my StairMaster since you embarrassed me back in August," Taylor said. "That laugh-a-thon through the Virginia hills still haunts me."

"How'd you know it was me before you turned around?" Terri asked.

"No, we Indians don't have super powers, if that's what you're wondering," said Hatch. "You wore the same perfume at Karen's funeral. *Happy* by Clinique."

Pointing to the axe, Taylor said, "Staying in shape?"

"Gray, you're not one for small talk," Hatch said. "I believe that was rule number one when we first met."

As instructed by the DDI, Gray Taylor took mental notes of Hatch's every comment and mannerism. He'd only met Hatch on three occasions, and that had been almost three months earlier, but still, he noticed that Hatch's black hair had grown considerably longer. He seemed more muscular and at ease.

"Y'know," Hatch said, stroking his chin, "it's almost like you two are surprised to see me, which is a little odd, because this is where I live."

"We were worried about you," Terri said.

Hatch chuckled. "Is that a fact?"

"Nobody's heard from you in a while," Taylor said.

"Jack's people became a running joke around the rez," Hatch said, shaking his head. "I made up some bullshit story about the FBI watching me because of what went down in New York. I'm still shocked nobody shot one of them. The white man is the devil, remember?"

"I bet they weren't hard to spot," Terri said.

"Little green men from Mars would have had a better chance of blending in with the natives," Hatch said. "You two want something to drink? There's not a doubt in my mind you're itching to get inside."

"Sure, works for us," Terri said.

Thump. Hatch buried the axe's blade into the stump, glanced over at Gray Taylor, then turned for the house.

The interior of the log cabin was larger than one would have imagined from the outside. There were three bedrooms and two baths, and except for a few photographs of Karen placed on the fireplace mantel, very little of Hatch's Charlottesville life seemed to have followed him back to Low Dog's home.

The great room, directly off the kitchen, had a two-story stone fireplace, the primary source of heat. It was tastefully decorated with Native American artifacts and included a wall filled with hardcover books—mostly U.S. history. Watercolor paintings and sketches of the area hung on another wall. The floors were blond pine, most of which was covered by two oriental rugs. A simple rocking chair sat in front of the burning hearth, with the book *The Earth Shall Weep: A History of Native America* by James Wilson on the nearby end table. Two large skylights brightened the room with natural light. Another door opened to a small greenhouse filled with vegetables and a variety of roses.

Taylor pointed to a bunch of pink and white roses. "Is that Low Dog's Cajun Moon?"

Smiling, Hatch said, "Nice memory, Gray. Look at you."

"I love this place," Terri said, turning in a full circle.

"Nothing like the Dakota, but it's home for now," Hatch said, leading them into a massive kitchen with Corian countertops. The appliances were new, and a long wooden table, apparently hand-crafted, was the centerpiece. Opening the refrigerator, Hatch removed two bottles of Mayer Brothers water and handed them to his guests. "Took us about two months to renovate the whole place," he said. "Convincing Low Dog to go along with the changes was a tough sell. He's old school. Even though I paid for everything, he prefers simple."

"Still no phone?" Taylor took a sip from the bottle, his eyes moving over the contents of the rooms.

Hatch shook his head. "There's no cell service on the reservation," he said. "It's an ongoing fight with AT&T and Verizon. Our chief wants to squeeze big business by charging an arm and a leg for the tower."

"You mean Chief Blackburn?" Terri said, one eyebrow arching.

"You've done your homework," Hatch said, taking a seat at the kitchen table.

"Your fearless leader gave us directions from Irving," Taylor said as he and Terri sat down.

"Feathers on a frog," Terri said, imitating Blackburn's accent and inflection.

"He's not my leader," Hatch said, not attempting to hide his bitterness. "He's been lining his pockets for years. You should see the palace he lives in. Shit, I'm shocked he even talked to you *white* people. From his point of view, you're all out to get us. The U.S. government is the evil empire; President Thorn is the antichrist."

"I don't think he liked me," Taylor said, smiling.

Terri chuckled. "He tried to intimidate my man. I could smell the testosterone."

"The chief's political platform is based on fear," Hatch said.

"What's that mean?" Terri asked, turning serious.

"The world is out to get the Indians," Hatch said, "but I am here to protect my people. Blah, blah, blah. Vote for me."

"Just another politician," Taylor said.

"Low Dog and Blackburn have had a running feud since I was a kid," said Hatch. "Their visions of the tribe's future couldn't be farther apart."

Terri leaned over the table. "You can always run for—"

"Okay, stop," said Hatch, raising his right hand. "Terri, please. You two didn't come all this way to talk about the Native American government, political principles, or the plight of the Seneca Nation. I take it Jack sent you guys? Am I right?"

"Pretty much," Taylor said, nodding.

"I am not going back to the Central Intelligence Agency," Hatch said, the words coming forth like a steady drumbeat.

"Hatch, he's worried about you," said Terri.

"I'm doing fine. Look around. Simpler is better. Low Dog's philosophy is right."

Taylor cleared his throat. "If you say so."

"And here comes the pitch to return to the Agency," Hatch said to Terri. "I can see it in Gray's eyes."

"I wish it was that simple," Terri said, patting Hatch's hand.

"Hatch," Gray Taylor said, leaning on his elbows, "in the past week, three people, all associated with Anthony DiFilippo and Vincent Tagliafero, were murdered in New York. The media is going crazy."

Hatch cocked his head. "Are you saying somebody made a connection between Karen's murder and these—?"

"No, not exactly," said Terri.

"Not exactly?" Hatch said, looking at Gray Taylor for confirmation.

"One of these guys, Johnny Cercone, was shot with a high-powered rifle from about 325 yards away in a brisk wind," said Taylor. "A perfect headshot only an expert marksman can make."

"So Jack immediately points a finger at Kevin Easter?" Hatch said, sitting up a little straighter. "Seriously, is that why you're here?"

Terri and Gray Taylor traded quick looks.

"Should I feel offended or honored?" Hatch asked, exhaling audibly.

"It sounds preposterous when you put it that way," Terri said, giving her husband another sideways glance.

"But here you both are nonetheless," Hatch said. "Four hundred miles from home."

Gray and Terri Taylor said nothing.

"Are we really having this conversation?" Hatch asked, incredulous. The chair scraped against the wooden floor. Making his way into the great room, he grabbed the steel poker and thrust it angrily into the fire. The seasoned cherry wood popped and sparked.

Terri said, "Clearly you can't be in two places—"

"We don't own a television, and I haven't used my laptop in . . . well, since before I got here," Hatch said. "No land line, no cell towers, no FiOS means no Internet; you might say I've exited the information superhighway. And *The Buffalo News* doesn't deliver to the reservation. I'm totally out of the loop. As insane as it may sound, I actually like it that way. Less is better from my point of view."

"The third man killed was identified as Donald Biasucci. That murder took place within the past few hours," Taylor said. "He was shot at point-blank range around noon in a Brooklyn motel room."

"Which exonerates me," Hatch said, rubbing his hands together. "Yippee!"

"Jack thought—"

"Forget what Jack thinks. He's not here. What do *you* think, Gray? What do you think, Terri? That's all that matters to me right now," said Hatch, clearly agitated. "I had nothing to do with any of this. I've been here, chopping wood, reading, shooting targets, and taking pictures. I go on long walks to remote places on the rez. I camp alone. I keep to myself. I'm trying to heal." Pausing for a moment, he added, "But I'd be lying if I said I was sorry about their deaths. Can we please move on?"

"I second the motion," Terri said.

For the next hour, all three of them slid into easier conversation.

Low Dog had recently been hospitalized for pneumonia, but he was doing much better. The old shaman was being released Sunday morning. Steven was in Saudi Arabia, where his company was running security on a new oil refinery scheduled to go online by the end of the year. Hatch had sold some of his black-and-white photographs to an art gallery in Buffalo's Allentown section, known for its eclectic clientele. Sydney King, a local TV reporter from the ABC affiliate, had even interviewed him for a piece. *The Buffalo News* was going to run an in-depth profile.

There was nothing to suggest that Hatch was lying, or had partnered with some unknown accomplice, or had even left the reservation for any significant amount of time.

"When's the last time you talked with Steven?" Terri asked.

"Steven?" Hatch said. "No, Terri, my brother isn't running around New York

City, killing the bad guys who allegedly had something to do with Karen's murder. It's preposterous and offensive to even suggest like that. Come on! You're wasting your time here."

"Sorry," Terri said quietly, reaching for her bottled water.

"The morning Steven flew out of Buffalo was the last time we talked," said Hatch. "I drove him to the airport over two months ago. Satisfied?"

Taylor said, "You have to admit that there's a serious coincidence—"

"Gray, if you use that walks-like-a-duck, quacks-like-a-duck analogy, I'll be tempted to impale you with the fireplace poker. You have the wrong person. I'm not your killer or even a person of interest. The same goes for Steven. Yes, we're close, but he doesn't have a dog in this fight. There's something else going on here."

"How'd it go, Gray?"

Gray Taylor, back behind the wheel of his Porsche, had waited until he and Terri hit the New York State Thruway before updating Jack Slattery. They were about ten minutes north of the Cattaraugus Indian Reservation, and the sun had already dipped below the Allegheny Mountains. Taylor let up on the accelerator, stepped on the clutch, put the sports car into fourth gear, and stomped on the gas. The speedometer pushed eighty, yet the engine wasn't even close to redlining. He engaged the cruise control.

"Chopping wood, reading, hiking, playing with his new cameras," Taylor said. "Exactly what he said he'd be doing. Hatch is off the grid. He's showing his photo collection in a local art gallery next summer. The kid is talented, Jack."

"He's pretty much divorced from the outside world," Terri said, bending over the BlackBerry. "He misses the hell out of Karen, obviously, but he seems to be getting on with his life. I'm envious. It's hard to take yourself out of our game without regrets."

"If there's still any burning anger toward the killer or killers," Taylor said, "he's good at hiding it."

"He was actually there. That's good news," Slattery said, though he sounded as if he disbelieved his own assessment.

"But totally unexpected," Taylor said, finishing his boss's thought.

"Nothing in this world should surprise me," Slattery said, "but I would have bet the ranch—"

"So who the hell is playing Terminator in New York?" asked Taylor. "And why?"

"Any reason to believe it could be Steven?"

"We've been over this," Taylor said, pulling around a slower-moving Mack truck. "Why would he do it? What's his motive? Killing people is a dirty, dangerous, messy business. And it's a hard thing to do . . . and even harder to live with."

"He has the military background," Slattery said. "And he's an expert marksman. I've checked."

"You're reaching, Jack," Terri said.

"Steven and Hatch are pretty tight," Slattery said. "Big brother was always looking out for baby brother when they were kids. And little brother was, and probably is, in a lot of pain."

"Hatch told us that Steven's in Saudi Arabia," Terri said. "You can have one of your people check out his story. Shouldn't be all that difficult."

Taylor cleared his throat. "Jack, how about that Bobby O'Rourke fella? He was allegedly playing with Mafia money. Maybe one of his buddies—"

"We're quietly checking it out," Slattery said. "But from what we've learned so far, he was just a gambler who got in over his head. And it wasn't his first time. None of O'Rourke's friends are even remotely connected to this problem." Taylor heard the DDI shuffle a few pages. "Did you meet Low Dog?"

"No. He's in a local hospital with a mild case of pneumonia," Taylor said. "He's getting out on Sunday."

"Don't you dare tell us you think an elderly shaman is behind this," Terri said.

"It hadn't crossed my mind," Slattery said.

Terri cupped her hand to her mouth and whispered to her husband. "Liar."

"Since Kevin isn't involved," Slattery said, "it's not our problem—that's the good news."

"The bad news," Terri said, "is some unknown person, who happens to be a very talented assassin, is killing off the Mafia in New York, and nobody has a clue who it is."

"Jack, is that really a negative?"

Slattery didn't answer the question. He suspected that his own statement— Kevin isn't involved, it's not our problem—wasn't altogether true. A high-ranking DEA official had insisted on a meeting—off the record—first thing Monday morning. This official had a laundry list of questions about certain Mafia soldiers dying on the streets of New York.

"You want us to stick around the area?" Taylor asked.

"Find yourselves a nice hotel near the reservation," Slattery said. "I'll be in touch."

CHAPTER 28

Bronx

Even in a house of God, Anthony DiFilippo couldn't find relief from the relentless storm playing out in his mind. All these murders, committed by a cunning adversary he'd yet to identify, threatened his position within the community, but more importantly, family, friends, and colleagues appeared to be in danger. For the time being, he watched on the sidelines like some third-string college quarterback, fearful of what terrible mistakes he might make if thrust into the game.

His people might demand a swift, brutal, and very public display of retaliation. If that took place, old wounds in formidable adversaries could be torn open. Blood would be spilled. The fragile peace of the past decade would be broken like priceless figurines smashed against a hearth. Payment of past debts—plus a little interest—might need to be made, and a number of families in the underworld community undoubtedly would suffer unless cooler heads prevailed.

Like any bona fide leader under attack, Tony D kept his emotions private. His grieving family didn't need another burden to shoulder—not now. So the don, seated in the front row of St. Andrew's Church, wrestled with his conflicted views and expanding list of potential enemies while hundreds paid their respects to Johnny Cercone. Most were still unaware that Woody had been murdered, or that they'd be attending not one, but two more services early next week.

Father Francis Stanley, an elderly Catholic priest, wore a stone-faced death mask throughout the early portion of his sermon. Touching on the sanctity of life, relationships with our fellow man and God, and the demise of social values, he droned on, making a strong case to St. Peter that Johnny's soul should pass through the pearly gates into heaven.

"How far can faith take us?" Father Stanley shouted at the congregation, his face reddening with his climax. Pounding the lectern, he said, "When does the end justify the means? Such a senseless death for such a young man . . ."

When does the end justify the means? Staring blindly at the casket, Tony D began to consider his options: a full court press, squeezing everyone, or playing it safe by hiding behind his army. He reached over and lightly patted Mara's hand.

No words could describe the invisible cloud of fear that now enveloped him.

Thirty minutes later, five Italian men, all wearing dark suits, carried Johnny Cercone's coffin through St. Andrew's central portal. Woody, one of the designated pallbearers, was conspicuously absent. The funeral director, Roland Triamante, and his two sons guided the men down the short sidewalk to the black hearse idling at the curb. Film crews from the local Fox, ABC, NBC, and CBS affiliates were camped out on opposite sides of Gerard Avenue. Dozens of journalists and photographers, their telephoto lenses trained on the exiting congregation, went to work.

Hands in his coat pockets, *Post* reporter B. J. Butera stood with his competition.

And the hunter, crouched beside a car's bumper, focused his Nikon F5 on each of the five pallbearers' faces as they moved the casket into the cold afternoon.

Emerging from the historic Catholic church, Tony D squinted in the sunlight, then quickly slipped on a pair of Ray-Bans.

"There he is!" one journalist shouted, elbowing his cameraman. "Don't you fucking dare screw this up." The throng of spectators pressed forward. Three New York City uniformed cops, arms outstretched, shouted for the curious onlookers to back up and stay on the sidewalk.

The don guided his weeping sister-in-law to the first limousine parked behind the hearse. Mara slid in beside her.

And then Tony D did something entirely unexpected. Straightening his winter overcoat, he stood erect, removed his sunglasses, and stared defiantly at the group who'd come to invade his privacy. *Are you over there, watching this spectacle, Mr. Invisible Man?* he thought.

"Jesus," one journalist said under her breath, "is he staring at me?"

B. J. laughed at his colleague's stupid comment. It was a nervous laugh.

Expressionless, the hunter shot another dozen frames. "Smile, Tony," he said. "You ain't seen nothin' yet."

Having delivered his silent query, Tony D finally climbed inside the limo beside Mara.

Brooklyn

The medical examiner kept a watchful eye as Donald "Woody" Biasucci's body was loaded into the back of a Mercy Ambulatory vehicle. Part of his job was to make sure the chain of evidence remained unbroken. It was about four o'clock, and the other members of the CSI team began packing up their equipment.

Detective Katherine Montroy, still sipping her very cold Dunkin' Donuts coffee from a Styrofoam cup, patted Dwayne Espinoza on the back. "*Mi amigo*, you worry way, way too much," she said. "Did you tie up all the loose ends?"

"Christ, I hope so," Espinoza grumbled. "But I'm sure some clever defense attorney will still rip me to shreds if they get the chance." He picked up his silver physical evidence kit.

"At least you get to leave," Matthew Philips said. "Our night is pretty much shot."

"Let the interview process commence!" Montroy said loudly, as if introducing two prize fighters to an auditorium filled with ravenous fans.

"Do you ever have a bad day, Kat?" Espinoza asked glumly.

"Hmm, my pet goldfish died when I was eight. Does that count?"

"Kat, I'll handle the naughty bunch of guests in the registration area," said Philips. "You take the nearby rooms." From his coat pocket, he removed a silver key, which was attached to a plastic Iron Man action figure. He handed it to his partner. "Pass key. The owner assures me it fits every door in the place."

"I'm such a lucky girl," Montroy said, rolling her eyes.

"Take a uniformed cop with you, Kat," Philips said. "I wouldn't be surprised if one of the guests tries to rabbit. We're talkin' johns and—"

"Okay, Dad. I think I can handle my end."

Chuckling and shaking his head, Espinoza said his goodbyes and disappeared into the parking lot. Philips took a long drag on his cigarette and headed for the Sunset Inn Motel's office and registration area.

Katherine Montroy spotted a patrolman, a black guy, handsome, about thirty, standing inside the yellow crime scene tape, studying the carnival in the street. "Hey, can you give me a hand, Officer?" she shouted.

The policeman, who looked genuinely pleased to be called upon, nodded, then hustled across the lot, but he was held up as the ambulance transporting Biasucci's body moved in front of him.

Fingering the pass key in front of Room 126, right next-door to the room in which Woody had been murdered, Montroy had just raised her fist to rap her knuckles against the cheap wood when the door opened.

Startled, Montroy dropped Iron Man, which bounced off the cracked concrete sidewalk. "Shit," she mouthed, instinctively reaching for her gun.

Harlem

The longer Lawrence Luther Wright took to digest the facts, the more he believed Anthony DiFilippo was *not* responsible for the Harlem warehouse explosions.

Along with the media, Lawrence Luther had been outside St. Andrew's earlier in the day, watching the don and his grieving family. He and Jamar Hightower, both concealed behind the tinted windows of a silver Cadillac STS sedan, had been double-parked a mere fifteen feet from the media.

"The man looks older than the hills," Jamar had said after Tony D slipped into the limo's backseat. Jamar pushed his dreadlocks back over his shoulder and looked over at his boss.

"Don't be fooled by appearances, Jamar," said Lawrence Luther. "Tony D's a lion. When the old man feels threatened, he'll retaliate, with plenty of soldiers at his disposal."

It wasn't the material loss that caused Lawrence Luther such anger and anxiety. Money was easy to come by. He'd simply raise the price of his product to recoup any short-term losses. Something far greater was damaged in the early-morning warehouse explosion: his street cred. That was all that distinguished him from the common drug dealer selling five-dollar hits of crack on any street corner in America.

This thing had to be fixed, and fast. But Lawrence Luther's brief conversation with the bomber had turned into the strongest evidence that Tony D was not involved.

Initially, Lawrence Luther had considered the braggadocio's behavior a sign of Italian arrogance. But if you're the don of the DiFilippo crime family, and you intend to get even for the murder of two of your key people, why make such an incendiary call? Sending a message was one thing. Starting an urban war was something altogether different. Tony D wasn't stupid, and violence, Lawrence Luther knew, had always been the don's last resort. In this cruel and unforgiving profession, Anthony DiFilippo was considered a gifted negotiator, a pacifist. Such an act of revenge wasn't his style.

Then again, Johnny Cercone and Fat Paulie Franco had been very close to Tony D. *Is the don acting now on emotion?* Again, that wasn't the old man's style. Besides, the Cercone kid had been absolutely no threat to his own organization. His business and Lawrence Luther's business focused on different markets. Tony D would know that.

A professional—a player who knew exactly what he was doing—had blown up Lawrence Luther Wright's new Harlem facility, not some thug looking to make a name for himself, or to get even for the deaths of Cercone and Franco. Lawrence Luther wanted—needed—to believe this. This expert—or maybe a team of experts—must have been monitoring his organization. But for how long? Tony D's men had been murdered during a forty-eight-hour period. And now, WCBS, New York City's fifty-thousand-watt radio super station, was reporting that Donald "Woody" Biasucci had been shot dead in a Brooklyn motel.

Sitting in the passenger seat of a newly purchased Cadillac parked outside Soul Food, a corner grocery store on Amsterdam Avenue in Harlem, Lawrence Luther looked at his gold Rolex. Four-ten. The windshield wipers, set on intermittent, slapped the drizzle aside.

Lawrence Luther swallowed the last bite of his spicy chicken sandwich, politely wiped his mouth with a paper napkin, and continued to watch the animated expression of Jamar Hightower, who listened to an informer on his cell phone.

"What else?" demanded Jamar, sitting in the driver's seat.

Lawrence Luther was almost entirely convinced that a third party had not only delivered this misfortune to his doorstep, but had also murdered Tony D's people. But why? To pick up the pieces once the skirmish was over?

Anthony, how do I convince you we have a mutual enemy? Lawrence Luther thought. *Or do you suspect this already?*

Jamar continued to speak with his mole. "Yeah, I'll make sure. Yeah, you'll get your money. Hey, have I ever fucked you over?" A pause. "You best keep your mouth shut, Gilligan! I'm not kidding." Pocketing the phone, he turned to his boss and said, "Cops figure there were five or six bombs, including the one attached to the Mercedes."

Lawrence Luther stared through the windshield into a decaying neighborhood. "What about the hooker who was with Mr. Biasucci before he was killed?"

"A teenager—calls herself Pebbles," said Jamar. "We're looking for her."

It was a late Saturday afternoon, and a few kids in the neighborhood were playing touch football in the wet street. "Look harder," Lawrence Luther said, his voice low, brusque.

"Yes, sir."

"Who's running Pebbles?"

"Don't know yet."

"What *do* you know?" Lawrence Luther crushed the brown sandwich bag and tossed it into the Caddy's backseat.

"That I can find this girl before the cops do."

"Make it happen."

"Boss, I was told that one of the detonators separated from the C-4," said Jamar. "Things coulda been worse. Gilligan tells me it's a military detonator—something the cops ain't never seen before."

Lawrence Luther's head slowly turned, as if the gravitational pull of the words grabbed hold of him. "Military?" he said, narrowing his eyes. "A detonator they'd never seen before?"

"That's what my boy tells me."

Stroking his beard, Lawrence Luther considered this new information for a few seconds. "I want Ms. Pebbles before anyone grabs her, Jamar. I'm sure DiFilippo's people are looking, too."

"We're on it. I have another guy hangin' around the Sunset Inn."

Lawrence Luther patted his friend on the shoulder. "Don't screw up, Jamar."

"It's being handled, Boss. Trust me."

"How about the name of the detective attached to Biasucci's case?"

Jamar looked down at the notes he'd scribbled on the back of a manila envelope. "Katherine Montroy and Matthew Philips. They're also assigned to the Paulie Franco and Johnny Cercone murders."

"And the gentleman investigating my warehouse? What's his name?"

Flipping over the envelope, Jamar said, "The homicide detective is Nick Benedetti—"

"No, the bomb expert."

"He's an arson specialist brought in by the fire department. Name's Brian McGowan. Spent some time in Iraq. You want to work with him?"

"We all have a price, Jamar. Find out Mr. McGowan's. And while you're at it, ask around about this Benedetti guy."

Brooklyn

"Jesus . . . please, don't shoot!" shouted the elderly, overweight man, his voice so shrill it sounded like a little girl's. Sweating profusely, he wore a white dress shirt that was soaked, and a wrinkled pastel tie that was much too short. His arms shot toward the ceiling. "I didn't—didn't do anything . . ."

Katherine Montroy exhaled explosively, shoved her SIG Sauer P229 back into her shoulder rig, and couldn't help but feel her heart hammering against her ribcage. "Sir, hey, take it easy," Montroy said firmly. "Please, lower your arms. I only want to ask you a few questions."

"That little skinny cop wouldn't let us leave," the man whined, pointing at Philips, who was stepping into the registration area. "Lady, it's not what you think."

"It's Detective Montroy," she said. "I hate 'lady.'"

"Sorry. Sorry."

The black cop jogged over. "How can I help, Detective?"

"Give me a sec," Montroy replied, raising her right hand like a grammar school crossing guard. She peered past the gray-haired businessman. Sitting on the bed was a young girl of about twenty. With unruly orange hair, hooped earrings, enough mascara to intimidate a party clown, and a short pink dress, she was smoking a cigarette that trembled, almost violently, in her hand. "Ma'am, are you hurt?"

"I just wanna leave," the girl on the bed said in a quivering voice.

The old man cleared his throat. "I'm married. Do you understand? I . . . I own a small insurance company not far from here. We're barely making ends meet. I've never done this before, Detective. Really."

"Jesus, will you please slow down?" Montroy said.

"If this, oh shit, if this ever gets out, I'm finished. My kids would never talk to me again and my wife would take me to the cleaners—"

"Sir," said Montroy, "let me start with one question, and maybe, just maybe, we can help each other through this mess."

The old man in the wrinkled dress pants swam for the life raft Montroy was about to toss into the shark-infested waters. "Okay," he said, letting the word draw out.

"The walls in this place are fairly thin. Did you hear anything odd or strange coming from Room 124 a few hours ago?" Montroy jerked a thumb to her right.

"You're damn right we heard things!" the girl yelled, apparently seeing her own exit strategy. She popped to her feet. "This chickenshit fat fuck wouldn't let me go. He even barricaded the door with that stupid dresser. I couldn't believe it."

"Y-yeah," the old man stammered, "because that lunatic pounded on our door, said something about a stolen Corvette—"

"What lunatic?" Montroy asked. "Sir, take a breath."

"The goddamned maid shows up right after things get quiet over there," the girl said, "and Mr. No Balls still wouldn't let me go. Thought we could hide out in here until all you guys did your thing and took off. And the fat bastard who owns this dump stood in the parking lot like a fucking sheepdog, herding people into his office or forcing them back into their rooms. We weren't going nowhere then. No way! Mr. No Balls screwed up. By the way, Buster, you still owe me eighty bucks—"

"There were two of them over there, Detective," said the old man, cutting off the girl. "One guy did a lot of yellin', the other was calm, scary calm—like a robot. When robot guy pounded on our door, he had an accent, maybe Chinese or Korean. Hell, I can't tell the difference. And at that point I just ignored him."

The girl said, "I coulda outrun—"

"Please," Montroy said, shooting the hooker a hard look. "One at a time."

"But once he got in that room," the old man went on, "I'm pretty sure his accent was gone. Disappeared. He talked like you and me—like an American."

"Did you hear specific words or phrases?" Montroy asked.

"A couple names," the girl said.

"Names?" Montroy repeated, thinning her eyes.

"Yeah," the old man said, nodding. "The spooky robot guy, your killer, asked, 'Is Anthony DiFilippo looking for me?' We both heard that. Right?"

The girl shrugged, then said, "Yeah, I heard it, lady—I mean, Detective."

"Sir," Montroy said, smiling, "I do believe you and I are about to cut a deal."

"What about me?!" the girl shouted.

"Both of you," Montroy said. "Chill. Tell me everything you heard, everything you saw, and your afternoon romp in the hay is forgotten."

"The guy drove away in a white Ford Explorer," the girl said, words clipped. She pushed the old businessman aside.

"Hey, excuse me!"

"Fuck off, Mr. No Balls," the girl said, "or I'll punch you in the throat."

The black cop stepped between them, but remained silent.

"Could either of you identify the killer?" Montroy asked. "Maybe a license plate?"

"It was parked on the street," the girl said. "Too far away."

"We only saw his back," the old man said. "He was wearing a hat and a leather jacket. Average height."

"A nice ass," the girl added. "Hard and lean."

Katherine Montroy turned to the uniformed cop and said, "Please tell Detective Philips I need him in Room 126 right away."

Parsippany, New Jersey

The patch of property in northern New Jersey that had become Patricia Durante's permanent resting place was now a small mound of dirt in a sea of headstones. Grass replanted over the gravesite had never really had a chance to germinate because of the scorching, rainless summer and the cold fall. It was about four-thirty, and the sun was warm on the hunter's face. It felt good.

The marble headstone, the name "Patricia Anne Durante" engraved in block letters, reminded its visitor of the pointless death that fueled his resolve, justifying a vengeance that had already taken the lives of five people. He knew there had been other options, other paths, but the deaths of Patricia Durante, Robert O'Rourke, and Karen Easter were ultimately his responsibility—his fault.

Hands folded as if in prayer, the hunter looked down at Patricia's headstone. His shadow covered most of the inscription: "Loving Daughter, Cherished Sister,

Devoted Friend." It reminded him of his own fragile world—how life can change in the blink of an eye.

From hours of surveillance tape, he'd learned of the evidence destroyed by a dirty homicide detective in the Twenty-Eighth Precinct, and of the large sum of money delivered thereafter. This detective had been given marching orders to deep-six the Rudy's Tavern triple-murder investigation once Vincent Tagliafero had been fingered for the deaths. The ballistics report from the Rudy's Tavern triple homicide would match the two handguns recovered from Tagliafero's body. A slam dunk.

Anthony DiFilippo had been the man behind this decision to sacrifice one nephew to protect another, and his criminal organization came away unscathed. The hunter would address this issue at another time. A nice letter to Mrs. DiFilippo might do the trick if things didn't play out as expected. Maybe he'd tell her personally.

A bouquet of pink and white roses—Cajun Moon, a hybrid tea—rested on the dirt at the base of Patricia's headstone. Dropping to one knee, the hunter gently rubbed a petal between his thumb and forefinger, then said, "From your secret admirer, Patty. They're really beautiful."

A few minutes later, the hunter walked briskly out of the cemetery to his idling SUV. There was much work to be done.

CHAPTER 29

Cattaraugus Indian Reservation

Kevin Easter tossed another log on the fire, pulled the screen closed, and returned to the rocking chair. His book, *The Earth Shall Weep: A History of Native America*, no longer appealed to him, and his tomato soup had gone untouched. The walls of Low Dog's cabin, even in the great room, seemed to have closed in since the Taylors had driven off about two hours ago.

Something felt terribly wrong.

Terri and Gray Taylor had planted a disturbing seed in his fertile mind. Since Hatch had been a boy, Low Dog had insisted that his grandchildren never ignore those unexplained feelings. But what could Hatch do? What were his alternatives? Living on the reservation left Hatch isolated.

He sat back in the rocking chair to think. "Goddamnit!" he finally said through clenched teeth.

Closing his eyes, Hatch drifted to another, happier time: a Halloween party with a group of friends. Patricia had dressed as Cleopatra, Karen as Dorothy from *The Wizard of Oz*, and Hatch as a shaman, with authentic Native American apparel. The war paint, beaded brow band, and multi-feathered war bonnet covered a good portion of his face and head.

Steven, on the other hand, had worn a Batman mask, black cape, and tights, all of which made him look utterly ridiculous.

Inspired by Hatch's costume, Patricia set off on a rambling tirade. "This genocide," she said, "began with the infamous Trail of Tears, and we still treat our Native American brothers and sisters like second-class citizens. And it's wrong!"

The fruity punch, fortified with grain alcohol from Sayre, Pennsylvania, helped lubricate her tongue. It was the first time Hatch and Steven had ever met Karen's sister.

"Genocide!" she exclaimed, her voice getting louder. "Goddamned murder. Another human catastrophe our . . . our country has conveniently forgotten. Do you know how many natives we've slaughtered in this country, Kevin? Do you know how many proud Indian nations were displaced or exterminated over a sixty-year period? Huh? Steven? Hello! Does your brother get it?"

Both of the Easter brothers nodded dutifully.

"Are you even listening to me, you guys?" Patricia said, her fruity drink spilling. "Hitler's Third Reich and his fucked-up freaks have the distinction of being modern-day butchers. But today, the nation of Israel has the financial support of the United States and a whole bunch of other western countries. We identify with the Jewish people and acknowledge the Holocaust. But what about *our* country? Huh? History books tell us that our forefathers, the settlers, are . . . were brave people who came to the New World for political and religious freedom. But historians conveniently forget to mention the senseless, barbaric murders of millions of these natives. This had been *their* home—undisturbed until *we* got here."

She pressed a finger into Hatch's chest. "What the hell separates our forefathers from Hitler's Gestapo, Kevin? Huh? Instead of concentration camps, we butchered these innocent people on *their* land—defenseless women and children. And nobody seems to give a shit! Even now! Most of these displaced Indians live in poverty. Do you two jokers know this? What's wrong with you?"

Patricia's chin had begun to tremble with rage. A few people at the house party appeared uncomfortable.

Hatch and Steven Easter glanced at each other again.

Right to the bitter end, Karen Durante let her older sister keep digging the hole. Smiling ruefully behind a glass of white wine, she enjoyed every single moment of the lecture.

"I have friends who are Apache," Patricia went on. "I hope you're not mocking these great people. What do you have to say about that? Huh?" She defiantly downed her drink and waited for Kevin Easter's reply, tapping her foot on the wooden floor. "Nothing. I knew it. Knew it!" Instead of responding with words, Hatch slowly removed the ceremonial headdress of the spiritual leader of the Seneca Nation Indian tribe. His fine black hair fell almost to his shoulders. His russet complexion and almond-shaped eyes left no doubt of his ancestral heritage. Steven removed his Batman mask and shrugged.

Patricia's mouth fell open. "Oh . . . my . . . God."

Karen handed her sister a ruby slipper. "Think this will fit in your mouth, Patty?"

"For a white chick, you're pretty smart," Steven said, kissing Patricia on the cheek. "You'd make a hell of a politician."

"I'll work on your campaign," Hatch said. "*Our* people could use your voice in Albany."

Wrapping her arm around Hatch's waist, Karen laughed. "Holy cow, did I forget to mention something about my boyfriend? Shame on me."

"I am such an idiot," Patricia said, slowly shaking her head.

"A drunken idiot," Karen said, pulling her sister closer. "It's okay."

"Ladies and gentlemen," Steven said, raising his cup of beer, "I think I've just fallen in love with Patty Durante."

Everyone at the party roared with approval. The Black Eyed Peas' "Pump It" played over the speakers, and people started to dance.

Steven and Patty were the first two on the floor.

Now, standing up from the rocking chair, Hatch seemed drawn to the large bay window facing the dark forest. The stars and moon were lost behind a thick layer of clouds. Steven's comment suddenly troubled him: *I think I've just fallen in love with Patty Durante.* It had sounded so innocent back then—but not now. *Could it be?*

He turned suddenly and gazed at the fireplace mantel. In a clear vase was one pink and white rose—from Low Dog's nursery. Cajun Moon. Terri had taken it from the greenhouse. Hadn't one of the mourners at Patricia's gravesite placed that rare subspecies on her casket?

"Steven? No way," he said, shaking his head. "Impossible."

A moment later, Hatch grabbed his winter jacket and headed for the door.

———————————

Forty minutes later, Hatch slid into the booth at Jan's Smoke Shop and considered some alternatives. Outside the plate-glass window, a light snow had begun to fall. The gas jockeys huddled together in a small wooden hut near the pumps. The restaurant was quiet.

A waitress sidled up to the table. "Hi, can I get you something yet?"

Pulled from his reverie, Hatch blinked, then looked up at the teenage girl and smiled. "Ah, hot tea."

"Sure." The dark-haired girl, whom he'd seen on the reservation before, returned a genuine smile, revealing a mouth full of colored braces. "I'll be right back."

"No rush."

The numbers Hatch had punched in at the pay phone had left him with more questions than answers. He was genuinely worried now. Taif Air Base in Saudi Arabia, Prince Sultan Air Base in Riyadh, and Al Udeid Air Base in Qatar were all dead ends. Steven hadn't reported to any of the three American bases, normal operating procedure even for a civilian working on behalf of the Saudi government and the powerful oil companies that controlled the region.

The hot tea was delivered. Hatch declined a menu. He'd lost his appetite even before Gray and Terri Taylor's Porsche had pulled out of Low Dog's driveway.

"That doesn't mean you're not staying in some fancy hotel, Steven," Hatch said, pouring sugar into his cup. "Right? And that sure as hell doesn't mean you're in New York City, doing . . ." His voice trailed off. "Shit." *Would I have known if you were quietly dating Patty? Did Karen know, or was she keeping it a secret because of our own troubles with her dad?* Dr. Durante hated the idea that one of his daughters was seeing a minority, so Hatch could only imagine the reaction if both girls had a crush on an Easter brother. *And what about the damn roses?* thought Hatch. *And you've been exposed to violence, Steven. That bullet broke your collarbone. It almost killed you.*

"Did you say something?" the waitress asked, wiping down a nearby table.

"Hey," Hatch said, looking at her nametag, "Becky, I know the rez doesn't have Internet service, so where do the kids go to get online?"

"The library, mostly."

"What about a Saturday night, like now? Is there a place I can bring my laptop?"

Becky leaned over the table and whispered, "Is it wireless?"

"Yeah."

"Park your car outside Kaz Brothers' Roofing, and you can pick up their signal. They have FiOS, and it's not password-protected yet. All the kids do it. It's a total joke—some nights the parking lot is full. Even the cops haven't caught on yet."

Hatch threw five bucks on the table. "Thanks, Becky."

Saudi Aramco, the state-owned oil company that hired Steven's security firm, SearchPath International, to protect the Ghawar, Safaniya, and Shaybah oil fields, had been Hatch's last option. Over the web, he'd gotten a half dozen key contacts and phone numbers at Aramco. Their own security division passed along the number for the SearchPath office.

A pleasant-sounding woman, in heavily accented Middle-Eastern English, answered the phone after the first ring. "SearchPath International. How can I help you?"

"Yes, hi, my name is Kevin Easter. I need to talk with my brother . . . Steven."

"I am sorry, sir, he is not in the office at the moment."

"When do you expect him back?"

"That is extremely difficult to say, Mr. Easter," said the woman. "Your brother moves around quite a bit. Sometimes with little or no notice. It is for security purposes."

"When was the last time he was there?"

"Oh, about five weeks ago, I think."

"Where are your new offices? Steven said you were working with Saudi Aramco, something about the Ghawar field—"

"We are in Riyadh. Our contract with Saudi Aramco expired about the time your brother returned to the United States back in August."

"You mean for my wife's funeral."

There was a long silence from the woman.

"Are you still there?" Hatch pressed the phone to his ear.

"Yes, I am here." Another pensive pause. "I . . . I did not know about your wife's death, Mr. Easter. Your brother is extremely private about his personal life."

Tell me something I don't know. Standing outside a closed gas station, Hatch stomped his cold feet on the wet pavement. It was a few minutes after midnight. The cold Canadian winds had picked up considerably in the past few hours. "Can you give me an idea as to when he flew to the U.S. back in August?"

"He left us on the eleventh. I remember because it was my birthday, and Mr. Easter missed the party, but he left me flowers. I am not sure when he arrived in America—he mentioned he had a few stops along the way."

Hatch considered this for a moment. "Did he leave you roses by any chance?"

"No . . . no, orchids. Very beautiful."

Patricia and Karen had been murdered on August 12, so Steven could have been in the United States that Saturday night. *Steven said he was in Kuwait, headed for Saudi. He also said Low Dog had called from the community center on the reservation. Were there missing days?*

"Is there a way I can get in contact with him?" Hatch asked. "The international cell number he gave me doesn't seem to work, and there's no voice mail set up."

"I am very sorry, Mr. Easter, but your brother's whereabouts are classified."

"Classified? Why?"

"I cannot answer that question either, I am afraid."

Exasperated, Hatch said, "Is he still in the Middle East?"

"Sorry, but—"

"I need to talk to my brother," Hatch said, impatient. "It's important!"

"What would you like me to tell him, Mr. Easter?"

"To call me!" Hatch shouted. "As soon as possible!"

"Of course," she answered pleasantly, although there was a trace of irritation in her delicate voice. "But it could take a day, maybe more, especially if he has traveled out of the region and not activated his satellite phone or e-mail, which I suspect he has not from what you have told me."

"Tell him to call my old cell number. It should be working by tomorrow." Hatch passed along the number and terminated the call. He jogged to his Pathfinder, thinking of the things he would need to pack for his trip to New York City.

CHAPTER 30

Bronx

"Goddamnit, Matty, this case is getting uglier by the hour," Katherine Montroy said, slamming Philips's office door closed. In her left hand, she waved Paulie Franco's ballistics report. In her right, she held Donald "Woody" Biasucci's new case file and *his* ballistics report. She dropped the folders onto Philips's cluttered desk. "Just got the update from Espinoza's assistant. Both of Tony D's people were shot with a nine millimeter, but the fucking guns are different. Striations, number of lands and grooves, height, width, and depth—not even close. The bore was even wrong."

Philips dropped his pen onto a lined legal pad, then peered apathetically over top his steel-rimmed glasses. His red eyes reflected a man who hadn't slept well in weeks. "Please, please, God," he said, "give this gorgeous lady the courage to shove a knitting needle through my ear. End my pain and suffering with dignity, oh Lord. Put me out of my misery, baby Jesus, before I hurt somebody. I know I'm missin' church again, and my wife's completely pissed—"

"Save it, Matty!"

Philips raised both hands in mock surrender. "My eighth-grade English teacher told me to be an actor."

"Maybe you're right. Maybe we have two assassins targeting Tony D's organization," said Montroy. "Maybe it's a whole army of these lunatics."

"Seriously, Kat, did you really think one guy was behind this?"

"I don't know what to think," Montroy said. "The evidence is so . . . so paradoxical."

"Hey, easy with the big words. I'm a product of a public-school education."

"On one hand, it looks like we're dealing with a real pro, and then, on the other, it seems as if our shooter is an amateur," she said. "He goes and kills Fat Paulie up close and personal, but leaves Michael Testa with only a bad headache. Same goes for Donald Biasucci. Our killer whacks Woody but lets the hooker, a likely witness, walk. He has scruples? Is that it?"

"I take it we haven't found Ms. Pebbles yet?"

"Paula Ward. A black and white visited her parents' house in Ronkonkoma about an hour ago, but they haven't seen her in almost four months."

"I couldn't even imagine my daughter—"

"There's a line these murderers don't seem to want to cross, Matty."

"Could be there's a bonus for limiting collateral damage?" Philips said, chuckling.

Throwing up her hands, Montroy said, "Why do I even bother?"

"Okay, let's revisit Mr. Charles Schechter and Ms. Melissa 'Kitty' Kaman," Philips said, opening a file on his desk. He cleared his throat. "Our lovebirds at the Sunset Inn Motel saw an Asian-sounding male, age twenty-five to forty, average height and slim build—who apparently has a nice ass—wearing a knitted ski hat and leather bomber jacket, leaving the scene of the crime. They heard him mention the name 'Anthony DiFilippo,' which pretty much comes as no surprise, since the deceased worked for said individual. They chatted about Easter, for some crazy reason—"

"And someone named Patricia," Montroy said.

"Biasucci yelled something like, 'I'm not fucking moving until you tell me what this is about.' And then the guy must have clubbed our buddy Woody in the skull, opening a nice-sized gash. They chatted for a few minutes, and our killer finished off Biasucci using a silenced pistol. How 'bout that?"

"Shit, I really thought we caught a break," Montroy said, shaking her head.

Philips closed the file. "What about the white Ford Explorer? I'll bet there's ten thousand of them in the area."

"Yeah, it's a long-shot," Montroy said, "but I contacted the New York City Department of Transportation about an hour ago and requested all surveillance and traffic tapes from the neighborhood surrounding the motel. If we get lucky, and the Ford SUV shows up, maybe we can follow this guy to his lair."

"Big Brother to the rescue."

"But the system has too many holes to really be effective," Montroy said with a shrug. "Shit, some of the damn cameras fail when it gets cold. Others are pointed in the wrong direction."

"And in some of our swankier neighborhoods," Philips said, "they make for good target practice by law-abiding juvenile delinquents."

"Those stupid cameras and Pebbles the prostitute are all we have, Matty."

"This is about gangland warfare, Kat, one underworld crime family kicking some ass and expanding their empire. And this family or gang, or the Christian Right, or the damn IRA brought in some big-game hunters—professionals who are quick and clean. Probably paid them some serious jack." Philips exhaled. "That's my theory, so why don't you and Tony D crucify me? I think you'd both enjoy the show."

Montroy settled back in a wooden chair that faced the desk. "If it's one guy, he's got a moral compass *and* a sense of humor."

"Assassins, comedians, priests—yeah, most are cut from the same cloth." Philips shoved an unlit Camel between his stained teeth and grinned.

"The shell casings the shooter leaves behind look like something you'd find in a Vietnam War museum. He planted them. Why? What's the point? It didn't slow the investigation down for even a second."

"I was told it wasn't even close to the .762 slug the techies dug out of Johnny Cercone's front door."

"Which makes me believe this guy—"

"Guys," Philips said.

"Whatever," Montroy said, tossing the morning newspaper on Philips's desk. "Check it out. These reporters are taking a run at everybody, especially me. I come across as a total moron in the *Times*."

Philips leaned to his left and picked up *The New York Post* from a pile of newspapers on the floor. "Want some advice, Kat?"

"I know, I know . . . stop talking to them."

"You'll catch on, Detective. In this business, less is more, especially with the sensational cases. Think Mark Fuhrman and O.J. Here, take a look at the news section."

The *Post* was having a field day at the expense of both Tony D and, to a lesser degree, the New York Police Department. The front page had a close-up of Anthony DiFilippo IV staring defiantly at the camera. As was usually the case, they ran a clever headline: "Will Tony D's Empire Strike Back?"

The long piece was as candid as the accompanying photograph of Paulie Franco's body slumped against the dashboard, with detailed descriptions of the Sunset Inn Motel—"Stop-N-Go Love Palace"—and the extravagant funeral for Cercone. With memorial services set for Fat Paulie Franco and Donald Biasucci later in the week, B. J. Butera, a reporter undoubtedly on the greatest ride of his professional life, speculated that this could be the beginning of a bloody conflict.

Montroy flipped a few pages and let out a long, disconcerted breath.

"Benedetti seems to be a busy boy," Philips said, pointing to another *Post* article. "'Two Dead in Arson Warehouse Fire,'" he read.

"Yeah, like we've been sitting on our fat asses whistling 'Dixie' all week," Montroy said, getting up from the chair. "Davis told me it was a serious meth lab. Lawrence Luther Wright ran the place."

Philips tilted his head forward and looked over his glasses. "Not my problem."

"You're a grumpy old man, Matty," Montroy said, leaving the office. "Let me know about the traffic cameras!" Philips shouted.

Bronx

The hunter's apartment was in the University Heights section of the Bronx on East Fordham Road, between Jerome Avenue and Grand Boulevard, ten blocks from Fordham University and three blocks north of the boarded-up business formerly known as Rudy's Tavern. The sun peeked over the steel, glass, brick, and stone structures to the east, creating an ominous red sky.

Red sky in the morning, sailors' warning, he thought.

Meteorologists might have an edge on the weather, but only the hunter and God knew of the chaos that lay ahead today.

Walking at a leisurely pace along Fordham Road, carrying a brown bag filled with groceries, the hunter wore a Yankees cap, tipped slightly downward to conceal his face. Beneath his leather jacket, he carried a loaded Smith & Wesson Model 29 with .44 magnum cartridges, made popular by Clint Eastwood's Dirty Harry. He crossed and re-crossed the quiet street, providing plenty of opportunity to cover his flank. Nobody followed him.

An elderly couple holding hands stood at a corner, waiting for the traffic light to change. They were dressed formally, as if heading to a morning church service.

Predominantly made up of students from nearby Herbert Lehman College, Bronx Community College, and Fordham University, the neighborhood was relatively safe despite being in one of the largest and most diverse cities in the world. Since the triple homicide in August, police patrols had stepped up their presence. Two cops currently walked the beat.

The transient nature of the surrounding area and centralized location made University Heights the perfect place for the hunter's base of operations.

Before he slipped the key into the outside door of his brick apartment building, his hard gaze swept the neighborhood. A coed walked toward one of the campuses, backpack slung over her shoulder. The hunter opened the steel door and took the stairs to the sixth floor, measuring each step, listening. He carefully examined his apartment door—especially the lock—but found no new scratches or evidence that it had been tampered with. He slipped in the key.

Once the door closed behind the hunter, and the apartment again plunged into darkness, he slid the two deadbolts in place and relaxed for the first time in the past two hours. Cardboard, secured with duct tape, kept out natural light. The floorboards creaked beneath his work boots as he crossed into the tiny kitchen.

Snapping on the overhead fluorescent light, he set the shopping bag on a butcher-block table and tossed his cap on the counter. He unloaded juice, sandwich meat, and apples into the old refrigerator. When the bag was empty, he grabbed a bottle of water and stepped into the living room.

He pulled the chain of the old lamp atop the metal desk, and the room lit up. It looked like a scaled-down version of the command center at NORAD. The walls were covered with street maps of Brooklyn, the Bronx, Manhattan, and even northern New Jersey. Red pins marked specific points of interest: Rudy's Tavern, the Hunts Point Market, the Harlem Warehouse on 145th Street, Woodlawn Cemetery, St. Andrew's Church, and the Ravenite Social Club. Photographs of these locations, along with snapshots of dozens of residences, were affixed to the wall.

On a second wall, more than a hundred photographs covered nearly every square inch of the faded flowered wallpaper. There was a flow chart, with Anthony DiFilippo IV as the primary target. Underboss Paulie Franco and three *capos*—Johnny Cercone, Donald Biasucci, and Louis Ciambella—had been secretly photographed in different venues, and their photos were just below Tony D's in a ten-layer pyramid of pictures. The FBI, DEA, and NYPD mob division would be hard-pressed to match the display. Unlike mug shots, the hunter's pictures captured charismatic and animated individuals going about their daily business, completely unaware they'd become potential targets.

There were many others: Lawrence Luther Wright, the man who controlled the flow of cocaine into Greater New York, stood outside his Harlem warehouse with two burly bodyguards and his woman driver. At least thirty influential gang members from the five boroughs of New York had made the wall. Every photograph had a number affixed to it—the lower the number, the higher the target value. Tony D was number one. Lawrence Luther Wright had originally been assigned number eighteen, but quickly moved up to number seven when his real influence became evident. Mara DiFilippo was number two.

There were Detective Katherine Montroy and her girlfriend, Tracy Fitzgibbon, both sitting on a park bench in Gramercy Park, and Detective Matthew Philips walking his dog, Trigger. One detective had a single digit, and the other was twenty-eight. The hunter's collection also included smaller photos: medical examiner Dwayne Espinoza, Detective Nicholas Benedetti, and twelve lower-ranking members of Anthony DiFilippo's army.

Franco (number four), Cercone (number three), and Biasucci (number six) each had a red X across their black-and-white photograph. Below the group of three, articles penned by B. J. Butera described the hunter's kills and the victims' background. Of the three capos, only the photograph of Ciambella was unmarked.

In baseball terms, Louis Ciambella (number five) was on deck.

The small living room-turned-command center included an Apple computer with three high-def flat screens—one constantly monitoring the front of the hunter's building—a Compaq laptop, a laser printer, a police scanner, a micro UHF transmitter, a bionic ear with a twelve-inch parabolic dish (used in the cemetery to record Tony D and the two detectives), an omnidirectional microphone with Bose headphones, a digital recorder, an acoustical jammer, a global satellite phone, camera equipment, and a CD burner for the hundreds of hours of recorded conversations. Inside a locked trunk beside his desk was the M40A3 semiautomatic rifle that had been used to assassinate Johnny Cercone.

There was also an MP5 assault rifle with a recoil compensator, a sawed-off shotgun, three handguns with silencers (all nine millimeter), enough C-4 plastique for three more bombs, two clones of Israeli-manufactured detonators, night-vision goggles, and Kevlar body armor. The hunter also owned professional locksmithing tools used to circumvent the elaborate alarm system inside Lawrence Luther Wright's warehouse. His military fatigues—something he'd yet to use because of the urban terrain—were neatly folded on an old trunk. Two hunting knives, still in their sheaths, lay atop a dresser near three wigs, along with enough cosmetics to easily make him into five distinct individuals.

He also had six more Vietnam-era 5.56 rounds that he'd stolen from Tony D's home three weeks ago. He wanted the don to know that his nemesis had been very near.

The hunter looked at his watch. It was 9:12 a.m. The National Football League had a full slate of games today. Many, including the New York Jets game, kicked off at 1 p.m. It was nearly time again.

CHAPTER 31

Bronx

Matthew Philips ignored the ringing telephone and concentrated instead on Terry Bradshaw and his colleagues on Fox's NFL pregame show. They were dissecting the New York Giants-Washington Redskins game, scheduled to begin at 4:15 Eastern.

"As you can see, my good friend Terry took one too many hits to the head," said Howie Long, retired Oakland Raiders defensive lineman-turned-studio analyst. "The Giants don't stand a chance against the Skins, especially with their offensive line in shambles. Heck, they're starting two rookies and a second-stringer with a bum knee."

The phone in his family room finally went silent, and the caller hadn't left a message. Relieved, Philips reached for his second beer of the day. Then his cell phone began to vibrate in his pants pocket. "C'mon, the wife's out shopping. Is a few hours of peace too much to ask?" he said, looking up at the ceiling.

The enigmatic Bradshaw laughed, turned to James Brown, who anchored the Sunday afternoon television show, and replied in folksy, Cajun-accented English, "J.B., did Howie just say *I* took too many shots to the head?"

Philips finally pulled his cell phone from his pocket and grimaced. He pressed the *send* button. "I'm kinda busy, Kat."

"Yeah, yeah, the Jets don't kick off for another forty-five minutes."

"You're on the clock." Philips got up from his favorite recliner and began to pace.

"We identified some prints off Biasucci's Corvette—couple of Bronx kids with short track records, minor stuff. I sent a car to their parents' residences."

"Good luck finding that needle in a haystack."

The Fox broadcast went to commercial, and Philips muted the sound.

"Jerome Brice and Thurman Thompson, both fifteen," Montroy said. "Maybe they can identify our—"

"Don't count on it." Philips picked up his bottle of perspiring Budweiser.

"And we may have gotten lucky with the traffic cameras," Montroy said. "They definitely have a white Ford Explorer leaving the area right about the time of Biasucci's murder."

"No shit."

"I've been invited over to the DOT substation on Court Street in Brooklyn first thing Monday morning," Montroy said. "They'll assign me an operator to run through the tapes."

"Want me to tag along?" Philips said. "Please say no, Kat."

"I can handle this all by my little self."

"Ya gonna let our Italian friend in on any of this?"

"There's really nothing to tell him yet, Matty."

"Maybe Tony D can help locate our two juvenile delinquents or that Pebbles girl," Philips said. "He did say his people outnumbered our guys something like twenty to one."

"Let me think about it. We can talk about it later."

"I'm putting my money on Pebbles," Philips said, reaching for his TV remote. He turned up the volume when the pregame show came back on. "She must have seen something. As for our two kiddy car thieves, may the force be with you."

"I'm betting on ATIS."

"The Advanced Traveler Information System?" Philips said, laughing. "That program ain't worth a shit. It's broken most of the time. Another waste of time and money."

"The Department of Transportation made some upgrades, Mr. Cynical. All the cameras, streaming and still images—especially the ones placed around Greater New York—have this new software that allegedly kicks ass."

"Fuck Big Brother." Matthew Philips laughed again, then terminated the call.

Manhattan

Jamar Hightower set his BlackBerry on the glass coffee table and turned to Lawrence Luther Wright. "The cops located Biasucci's Corvette in a Bronx chop shop on Tremont."

The two men sat in a tastefully decorated Manhattan penthouse, ten stories above Fifth Avenue. It had a breathtaking view of Central Park. The living room was adorned in black and white, with the only bright colors emerging from Jamar's red scarf and the image from the sixty-inch flat-screen television mounted on the white wall. Both men had been watching the first few minutes of the Jets-Patriots game.

Lawrence Luther grabbed the remote, and the TV winked off. "Any names?"

Jamar read his notes. "Jerome Brice and Thurman Thompson—teenagers who like shiny cars and personal property that don't belong to them."

"And?"

"Seems the cops want to have a word with these gentlemen—same as us."

Standing up from his white leather sofa, Lawrence Luther crossed the white Persian carpet and studied his pencil sketch of the Manhattan skyline, which he'd placed on an easel. He reflected on the satisfaction the simple artwork brought him. The hobby had become not only a passion, but also a necessary outlet from the constant pressures of his worklife. "'They promise them freedom, but they themselves are slaves of corruption; whatever overcomes a person, to that he is enslaved.' Peter, chapter two, verse nineteen."

Jamar looked over at his boss, puzzled. "Did you say something?"

"Just talking to myself." Lawrence Luther scratched his cheek and said, "Any more on this Pebbles girl?"

"Paula Ward," Jamar said. "Sixteen years old. Lived out on the Island up until about a year ago. Your typical suburban kid—parents divorced, daughter turns to coke, acquires a taste for crack, then finds an easy way to support her habit."

"How very sad," Lawrence Luther said tonelessly. He turned from his sketch and pointed a manicured finger at his closest associate. "I want them all, Jamar . . . before the police. Before anyone has a chance to talk to them. I want to make myself perfectly clear."

"It's being handled."

"And Mr. Brian McGowan? You find anything interesting on him?"

Jamar told Lawrence Luther about the backdraft that nearly killed McGowan. "From what I've been told, it messed up his face pretty bad," he said. "He's basically an independent contractor. Not much of a life. Wife left him after the accident."

"Satan has a special room for people like Mrs. McGowan."

"Praise be to Jesus."

"Can we purchase this man's services?" asked Lawrence Luther. "It might be a good thing to have an inside track on the investigation."

"Doubtful," Jamar said, getting to his feet and buttoning his coat. "McGowan's a Boy Scout. High school athlete, a short stay in college, a tour in Iraq, NYFD for a couple of years, the accident, and this consulting gig. He's making some nice money now."

"And that Detective Nicholas Benedetti?"

Shaking his head, Jamar said, "From what I've learned, he's very clean."

"Where you headed?"

"To visit Mr. Jerome Brice and Mr. Thurman Thompson," said Jamar. "Pit Bull's pulling the car around."

Brooklyn

Even before the twelve-year-old boy had made it the entire five blocks from his family's tenement to the urban playground, he was out of breath from running. He grabbed hold of the wire fence surrounding the basketball court and yelled, "Thurman! Hey, yo . . . yo, Thurman!"

Six teenage kids were playing a pickup game on the wet pavement. A tall, cadaverously thin boy wearing an oversized Lakers jersey, Kobe Bryant's number twenty-four on the front, took a shot five feet beyond the three-point line. The ball clanked harmlessly off the bent rim. "Shut your pie hole, you punk-ass bitch!" he shouted in a high-pitched whine. "Can't you see I'm workin' over here?"

"Cops wanna talk to you, Thurm," the boy said, glancing furtively over his shoulder, as if being followed by some dangerous predator. "They was at your momma's place. They asking questions 'bout you."

Thurman adjusted his Lakers cap but didn't appear all that concerned. Looking over at his best friend, Jerome Brice, he said, "What's up with this shit?"

Jerome, a squat, round-faced tenth-grade dropout, stuck his hands deep into his green cargo pants, then shook his head. "Don't know."

Ten feet from the basketball court, a silver Cadillac STS came to a stop at the curb. One of the players pointed it out, and everyone's attention momentarily shifted, their ball rolling harmlessly to the fence.

Two very big, well-dressed black men with nasty scowls exited the Caddy. A third, his hair in long dreadlocks, slid from the passenger seat, and there was absolutely no question he was the one in charge.

Jamar Hightower wore a black leather coat that touched the top of his Bruno Magli shoes. His red scarf fluttered in the cold breeze.

The twelve-year-old boy took flight, disappearing around the corner of a brick building without so much as a backward glance.

"Be cool," Thurman said, barely above a whisper. "I can handle—"

"Bite my bag," Jerome said quietly, his voice both nervous and impressed. "You see the bulge under that brutha's jacket? Got himself a hand cannon."

The three men strolled onto the basketball court as if they were entering a Fortune 500 boardroom, but this wasn't a hostile takeover—this was a shakedown, and all the kids seemed to sense trouble.

"Afternoon, ladies," said Jamar pleasantly. "Looks like you're all busy this fine afternoon, so I'll get right to the point." He jerked a thumb toward his two associates. "Me and my friends are looking for Thurman Thompson and Jerome

Brice. I was told they'd be on this court playing some hoops. Can you help me out?"

"Don't ring a bell," Thurman said, glancing at his ragtag group of friends.

They all nodded rapidly. Too rapidly. Mumbles of agreement followed.

Sighing regretfully, Jamar said, "Always the hard way. You boys ever hear of Mr. Lawrence Luther Wright?"

It was as if the fear of God swept onto the basketball court with a bitter wind. Lawrence Luther Wright had a reputation as vicious. Six sets of eyes grew wide. A few of the players turned to stone, while the others nervously shuffled their feet as if they meant to bolt. One of the bodyguards, Weekend, stood between the group of boys and the exit. Scaling the fence was the only option, and not particularly realistic.

"Don't know any Thurman," Jerome said, crossing his arms defiantly over his thick chest. "Or Jerome Brice. You musta got the wrong street, wrong court. Yeah, that's the problem here. Maybe these guys are over on—"

"I believe he's lying, Pit Bull," said Jamar, looking over at his colleague. "What do you think?"

The grim-faced man, who resembled a professional wrestler on steroids, leisurely wiped the dampness from his large bald head with a handkerchief, then smoothly removed his Browning Hi-Power handgun from his shoulder harness. He took two giant steps toward Jerome, grabbed hold of the boy's flabby forearm, and pressed the muzzle against his left eye. The teenager whimpered like a terrified puppy.

"I think you're *all* lying!" Jamar shouted, arms outstretched like a Baptist minister addressing his rapt Sunday parishioners. He walked over to Thurman and pulled him close. "My brutha, my brutha, you sure as shit don't look like the Kobe Bryant I saw at Madison Square Garden a few weeks ago. But you're wearing Kobe's number. That ain't cool."

Thompson opened his mouth, but nothing came out.

"Boy," Jamar said, "you're too damn short and too damn skinny to be Kobe. And no way on God's green earth do you play ball like my man Kobe. And what's with the name on the back of your jersey? 'Thompson'? Is that maybe a misprint?"

"I . . . I borrowed it." Thurman's nearly inaudible voice trembled.

"Kobe," Jamar said, letting the name draw out, "it's probably in your best interest to be straight with me, or your teammate is gonna lose more than just an eyeball."

"Why . . . why you guys lookin' for those kids?" Thurman stammered.

"Who said anything about them being kids?" Jamar said, a condescending smile stretching across his darkening face.

"I . . . I mean—"

"Mr. Thompson and Mr. Brice may have witnessed a serious crime—one Mr. Wright has an interest in," Jamar said. "We're lookin' for their help. Very simple."

Thurman cleared his throat. "Crime?"

"Murder. A white boy—an associate of ours—got himself shot dead at the Sunset Inn Motel, and we would like to understand why that unfortunate incident happened, maybe even find out who did such a wicked thing. We can even dig up a little reward money if that helps overcome any memory loss."

Some of the kids took quick glances at the chain-link fence, weighing their chances. Except for Jerome, who still had a gun in his face, all seemed to gravitate closer to one another, like a flock of sheep confronted by hungry wolves.

"Ladies, I can assure you that Mr. Wright would greatly appreciate your assistance," said Jamar. He now held a thick wad of money in the palm of his hand. He peeled off a one hundred-dollar bill. "Any takers?"

Jerome pulled away from Pit Bull. "A guy in a Yankees baseball cap gave us fifty bucks to steal the ride . . . the Corvette, I mean, but we didn't murder nobody," he said. "Man, I don't even own no gun. Neither does Thurm. The guy who gave us the cash—he gots to be the one who smoked your buddy. He was a Chinese dude—the one who paid us, that is."

Thurman shot his friend a murderous glance.

Smiling, Jamar said, "Winner, winner, we got ourselves a chicken dinner."

Pit Bull holstered his nine millimeter.

"Chinese dude?" Jamar shoved the money back into his coat pocket.

"Chinese, Jap, Korean. He was Asian," Jerome said, looking back over his shoulder. "Told us there was a bunch of coke in the car, too. He lied. Ain't that right, Thurm?"

Thurman said nothing.

"Kobe, so help me God, you're gonna talk," Jamar said, grabbing Thurman by the ear, "or I'll cut your balls off and mail them to your momma for an early Christmas present. You think she'd like that? Huh?"

Thurman shook his head. "No, sir."

"As for the rest of you chumps," Jamar said, "go home and read a book. Start with the Bible. Make yourselves useful. And ease off the violent video games."

Pit Bull chuckled.

He and Weekend dragged Thurman Thompson and Jerome Brice to the idling Caddy. The rest of the boys sprinted for the exit.

CHAPTER 32
Brooklyn Heights

Anthony DiFilippo sat alone in his Brooklyn Heights brownstone on Montague Street watching the third quarter of the Jets-Patriots game, hoping to temporarily step away from the problems he couldn't solve, at least not without further information. The quiet neighborhood, with its stone sidewalks and tree-lined streets, had been declared a historic district in November 1965. It had a spectacular view of the Manhattan skyline, New York Harbor, and the Brooklyn Bridge. And with neighbors like Mary Tyler Moore, Gabriel Byrne, Jennifer Connelly, and Bob Dylan, Tony D wasn't the only celebrity to be seen walking the streets on a warm summer evening, although he was considered the most infamous.

Three heavy raps on the wooden door returned Tony D to his immediate concerns, and he hoped his expected guest might shine some light on this mess. Muting the TV, he rose from his La-Z-Boy, tightened his bathrobe belt, and shuffled across the marble floor into the front foyer. He pulled the door open. "Come in, my friend," he said, smiling warmly.

Louis "Lady Luck" Ciambella had aged over the past week—the don could see that immediately. According to Mara, Tony D wasn't looking any better himself. Death—especially one's own—could wear on a man, and the nightmares had taken their toll.

Perhaps Ciambella was having nightmares, too. His brown eyes were rimmed in red, and his leathery features appeared frozen in a tight grip of debilitating anxiety.

"Tony," he said, "I would never have bothered you and Mrs. D, especially on a Sunday—"

"Mara's Christmas-shopping with her sister. It's not a problem."

"Really, Boss, if I didn't think it was important—"

"I could use some company," the don said with a shrug.

Stepping beneath the massive crystal chandelier that hung from a gabled ceiling two stories above, Ciambella closed the door and pulled a legal envelope from the inside pocket of his overcoat.

The don scrutinized the white envelope before accepting it. A name was printed neatly in blue ink across the front: "ANTHONY DIFILIPPO." He coughed, grimaced, and even touched his chest, albeit briefly.

"You should get that checked out, Tony," said Ciambella. "The cancer is going around these days, y'know—especially in Queens. Some say it's the water."

"Cancer's got bigger fish to fry, Louis," said Tony D, putting a reassuring hand on his friend's shoulder. "What have you got here?"

"About forty minutes ago, these three black fellas—two as big as Mack diesels—delivered this envelope to my house," said Ciambella. "My neighbor, Barney, he was scared stiff when he saw them coming up the driveway. The cowardly wop actually hid in his tool shed until they left. Anyways, one did all the talkin'—long dreadlocks, dressed like a businessman, polite. Said the letter had something to do with Woody's hit and the other problems we was havin' lately. He insisted I deliver this to you . . . immediately."

"What did you tell these unexpected visitors?"

"I said it don't work that way."

Chuckling quietly, Tony D nodded and said, "But here you are, nonetheless."

"Because Mr. Dreadlocks said the note was from Lawrence Luther Wright. That got my attention in a hurry."

Tony D considered this for a long moment. Just when you think you have your opponents figured out, a blitzing linebacker blindsides you.

"He said you'd do the right thing, Tony," Ciambella said. "That's what the guy with the dreadlocks told me."

"Take off your coat, Louis." The don coughed again. "Let me get you a glass of wine. You look like you've seen Satan himself."

"Satan ain't as big as them two, that's for sure. They was huge, Tony!" Ciambella peeled off his overcoat and hung it on the tree rack beside the antique grandfather clock. Two fedoras—one brown, the other black—hung beside the coat.

"Watch a little football," said Tony D. "The Jets look pretty good today. Do you have any money on the game?"

"You know I don't gamble no more, Tony." Ciambella grinned. "Ponies and dogs are mostly a sure thing."

"Of course they are. It's good to see you still have your sense of humor. I'll be right back."

Louis Ciambella sat on the blue-and-white-striped loveseat, his hands nervously fidgeting. He glanced briefly at Tony D's old gun collection, locked up behind thick glass. The football game remained muted.

A few minutes later, Tony D returned to the family room, which was adorned with Victorian era antiques. He handed Ciambella a glass of Shiraz. "To lost friends. *Salud*," he said to his captain. They each took a long swallow of the red wine. The don set his glass on the coffee table next to his favorite chair, then pulled the envelope from his bathrobe pocket. "Tell me what you make of this, Louis."

The envelope had been opened.

Ciambella took the note from his boss's fingers and silently read the neat printing:

Dear Mr. DiFilippo,

It's obvious we share a problem. Such senseless murders. Some unknown person has assaulted me as well. As you may know, one of my properties was destroyed early Saturday morning. Sir, this was not the work of a typical arsonist. A pro, with knowledge of explosives, had his hand in this.

Maybe we can help one another. You have a reputation for being a reasonable man. Call me on my cell: 203-555-9890.

I may have answers to our common questions.

God Bless,
Lawrence Luther Wright

Ciambella looked up when he was done reading.

Tony D met his gaze. "Your first thoughts, Louis?"

"I think Lawrence Luther Wright is a smart man."

"Why do you say that?"

"Because he's either setting a very sophisticated trap for you, or he's close to figuring out who murdered Paulie, Johnny, and Woody," said Ciambella, spreading his hands. "I choose the second option."

The don patted Ciambella on the shoulder. "I happen to agree."

"So . . . what are we gonna do, Tony?"

The hunter parked the stolen Ford Explorer on Pierrepont Place, two blocks from Anthony DiFilippo's brownstone, and swapped out the license plates he'd stolen in New Jersey. Double-knotting his Nike cross trainers, he zipped up his blue windbreaker, then started an easy jog through the historic residential neighborhood in the shadow of the Brooklyn Bridge. It was nearly three o'clock on Sunday afternoon, and though it was cold, the sidewalks were busy with people enjoying the sunny, crisp day.

Turning the corner, the hunter could see Louis Ciambella's black Hummer H2 parked at the curb in front of DiFilippo's home. A BMW 740L was also on the street. He could barely make out the two men—Tony D's bodyguards—sitting in the front seat of a Ford Taurus.

Directly across the street was a dark blue Plymouth sedan with two more men. Embers from a lighted cigarette were visible on the driver's side. After weeks of reconnaissance, performed with no fewer than four disguises, the hunter knew they were undercover cops, assigned not only to keep a watchful eye on the don's movements, but also to add an additional level of protection to the affluent neighborhood. On one particular run, the hunter—masquerading as an Asian man, just as he'd done during Biasucci's execution at the Sunset Inn Motel—had even seen the good guys and bad guys engaged in a friendly chat under a streetlight.

Except for Ciambella's sense of urgency, very little of this concerned the hunter. He'd been outside the *caporegime's* modest two-story home in Queens when the three men had visited. The hunter, about two hundred feet from the meeting, had just finished his task and was about to leave.

Through binoculars, wedged between some foul-smelling garbage cans, he'd recognized everyone on Ciambella's front porch. The conversation was brief. The man with the dreadlocks wore a red scarf. His name was Jamar Hightower, and he happened to be Lawrence Luther Wright's go-to guy. Jamar did all the talking. Pit Bull and Weekend stood quietly in the background. A white envelope was passed from Hightower to Ciambella.

Minutes after the silver Cadillac sedan left his Queens neighborhood, Ciambella pulled away from the curb in his Hummer.

Now, the hunter, ignoring the puddles from the preceding night, jogged past DiFilippo's brownstone, though his gaze took in all the players. His presence alarmed nobody, and he found this curious, especially because three of Tony D's key people had been murdered in the past week. He turned right at Montague Avenue, picked up his pace, and headed back to the stolen Ford. Starting the SUV, he retraced the path he'd just run.

Ciambella's SUV was now gone.

"Shit!" The hunter cursed himself for being too slow. He'd wanted Ciambella's Hummer to be parked right outside the DiFilippos' home—bigger bang for the buck.

So, instead of finding and eliminating tonight's primary target right now, the hunter headed back to his Fordham Avenue apartment, hoping the voice-activated bug planted in Tony D's fedora had picked up the contents of Lawrence Luther Wright's message.

Brooklyn

The persistent nightmare was in color now that Hatch had returned to New York City. In his dream, he opened his mouth and screamed for help, but no noise was emitted. It was like drowning in oil, he thought. He lunged at the young man—he'd been told his name was Vincent Tagliafero—who held the pistol in his shaky hand. The gun was pointed at Karen. In excruciatingly slow motion, a bright while flash bloomed from the muzzle, and the bullet punched through the stale air.

Every morning when he awoke, Hatch felt he was another second closer than in the preceding night's vivid dream, but still hundredths of a second too late—an eternity that separated life from death—as the .38-caliber slug struck Karen in the head, and a pinkish mist splashed across the mirror behind the ornate bar. Always, Hatch caught his wife before she crumpled to the wooden floor inside Rudy's Tavern. He held her in his arms, gazing into her dull blue eyes, knowing that his own life would never be the same.

In a tiny voice that resembled a child's, Karen whispered the words that had driven him to the brink of madness these past few months, words that had forced him to reëvaluate his existence in this world—wisdom that he couldn't ignore any more than he could change the color of his skin.

"Patty loved him the way I still love you, Little Crow." Through bloodstained teeth, Karen had repeated this cryptic message every night since Hatch had learned about her murder. And each time, Karen had smiled the moment before she'd closed her eyes and died in his arms.

Patty loved him the way I still love you, Little Crow.

"Who?" Hatch asked his dead wife each morning. "Help me out here, Karen."

Because of the Taylors' unexpected visit, because they'd not so subtly questioned his role in the New York City murders these past few days, because Steven was unaccounted for, and because of the Cajun Moon roses, Hatch thought he understood the meaning behind Karen's peculiar message. More importantly, he realized once again where his life was headed. He'd found purpose.

Hatch had visited Low Dog in the hospital on Sunday morning and told the elderly shaman he was leaving. He wouldn't say for how long or where he was headed and Low Dog knew better than to ask.

"Evil comes in many faces, Little Crow," the old man said quietly, sadly, as if he'd never see his grandson again.

"Yes it does, Grandfather."

There was no heavy embrace, or firm handshake, or even a gentle kiss on the cheek. And Hatch was out the hospital door, angrily swiping a tear from the corner of his eye, suspecting no good would come of his journey.

By noon, Hatch had packed his gear into the Pathfinder. He was headed east on Route 86, the bright afternoon sun in his eyes, the CD player empty; he needed this time to formulate a plan. The trip between the Cattaraugus Indian Reservation to New York City was about four hundred miles. By 10:45 p.m., a handwritten note had been personally delivered to a friend.

The hunt for Steven had begun.

CHAPTER 33

Manhattan

G ray Taylor tossed his overnight bag into the walk-in closet, then kissed Terri on the lips. Like a felled tree, she toppled onto their king-sized bed. It had been a long, exhausting, and exhilarating two days—a trip both had agreed on while driving over the George Washington Bridge, with the breathtaking Manhattan skyline to their right.

Instead of coming directly home late Sunday morning, they'd stayed at Niagara-on-the-Lake in Ontario, Canada. They'd toured a winery, visited Casino Niagara (which had turned into the Seneca Indians' featured gaming property), had a spectacular Italian meal overlooking the lighted falls, then made love back at their bed and breakfast, the Post House Inn.

Still wired from the seven-hour drive, Taylor said, "I'm gonna catch the local news, maybe ESPN. Don't wait up." He laughed.

"Turn off the light, Mr. Happy," Terri said, pulling the comforter over her head.

"Anything for my queen."

A mumbled response came from beneath the blankets.

"I'll let that one slide, Your Grace." Taylor closed the door.

A moment later, Taylor flicked the wall switch and the kitchen's bank of fluorescent lights popped on. He was immediately drawn to the handwritten note sitting on the marble countertop near the toaster. Bending at the waist, he read the words without touching the paper:

This is not your problem, Gray.
Stay out of it. I'd hate to see you get hurt.
The same goes for Jack and his people.
I appreciate your concern, but you can't help.—Hatch

Kevin Easter had not only returned to New York City since their visit to the reservation, but he'd actually broken into the fortress of the Dakota. *This is not your problem, Gray.* What exactly did that mean? *Of course it's my problem. For Christ's sake, Hatch, you just made it my problem.*

Were Steven and Hatch in this together? Why the warning? Had visiting Hatch triggered something? Apparently so.

Rubbing his unshaven chin, Taylor looked at his watch: 11:03 p.m. There was a great deal to think about before phoning Jack. "What should I tell him?" he said aloud. *What exactly is the truth? Should I wake Terri?*

With questions outnumbering answers, Gray Taylor sat back in his overstuffed leather chair, turned on the TV, and powered up his PC. The up-to-the-minute news scrolling across the bottom of his flat screen caught his attention. "Jesus," he muttered. Taylor pointed the remote at the TV. The ABC affiliate returned to the local news.

"And this late-breaking development," the anchorman said in a deep, authoritative voice, "is being streamed to us live from a residential neighborhood in Queens. It appears as if an explosion has killed . . ."

Increasing the volume, Taylor slid to the front of his chair after he heard the name Anthony DiFilippo.

The dark-haired anchorman with unnaturally white teeth continued with the story as the live video focused on the charred remains of a late-model Hummer H2—one that had been owned by Louis Ciambella, a *caporegime* in the DiFilippo crime family. The smoldering wreckage, parked in the driveway of a modest two-story home, was now bathed in the glow of the NYPD's halogen lights, there to assist the CSI team. Because the explosion and fire had been so intense, it wasn't certain how many people had died in the attack.

The anchorman went on: "Mrs. Cathy Ciambella has reportedly told investigators that her husband, Louis, returned home around nine-fifteen this evening. Sitting in his parked SUV, he was apparently having a conversation on his cell phone when the explosion took place. Eyewitnesses, including a neighbor, Mr. Barney Santorelli, said the immediate area shook as if there had been an earthquake, and a fireball climbed more than thirty feet into the sky."

"Fuck," Taylor said through clenched teeth. He pressed the TV remote, and the CBS news affiliate replayed much of the same story, adding no new details.

There was another clip of the twisted steel and smoldering upholstery. "This is the fourth member of Anthony DiFilippo's organization to be killed since the day before Thanksgiving," an attractive brunette reporter said with a frown that looked strangely like a smile. She was live from Ciambella's driveway. In the background, firemen sprayed water on a hot spot.

"Thank you, Lauren. Sports is next," said the reporter's colleague back at the station. "When we return, Mike will tell us how the Jets and Giants—"

Taylor turned off the television. He took in a deep, cleansing breath, then slowly exhaled. He got up from his chair, crossed the carpeted room, and looked out the window into Central Park. A full moon hung in the southeastern sky. "Hatch, I have a feeling this is gonna get nasty . . . for both of us."

CHAPTER 34

Brooklyn

Lawrence Luther Wright slid into the backseat of the BMW 740L. A thick-necked Italian man in a fashionable dark suit closed the heavy door behind him. The dome light slowly dimmed, leaving both Lawrence Luther and Anthony DiFilippo waiting in the car, bathed in the moon's glow.

"When I was a boy," Tony D said reflectively, "me and my friends came here almost every day in the summer. It was like a second home." The don cleared his throat and looked out the window at the Coney Island Amusement Park, now closed for the season. "I loved it here."

A few roller coasters rose into a black, ominous sky, and the full moon hung over the Long Island Sound like a giant illuminated plate. The beach was deserted, and all the concession stands were boarded up. Trash and leaves skidded across the lot with the stiff easterly breeze.

"I actually lost my virginity in the back of my best friend's Mustang convertible over in that parking lot."

Lawrence Luther slowly turned his head to follow Tony D's outstretched arm. He remained respectfully quiet. He knew he was safe, even though the don's bodyguard—Marco was his name—had taken his handgun. Three of his own men, including Jamar, were in the recently purchased Mercedes G500 SUV parked behind the BMW. Two more of his people were hidden in the same amusement park the old man quietly reminisced about.

Turning his body to face his guest, Tony D said, "My best friend, the one who owned the Mustang, was Paulie Franco. All those Coney dogs probably contributed to his nickname. I'm going to miss him, Mr. Wright. Life was a whole lot easier when I was a kid."

"Not for me," Lawrence Luther said without hesitation.

"I appreciate your candor." The don coughed into a linen handkerchief. "I also appreciate your reaching out to me."

Although they were rivals in some areas, they respected one another. It was never easy being a leader of men, regardless of one's goals or business model. One needed to experience the job to firmly grasp the pressure and isolation.

"Thank you for coming, especially on such short notice," Lawrence Luther said.

"We share a problem, you think?"

"Yes, sir."

"Why would you believe such a thing?"

"A few nights ago, somebody planted bombs under both my Mercedes Benz and a building I own in Harlem—military-grade C-4 with sophisticated detonators, one of which survived the explosion."

"Yes, I read about the fire in the newspaper."

"Sir, the man responsible for these attacks taunted me. He said, 'That's for Johnny and Fat Paulie,'" Lawrence Luther said. "This man circumvented a very elaborate security system, including armed sentries and nearly twenty employees. He called my private cell number and counted down the seconds before my facility blew up. And he gave my people enough time to clear the building, which still puzzles me."

Tony D's eyebrows pinched together. "Michael Testa, who was Paulie's bodyguard, got himself a concussion and his feelings hurt, but nothing worse. I'm still not sure why he was allowed to live."

"The media got that story right, then."

Nodding, Tony D said, "Why should you doubt this bomber's statement? Why not put a bullet through my head and be done with it?"

"Because I'm fairly certain you had nothing to do with the attack, Mr. DiFilippo," said Lawrence Luther. "Sir, it's not your style. Someone is playing us. We're both veterans of the streets. We're educated men. We know that any serious conflict disrupts business. Frankly, I'm in this to make money—lots of money. Again, forgive me if I've stepped over a line by assuming anything, but I suspect you have a similar mindset. This man—"

"I think of him as a ghost," Tony D said quietly.

"Sir, yes, this *ghost* wants us at war against one another."

"Why?"

"The *why* doesn't concern me, Mr. DiFilippo. It's the *who*. I want him—and anyone associated with him. I want them dead before others are pulled into the fight, which seems like the natural course of events."

"When you refer to others, are you speculating?"

"No, sir. I've had some of my most reliable people asking a lot of questions. It appears as though a few key members of some local gangs have also been killed by different means," said Lawrence Luther. "The news organizations are not so fast to report on some nameless figure, especially a minority. Your organization gets all the ink because the Sicilian Mafia is always an intriguing subject."

"Raise your flag and somebody is bound to shoot it down," Tony D said. "I've never sought notoriety. My predecessors learned the hard way."

"A Gangster Disciple leader was stabbed in the heart this morning," said Lawrence Luther. "His girlfriend found him in bed that way when she got up for church. Our ghost identified, targeted, hunted, and murdered this man. I'm sure of it. The Latin Kings report they've had some trouble, too, but won't discuss the details. Even Los Solidos and the Ñetas have incurred casualties, and now they're beginning to think *your* organization may be behind it."

"Why me?"

"Some believe you're retaliating for the murders of Cercone, Franco, and Biasucci—"

"I've given no such orders," the don said, an edge to his voice. "And none of my men would be stupid enough to move against—"

"Sir," Lawrence Luther said, raising one hand, "I think we're both victims here. I also think this is only the beginning. If we can put an end to this before our ghost gets up a head of steam—"

Tony D's cell phone rang. He narrowed his eyes. "Please excuse me for just one moment. Very few have this number."

Though apparently irritated by the intrusion, Lawrence Luther nodded.

Tony D pressed the *send* button and put the phone to his ear. "Yes?" A long pause while he listened. "Please . . . Mara, please calm down." Another pause, and the don shifted his weight. "Yes, I did hear you. I'll send some people to your sister's house as soon as I hang up. They'll stay outside in the driveway. Don't leave. Yes, I'm safe. I'll be there within the hour." He folded up the phone.

Lawrence Luther remained quiet. The don appeared to consider his words. "My good friend, Louis Ciambella—his SUV was blown up," Tony D said quietly. "According to my wife, it's all over the news. She thought maybe I was in the truck with him."

"Is he okay?"

"Witnesses say Louis was in the vehicle when the explosion took place."

"I'm sorry, Mr. DiFilippo."

"I need one moment to make a call."

"Take as much time as you need."

When the don was finished making arrangements to have his wife protected, he folded the cell phone closed and slipped it back into his pants pocket. His voice was strong, businesslike again. "I believe Louis's death reinforces your theory, Mr. Wright."

Lawrence Luther said nothing.

Tony D's gaze moved over the Long Island Sound. "The police are looking for two teenage boys from the Bronx. Do you know anything about this?"

"Jerome Brice and Thurman Thompson. I've had a heart-to-heart with both."

"We've been looking for them, along with the young prostitute who had been with Woody."

"Her real name is Paula Ward, a high-school dropout from Ronkonkoma."

"That much I knew," Tony D said, frowning. "Mr. Wright, you seem to be one step ahead of me and the authorities."

"Brice and Thompson say that an Asian guy with a gray driving cap and brown leather jacket paid them to steal Mr. Biasucci's Corvette minutes before your man was murdered. Biasucci was with Ms. Ward—Pebbles—when our ghost interrupted them."

Tony D cleared his throat. "So these young boys were used as a diversion?"

"Yes, sir. They had no idea they were being played."

"Do you think an Asian gang brought in some outside talent?" Tony D asked, turning back to look at Lawrence Luther.

"Of all the New York gangs, the Akrho Pinoy, who started in L.A., would have the easiest access to a professional like this," Lawrence Luther said. "They're flush with cash from the lucrative heroin market, and they've had their eyes on the New York City market for years. They're in Boston and Providence already."

"I had been leaning toward the Russians," Tony D said with a shrug. "But why target my people when we have nothing to do with illegal drugs?"

"That I couldn't answer."

"And for what purpose? Why so aggressive?"

"Why did Hitler try to take over the world, Mr. DiFilippo? It's all about power."

But Tony D also thought about a recent conversation he'd had with his detective friend. A white Ford Explorer had been identified as the vehicle the ghost had used after murdering Biasucci. They'd caught a break with the Department of Transportation cameras, and were hoping for a lot more help on Monday morning. Nevertheless, something tugged at him like a fishhook in his brain. What was really going on here?

"Maybe it's something we've missed," Tony D said, tapping his fingernail against the window.

"I'm not sure I know what you mean."

"Some unknown organization hires a professional killer," said Tony D. "They intend to start a war, targeting my organization, blaming me for any type of retaliation, and then they drag you into it. When the shooting stops, they pick up the pieces."

"We're big targets."

"Apparently so. And you say others have been attacked."

"I'm not one for handing out advice, but I'd be careful if I were you, Mr. DiFilippo."

For a long moment, both men sat in silence, digesting all the information.

Tony D finally said, "So, my new friend, what do we do about this ghost?"

Smiling ruefully, Lawrence Luther Wright said, "Sir, I'm glad you asked."

CHAPTER 35

Brooklyn

Standing in the front yard of Louis Ciambella's neighbor, B. J. Butera dropped to one knee and studied a charred piece of something he suspected came from the Hummer H2. It looked like a part from the transmission or the steering gear, or maybe it was a piece of the suspension. The damage was too extensive for his untrained eye.

B. J. turned to the photographer who'd been assigned to him. "Tommy, does this smell funny to you?"

Tom Whieldon, a young intern from New York University holding a digital Nikon, crouched, wrinkled his nose, and said, "Yeah, like something my dad might burn on the grill."

B. J. jumped back as if he'd just been burned himself. "Shit, is that a bone?"

Whieldon, moving away from the blackened object, dragged his fingers through his long blond hair and said, "Dude, you're kidding me, right?"

B. J. pulled a pen from the inside pocket of his leather jacket and poked at the three-inch-long object, which resembled a branch. "Oh, man, for a second there, I really thought I was gonna lose my breakfast," he said. "It's steel. Christ. Has to be from the goddamned Hummer."

"Breakfast?" Whieldon said. "Hell, B. J., it's four in the morning. I just got back from an all-night kegger." He focused his expensive camera on Ciambella's neighbors, who were huddled near the road behind the yellow crime scene tape, and fired off another half dozen shots.

"Hey, get the hell out of my fucking yard, you little bastards!" Barney Santorelli shouted from his front porch.

"Sorry!" B. J. yelled, heading back onto the street, Tommy trailing.

"Could the guy at least put on some pants?" Tommy said under his breath.

Onlookers watched the CSI team, two detectives, and the television crew go about their jobs. The NBC affiliate was set to broadcast during the early morning show. The white van with the multicolored peacock painted on both sides had a satellite dish mounted on the roof.

Many of the curious had gotten cold, and the crowd had thinned in the past hour. Some griped that this crime scene wasn't as exciting as those on television. Others drew their own conclusions about Louis "Lady Luck" Ciambella's violent death. The bomb theory had taken first prize.

"I love the smell of napalm in the morning," B. J. said, chuckling.

Whieldon lowered his camera. "Huh?"

"Kids," B. J. said, shaking his head. "Goddamned punk-ass computer generation with no appreciation for history. Please tell me you've heard of Francis Ford Coppola."

"Oh, sure, he makes great linguini," Tommy said, grinning.

"Asshole," B. J. murmured.

For the benefit of a young forensic technician, the chief criminalist assigned to the case pointed out a specific hunk of charred SUV about fifty feet from the hole in Ciambella's blacktopped driveway. Detective Katherine Montroy sipped something hot from a Starbucks cup while conversing animatedly with Brian McGowan, also assigned to the explosion. Matthew Philips stood next to an NYPD photographer, who took about ten shots of the undercarriage, which now hung precariously in the lower branches of the Santorellis' maple tree. The residential street was blocked off in both directions, but that didn't stop a steady stream of sightseers.

"It's like déjà vu all over again!" B. J. yelled from behind the yellow tape once Detective Montroy had walked away. "New York's finest keepin' you occupied, Brian?"

"Busier than that stupid Energizer Bunny!" McGowan shouted back. He walked over and shook B. J.'s hand. "I shit you not, this city is absolutely, positively going to hell. Maybe moving back wasn't such a bright idea."

"This *is* hell, brother. Didn't you get the memo?" For a quick moment, B. J. found himself staring at the purplish, lumpy flesh on McGowan's face and neck, but McGowan, who looked exhausted, didn't notice or didn't care.

"Memo?" McGowan laughed. "Not bad, B. J."

"Anything attention-grabbing for this reporter to report?"

"An obliterated Hummer H2, pieces of the driver in his front yard, nosy neighbors, and a bitchy detective who apparently doesn't want to be here." McGowan smirked. "Breakfast of champions."

"Maybe Detective Montroy is feeling pressure from the brass."

"Hey, Brian!" Katherine Montroy yelled from Ciambella's front door.

McGowan turned around, then placed a hand to his ear. "Me?"

"Get Mr. Cub Reporter off the property," Montroy shouted, "or I'll have him arrested for trespassing!"

"You got it." McGowan turned and smiled. "Looks like you two are old friends."

"We've been assigned to some of the same crap over the last few months. You know the saying: One man's garbage is another man's treasure."

"And you're the trash collector?" McGowan said, grabbing his friend by the elbow.

"So why the funny face, Brian?" Butera asked once they'd slid under the crime scene tape. "You swallow another canary?"

"We're still off the record, right?"

"C'mon, man, have you ever seen anything in the paper or on the website about any of—"

"The short version," whispered McGowan, "is this looks like the same bomber from the Harlem warehouse. It's way early, but the blast has a C-4 footprint, and it smells exactly like the stuff that came from the drug lab. I took residue samples, even found brown plastic pieces that look strangely familiar. Sorry, no detonator this time—nobody can get that lucky twice."

"Have you identified the other one?"

Shaking his head, McGowan said, "At first I thought it was Israeli-made. But it's only a great knockoff."

"What does that mean?"

"Think of it as an aftermarket car or truck part," said McGowan. "You have OE, original equipment, and companies who copy the OE. That's what we got here."

"Like generic medicine?"

"Exactly."

"Can I go on the record with that?"

"Not yet," said McGowan, briefly glancing back over his shoulder. "Soon."

"Okay, so this has to be a power grab, right? Somebody's looking to expand their criminal empire?"

"I'm no expert when it comes to the underworld, but this guy seems to be plugged into organized crime's key players," said McGowan. "Lawrence Luther Wright, the badass drug kingpin, owned the Harlem building, and Louis Ciambella, a.k.a. Anthony DiFilippo's captain, won't be eating ravioli at his momma's house tonight."

"Listen to you, all cynical and sarcastic about this perfect world we live in. Damn, it's good to have you back, Brian."

McGowan leaned closer to B. J. and whispered, "Ciambella and his dead colleagues didn't make their money selling wholesale plumbing supplies, and we all know it. My man, let's not fool ourselves here. These people kill, extort, and intimidate for a living."

"But, shit, nobody deserves to die like this guy did."

McGowan didn't respond.

B. J. narrowed his eyes. "Hey, you're sitting on something, big fella. I can tell."

"Last night," McGowan said, "a smaller bomb took out an abandoned building in Long Island City, but not enough to damage the neighbors' houses. This time it wasn't C-4. Good old-fashioned dynamite. A gang called the Ñetas, another player in the trafficking of coke, allegedly took over the property a few months ago. It was their base of operations."

"So somebody decided to strike back? Is that what you're thinking?"

Pursing his lips, McGowan shrugged. "Don't know yet."

"Ciambella's background, Lawrence Luther, the Ñetas—how do you know all this?" asked B. J.

"Everyone at a crime scene talks too much," said McGowan. "Nick Benedetti is pulling things together. Detectives Montroy and Philips are involved, too."

"What else?"

"Ciambella makes four by my count on the Tony D side of the ledger sheet."

B. J. lightly grabbed his friend by the arm, guided him past his parked Volvo, and escorted him behind a giant oak tree near the road. "Seriously, Brian, let me run with this story," he pleaded. "You can't be the only one putting two and two together. And Benedetti must have a few pet journalists in his pocket. These criminals are on the verge of war."

"The cops don't have any suspects, B. J., and you might tip off the wrong people," said McGowan. "Is it another mob family, or maybe this Akrho Pinoy gang? Or the Bloods? What about the Triada family in Queens? Just about anybody could have started this fucking thing."

"Akrho Pinoy," B. J. said, committing the unfamiliar name to memory. "Never heard of that one."

"Give me two days—forty-eight hours," McGowan said. "By then I should know a whole lot more about the investigations and how they may or may not be connected. And maybe we'll have some physical evidence to support the story—way more than the detonator. Let the cops do their job."

"Won't you get in trouble for leaking?"

"Let *me* worry about that."

Gloved hands in his coat pockets, his long hair tucked under a dark blue ski hat, Kevin Easter stood outside the yellow crime scene tape with a small group of neighbors and curious onlookers, watching the Louis Ciambella investigation play out. He was beginning to put names with faces. Detective Katherine Montroy, who'd regularly been quoted in the New York newspapers, along with another detective, Matthew Philips. Nick Benedetti. B. J. Butera—Hatch had read his laminated press pass hanging around his neck. Butera and a *New York Post* photographer were now talking to a red-headed arson investigator. He'd yet to get the investigator's name, but overheard bits and pieces of his conversation with Butera. The ugly scars on the redheaded man's neck and face left no doubt he'd been in a terrible accident.

Pieces of the Hummer were scattered over three lawns. *Overkill,* Hatch thought, wondering again if his big brother could really do such a thing.

And then an elderly white-haired woman, frumpy and disheveled, wearing a faded house coat, stepped out of the Ciambella residence. She was being assisted by two very large men, who carried her to a green BMW parked at the curb.

"We love you, Cathy!" a woman next to Hatch shouted to Mrs. Ciambella.

"God bless!" a hoarse male voice called out.

There were other heartfelt words from other concerned neighbors. Cathy Ciambella seemed to hear none of it—and if she did, a response never came as she was delicately guided into the BMW's backseat.

Seconds later, the luxury car sped out of the residential neighborhood.

"Louis was her whole life," said the woman who'd spoken earlier, blotting each eye with a tissue. She started to weep. "And . . . and she's got no children to help her."

"Funniest guy I've ever known," the man said to some of the male onlookers. "The Ciambellas celebrated their thirty-first wedding anniversary last month, and Louis gave Cathy this giant teddy bear . . ."

Hatch's mind drifted back to his own wedding day. The small reception—forty-eight guests attended—followed the brief Catholic ceremony. Because money was short, the party was held at a friend's house in Charlottesville. And except for the weather—two inches of rain had fallen in a twelve-hour period—the day and evening had been perfect. Steven had been the best man; Patty, the maid of honor.

And then the band made the critical mistake of leaving their instruments and equipment unattended while taking a break. The new bride, radiant in her white dress, picked up a violin and started playing the Beatles' "With A Little Help From My Friends."

Patty joined her sister on vocals: "What would you think if I sang out of tune? Would you stand up and walk out on me?"

Steven joined in at the second line: "Lend me your ears and I'll sing you a song, and I'll try not to sing out of key."

And then just about everyone huddled under the backyard tent sang the chorus: "Oh, I get by with a little help from my friends. Mm, I get high with a little help from my friends. Mm, I'm gonna try with a little help from my friends."

"What do I do when my love is away?" Hatch said softly, pulled back to the present, and to Louis Ciambella's gruesome death. The memory brought a genuine smile to his lips. "Until our wedding day, Karen, I didn't even know you played an instrument. You were always full of surprises."

CHAPTER 36

Manhattan

Gray Taylor's sweat-drenched T-shirt clung to his hard body as he moved past the halfway point of a workout begun at 5:30 a.m. The StairMaster, which stood in the middle of their brightly lit home gym, blinked a warning: "HILL CLIMBING IN ONE MINUTE."

His right knee had a partially torn ligament from an especially dangerous job in Calcutta two months earlier, and it had become sore. Ignoring the pain, Taylor pressed a white button on the computerized display panel and pushed harder. A new message appeared: "23 minutes, 15 seconds—421 steps completed. 21 minutes, 45 seconds remaining."

Leveling off at eighteen steps per minute, Taylor wiped his face with the towel hanging around his sweaty neck and renewed his assault on the machine.

WABC radio, a news/talk station focused primarily on sensational stories affecting the Tri-State area, played on the surround-sound speaker system. The famous—particularly local politicians, union officials, and grotesquely overpaid athletes—were not immune from callers' verbal attacks, which included many commuters with an axe to grind.

Although this morning's discussion focused on the mayor and his relatives, who'd purportedly been given cushy government jobs, what interested Taylor most was the news update that came every ten minutes. He'd learned very little since last night's report on the explosion that had obliterated Louis Ciambella's SUV. It had been confirmed that Mr. Ciambella had been sitting alone in the Hummer. Eight hours later, forensic experts were still picking through evidence.

An aggressive ABC reporter asked Detective Matthew Philips if he thought Ciambella's death was related to those of the other members of the DiFilippo crime family.

Philips snorted. "Ma'am, we're obviously looking at everything."

"Some believe this killing spree is coming from a rival family muscling in on Anthony DiFilippo's operation, which allegedly controls the Teamsters at the

Hunts Point Market," said the reporter.

"For Christ's sake, honey, stop making things up," Philips said, exasperated. "Why don't you idiots practice a little patience for a change? A man died here last night. The man had a wife. How about a little respect from your—"

Laughing after the piece was cut short, the morning anchor said to his listeners, "Well, ladies and gentlemen, that's why we have a six-second delay."

"Bravo, Detective Philips," Taylor said, sweat dripping off his face.

"God, I love a man who talks to himself," said Terri. She'd been leaning on the doorframe.

"Ah, the lady of the house is awake," said Taylor, "and she has herself a ponytail, which can only mean game on."

"So what's all this business about another DiFilippo disciple getting himself killed?" Dressed in a Nike sweat suit, Terri climbed aboard the treadmill next to her husband's StairMaster, pressed a few buttons, and started off on an easy jog.

Taylor considered the question, sighed, then told his wife all he knew about Louis Ciambella's violent death—and Hatch's note.

"How the hell did Hatch get into the Dakota?" Terri asked, shaking her head.

"If you see him, please be sure to ask. Nobody let him in."

"Primary suspect or accessory," said Terri firmly, quickening her pace on the treadmill, "I won't—will not—can't believe Hatch is involved in any way in these murders."

"Terri, c'mon. We barely know Kevin Easter."

"Call it women's intuition."

"Have fun explaining away his note," Taylor said, his voice rising. "It's a warning. He wrote, 'This is not your problem, Gray.' How else can you interpret it?"

"He's trying to protect his brother. Period. Why else would Hatch sprint back to New York? This is about family."

"Steven's involvement doesn't make any sense, Ter. What's his motive? Make Hatch feel better? Even with Steven's military background, is he mentally capable of killing so many people?"

"Now you're just being naïve," Terri said, her face darkening and jaw muscles flexing. "You know firsthand what some people are capable of. It only takes a little push in the right direction."

Taylor nodded, understanding.

"Obviously, there are a few exceptions to the rules," Terri said. "Look, I'm not itching for a fight, Gray. I'm just stating the obvious. Our visit set things in motion for Hatch."

Taylor stepped off the StairMaster. "Okay, then, it comes down to a few theories," he said. "Hatch is in the city to stop Steven, or they're in this thing together, or Hatch has another partner he's trying to protect—"

"Your last assumption is ludicrous," Terri said. "Do you really think Hatch would contract out something like this? Not a chance."

"Or maybe he's here to get a fucking front-row seat to street justice."

"Hatch was minding his own business until we showed up," Terri said. "Now you think his involvement is *your* responsibility. That's what this is all about. Am I right?"

Taylor nodded again.

Terri said. "Can I give you my opinion on something far more important to me?"

"Do I really have a choice?"

"I don't like what's happening to you, Gray," Terri said, picking up her pace on the machine. "You're more uptight than you've been in a long, long time."

"More of your women's intuition, babe?"

Terri shook her head. "I see it in your eyes."

"He's got to be back in the city to stop Steven," Taylor said, ignoring Terri's comment. "When we mentioned Steven, he got protective. He was mad at us for even bringing it up. This whole mess suddenly got personal for him."

"And apparently for you," Terri said firmly.

"What the fuck does that mean?" Taylor shot back.

"My God," Terri breathed, "are you hearing yourself? Talk about defensive!"

"I have no idea what you're saying!"

"Kevin Easter is a big boy with his own moral compass," Terri said. "I'm telling you this isn't your fault, Gray, and it's not your problem. And frankly, I don't appreciate your tone. You're coming across as a bully."

Taylor, his hands clenched in tight fists, said nothing.

"Jack will see things from a different angle," Terri said. "He usually does."

"Doubtful," Taylor said barely above a whisper.

Terri pressed a button on the treadmill and the machine slowed to a stop. "I'm outta here."

"What's up with you?"

Terri stepped off the treadmill, crossed the room, and turned off the radio. When she spoke again, it was in a tone that closely resembled sadness. "I'm really worried, Gray."

"Yeah, Hatch could be headed down—"

"No," Terri said, "it's you I'm concerned about."

"What are you talking about?" Taylor's voice had taken on a hard edge, like a wild animal baring its teeth.

"Please don't lose yourself in this," Terri said quietly. "I know how you get when things turn personal. And this one *is* personal."

"I can handle—"

"No!" Shaking her head, Terri was at once resolute and on the verge of tears. "If you somehow end up in that, that . . . if you return to your old self, I'm—well, I'm not sure I can go through that shit again."

"Terri. Hey—"

"It's a period of our life that still haunts me," Terri said, biting down on her lower lip. "I'm sorry, but you need to hear this from somebody who . . . who loves you unconditionally."

"I never meant for your family to be pulled—"

"Just be careful," Terri said, raising one hand. "I know you're very fond of Hatch. I watched you two at breakfast that morning, and then again at the funeral. He's become like your little brother. You're emotionally invested in him now. That's rare for you."

"I'll be fine, Terri." The words emerged with a sharp edge. "His problem has nothing to do with what we went through."

"You're wrong."

"I'm not wrong!"

"If Jack turns this into an op, and you're point, I'd rather not be around until it's over. What you were forced to do—I'm not sure you ever fully recovered." Terri walked to the far end of the home gym, then turned back to face her husband. "If Jack wants you to take care of this, and you agree to, I'm going to visit my sister. I'll need to distance myself from the situation."

"Terri—"

"It's because I love you, Gray," she said, dragging her sleeve over her eyes.

"Why are you being so—"

"I'll be back to help pick up the pieces when this is finished." And Terri was out the door.

Gray Taylor contemplated Terri's words for nearly ten minutes. *I'm not sure I can go through that shit again. A period of our life that still haunts me.* He stripped off his drenched T-shirt and threw it against the wall. "Goddamnit," he said through clenched teeth.

"Jack, the note was on my kitchen counter when we got home last night!" Gray Taylor shouted into his phone, his mind drifting back to his confrontation with Terri. *What you were forced to do . . .*

It was now a few minutes after six o'clock in the morning, and still dark outside his study at the Dakota. Wearing a light blue Adidas sweatshirt, jeans, and tennis shoes, Taylor sat behind the large wooden desk. He'd already showered and shaved, and was now drinking his first cup of black coffee.

"Read it again," Slattery said.

Taylor did so.

"Scan the document and send it to me as an e-mail attachment," Slattery said. "I'll be in my office by six-thirty. I'll see if there's more on Ciambella's death that may interest our investigation."

"*Our* investigation?" Taylor said, getting up from his chair.

"Like it or not, we're unofficially involved, Gray."

"All because of what I've told you? Hatch doesn't even work for you, Jack."

"But he did," Slattery said. "And there are a few other fun facts I've recently become aware of. We checked Steven Easter's passport. According to Saudi officials, he left their country almost six weeks ago."

"Shit, I don't like the sound of that."

"Customs isn't sure if he returned to the U.S."

"How can that be? Where did he go?"

"From Saudi to Kuwait, United Arab Emirates, Qatar, Iran—"

"Over what period of time?"

"Three days," said Slattery. "It looks like Steven crossed in and out of these Middle Eastern countries, and a few others I didn't bother to mention."

"Why is he on the move?"

"Maybe he's busy," Slattery said, sounding anything but convinced. "Maybe he's trying to cover his tracks for some reason."

"So we have no idea where he is or what he's doing?" Taylor said, incredulous. "Or if he's somehow slipped into the States under our radar?"

"It seems fairly obvious what he's doing."

"C'mon, Jack, there has to be another explanation. There was a point in time when you thought Hatch was behind this. Remember?"

"Gray, give me one other reason why Kevin is back in New York City. Give me one other reason for a handwritten note personally delivered to you, warning you to back off." There was a long pause from the DDI. "I didn't think so."

"Has anyone taken the direct approach by calling Steven's office?"

"If Steven Easter is a vigilante in New York City, I'd hate for him to know we're looking for him," said Slattery. "But we have made some discreet inquiries, and nobody seems to know where he is, or at least his employees aren't talking— yet. Playing this one close to the vest makes your job a bit easier."

"This is unreal. With all our security, how do you fall off the grid and still stay mobile?"

"I'm looking at a possibility that involves another government agency," Slattery said. "Something that recently came to my attention."

Taylor considered this for a moment. "What do you want me to do?"

"Sit tight," said Slattery. "I'll e-mail you any new developments, including the police reports and other documentation of the Ciambella investigation. If you need to leave your apartment, keep your encrypted PDA close."

"Yes, sir."

Slattery cleared his throat, then said, "I have something important I need to ask you, Gray."

"The answer is yes," Taylor said, his lips pressing into a tight, colorless line. "I can handle the situation."

"Even if things turn, ah . . . complicated?"

Taylor stared out his window to the east. The sun had yet to come up and Central Park was still dark this last Monday morning in November. "Yes." Taylor's answer came out like a bullet.

"It seems like you and Kevin hit it off."

You're the second person in the past hour to bring that to my attention—both people I love and respect.

"I can handle things, Jack."

Brooklyn

Though Kevin Easter, sitting on a double bed, watched the busy city street through a dirty window in the Grand Avenue Holiday Inn, a two-story hotel in Queens with wireless Internet access, his mind was elsewhere—specifically, on his brother. Around the small room was all the equipment he needed to find Steven: laptop, printer, recorder, Garmin GPS, maps of the five New York boroughs, Nikon 2DX, and the information he'd begun to collect on Anthony DiFilippo's organization. The Buckmaster hunting knife and the Glock 9mm were tucked in the backpack he'd last used on Andros Island.

Hatch had yet to hear back from Steven. This reinforced his theory: His brother was somewhere in the Big Apple, and he was killing people he thought had been involved in the murders of Karen and Patricia. It was the only reasonable explanation.

Patty loved him the way I love you, Little Crow.

The Cajun Moon roses, the Internet articles Hatch had read from *The New York Post* archives, the Louis Ciambella crime scene, and Steven's presence at Karen's funeral on such short notice all seemed to confirm his dead wife's nightly message.

Gray Taylor and Jack Slattery must have come to the same conclusion by now.

The mission was simple: Hatch needed to find his brother before anyone else did.

He grabbed his gear and, ten minutes later, he was out the door.

CHAPTER 37

Bronx

Lawrence Luther Wright sat on a wooden bench in the early morning sunshine. He was on the Bronx's south side, in St. Mary's Park on East 149th Street and St. Ann's Avenue. Behind his Serengeti sunglasses, he glanced over at an elderly blue-haired woman. She wore a suede jacket and gray slacks. Sitting on a painted bench near the swing set, she nibbled a muffin while reading *The Wall Street Journal*. Every moment or so, she peered over her newspaper at the two black men leaning on the silver Cadillac STS parked at the curb, and each time, she thinned her eyes, sighed heavily, then went back to reading.

Pit Bull reached under his long winter coat when he first glimpsed Anthony DiFilippo strolling down a footpath through the park. The Mafia don came unescorted.

"Easy," Jamar said, patting the big man on the shoulder.

Pit Bull kept his eyes fixed on the Italian mobster. "My brother, the days of me takin' anything easy are officially over," he said. His voice was so deep that the words seemed to vibrate in the crisp air.

"The boss is gonna fix this thing, Pit Bull. You watch."

Tony D, a black trench coat thrown over his right arm, sat down beside Lawrence Luther. The elderly woman who'd been reading the *Journal*, having apparently seen enough, folded up the newspaper and left St. Mary's Park in a slow, shuffling gait, grumbling something indecipherable under her breath.

The don set his silver briefcase down between the two men and gently placed his fedora on his lap. "Good morning."

"No, it's not," Lawrence Luther replied in a sharp, clipped tone.

Tony D looked up into the blue sky. "Could have fooled me."

"Your ghost apparently wasn't through after he dispatched Mr. Ciambella last night," said Lawrence Luther, his vigilant gaze moving over the park again. "One of my very close associates didn't show up for work this morning, and he's never late, never misses a day. He was found in his bathtub about an hour ago. Drowned."

Tony D said nothing, although his jaw muscles tightened.

"My colleague was not an easy target, Mr. DiFilippo, unless, of course, you used a gun, and it better be a big gun. He was a physical specimen—a retired professional boxer. Our ghost is not only smart and well-trained, he's tough."

"All the more reason to finish this."

"Obviously."

"What you requested is in the briefcase," Tony D said, glancing over at the two bodyguards. "I encourage you to move quickly, Mr. Wright. I have two more funerals to attend after Paulie's today, a wife who insists we retire to Florida, and an organization that appears rudderless. My people are uneasy. They don't see me addressing the problem."

"The wheels are in motion," Lawrence Luther said evenly.

"The information in that briefcase came from a detective who's been working on these cases . . ."

The hunter watched and listened to Lawrence Luther Wright and Anthony DiFilippo from eighty feet away. He was near the wooden playground that, according to a bronze plaque near the entrance to St. Mary's Park, had been erected and paid for by the Neighborhood Watch Program in August—the month that had forever changed the course of his life.

A few small children with their parents or babysitters played on the swing set. Wearing a baseball cap, one father, holding an expensive camera, took shots of the kids and some of the dormant oak trees.

The hunter's less expensive Nikon, meanwhile, recorded twelve perfect frames of Tony D and his new partner conducting their second business meeting in as many days. He hadn't expected this alliance, but it changed nothing—his plan remained intact. It was essential for DiFilippo to feel the pain of personal loss before Judgment Day. Maybe it was time for his lovely wife to receive an anonymous letter suggesting that Tony D had something to do with Vincent Tagliafero's murder—maybe. Or he could just kill her.

Tony D would be stripped of everything and everyone he loved. The plan was to break the old man, then kill him in spectacular fashion.

Instead of focusing their attention on the "professional" or "ghost" or "player" wreaking havoc on their lives, the two heavyweights of the New York underworld planned their own form of retaliation on the suspected masterminds of the recent attacks. That, at least, the hunter had counted on. It's why he wore a disguise.

Lowering the camera, the hunter adjusted his earpiece.

"I'm not sure how long the NYPD mob division can be kept out of this," Tony D said to Lawrence Luther. "I have influence, but it's finite. According to my detective friend, the chief wants answers. Pressure is coming from a number of people, including the mayor, if you can believe that. Many in the police department figure I'm about to go to war against another family. And nobody wants that kind of blood on the streets."

"Have your police buddies mentioned me or my organization?" Lawrence Luther asked, stroking his neat beard.

"No. Supposedly, they haven't connected your problems with mine—at least not yet."

"It's only a matter of time," Lawrence Luther said, pursing his lips. "The media might figure it out first."

"Unless we put an end to the attacks in the next couple of days."

"Have you shared our theory with anyone?"

"Not even with my wife," Tony D said. "A few subtle questions have been directed toward the fire department and the arson specialist, but it hasn't led to anything worth mentioning."

"Time is too short to recruit a guy like Brian McGowan," said Lawrence Luther. "One of my advisors tells me he's a Boy Scout. Same could be said of Detective Nick Benedetti."

"Yes," Tony D said, "we've come to the same conclusions."

Gesturing toward his two associates outside the park, Lawrence Luther said, "As you can see, my people are incredibly anxious. Look at those damn fools. Each of them has his finger on the trigger, literally and figuratively. They don't trust anyone—you included. They think you'll eventually turn on me."

"Their opinions don't concern me, Mr. Wright. Do *you* trust me?" Tony D coughed, then grimaced. "That's what counts."

"Do I have a choice?"

"If you'd like, you can handle this ghost by yourself."

"I'd rather we work together. Something tells me we're running out of time. The attacks are coming quicker now."

"My preference is to stay the course and keep the lines of communication open."

Lawrence Luther nodded, stroked his beard again, then said, "Agreed."

"What you'll find in that briefcase is a sign of good faith."

The internal reports, copied from the New York Police Department's special investigative unit, focused primarily on the gangs of New York. One needed a top-level clearance to access the files through the IBM mainframe. Tony D's contact had taken a great risk accessing the program to gather the required information.

For the next ten minutes, Lawrence Luther silently flipped through classified police files dating back almost eighteen months: arrest reports, the D.A.'s files and objectives on certain repeat criminals, plea agreements, convictions, surveillance photographs, dozens of rap sheets, informants, and even profiles by psychologists and psychiatrists working with the NYPD. Asian men with connections to a gang called Ho Chen Dauwau—the Blood Brothers—and the gang Lawrence Luther had mentioned the night before, the Akrho Pinoy, were at the heart of most of the classified data, notes, and background material. Numerous drug charges—specifically heroin-related crimes—seemed to be the common thread throughout. There was little doubt that the Akrho Pinoy now controlled the heroin trade in the five boroughs, Long Island, and northern New Jersey.

But Akrho Pinoy, according to the detective's handwritten note, had other interests: extortion, gun-running, prostitution, gambling—a list that seemed to expand monthly. And they coveted growth.

"Shame on me," Lawrence Luther said, shaking his head. "I didn't know these punks were moving up in the world so quickly. Makes me wonder what else I'm missing."

"You're not the only one."

Lawrence Luther pointed to a photograph of a gaunt Chinese man with a pencil-thin mustache, long dark hair, and hard black eyes. "This is probably our guy."

Tony D looked over. "Roger Tai. He runs the New York chapter now."

"His predecessor was found in a shopping cart last summer."

"Minus his head."

"They're animals, Mr. DiFilippo. Most have no sense of godliness."

"There are additional notes on the back of each picture," said Tony D. "His organization has a history of farming out some of their bloodier work, being seen in public while the job takes place."

"Seems about right for a snake like this." Lawrence Luther flipped over the photograph. "Tai looks older than twenty-nine."

Tony D glanced over at a man taking pictures of some of the wood carvings—mostly of exotic animals—by local artists. "Mr. Roger Tai believes he's bulletproof," he said, turning back to look at his new partner.

"Only Superman can make that claim," Lawrence Luther said, smiling for the first time. "And we all have a little kryptonite in our lives."

"True."

"We target Roger Tai, and if it takes a few buddies to get his attention, so be it. I want these parasites out of my city."

"Our city," Tony D said in a raspy hush.

"Yes. Out of New York and back to Los Angeles before Christmas."

Forty minutes later, the two men shook hands and went their separate ways. Carrying the briefcase out of St. Mary's Park, Lawrence Luther slipped into the silver Caddy's backseat. Anthony DiFilippo's BMW 740L met the don at the curb.

The hunter packed up his gear, including his recording equipment, waited thirty minutes, then headed to his vehicle parked a block away.

Brooklyn

The young dark-haired woman running her fingers over the keyboard at lightning speed looked more like a swimsuit model than your typical computer nerd. Neesa Saul happened to be both. Though only twenty-six, Neesa oversaw the Advanced Traveler Information System for the New York City Department of Transportation. The modeling gigs took place at night and on weekends.

"I bet you never missed a deadline in college," Detective Katherine Montroy said, rolling her chair closer to Neesa's workstation.

"Barely got through NYU," Neesa said with a shrug. "Look where it got me."

They were in the ATIS command center on Court Street—on the third floor—facing at least fifty hi-def monitors on a single giant wall shaped like the inside of a bowl. Every monitor showed a different road or intersection, placed somewhere around the five New York City boroughs: Queens, Brooklyn, the Bronx, Manhattan, and Staten Island. Some monitors were in black and white, but most displayed in color. NASA personnel would be envious of such technology, and the way traffic was quickly and expertly diverted and rerouted around accidents, road construction, or even normal congestion.

"This guy you're after," Neesa said, eyes on her keyboard, "is he a murderer?"

"A person of interest," Montroy said. "Very serious interest."

Neesa clapped her hands together. "Okay, let's catch a bad guy."

Every few seconds, one or more of the screens would flash from one site to another, while at least ten employees tried their best to observe a small fraction of the 5,800 miles of streets, 789 bridges, 12,000 signalized intersections, and millions of people who depended on the New York City transportation infrastructure each day. It was still rush hour on Monday morning, so almost every street, highway, and intersection was filled with traffic. Even so, the large room was relatively quiet.

"Okay, there's your white Ford Explorer on Coney Island Avenue, two blocks from the Sunset Inn Motel." Neesa clicked a few keys, and the monitor changed to another location.

"That was fast," Montroy said, leaning closer to the large computer screen. In the bottom right-hand corner was a timestamp: "NOV 27-11:50 a.m." It clicked to 11:51 a.m. as the Ford SUV moved in and out of the shot.

"Here it is again," Neesa said, "headed south on Ocean Parkway." Eleven fifty-four.

"Can you freeze it?" Montroy flipped open a small pad.

The timestamp and the white Ford Explorer stopped at 11:56 a.m. "You want a close-up of the license plate?" Neesa said, dragging her mouse, then clicking a few more keys. "I can even make you a hard copy."

"Holy shit," Montroy breathed. It was a New Jersey plate. DRN 2866.

"I'd try for a better shot of your driver, but the windows are tinted," Neesa said. "Hmm, they actually look illegal to me. And the driver's not using the E-ZPass lanes. Probably a smart move."

Montroy flipped open her cell, then punched in Matthew Philips's number. "Matty, it's me. Look, I want you to run a plate." She passed it along. "Yeah, I need it, like, right now." She hit the *end* button, shoved the phone back into her coat pocket, and murmured, "Men."

"Yeah, I'm thinking of trading in my lame-ass boyfriend for an older model. Maybe a guy with an actual career."

"Looks, brains, and common sense," Montroy said. "Neesa, you got it all."

"I like to think so," Neesa said, sitting a little straighter.

"Okay, let's see where our driver goes from here," Montroy said. "Roll 'em."

More clicks of the keys revealed another location the white Explorer had passed. It moved west on the Shore Parkway at 12:02 p.m., across the Verrazano Bridge at 12:21 p.m., onto the Staten Island Expressway at 12:24 p.m., then to the Goethals Bridge into New Jersey by 12:48 p.m.

"That's the best I can do," Neesa said, turning her chair to face Montroy. "Jersey uses a different system, and we don't have access to their cameras. But I can get you the right person to talk to."

"I'd appreciate that," Montroy said as her phone started to ring. "Sorry."

"No problem."

Montroy looked at the LCD screen, and then hit the *send* button. "Tell me it's not stolen, Matty."

"I'm looking at my computer now," said Philips. "Two-thousand six Ford Explorer. White. Jersey plate DRN 2866—"

"C'mon, c'mon, I don't have all day."

"Kat, the plates belonged to a 2002 Chevy Suburban—owner lives in Paterson. The Explorer might be the one ripped off from a college kid who lives with her parents in Red Bank, but goes to Rutgers. She's not sure how long it was missing because it was parked on campus and she rarely uses it. That's the only white 2006 Explorer reported missing in New Jersey. I have five in New York, but they're nowhere close to the Apple: Fulton, which is northwest of Syracuse; Rochester;

Williamsville, near Buffalo; Cortland; and a town called Lake Placid."

"Can you contact the Jersey State police and tell them we're looking for this vehicle?" Montroy said.

"I think I can help you out," Philips said with a chuckle. "If they actually find this Explorer, you want them to grab the guy?"

"No!" Montroy said a little too loudly. "Just let us know. Gotta go."

"You're very welcome," Philips said sarcastically.

Neesa handed Katherine Montroy a slip of paper. "Here's a phone number for the gentleman who heads up New Jersey's DOT," she said. "Tell Max I sent you, Detective. He's been hitting on me for nearly a year now. Sixty, married, two adult children. Reminds me of Archie Bunker, but cute in a creepy way."

"Archie Bunker?" Montroy said, cocking her head. "What about a nice trust fund kid from the Upper West Side for you? Perhaps someone closer to your own age?"

"I'm available, Detective. Feel free to pass out my phone number if you come across such a creature."

"Done."

"Listen," Neesa said, leaning closer to Montroy, "I have a new program that enables us to locate a vehicle if it comes back into our jurisdiction—a little something I've been working on. You want me to run it for the next few days?"

"How reliable is it?"

"If your white Ford Explorer comes back into New York City and he hasn't changed the license plates, I'll find him."

"Do it."

CHAPTER 38

Manhattan

Gray Taylor wandered about his home office holding a handful of files from Jack Slattery, committing much of the information and photographs to memory. He was glad Terri had left for Pennsylvania to visit her sister. She didn't need to see his fastidious preparations or mindset. They could both use a little space now that Hatch's note had brought Taylor fully into the crisis.

Jack's information included in-depth reports from a number of police assigned to investigate the deaths of Johnny Cercone, Fat Paulie Franco, and Donald Biasucci, and preliminary information on the car bomb that killed Louis Ciambella. Images of each man and the murder scene were displayed in graphic detail all over Taylor's cluttered desk. And the incidents began to make sense.

A history buff, Taylor was reminded of the first few days of the Gulf War. When General Colin Powell confidently addressed a national audience made up of anxious Americans, an international hero was born. Powell stated that his single purpose was to free Kuwait from Saddam Hussein's ruthless grip.

"We are going to cut its head off, and then we are going to kill it," General Powell proclaimed, referring to the Iraqi army and Saddam's overhyped Republican Guard.

Steven appeared to be playing by the same rules, Taylor thought.

Taylor laid a few pages beside the black-and-white pictures, then picked up the Anthony DiFilippo profile, along with detailed information on his diverse organization.

The CIA field operative spent the next hour delving into a comprehensive look at the Mafia don's life. The deeper he looked, the more impressed and puzzled he became. Tony D had never been arrested for anything serious—only a traffic violation twelve years earlier.

"Can you really be that smart, Mr. DiFilippo?"

Taylor hit his cell phone's speed dial, number seven. The phone rang twice.

"You'll have to make it quick, Gray," Slattery said. "I'm on my way to meet with the director. There's a few things you should know about an ongoing New York op, but I need permission to get you clearance."

"Sir, I'm getting the impression there's more here than meets the eye," Taylor said, falling back into his leather chair. "I'm no expert on the subject, but it seems like DiFilippo either leads a charmed life, or he has a guardian angel or two."

"You might say that."

"And these guardian angels were undoubtedly blindsided when Steven Easter—or some unidentified vigilante—paid a visit to New York."

"Your Mensa membership won't be revoked anytime soon, Gray. You're on the right track."

"I could use more background on DiFilippo."

"Way ahead of you," said Slattery. "A courier should arrive at your place in the next thirty minutes."

Exhaling heavily, Taylor said, "He'll hunt tonight, Jack."

"Why would you say that?"

"Because that's what I'd do. This guy wants to keep everyone on edge."

"Do you think Anthony DiFilippo is the target?"

"Doubtful. Not yet," said Taylor. "But I wouldn't be surprised if Mara DiFilippo is on his short list, or even the don's children. Killing people close to him—this is all about inflicting pain."

B. J. Butera looked down at his cell phone and smiled when he recognized the incoming call. Pressing the *send* button, he cupped his hand to his mouth and whispered, "Please tell me you've finally connected the dots." He glanced furtively around the busy *New York Post* newsroom, but nobody was within twenty feet of him.

Brian McGowan, sitting in his Volvo sedan, was on the Robert F. Kennedy Bridge headed into Queens. "I'm in gridlock, and it's only noon," he said, aggravated.

"Did you get your results back?"

"What results?" Turning down the radio's volume, McGowan laughed quietly.

"You're not funny, Brian. Was there C-4 at both sites?"

"Got ourselves a match . . . but not officially. Same for a small house in the Bronx. That's the good news," said McGowan.

"I can't run the story—that's the bad news."

"Not yet. Be patient—"

"Brian. C'mon, somebody's gonna beat me to the punch."

"I told you this morning I'd have things buttoned up in forty-eight hours.

Even the detectives on the case don't know what I'm sharing with you."

"I can't wait two days," B. J. said in a loud whisper.

"Okay, give me until tomorrow afternoon. Maybe then I'll have something tasty."

"Yes!" B. J. exclaimed, pumping his fist in the air. "I could kiss you on the lips."

That comment produced a few sideways glances in his direction.

"You might want to get yourself a new girlfriend," said McGowan.

"Yeah, sure, right after you jump back into the dating pool," B. J. said. He winced at his own comment.

Traffic suddenly began to move. "I swore off the ladies," said McGowan. "Catch ya later."

Gray Taylor had just laid his half-eaten tuna sandwich on his plate when his BlackBerry began to vibrate on the desk. He picked up the phone, scrutinized the four-three-four Charlottesville, Virginia exchange, and thought: *The kid is full of surprises.* He brought the phone to his ear and said, "Glad to see you're once again a loyal Verizon customer."

"I hope you didn't fire your doorman because of me," Hatch said, walking down Grand Street near the entrance to the Williamsburg Bridge.

"Do I want to know how you got into my place?"

"Rappelled off the roof. I left behind a few reminders you might want to take care of."

"Yeah, right," Taylor said. "From the sound of it, you're still in the city."

"I'm here until it's over." Hatch let out a long breath. "Please take my advice, Gray. Back off. That's why I'm calling."

"Why would you even give me a heads-up with your note?"

"Because I consider you a friend. You and Terri helped me through a rough time last summer. And since Jack has you playing babysitter again, I didn't want you to get hurt. When I'm done with this call, I'm turning off my cell. Tell Mickey and the rest of his geeks to chill. They won't be able to find me electronically. I'm stepping off the grid until this is over."

Taylor got to his feet. "Why is Steven doing this, Hatch? I don't get it."

"Your question covers a lot of ground. It insinuates even more."

"Would it be fair to ask just how deep you are in this whole mess?"

"What do you mean?"

"Is this a rescue mission, or did you lose your mind completely?" Taylor asked. "Terri insists you weren't involved until we got you involved. I happen to feel the same."

"Let's just say that your visit opened my eyes to a disturbing possibility."

Taylor looked out the window toward Central Park. A guy on stilts playing a guitar ambled down a footpath. "How will you find him?"

"Probably the same way you would."

"Hatch, we're all really worried about you. Me, Terri, Jack."

"I'm gonna do this alone."

"Let me help," said Taylor. "We can do this together, quietly. I know my way around New York."

"No."

"Why?"

"It's pretty simple, Gray," Hatch said, his voice very low. "This is my fault. This is my problem, not yours. I work by myself. You read my file."

"Karen and Patricia were in the wrong place at the wrong time!" Taylor shouted. "You know that! How can *you* be to blame?"

"Stay out of this for another forty-eight hours, Gray. That's all I'm asking."

"I can't do that, Hatch. And if you don't come in . . ." Taylor's words trailed off.

"I hear you loud and clear," Hatch said. "Your loyalty to Jack is commendable."

It goes way beyond that, kid. "And when you find Steven? Then what?"

"It's over."

"Over!" Taylor yelled. "Can you be a little more specific? Hatch, be serious here. There's not a chance in hell we can just let your brother walk away from this. If Steven is really behind these killings—which apparently you think he is—then he has an enormous debt to pay." Taylor paused. "Your brother is going to prison for life." *Or I'll be killing him.*

"Stay out of this," Hatch repeated, then terminated the call.

Gray Taylor laid the BlackBerry back on the desk, picked up his sandwich, then tossed it back on the plate, having lost his appetite. "You don't fucking get forty-eight hours."

A moment later, Taylor found himself drawn to his balcony. Stepping outside into the cold afternoon breeze, he looked up at the Dakota's granite and marble facade. And there it was: A piton had been hammered into the rock about five feet above the Taylors' apartment; another was near the roofline. Mountain climbers used the eight-inch steel spikes—like the two Easter had left behind—to help scale particularly dangerous cliffs.

"I'll be damned," Taylor said, his breath clinging to the cold air. "You're pretty good, Hatch. But I'm still coming for you."

CHAPTER 39
Brooklyn

Though two o'clock on a Monday afternoon, candlelight still flickered inside Katherine Montroy's bedroom. The blinds had been pulled to enhance the ambiance. The workday—it had started around midnight—had blessedly ended before 11:30 a.m., after calls had been made to Matthew Philips, Brian McGowan, and Nick Benedetti. None of them, including Max at the NJDOT, had anything new to report on Louis Ciambella's murder, the white Ford Explorer, or the possible underworld war, which now appeared inevitable.

Sweet-smelling incense languidly moved into the brightly lit hallway where the man in the balaclava stood. Music—the hunter recognized the Steely Dan album, *Aja*—was playing throughout the modest Brooklyn apartment.

Chinese music always sets me free. Angular banjos sound good to me.

Dry, dispassionate eyes, like those of a shark, stared from behind the balaclava. Wearing dark green jogging attire with a blue windbreaker, black running shoes, and Lycra gloves, he had the Beretta 9mm with the sound suppressor resting against his rapidly beating heart. The hunter closed his eyes, leaned against the wall, and listened to the couple making love.

Then something unexpected took hold: A pleasurable memory, like a fountain, welled up in the hunter's mind, and he was but a hapless passenger.

———

Self-conscious about her naked body, Patricia Durante pulled the silk sheets to her neck and bit down on her lower lip. He wondered again how such a strong-minded and intelligent woman could be so uncomfortable with her appearance. He found Patricia extraordinarily beautiful, and unlike many in their generation, she wasn't superficial or materialistic. Fame, she had explained, had come at great expense—for her, a life outside of the theater didn't really exist. A *New York Post* feature on Patricia had brought more unwanted media attention and a few new critics. She was, Patricia had recently confided, painfully alone when the lights of the theater dimmed. But not anymore.

Like her sister Karen, Patricia didn't measure her friends by the color of their skin, their body type, their job title, or their portfolio. Depth of character—flawed character, he'd quickly learned—made their attraction absolute.

They had decided to keep their relationship a secret, at least until it had grown roots. Dr. Durante, Patricia's overprotective father, still struggled with Karen's marriage to Hatch. And like Hatch, he would never measure up.

Patricia's black hair was splayed over the pillow like a *Victoria's Secret* pictorial, yet there was nothing contrived or phony here. Her full breasts, hidden beneath the sheets, bright blue eyes, freckled nose, and even her twisted smile seduced him.

"Do you believe in love at first sight?" Patricia asked.

"Not until I met you," he said without hesitation. He sat on the edge of the bed.

"How about destiny?"

"I believe in choice."

"What about your brother? What will he say?"

He pondered the question, chuckled, then said, "He's a little bit country, I'm a little bit rock 'n' roll."

"So he'd be supportive?"

"He's gonna say I'm dating way above my pay grade."

Laughing, Patricia said, "Can I tell you a secret?"

"Sure."

"It's not meant to embarrass you."

"I can handle it . . . probably . . . maybe." And he smiled. It was an anxious smile.

For some inexplicable reason, Patricia Durante suddenly looked on the verge of tears, and she pursed her lips for a long moment before speaking. "I've loved you from the very first moment I laid eyes on you," she said. "Don't ask me why or how . . . I just did. I can hardly believe I'm even saying this out loud."

"I know exactly how you feel," he said sheepishly.

"Move to New York. Move in with me." Patricia was suddenly excited.

"What about my job?"

"I make enough money to support us both—"

"It's not the money, Patty. People depend on me," he replied, exhaling audibly. "It's not that simple."

"Of course it's that simple. We'll work things out."

"God, I love you."

Patricia folded back the sheet, exposing her naked body. "Show me."

A cold, hard rain suddenly attacked the Bronx apartment window, as if let out of a cage. Candlelight danced across their faces. Distorted shadows mirrored their lovemaking. Two lonely people lucky enough to find something very special in the world.

But it wasn't going to last.

Everything came to a horrifying end at Rudy's Tavern on a hot August night. And like Lazarus waking from the dead, the hunter was pulled back to the present. Imaginary steel bands tightened around his chest, squeezing the air from his lungs. Standing in Katherine Montroy's apartment, dressed as he was, he was exposed. Cops like her usually had a gun nearby—he could no longer afford to fantasize about what might have been. Patricia was dead and buried, along with his dreams—their dreams.

The silenced Beretta trembled in his right hand. His left hand fingered the Vietnam-era shell in his pocket. Looking down at the gun, he cursed his frailty. *Breathe. Take it easy. Calm down. Goddamnit, take a deep breath.*

A minute passed before the hunter regained control. He considered leaving the apartment, but understood the time was now—killing Montroy would grow more difficult the longer he waited. The nightmares, lack of sleep, and stress had already begun to impair his judgment. He'd lost nearly ten pounds in the past six weeks.

The hunter had been living on the razor's edge since returning to New York. Decisions came with greater effort now. Days and nights ran seamlessly together. His victims had whispered his name even in the daylight. Guilt was the lead role, he knew, and remorse weighed heavily on his mind, just as he thought it might. He tried not to care. Exhaustion helped him forget.

The hatred the hunter held for those who had destroyed his life kept him moving forward. He had to kill everyone involved in Patricia's death, and that included Katherine Montroy, the detective who'd promptly turned her back on the investigation after Vincent Tagliafero's body had been discovered at the Hunts Point Market. Surely she was the one who'd been leaking information to Anthony DiFilippo, receiving large sums of money in return.

Tony D had paid fifty thousand dollars for information on the Chinese gangs working New York. That money had gone to Montroy, Philips, or Nicholas Benedetti. The hunter couldn't be sure which. Uncertainty kept the hunter on a short leash, but that rope was frayed, ready to snap.

Do it, he demanded of himself. *Eliminate the source of your pain.*

Soft moans emanated from Montroy's bedroom.

The hunter tilted his head back and stared at the dark hallway ceiling. *Leave. Abort. Let it go. Run! Maybe she isn't dirty.* Maybe it was Philips who had entered into a dangerous relationship with Tony D.

Gripping the pistol with both hands, the hunter stepped into the bedroom. In the candle's flickering light, he watched the two women in lovers' embrace, their mouths locked in a deep, passionate kiss.

The hunter stood frozen. The room, though consumed with some erotic incense, still carried with it the strong aroma of sex. Memories of his own love duet flashed again, like blue lightning rocketing across a midnight sky.

Montroy's hands came up to her partner's breasts and gently squeezed each nipple. Eyes closed, Tracy Fitzgibbon moaned, low and guttural, and quivered briefly.

Leveling the pistol, the hunter pointed at Montroy's head. Twelve feet away. An easy shot. The larger woman's face was bathed in sweat.

Hands slapping against the mattress, Montroy clenched the sheets.

The gun suddenly stopped trembling in the hunter's steady hand.

And a cell phone on the dresser rang.

CHAPTER 40
Coney Island

Through night-vision binoculars, Kevin Easter, hunkered down in a lifeguard tower, watched the unmarked Ford Taurus pull up behind the luxury BMW he'd been following for most of an hour. Both vehicles were parked near a boarded-up concession stand about two hundred yards from the Long Island Sound.

It was a perfect place—secluded, dark, and quiet—for a clandestine meeting between two people who should have been natural enemies.

"I've seen you before," Hatch said softly. "Yes, you were at the Ciambella crime scene. What are you doing here, Detective?" The ex-CIA field operative adjusted his eight-inch parabolic dish and headset to better hear and record their conversation. Then he replaced the night-vision binoculars with his Nikon and its telephoto lens.

Anthony DiFilippo IV exited the BMW's backseat, closed the car door, then shoved both gloved hands into his long coat. His scarf fluttered in the ocean breeze. He smiled ruefully when the detective came his way. A very large bodyguard stood dutifully at his master's side, like an angry dog ready to strike if let off its chain.

Click, click, click, click. The high-speed shutter softly whirred, and Hatch's new Nikon began recording the surreptitious meeting.

Brooklyn Heights

These were the unglamorous moments CIA novels, suspense thrillers, and Hollywood movies rarely touched upon. Stakeouts—regardless of the time or place—were typically lengthy and mind-numbing. Nonetheless, those in the intelligence-gathering community deemed them a necessary evil. Firsthand knowledge of an opponent's intentions were critical, particularly when a life hung in the balance—just as Gray Taylor suspected Anthony DiFilippo's did.

But Tony D was not going to die—not tonight, and not on his watch. Just as the *NBC Nightly News* was coming on, CIA Director Timothy Walsh and Deputy Director for Intelligence Jack Slattery were giving him clear and precise orders over a secure conference call line.

"Protect Anthony DiFilippo at all costs," Director Walsh said. No surprise there. And his explanation confirmed, for Taylor, his suspicions that someone powerful had been protecting the don for a good number of years. "Our involvement in this affair must never be made public, Mr. Taylor. Do you understand?"

"Yes, sir."

"This office will not contact, notify, or collaborate with any other government agency," the director said. "You're on your own, son. And if you get caught or you're implicated, we'll disavow."

"I understand," Taylor had said into the phone, looking out again at Central Park from his study.

"If *anyone* gets in your way," Slattery had said, "eliminate them with prejudice. Protect the subject—that is your primary objective, Gray. We're not in the business of giving anyone a head start. Steven Easter has to be stopped before the damage is irreparable. He's very close to exposing this alliance. If that happens, for lack of a better phrase, we'll never get the toothpaste back in the tube."

"Stability in the northeast U.S. could be compromised if Mr. DiFilippo is removed from his position in the family," Director Walsh said.

"Yes, sir," Taylor replied. "What if we brought Tony D into protective custody—send the don and his wife on some international vacation? It would get them out of the line of fire."

"Mr. Taylor, there's always a chance Steven Easter would go underground until Mr. DiFilippo returns to his daily regimen," the director replied. "Prolonging the fight will not end this war."

"Anthony DiFilippo doesn't take vacations," Slattery said. "A significant change in routine would surely tip Steven off. It could also be seen as a sign of weakness by Mr. DiFilippo's enemies. He'd be running away from a war that's already begun."

That conversation had taken place almost eight hours ago. It was three in the morning now. Taylor was cold and hungry, two conditions that often went hand in hand with such assignments. He'd positioned himself in a vacant second-floor brownstone apartment on Montague Street, directly across the road from the DiFilippos' home. The SIG SSG-3000 sniper rifle with Hensoldt scope leaned against the wall near the open window. The Steiner night-vision binoculars and the newly developed handheld DKL system, which remotely tracked human heartbeats through the target's electromagnetic field, made his job easier.

Two CIA field operatives, handpicked by Slattery, were driving up from D.C. They'd assist Taylor in protecting Anthony and Mara DiFilippo.

The upscale neighborhood was quiet, but Taylor wasn't alone. Two of Tony D's bodyguards sat in a blue Pontiac sedan parked at the curb. An unmarked police car was also on the street, but the cop behind the wheel had been sleeping fitfully for the past hour.

The DiFilippo household was dark and quiet. According to the electromagnetic footprint created by their beating hearts, Tony D and his wife had been in bed since midnight.

The possibility of having to kill Hatch—a friend—had begun to tug at Gray Taylor, awakening ugly memories.

CHAPTER 41

Bronx

At nine o'clock Tuesday morning, Matthew Philips arrived at the Twenty-Eighth Precinct. One corner of his wire-rimmed glasses was taped together, and he had a nasty scrape on his chin. Large purple bags sagged below each eye. His thin, oily hair was a disheveled mess, and his white shirt and tan slacks were wrinkled, as if he'd slept in them. There was even dirt on one knee. An unlit cigarette trembled in his hand. The past two weeks had taken their toll. . After reading the *Post's* front-page article, he found himself in a thoroughly foul mood.

"Hey, any of you guys seen Detective Montroy?" he shouted, turning in a slow circle.

"Jesus, Matty, when did you start giving a shit about anyone?" said a uniformed officer at the coffee machine.

Philips looked at his watch. Katherine's shift was supposed to start at eight. She was never late.

Manhattan

The New York Post was delivered to Lawrence Luther Wright a few minutes before seven o'clock Tuesday morning. Jamar Hightower closed his boss's apartment door around eight. His smile couldn't be ignored.

"We're having a good morning, brother?" Lawrence Luther said, patting the younger man on the shoulder.

"Couldn't be better, Boss."

"Coffee?"

"Maybe after you read the article," Jamar said, removing his jacket. His dreadlocks fell back over his shoulders. "You'll find the front page interesting."

New York's most notorious cocaine distributor resembled a black version of

Hugh Hefner this morning. He wore a silk bathrobe with the initials "LLW" monogrammed on the breast pocket. The pink bunny slippers, though, didn't fit the man's persona. Jamar was caught stealing a peek.

Lawrence Luther gestured toward the bedroom. "They belong to a lady friend."

"Thought maybe it was some new fashion statement," Jamar said, handing over the *Post*. He chuckled. "I was kinda thinkin' about gettin' me a pair."

"I'll add it to your Christmas list. You've been a good boy this year."

Both men found a seat on the white leather sofa. Unfolding the newspaper, Lawrence Luther stared at the front page. B. J. Butera's story brought forth a satisfied smile, like that of a teenage boy reading his name in print for the first time. "Nice headline," Lawrence Luther said. "YOUNG PUNKS ON DOPE!"

"It fits these dead assholes," Jamar said with a shrug.

Lawrence Luther turned to the second page and read parts of Butera's article out loud: "Monday night, five Asian-American men were gunned down while having dinner at Sam-Poo, an upscale restaurant in Chinatown. Among the dead was Roger Tai, owner of Clean Free Dry Cleaning, who allegedly had ties to Akrho Pinoy, a Chinese gang that controls the heroin drug trade in many cities in the northeastern U.S. ...."

According to the article, at approximately 9:40 p.m., three men brandishing assault weapons, their faces covered by ski masks, came through Sam-Poo's kitchen and ambushed the men—all purportedly Akrho Pinoy gang members—who, though armed themselves, never had a chance to return fire. The owner, Sam Chent, was unharmed, as were his six employees and twelve other patrons.

Three other gangs—Latin Kings, Gangster Disciples, and Ñetas—were also mentioned in the article. All had violent track records. All were considered suspects in the killing.

Lawrence Luther's pleased grin had yet to fade. "Well done."

"This city can be a jungle, Boss. Mr. Tai got careless."

Raising his arms like Moses addressing his pious followers, Lawrence Luther Wright thundered, "'Then I thought I would pour out my wrath upon them and spend my anger against them in the midst of the land of Egypt.'"

"Ezekiel," Jamar said. "Chapter twenty, verse eight."

"Look at you, my brother. You've been reading the good book."

"Every night."

"Praise be to heaven," said Lawrence Luther proudly. "The righteous one has saved another soul."

A young female voice called out from the bedroom. "You gonna untie me, baby?"

"She's got a long way to go to catch up to your faith, Jamar."

"Boss, I believe Mr. DiFilippo owes us for this one," said Jamar.

His attitude darkening, Lawrence Luther let out a long breath and said, "I'm not so sure he'll see it that way."

"What do you mean?"

"Let me finish with my guest and I'll explain," Lawrence Luther said. "Give me an hour."

Brooklyn

"Hello?" The word came out of Katherine Montroy's mouth in a dry croak, as if it had been dragged along on sandpaper.

Though it was now almost quarter after nine Tuesday morning, Montroy had yet to get out of bed, and the flu had nothing to do with her missing work. It was the mental anguish that made her retch and dry heave into the plastic bucket most of the night. She was thankful that Tracy had worked the night shift. The memory of yesterday afternoon's lovemaking had all but disappeared.

The female caller appeared puzzled. "Yes, um, I'm looking for Detective Katherine Montroy," she said hesitantly. "I must have dialed the wrong number. Sorry."

"This is Detective Montroy. Who is this?" *Restricted call* had come up on her display screen.

"Neesa. Neesa Saul. From the NYCDOT."

"Oh, hey. I'm sorry, Neesa," Montroy said, her feet hitting the carpeted floor. "Yeah, I . . . I have the flu or something." It was the second time this morning that she'd lied.

"You sound awful," Neesa said. "I'd call you tomorrow or later in the week, but this probably can't wait."

Montroy recognized the woman's sense of urgency and excitement even before all the words were out of her mouth, and suddenly she felt invigorated. "Neesa, did you find something? Your buddy Max hasn't been much help."

"That white Ford Explorer crossed over the George Washington Bridge about an hour ago," Neesa said. "It headed east into Manhattan. And now it's parked on Grand Boulevard in University Heights in the Bronx."

"No shit!"

"You can't miss it," Neesa said. "I'm guessing it's about eight blocks from Fordham University."

"Did you get a shot of the driver by any chance?" Montroy asked, stumbling to her feet and yanking open the closet door to find some clothes.

"Our camera is almost a block away," Neesa said. "I can barely make out the back bumper, but it's definitely the right SUV. I'm looking at it in real time."

"How long has it been there?"

"I dialed you the minute it parallel parked, Detective."

CHAPTER 42

Brooklyn Heights

G ray Taylor looked at his BlackBerry, then thinned his eyes. He thumbed the *send* button and brought the phone to his ear. "This is your definition of stepping off the grid, Hatch?"

"Not exactly."

Taylor sighed. "Unless you have something constructive to say, like maybe you've come to your senses and we can work this out together, I'm kinda busy."

"Are you familiar with Daniel Webster?"

"You mean the guy who wrote the dictionary?" Taylor got to his feet, but kept his vigilant gaze fixed on the Brooklyn Heights neighborhood. It was 7:47 a.m. The eastern horizon was bright with a new day. Tony D had yet to leave his home, though Taylor suspected he would soon.

"Mr. Webster was a great scholar and American statesman, Gray," said Hatch. "I expected more from a smart guy like you."

Taylor picked up the handheld DKL unit and pointed it at DiFilippo's brownstone. Two heartbeats. Both had been on the move for about an hour. *No diversion.* "Let me buy you breakfast, Hatch. We can compare notes."

"Had two PowerBars, a Baby Ruth, and an orange Gatorade," Hatch said. "Seriously, what do you know about Daniel Webster?"

"Not much."

"I'm only going to say this once, so listen up. Bear with me for a min—"

"This isn't a game," Taylor said, a flare of temper escaping.

Hatch cleared his throat and said, "'There is no evil we cannot either face or fly from but the consciousness of duty disregarded.'"

"Your point?"

"You know who told me to memorize Webster's quote?"

"Your third-grade English teacher?"

Chuckling, Hatch said, "Not bad."

Taylor peered through his binoculars. Tony D's bodyguards still sat in the

Pontiac. A colleague had delivered them breakfast from Burger King. "Little Crow, you're boring the shit out of me."

"Jack quoted Webster the day he hired me," Hatch said, turning somber. "Took me a long time to understand its meaning or why the boss thought it was so damn important. 'Consciousness of duty disregarded.' It's eloquently said, and terribly complicated in practice, once the bullets start to fly—don't you think?"

"Is it too much to ask for you to go back to Buffalo?"

"You're going to kill my brother."

"I have no intention of killing anyone," Taylor said. "But I will stop him—"

"I believe Jack's exact words were, 'Eliminate *them* with prejudice.' Them!"

How in hell did Hatch eavesdrop on a conversation encrypted by no fewer than 268 million codes?

"Jesus, Hatch, you can pick through anyone's conversation and come to your own conclusion," said Taylor. "It's like the media taking something out of context. Let me help you."

Hatch didn't respond.

"Still there?" Taylor said, his hard gaze continuing to survey Tony D's neighborhood.

"Gray, are you having a good time in the brownstone across the street from Mr. DiFilippo's home? Hmm? Bird-watching with the People Finder Unit, maybe?" said Hatch. "I could have busted you. One phone call to the cops and the whole world would descend on your position. Tony D and his minions would think *you* are the guy wasting his people, especially with that sniper rifle to your right. CIA might be implicated. Things would get messy, and Jack hates messy."

"Since you were listening in on my private conversations, you know my primary objective is to protect Anthony DiFilippo."

"I had no idea a mob boss could be so important to the U.S. government."

"We live in a strange world."

"Let it go, Gray. Walk away for just a day. One day."

"You know I can't do that. Stop asking," said Taylor, searching the area with his binoculars.

"Did you see this morning's paper?" Hatch asked. "Probably not, unless you have home delivery over there."

Taylor felt like ice water had infiltrated his blood. He shivered. "Now what?"

"This situation took another bad turn last night." Hatch read the *Post* headline and a few paragraphs of B. J. Butera's article.

"It's only going to get worse," said Taylor.

"One way or another, it will be over soon," Hatch said. "Believe me."

"Why should I?"

"You've seen my file. I'm pretty good at finding people."

Adjusting the binoculars, Taylor said, "Have you spoken to Steven?"

"Keep your two associates out of the way, Gray."

Taylor let out a long breath, then said, "The acts of this life are the destiny of the next."

"Don't tell me you're reciting Mr. Webster. That'd be too weird."

"I thought you would recognize your own grandfather's advice."

"You called Low Dog?" Hatch was incredulous, angry. "Why?"

"Fair is fair."

"What the fuck does that mean?"

"You left a note for me and Terri. I owed you one, pal. This is about family now," Taylor said. "Your stubbornness brought this upon a bunch of innocent people, including *my* wife, who happens to care for you. Why not get everyone we love involved in this disaster? You and I know this is gonna end badly, and I felt like your grandfather needed to hear it from the man who's going to finish it—unless you do the right thing and stand down. Go home."

"I can't do that!"

"Take care of yourself, Little Crow." Taylor terminated the call.

CHAPTER 43
Manhattan

The manila envelope was propped up on B. J. Butera's cluttered desk when he arrived at the newsroom a few minutes after ten o'clock Tuesday morning. A colleague walked by and patted B. J. on the shoulder. "Kid, you're on one heck of a roll," said the rotund man with the graying goatee, a veteran *New York Post* sports reporter. "It's probably time to ask for a raise."

Picking up the thick envelope, B. J. felt a bulge. No return address, no postmark—only his name printed on the front in neat block letters: "MR. BUTERA." *Mister? Nobody calls me mister.* He scanned the large newsroom in search of the practical jokester. Until a few months ago, he'd have been lucky to get a grunt of acknowledgment out of the senior staff around this place. He shook the envelope, then finally peeled back the top.

A few moments later, B. J. covered his mouth to stifle a girlish giggle. "Holy shit." What he found inside almost certainly guaranteed another front-page story and more recognition from his peers. This was the big one—his Watergate. A raise was indeed in order.

He slowly got to his feet and tried to identify Deep Throat. A cluster of people huddled around the coffee machine. Others watched *The Today Show* from a few televisions hanging from the ceiling. Most, however, sat in their cubicles staring blankly at computer screens, typing or talking on the phone.

The photographs drew his attention again. "Thank you, God," he whispered.

About ten feet away, a new face pushed the mail cart through the newsroom. "Yo, yo, mail guy!" B. J. shouted, cupping his hand to his mouth. The young man tossed a small cardboard box onto a desk and looked up. Tucking his long black hair behind one ear, the Native American pointed to himself. B. J. waved the envelope. "Did you put this on my desk?"

"Heck, I don't remember." And off he went, softly singing a Beatles song. "I get by with a little help from my friends . . ."

B. J. turned back to this unforeseen and startling gift. Laying the two five-by-seven photographs on his desk, he studied them—but also made sure nobody else caught a glimpse of his journalistic gold. All the while, like a magician, he flipped the CD from one finger to the next, considering his options.

"I need a quiet place," he murmured.

Brooklyn Heights

Sharks and Minnows.

As a kid growing up in the Bronx, it had been a game Anthony DiFilippo and his buddies, including Fat Paulie Franco and Louis Ciambella, had played regularly in the cool waters off Coney Island. One shark devouring a school of minnows. Each time they'd played, Tony D aggressively lobbied to be the shark. It was a position he'd savored his entire life.

Now, sitting at the kitchen table, the don nibbled a piece of toast while reading *The New York Post*. Flipping to the second page of the article, he was reminded of his favorite summertime game as a youth, and then sighed deeply. The rules in his structured life had been perfectly clear: To play Sharks and Minnows properly, there could only be one shark.

Lawrence Luther Wright didn't appear to be the type to abdicate his lofty position in the community—not by a long shot, especially now that the adept drug dealer had dispatched Mr. Tai and four of his associates in such short order.

"Very, very impressive, Mr. Wright," Tony D said, reaching for his mug of hot coffee. "You're a very dangerous man."

For Tony D, it was a fairly easy decision: one shark in the water, one alpha wolf in the forest, and one powerful man to control the New York underworld. Darwin's law—survival of the fittest—was the natural order of things, especially when his own life depended on it. Even if the don could somehow ignore Lawrence Luther's emerging reputation and power base, he knew other people far more influential than himself would not. As Tony D saw the situation, he had an obligation—a *duty*—to rid society of miscreants like Mr. Wright before they grew too dominant. Weeds needed to be pulled out at the roots. Although he loathed violence, his own survival depended on tending to his garden with extreme diligence.

Anthony DiFilippo picked up his special cell phone and punched in eleven digits—it was a long-distance telephone number that changed every month, whether he used it or not. Only the two-zero-two area code remained the same.

A curt-sounding woman with a trace of a Cajun accent answered after three rings. "I've been expecting this call."

"Because of the article?" Tony D said, pushing the newspaper to the side.

"The media coverage concerns us."

"It's always temporary in this city. We've been through this dozens of times."

"We're monitoring the situation."

"Obviously."

"Internet reports, the *Post*, and *The New York Times* have been especially unkind to your organization, Tony. Fox picked up on the story this morning and took it national. You're coming across as weak. That's a bad thing for a man in your position."

"It's being handled."

"This incident at the Chinese restaurant—was it your doing?"

"Not directly," Tony D said slowly, getting up from the table.

"I'm afraid some of my colleagues feel you're losing your edge—"

"This dog has not forgotten how to hunt," Tony D said, cutting off his handler.

"Would you like to share your plan with me?"

"No." Coughing, Tony D cleared his throat and said, "Have I ever let you down?"

Bronx

Detective Katherine Montroy parked her unmarked Taurus on Grand Boulevard, lowered the visor, then sat low in her seat. It was a few minutes after ten o'clock Tuesday morning. Nine vehicles ahead was the white Ford Explorer. Apprehending this murderer would go a long way toward saving her soul, she knew.

And she needed to do this alone.

CHAPTER 44

Manhattan

"Where the hell are you, B.J.?" Howard Stapleton shouted into his telephone. "I can barely hear you, B. J." The spike of emotion was rare from a man who didn't work for a paycheck. Stapleton closed the heavy glass door that separated the noisy newsroom from his corner office, which overlooked the Avenue of the Americas.

"My car," B. J. Butera said again. "I'm in the parking garage."

The tall, athletically built, gray-haired man in the dark blue Mantoni sports jacket didn't need a second invitation. As the editor in chief of *The New York Post*, he'd been involved in the business of journalism for thirty-seven years—long enough to smell something major percolating. And Butera, who also happened to be on a real hot streak, had never sounded a false alarm.

Stapleton's voice returned to its typically poised timbre. "What level?"

"Two. East side of the building. I'm still driving my crappy Toyota." *But those days are coming to an end.*

Bronx

The hunter, gloved hands in his jacket pockets, crossed at the intersection from East Fordham Road over to Grand Boulevard, his head on a swivel, eyes always searching for signs of danger in the relatively quiet neighborhood. And just as he reached the curb, he saw two of Tony D's men sitting inside a café, drinking coffee from paper cups, no doubt watching his vehicle.

Zebras galloping down Fifth Avenue on a sunny Sunday morning would have looked less conspicuous than these two, he thought.

How did they find me? The hunter remained calm, though his heart began to pound against his ribcage. It was crucial to act normally.

These two men—Marco and Salvatore—had found the hunter's stolen SUV, but had yet to locate his base of operations. Most importantly, they hadn't spotted him. Not yet. It didn't matter how they'd gotten this far—only that he needed to leave the neighborhood without bringing undue attention to himself. But he also couldn't leave empty-handed; there were items in his apartment that needed to be retrieved sooner rather than later.

A few yards from the stolen Ford, he dropped to one knee, removed his leather gloves, and began retying his boots' laces, searching for more of DiFilippo's people. The hunter then pulled his Yankees baseball cap down, stood, and glanced at his watch through his sunglasses, as if forgetting about some previous engagement. Turning, he began covering old ground, knowing that every step away from these goons was another step in the right direction. Once he turned the corner onto East Fordham Road, he'd slip back into the building where he was staying.

"Hey! Hey you!" a woman shouted from up ahead. Her voice was loud, firm, and commanding. She was climbing out of a Taurus parked at the curb on the other side of Grand Boulevard.

The hunter barely looked up, yet instantly recognized Detective Katherine Montroy. *Shit!* He turned and sprinted back toward the café, hoping to pass Tony D's men before they could get outside.

"Stop!" Montroy yelled, reaching for the SIG Sauer P229 handgun in her shoulder rig. "Police!" She swung her arm around and up, took careful aim, and fired the 9mm once.

The hunter stumbled, then went down, face first, his chin hitting the concrete.

As Tony D's soldiers knocked over a table, heading for the café's front door like bulls leading a stampede; as pedestrians on the street stood motionless or ran, ducking into doorways or behind parked cars; as most drivers drove on, oblivious to the shooting, an elderly white-haired woman in a light sweater and pink pajama bottoms, short and frail looking, stepped from her apartment building onto the sidewalk, between Montroy and the wounded man on the cracked concrete. He was rolling over.

At one end of a leash, the elderly woman did her best to control a full-grown Irish Wolfhound, weighing in at a good 110 pounds.

"Lady, get out of the way!" Montroy screamed, pointing her pistol at the ground.

"You can't talk to me like that!" the woman yelled back. "Who the hell do you think you are?"

The hunter struggled to his feet. The 9mm slug had not exited, but there was very little blood on the sidewalk, and his adrenaline minimized the pain. The moment he was up, he was moving again, wagering his life that Detective Montroy wouldn't take a chance and fire her weapon unless she had a clear line of sight past the angry elderly woman and the big dog.

"I'm a cop!" Montroy yelled. "I'm after that man! Behind you! Look!"

The elderly woman painstakingly shuffled around to face the other direction, and covered her mouth as if to stifle a scream—then accidentally let go of the leash. The gray and white dog galloped between two parked cars and into oncoming traffic. A postal truck hit the brakes, locking up the tires, and screeched to a stop, nearly clipping the animal. A chorus of horns, echoing off the buildings, followed.

Tony D's two men lumbered across the street and onto the sidewalk, but the hunter had already turned the corner and disappeared.

"Where the fuck did you two assholes come from?" Montroy demanded, shoving her SIG back into the shoulder harness. "Who told you about this?"

"Watch your mouth, Ms. Montroy," Salvatore said in a low growl, his right hand clenched in a tight fist.

Marco removed a cell phone from his coat pocket and fingered a few buttons. He waited a moment, then said, "He got away, Boss."

"You can tell the old bastard it's one and done for me!" Montroy shouted. "I'll never take his fucking money again! Never!" Rage and frustration had taken hold. And then the tremors began. A long exhalation followed. "And he can take his threats and shove them up both your asses!"

The two DiFilippo soldiers turned and walked toward East Fordham Road without responding again, unaware that their Buick sedan was parked right in front of the apartment building that housed the hunter's lair.

Montroy went back to her own car, slipped into the driver's seat, and pulled the door closed, trying to calm down. The unidentified assassin who'd been targeting Tony D's people wouldn't return for the stolen Explorer, and living in this massive city, where parking places on the street were considered territorial gold, he could be hiding out at least five blocks in any direction. How many cops would it take to secure such a wide area, where apartment buildings rose twenty, even thirty stories high?

Having made her decision, Montroy made the call to her precinct captain, requesting backup near Fordham University—as many police officers as the department could spare. She'd wounded a very dangerous suspect, one who may have been responsible for multiple homicides. When she ended the call, Montroy was back out of her car, looking in through the Ford Explorer's tinted windows. There was nothing on the seats or floorboards.

Montroy flipped open her phone again and reported that she'd found a stolen vehicle used in a recent series of serious crimes. It needed to be impounded. Perhaps they'd get lucky with a fingerprint or a hair sample. She doubted it, though—Tony D's "ghost" was much too clever.

Waiting for the troops to arrive seemed like an eternity. Finally, lights flashing, siren wailing, the first patrol car rocketed down Grand Boulevard just as her adrenaline started to bleed off. Regardless of the way Montroy sliced it, this day was going to be hard to explain.

Manhattan

Howard Stapleton and B. J. Butera sat in the dark green Toyota, listening to the twenty-three-minute CD. It was the second time for Stapleton and the fourth for B. J. The clarity was marginal, but good enough to understand the edited conversations from the three individuals who'd apparently been secretly recorded and photographed on two different occasions. The narrator's computer-altered remarks and astute observations came in loud and clear.

The two journalists made a few comments of their own as the CD played on. B. J. scribbled furiously on a yellow legal pad. Tugging at his chin, Stapleton continued to study both photographs.

When the second conversation ended, B. J. ejected the CD from the car stereo. He turned to his boss, an animated expression plastered on his unshaven face. "Looks like Christmas came early, Chief."

"Well, I do agree that you have yourself one hell of a Deep Throat. Any ideas who it could be?"

"I . . . man, I wouldn't have a clue."

"An admirer of your recent work, possibly? I'm particularly fond of this guy's sense of humor, B. J." Stapleton picked up the handwritten note: "'DIS-ORGANIZED CRIME?' He's trying to steal my thunder. It's definitely tomorrow's headline *if* you can pull it off."

"Pull what off?"

"Son, as the proverbial saying goes, you better get your ducks in a row before we run with something this hot," Stapleton said, pursing his lips into a tight grimace. "You're publicly attacking some very powerful people, and that means the reputations of a bunch of folks would be swinging in the balance. You, me, the paper, the goddamned holding company that owns *The New York Post*—none of us can afford to get this one wrong. Our legal eagle insists we take too many risks as it is."

"Fuck him," said B. J.

Slowly shaking his head, Stapleton replied, sternly, "No. That's not how it works, B. J., and you know it. He'll fuck you right to the unemployment line, but only after he drives the bus over you a few times. This needs to be done right.

Understood?"

B. J. nodded.

"I hope so," Stapleton said.

"Shit, what does my source want out of this?" B. J. said, getting back to the manila envelope.

"Could be a cop who's fed up with the system, or someone with a bone to pick with the detective in the picture."

They both looked at the photograph of Detective Katherine Montroy, standing in a deserted parking lot. It was dark, but the images were clear in ghostly shades of green. A rollercoaster from Coney Island's amusement park stood in the background.

The shot had been taken last night, according to the timestamp.

Reputed mob boss Anthony DiFilippo IV was accepting a thick envelope from Montroy.

"Or my guy's an old-fashioned Good Samaritan," said B. J.

"He has night-vision technology," Stapleton said, tapping his manicured fingernail against one of the photographs. "He was also a good distance away but had the ability to listen in on their conversation." The editor in chief turned the picture over and read aloud the printed message: "'Anthony DiFilippo and Detective Katherine Montroy at Coney. Fifty grand was offered for information on Chinese gangs in NYC. You wrote about the results, Mr. Butera.'"

"The CD tells us why Tony D wanted the info," B. J. said. "The photos show us how he got the information and who's involved. This morning's article describes the bloody aftermath. Five Asian gang members—all dead. Sir, I'm ready to rock and roll."

"Ease off the accelerator," Stapleton said, leaning his head against the seat, then folding his hands.

The second photograph—this one in color—was of Anthony DiFilippo and Lawrence Luther Wright sitting on a bench with a silver briefcase between them. According to the notation, they were in St. Mary's Park. In the recording, both men discussed a very serious problem: Roger Tai, the leader of the Akrho Pinoy gang.

"Tony D didn't want to get his hands dirty," Stapleton said.

"Which doesn't make sense," B. J. said. "Four of his top men—an underboss and three captains—got whacked. Wouldn't the don feel the need to exact his own revenge?"

"If you really think about it, B. J.," Stapleton said, "when's the last time DiFilippo resorted to violence? He's got a reputation for being dangerous but doesn't really deserve it. War is a young man's means of solving problems. Tony D turned to diplomacy when he took over the family."

"But aren't reputations won and lost in times of crisis?" said B. J. "Street cred, baby."

"Maybe the cops are watching the don too closely."

B. J. pointed to the photo. "Not that closely."

"Or Mr. DiFilippo doesn't have the right people in place yet," Stapleton said. "Soldiers he can trust. Filling those management positions can't be easy."

"So . . . Tony D enlists Lawrence Luther Wright? Really?"

"The don buys the information on Tai's outfit, and Wright's people go to work." Stapleton let out a long breath. "Deep Throat is making this way too easy, B. J."

"Sir, c'mon. You're taking all the fun out of this."

Turning his head to look B. J. directly in the eyes, Stapleton said, "You have a photo of Ms. Montroy and Tony D, another one of Lawrence Luther Wright and Tony D, five dead Akrho Pinoy gang members, an explosion that destroys Mr. Wright's new Harlem drug operation, another bomb that pretty much turns Louis Ciambella into vapor, three more dead members of DiFilippo's crew, allegedly more than a few dead gangbangers—"

"It's a war," B. J. said, spreading his hand. "Simple as that."

"Here's the rub," Stapleton said. "How can we be so sure everything's connected? Why are DiFilippo and Wright so quick to identify Roger Tai's organization? Who tipped them off?"

B. J. dragged his fingers through his thick blond hair, considering his next move. "What if I can prove the Harlem bombing and the explosion that killed Ciambella used the same material?"

"That would support your theory. One bomber."

B. J. jotted down some notes.

"For God's sake, B. J., keep things quiet," said Stapleton. "This story has to be done right."

"I know, Chief. I will."

"It still doesn't tell us who Deep Throat is."

"Does it matter?"

Stapleton again puzzled over the question. "I'm not sure," he finally said.

"Sir, with all due respect, isn't second place the first loser? We need to move on this story before—"

"Look," Stapleton said harshly, "I need to talk with our legal department. In the meantime, you start pulling things together. Please be discreet. I don't want you looking for confirmation or comment from Montroy, Philips, or Benedetti. Not yet anyway."

CHAPTER 45

Bronx

Curiosity may have killed the cat, but a routine can just as easily kill a man. Johnny Cercone, leaving his apartment at nearly the same time every morning, was one such example.

But Matthew Philips, a man who'd dedicated his entire adult life to capturing killers with bits and pieces of disjointed data, relevant facts, and witness accounts, rarely applied the "habit theory" to his own life. Why should he? When was the last time a New York City detective had been murdered?

A nagging itch, on the other hand, compounded by memories of his ugly confrontation with two of Tony D's thugs, had followed Philips throughout the day. Fellow police officers steered clear of their ornery colleague, whispering about his disheveled appearance. Philips's hands shook so violently by three o'clock that lighting a cigarette was all but impossible.

He realized now that his sixteen-year association with Tony D had become a crushing burden to his conscience. The don had always wanted insight on his enemies and updated information on the New York narcotics trade, and the enormous sums of money Tony D offered in return were too good to pass up. Like a heroin addict, Philips promised to quit cold turkey after the next score. That never came to pass. But Philips had recently discovered there was indeed a line he would not cross.

Tony D wanted files and photographs of the Chinese gangs. These were people he wasn't just going to intimidate or incriminate on trumped-up charges, but men he considered a threat to his organization—men the don almost assuredly had targeted for assassination.

Philips had never lied to the don until that request reached him two days ago. He tried to explain that such sensitive information was impossible to obtain without secure clearance, which Philips didn't have.

Tony D evidently found another avenue to get the answers he coveted. And those results were plastered all over the front page of this morning's *New York*

Post. Tony D, without Matthew Philips's assistance, had gotten his revenge in spectacular fashion, but that wasn't the end of it.

Now the don demanded sensitive files gathered from neighboring police precincts, including the mob division. This morning, Philips had lied again, this time to two of DiFilippo's people outside a Super Saver pharmacy, telling the grim-faced soldiers he couldn't deliver on that request, either. It had been the second time in two days he'd denied Tony D, a pattern that could not be explained away.

The don would be extremely disappointed, one of the thugs, Marco, mumbled a few times. Then he punched the detective in the kidney—repeatedly.

"Maybe your skinny wife will have an unfortunate accident if certain files don't find their way to the boss," Marco said.

So Philips threw them a bone: Neesa Saul, the supervisor at NYCDOT who coordinated the traffic cameras, may have uncovered something important. Katherine had given him the name yesterday. Saul had a special program she hoped would help find the infamous white Explorer.

Tony D's thugs appeared satisfied. Marco relayed the information to his boss, and they left him alone.

After the brief altercation, Philips considered telling Katherine everything. She was a good cop and a great detective, who didn't deserve to have her reputation tarnished if this unholy relationship became public or turned south. They were friends. Early retirement seemed like the only option, but only after he explained the situation to Katherine. His partner deserved to know the truth.

Pulling on his trench coat, Philips headed out the Twenty-Eighth Precinct's front door without acknowledging any of his colleagues.

Fifteen minutes later, Philips tossed back his second shot of Jack Daniel's and chased it with Red Dog Ale. The effects were instantaneous as the alcohol coursed through his bloodstream. He set the empty glass on the oak bar and extended his fingers, palm down. The tremors had disappeared. It was like a magic trick. Even his heart seemed to be beating normally. He smiled for the first time since rolling off the couch this morning.

"Bad day at the office, Matty?" the sociable bartender asked in Russian-accented English. Maxim Pokryshkin had a gaunt, pale face, a graying goatee, and crew cut. He placed another shot of Jack Daniel's in front of his only customer. "My friend, you do not look so good."

Peering over his bent glasses, Philips said, "Max...I'm thinkin' about retiring—gettin' out before there's nothin' left of me."

Leaning on the cash register with an unlit stub of a cigar clamped between his stained teeth, Pokryshkin, who wore a white apron and a concerned expression, drew another Red Dog from the tap and pushed the glass of beer in front of Philips. "On house, Matty. Make you think clearer."

"You're a saint." Philips reached for the draft and took a long pull. The shot of Jack came next, and Maxim was right—he *was* thinking clearer.

It had all begun so innocently sixteen years earlier. Newly promoted Detective Philips had found a large manila envelope tucked in the front door of his one-bedroom ground-floor Brooklyn apartment. He flipped through a bundle of crisp twenties—five thousand dollars in cash. When he turned around, he saw a handsome salt-and-pepper-haired man sitting in a black Chrysler sedan, parked at the curb. The driver of the car nodded once and casually drove off.

That man was underboss Anthony DiFilippo IV, who, even then, had his sights set on the top position in New York's largest crime family.

Philips should have returned the money. He didn't. The package, like a forlorn lover, had called out to him that night. He was engaged to be married, and the cash would come in handy for a number of things. In fact, the timing was perfect.

Like any mutually beneficial relationship, each party depended on the other. Philips passed along delicate and sometimes classified information, which included ongoing investigations that implicated Tony D's enemies and even members of his own crime family. Through the years, the envelopes became thicker as Philips brought Tony D tidbits on specific competitors and enemies who intended to move in on the family. This reliable pipeline helped Tony D identify problems at an early stage, long before they could take root, and because of this surreptitious link with Philips, Tony D developed a growing reputation for keeping the peace through shrewd negotiations. This status solidified once he became the most powerful underworld figure in New York City.

The triple murder at Rudy's Tavern was a perfect example of how their system worked. Both Johnny Cercone and Vincent Tagliafero were involved in the Three Tenors murders—no question about it. Forensics found their fingerprints, along with other identifiable markers, at the scene. An eyewitness, who subsequently changed his story after his son's college debt had been mysteriously satisfied, observed two men leaving Rudy's in a hurry. The Corvette's plate number and the color of the sports car had matched Cercone's vehicle. Those details had been relayed directly to Tony D from Philips a few hours after the three murders.

"Tony, one of your nephews has to take the fall," Philips said a few days later. "I'm sorry."

Then, a week passed, and Vincent Tagliafero's body was found behind a vacant warehouse at the Hunts Point Market. At most, Philips had thought the don would have Tagliafero or Cercone arrested—never did he think that the don would order the death of a family member. Philips had directly facilitated a murder.

Only then did he realize how dangerous Anthony DiFilippo could become.

Philips had been told about the order the night before the Tagliafero hit. Unfortunately, Katherine Montroy was called to the crime scene, unknowingly thrusting her into a very volatile and precarious situation—yet everything seemed to have worked out. The murder weapons were located on or near Tagliafero's body and positively identified as the guns used to kill three people at Rudy's Tavern. Montroy had gotten a little aggressive with her onslaught of questions, specifically of the ballistic reports, but even that issue seemed to fade away after Montroy received much of the credit for solving the triple homicide.

Once Tagliafero had been buried, the media, satisfied, quickly turned to another sensational story, and the murders of Karen Easter, Patricia Durante, and Bobby O'Rourke were all but forgotten. Technically, the Three Tenors case was still open—a second shooter could have been at the scene—but the mob division had other cases and more pressing issues. Who's to say Tagliafero didn't use both guns?

Since then, information on the Vietnam-era shells left behind at the crime scenes, the two teenage boys who'd stolen Woody Biasucci's car, Pebbles's identity, and the white Explorer was passed directly from Philips to Anthony DiFilippo.

And for his trouble, Philips found himself growing richer.

Maxim Pokryshkin, standing at the far end of the bar, poured pretzels into a small wooden bowl. Frank Sinatra sang quietly on the radio.

Easter and Patricia? "Karen Easter and Patricia Durante," Philips said out loud, staring at his empty beer glass like it was some crystal ball. "And *Tony D.*" *The guy who murdered Woody Biasucci forced him to recite* names. *"Easter" had nothing to do with a holiday—it was a name.* "A person's name!"

"You okay, Matty?" Max asked, screwing up his face. He slid the bowl in front of his only customer.

"Now I am," Philips said, clapping his hands together. "Yes!"

At half past three, Matthew Philips slapped a twenty-dollar bill on the bar, thanked Pokryshkin for a lovely chat, and headed back into the cold November afternoon. Squinting in the brightness as the door to Lucky's Lounge closed behind him, the detective was bombarded by the ceaseless noise of the Bronx neighborhood—a chorus of car horns, a barking dog, and a Hassidic Jew yelling at the mailman from a second-floor window. Philips filled his lungs with fresh air.

"Hey, Detective Philips!" a man shouted from the open window of a black Toyota Tundra. The SUV was double-parked outside the small tavern. Traffic was light, the mailman had turned the corner, and the old Jewish man was gone.

Philips brought his hand to his face, blocking the sun that peeked over the brick apartment building to the west. "Do I know you?"

"We haven't met, but I have something to tell you about Katherine Montroy."

"Kat?" Philips froze.

The driver of the older Tundra wore a Yankees baseball cap, pulled down to cover much of his face, dark sunglasses, a cream-colored scarf around his neck, a brown leather jacket, and a beard. "Yep," he said, "I'm pretty sure you'll find it interesting."

Philips shuffled over to the SUV and leaned into the passenger-side window. "Hey, asshole, your guys already made their point this morning. Tell your boss to back off. I think I figured out why all this shit is happening—"

"I almost made a terrible mistake with Ms. Montroy," the hunter said, reaching underneath his jacket. "I was a breath away from killing her. And then a strange thing happened—I got cold feet, couldn't pull the trigger. My weakness saved her, Detective Philips—and it almost cost me my life."

"Are you nuts?"

"Your partner was an innocent bystander until you dropped the ball. Tony D offered to pay Montroy fifty grand for files on a few Chinese gangs, then threatened to hurt her girlfriend when she balked. And you made the introduction at the Woodland Cemetery. Interesting, huh?"

Philips's face darkened. "I don't believe you," he said in a less than convincing tone. Tony D had gotten his information from somebody. He knew Katherine couldn't be bought, but everyone had a breaking point.

"Of course you believe me," the hunter said.

"If you're trying to scare me, it's not work—"

"All this time, I was looking at your bank accounts, maybe something offshore—anything to tie you to DiFilippo. And I'll be damned! You went old school—buried your booty like a damn dog."

"Are we finished here?"

The hunter smoothly removed a silenced Glock 9mm from his shoulder rig and pointed the weapon at Philips's chest. "Just another minute."

"Hey . . . okay, I didn't mean nothin'," Philips said, raising his hands.

"For the past few weeks," the hunter said evenly, "I thought Montroy was the dirty cop, when all along it was you, Detective Philips. *You* destroyed and manipulated evidence at the Three Tenors homicide. *You* took payoffs from Anthony DiFilippo. *You're* the one with a steamer trunk filled with cash under the floorboards in your shed."

"I have no idea what you're talkin' about."

"Please, must we play such games?" the hunter said, mimicking a phrase he'd heard while recording Anthony DiFilippo.

Detective Matthew Philips's eyes widened, yet he didn't respond.

"For the record, no, I'm not a cop, and I don't work for Tony D, but the don is apparently looking for me. And this belongs to him." In the hunter's gloved hand, he held a Vietnam-era shell from an M16.

As if a few giant puzzle pieces had slid into place, Philips suddenly understood who he was talking to. Easter, Patricia, Tony D. "You . . . Jesus, you're the guy . . ."

"Well done, Detective."

"But—"

"Like I said, Ms. Montroy got very, very lucky."

"Please tell me you didn't hurt her."

"She's fine." Cocking his head, the hunter paused for a moment, then said, "I'm not exactly sure how Ms. Montroy found me, but she did—even shot me in the ass. I barely got in and out of my apartment with the stuff I need to finish this thing. Your partner is a very smart woman, Detective Philips."

Philips closed his eyes. He was tired of the lies, his job—tired of just about everything. "Christ, this is all because Vincent Tagliafero and Johnny Cercone killed your friends back in August," he said, barely above a whisper.

"Yes," the hunter said firmly.

"Why? Who were these people to you? Where do you fit in?"

"Patricia Durante was going to be my fiancée," the hunter said through clenched teeth. "You people ruined my life."

Defeated, shoulders slumped, Philips slowly shook his head. "My God."

"And you, Detective, helped deflect the blame away from Cercone—you and Anthony DiFilippo, and—"

"I'm sorry—"

"That makes two of us." The hunter squeezed the trigger twice. The sound, like pressurized air released from a compressor, was lost in the bustle of the Bronx street. Two bullets thumped into Philips's chest and exploded out his back, violently knocking him into a cluster of garbage cans.

He died staring up at the sunny November sky.

CHAPTER 46
Brooklyn Heights

In spite of the circumstances of her marriage and the murmurs and chilly glances from her wealthy neighbors, Mara DiFilippo had always stood by her husband. Never once had she questioned Anthony's love for his family, nor did she probe into his business, even when the voracious New York tabloids accused him of horrible acts. As of late, those media attacks had come with greater frequency.

And maybe it was only a coincidence, but the flame of passion behind Anthony's brown eyes had gradually diminished over the past three months. It was obvious to her that something was terribly wrong. The murders of her two nephews, Vincent Tagliafero and Johnny Cercone, followed closely by the deaths of Paulie Franco, Donald Biasucci, and Louis Ciambella, along with an endless stream of nightmares, had darkened her husband's personality. He'd even stopped talking about his problems, which only made matters worse.

Mara tried to blame his health, and his upcoming surgery at Sloan-Kettering Hospital, but finally came to another conclusion: The storm Anthony had mentioned five or six weeks ago had finally come ashore.

And like any major hurricane, this one had a name: Gray Taylor.

The dinner dishes had been cleared. Mara DiFilippo joined her husband at the kitchen table.

"More wine?" Tony D asked, reaching for the bottle of Shiraz.

Fingering the small envelope in her apron pocket, Mara said, "No thanks."

"You okay?"

Their eyes met. The envelope appeared in Mara's right hand, as if by magic. She slid it across the white tablecloth. Her simple wedding band—the one Anthony had given her almost forty years ago—came next.

And then the teapot began to whistle.

Leaning close to her husband, Mara said, quietly, "I want you to whisper, Anthony. The teapot should help."

Tony D narrowed his eyes. "Help with what?"

Mara's barely audible voice quavered. "I think our conversations have been monitored for the past few weeks."

"Why would you say that?"

"Shhh. I need you to lower your voice."

Tony D gestured toward the envelope and ring. "What are you doing?"

"Anthony, you've protected and loved me, given me stability and purpose, helped me raise three wonderful children, but I will *not* attend *your* funeral," said Mara decisively. "Not now. As it is, I'll be spending more than enough time at St. Andrew's over the next few days."

"You worry too much," Tony D said with a tight smile, leaning back in his chair.

Shaking her head with firm resolve, Mara said, "Apparently, I don't worry enough."

"You're not making any sense, Mara. What's gotten into you?"

The whistling teapot grew louder.

"You're scared, Anthony. You've been scared for almost three months. I can see the fear in your eyes. And those damn dreams of yours are almost real to you. You toss and turn most nights. That's never happened before."

"You're—"

"Don't you dare tell me I'm wrong," Mara said through gritted teeth.

Tony D reached for his wife's hands, but she recoiled. "Mara, honey, it's the cancer," he said. "I guess I'm just a little spooked."

"No," Mara said, shaking her head. "No. Your nightmares came before the diagnosis—long before we scheduled the operation with Dr. Brightly. Vincent's death triggered something in you. Don't lie to me, Anthony. My eyes are wide open now."

"If you really need to know, the problem was cleaned up last night."

"You're wrong," Mara insisted. "It's not over."

"I'm sorry," Tony D said, as if he hadn't heard his wife. "I didn't want you to be concerned—"

"The envelope isn't from me."

Tony D said nothing, although one thick eyebrow inched upward.

"I was told to deliver it to you," Mara said. "A man gave it to me at the supermarket."

The don glanced at the white envelope. *Another message from Lawrence Luther*

Wright? Detective Philips, maybe? "What man?" he said. Though his voice remained a whisper, it took on an abrasive edge. Tony D's business persona seldom crossed over into his personal life.

"He was tall, with close-cropped blond hair," said Mara. "He stopped me in the produce aisle. He looked like he came straight out of some military pamphlet—big, like a football player. Very handsome and well-spoken—introduced himself as Gray Taylor, even showed me his driver's license, and politely asked me to deliver this envelope to you before the day was over. Mr. Taylor said our lives depended on it."

"Some lunatic threatens you—"

"Shhh." Mara raised her index finger to her lips. "He was very gracious—a complete gentleman. He acted as if he genuinely cared about your safety . . . and mine. He insisted our house is 'under surveillance'—those were his exact words."

"Our home is always being watched, Mara. You know that."

"Recorded with high-tech audio equipment."

Tony D considered this for a moment. "This man told you all of this in a brief conversation . . . today?"

Mara nodded. "At Jubilee Foods."

"Right," Tony D said dismissively, turning the envelope over.

"Anthony, you're being an ignorant ass," she said, exhaling audibly. "With everything you've been through, tell me this isn't out of the realm of possibility."

"And your wedding band? What's that about?"

"It's time to retire. Blame the cancer. You can't keep up this charade—"

"Mara, important people depend on me. You know that," Tony D said. "Cancer is no reason to walk away from my life."

"Our life!" Mara's gaze dropped to the envelope. "I have a feeling things are about to change . . . for both of us."

Tony D was incredulous. "Because of some cryptic message delivered by a guy you don't know?"

"Me or the business—it's your choice, Anthony. I'll give you until tomorrow night." Getting up from her chair, Mara turned off the flame below the teapot and left the kitchen without her wedding band.

Alone at the table, in a room steeped in silence, Tony D studied his name printed on the white envelope: "Anthony DiFilippo." The muscles in his neck and shoulders suddenly began to ache, and then the troublesome cough was back. He finished off another glass of red wine and finally unfolded the handwritten letter:

Dear Mr. DiFilippo,

Your efforts to alleviate a mutual problem are focused in the wrong direction. Another player is responsible for the deaths of your people. We should talk tonight: Rockefeller Center, east side of the ice rink. 10:00. Please be cautious. Check your clothing for bugs. When you contact your people, be especially discreet. I'm sure your home and vehicle continue to be closely monitored by a very talented adversary. I work for the CIA. Verify my story with your handlers if you must.

Gray Taylor

Brooklyn Heights

As he'd done the night before, Kevin Easter watched Anthony DiFilippo's neighborhood from the safety of a high-rise apartment building one block away. The distance was well outside the reach of Gray Taylor's heartbeat-tracking DKL unit, not to mention the sniper's rifle the older man had been trained by the CIA to use. Hatch hadn't seen any sign of Taylor this evening, although the regular watchers—Tony D's bodyguards and local cops—were back in their usual positions. He'd considered phoning Taylor, but thought better of it. Hatch hadn't changed cell phones, and there was always a small chance CIA techies like Mickey Aldridge could triangulate his position. In fact, his cell had again been turned off and shoved in his duffle bag. If need be, Hatch could always use a payphone.

He sat on an upturned wooden box in the dark and watched through his telephoto lens, waiting for something he didn't really expect to happen tonight. Tony D's home was protected by armed men, and no reasonable hunter would attempt to circumvent such defenses—yet here he was nonetheless, because he didn't have a better starting point.

You needed a good place to begin. Low Dog had taught Hatch that when he was just a boy.

"Animals of the forest, like most men, are creatures of habit, Little Crow," the shaman had stressed. Hatch and his grandfather were both in a tree stand, high above a deer path, their breath clinging to the still air. The sun had yet to rise that cold Thanksgiving morning, but still Hatch had seen the fresh tracks in the snow before ascending the ladder two hours earlier.

As a boy growing up on the Cattaraugus Indian Reservation, hunting was an important step—the first test in becoming a man. But Hatch wanted nothing to do with killing—squirrel, rabbit, deer, black bear, it didn't matter. Taking a life felt wrong, he'd said to his grandfather. But Low Dog, his guardian and mentor, had insisted. Venison would feed them for an entire month.

As the first shadows appeared that frigid morning, a ten-point buck appeared on the path. Low Dog quietly elbowed his grandson, and Hatch raised the bow he'd made from a cherry tree on their property.

The arrow flew true, but the shot wasn't clean.

Low Dog and Hatch followed the blood trail for nearly an hour. They found the buck thrashing about, tangled in a thick briar patch. The broken arrow had pierced its neck. Hatch never forgot his own reflection in the buck's incredibly big brown eyes. The beautiful creature with its stately antlers lay in a snow drift, bleeding out, struggling for breath, suffering—all because of Hatch. He'd never felt so small, so scared, or so ashamed, and he remembered how he wanted to pull the arrow from the buck's neck, help it to its feet, and send it back into the forest where it belonged.

Low Dog handed his young charge a Buckmaster hunting knife. It was heavy and sharp. Shaking his head defiantly, Hatch threw the knife into the snow.

"You must," Low Dog said, gently patting his grandson on the shoulder. "This great animal gave its life for you, Little Crow. It suffers, and you must stop its suffering."

But when the tears fell, Hatch bolted into the woods, humiliated for being so weak.

Pulled back into the present of his temporary residence, Hatch knew that his big brother had felt no such attachment to the animals that provided food for their family. But could Steven kill another human being? Could brothers really be that different?

But then again, didn't his own professional work—photographing enemies of the United States—help facilitate some of their deaths? Isn't that exactly what he'd done today with his message to Lawrence Luther Wright?

Hatch turned his binoculars back on the DiFilippo home, remembering Low Dog's words: *Animals of the forest, like most men, are creatures of habit, Little Crow.* Hatch knew the elderly shaman was right again.

CHAPTER 47

Bronx

Sitting in the vinyl booth, Brian McGowan slipped the menu back in-between the plastic bottles of mustard and ketchup. As a kid growing up in the Bronx, the Arthur Avenue Deli, which also doubled as a candy store and ice-cream parlor, had been a routine stop on his way home from grade school.

Now, McGowan drummed his fingers on the table, his gaze drifting to the busy street, then back to B. J. Butera. "Somebody actually photographed DiFilippo and Montroy with night-vision equipment? And this person had the pics secretly delivered you?"

B. J. nodded. "Man, it's fucking unbelievable."

"Makes me wonder who else got a look at those photos," McGowan said, reaching into his jacket pocket and removing three white pills. He tossed them in his mouth and washed them down with his glass of water. "I have a monster headache."

"Take your troubles to Jesus," B. J. said in a quirky melody. He grinned.

"Hell," McGowan said, staring out the window, "is this evidence being handed out to multiple reporters or what? Do the cops have 'em yet?"

"If it is out there, you can bet the ranch Tony D knows."

"I have an opinion," said McGowan. "Interested?"

"Absolutely."

"Look at the big picture for a minute."

"I am, Brian, from like a hundred different angles. Christ."

"Okay, well, I think we're dealing with a couple of people, B. J. The shooter and a bomber. A team. And one of them sent you the envelope. Maybe he wants the killings to end—call it buyer's remorse."

"Dude, are you drinking the Kool-Aid or what? Where'd ya come up with that?"

"Your Deep Throat has night-vision gear and balls as big as Montana," said

McGowan. "Photographing Anthony DiFilippo and Lawrence Luther Wright on a park bench? Recording them? C'mon. And he got that envelope to you without being seen. You said there was no postmark."

"Correct, Inspector Gadget."

"The assassin used a sniper's rifle and made a world-class shot—"

"In the snow."

"Yeah, and then there's the bombs. Same residue at a few of the scenes. But can one guy be in so many places? Doubtful. It feels like some rogue military guys are cleaning up the streets. And now one or both want the world to know their motive. Maybe they've taken it as far as they can . . . or want."

"Truthfully, one guy or two, it really doesn't matter that much to me," said B. J. "Not yet."

"Keep your eye on the prize, B. J. Your story is about killing underworld figures—bad guys, pond scum."

"Can you go on record that the same C-4 was used at multiple sites?"

Smiling, McGowan said, "Same detonators, too. I found another piece at the Long Island City bombing."

"Brian, you have to know you're sticking your neck out."

"This ugly neck?" McGowan reached into the front pocket of his hoodie and tossed a white envelope onto the table.

"What's in it?"

"Confirmation, verification, proof. Call it what you want. That's a copy of my internal report." McGowan shrugged. "I suspect a crazy story like this will get you another front page."

"Unless the Pope disavows the existence of God."

The waitress delivered two pastrami sandwiches. B. J. ignored his meal, pushing the plate aside. He folded his hands and leaned over the table. "So, can I quote you? Anonymous source?"

"What's the point? People in the NYFD are going to know where the leak came from."

"Why are you doing this?"

"Because it's the right thing to do, my man. It's about exposing these arrogant mobsters for who they are. It's about the truth. You know me—always trying to be the good guy. I'm the white knight, remember?" McGowan bit into his sandwich.

"And what is the truth?"

"Anthony DiFilippo's people are criminals, and somebody decided to do something about it."

"But what about this so-called military hit squad?" B. J. asked. "If they're not working for the Akrho Pinoy or some other gang, what's the real motivation? Why start a war in the first place? We're back to that."

"Oh, I'm sure you'll figure it out, B. J."

CHAPTER 48

Manhattan

The eighty-foot-tall Norway spruce from northern Vermont towered over Rockefeller Center's historic skating rink. The restaurant that overlooked the ice was filled with shoppers and tourists searching for an early taste of the holiday spirit. It was an excellent location for two people to have a private conversation in a very public venue.

Watching about thirty skaters enjoy the yearly tradition, Gray Taylor, gloved hands in his leather jacket, stood at the east end of the ice rink. It was unseasonably cold, yet nobody around him seemed to be complaining. High above the city's skyline, the moon was one night away from full.

Spectators cheered as a redheaded teenage girl—her hair pulled back in a braided ponytail—completed a beautifully orchestrated double jump. Her wide smile was as contagious as the festive atmosphere.

Out of the corner of his eye, Taylor watched the heavyset white-haired man slip in beside him. Taylor turned and brought his index finger to his lips. Next, a small wand, about the size of a ruler, appeared in his hand. Tony D watched as the metal detector moved over his entire body, as if he was passing through airport security.

There was a faint beeping sound when the wand reached Tony D's fedora. Taylor stuck out his hand, palm up. Tony D removed his hat and handed it over. Folding back the inside hatband, Taylor pointed to the thin wire.

Shaking his head, Tony D frowned.

Taylor tossed the fedora into the closest garbage receptacle and returned to the rink. "We can talk freely now, although I suspect we're being watched."

"My home is swept twice a week," said Anthony DiFilippo.

"The technology to locate that particular bug doesn't officially exist."

"Why am I not surprised?"

"I'm Gray Taylor." The big man stuck out his hand. "Thank you for coming, Mr. DiFilippo. I know trust doesn't come easy for a person in your position."

Tony D momentarily regarded Taylor, then reached out his hand. "You made quite an impression on Mara," he said. "She happens to be a good judge of character."

"Sir, your wife has an amazing inner beauty."

Managing a chuckle, Tony D said, "I married up."

"Then we have something in common." Taylor's hard gaze quickly moved over the crowd. The only danger he sensed was from DiFilippo's two bodyguards. Like angry pit bulls at the International Cat Show, both men appeared completely out of place.

There was no sign of Hatch or Steven.

"Mara's the only reason I'm standing here, Mr. Taylor. And I did check up on you."

"I apologize for involving your wife," Taylor said. "Knocking on your front door would not have been a wise move. Many eyes watch your home, and I needed to get your attention in a hurry, quietly."

"You've certainly done that," Tony D said. "The same goes for the men who've been following me around throughout the day."

"They're for your own protection."

Tony D gestured with his chin to the two Italian men standing next to an elm tree. "As you can see, I have my own security."

"Sir, with all due respect, they can't stop the person who intends to kill you."

"You may be right," Tony D said. "I was under the impression that the head of the snake was cut off last night. I read something about a multiple homicide of some gang members in Chinatown."

"You and Mr. Wright targeted the wrong organization," Taylor said as directly as he could. "It was all part of the real shooter's plan—starting a war within the underworld community, then killing your wife, maybe your children if they're accessible, then you."

"Mara? My kids? What in God's name do they have to do with any of this?"

"This whole thing is about inflicting pain. On you."

Tony D cleared his throat. "And what's your part in all of this, Mr. Taylor?"

"I'm here to save your life."

"Why am I so important to you?"

"Your place in the community brought your problem straight to Director Walsh's attention."

Tony D sighed. "I suspect you know who this assassin is and why he's killing my associates."

"We believe so," Taylor said. "He served in the Marines—special ops–but he's a civilian now. We're in public because I wanted him to understand that I've made contact with you, but I didn't want him to know what we were discussing. So you might want to cover your mouth when talking."

Tony D did just that. "You still haven't told me why this is happening."

Over the next ten minutes, Taylor explained everything he knew and, from that, everything he'd deduced.

Tony D shook his head regretfully when Taylor was finished with his account of the situation. "All this death because of my dimwitted nephew and my response to that tragedy at Rudy's Tavern?"

"Yes, sir."

"It was an accident, Mr. Taylor—and a horrible one at that."

"Sir, it's clear to me, and others, that Steven Easter wants you to suffer, just like his brother is suffering." Taylor paused. "And like I said, Kevin Easter has now become an integral part of this. How Kevin intends to intervene is anyone's guess. There's a very high probability one or both of them are watching us right now."

"Spooks," Tony D said sarcastically, glancing around the festive area.

"Kevin is considered one of the best hunters of men in the world," Taylor said. "Steven learned his trade over in Iraq before starting a security firm. Both, I can assure you, know their stuff. Both are off the grid."

"Meaning?"

"No one knows where they are, and they don't intend to be found."

Tony D coughed, the sharp ache in his chest evident in his face. "This man has done . . . done a fine job of getting me back, Mr. Taylor."

"He's not finished."

"Why me?" the don asked, spreading his arms. "Why Paulie, Donald, and Louis?"

"Because *you* helped cover up the truth, just like Matthew Philips helped sweep the homicides under the carpet. Your colleagues were murdered because they worked for *you*. And you loved these men."

"Steven Easter knew Matthew was involved?"

"I suspect that's why Detective Philips was murdered this afternoon," said Taylor.

"I heard about Matthew's death about an hour after it had taken place," Tony D said. "Long before the media sank their teeth in the story."

"I'm not surprised."

"But I didn't think it was connected to the bigger picture," Tony D said. "And now you're telling me that Mara could be targeted? I need to make a call."

"We took your wife to a safe house two minutes after you left your home."

"Shows just how vulnerable I am." Tony D cleared his throat again, shrugged, then said, "If what you're saying is true, you might want to protect Detective

Katherine Montroy. She could be a target now."

"She's on the take?"

"We tried to bribe her, Mr. Taylor, and when that didn't work, we threatened her," Tony D said. "One of my people promised to hurt Ms. Montroy's girlfriend if she didn't cooperate. She wouldn't take the money, but we all have pressure points."

Taylor removed his BlackBerry and made a quick call to one of the CIA colleagues who'd picked up Mara DiFilippo, making arrangements to do the same for Montroy and her girlfriend. "Sir," Taylor said after sliding his phone back into his coat pocket, "if not for your unique relationship with the Drug Enforcement Agency, and specifically with Administrator Blum, I can assure you we would not be having this conversation or taking all these precautions."

"Is there anything you don't know about me, Mr. Taylor?"

"You're considered a serious asset in this part of the world," Taylor said. "Deputy Director for Intelligence Slattery was briefed just a few days ago about the arrangement you have with Administrator Blum. Mr. Slattery feels you've bitten off more than you can chew. Your handlers apparently agree."

"They may very well be right," Tony D said soberly. "Who else is involved in this?"

"Mr. Slattery and me," Taylor said. "I can't speak for the DEA, but they've kept knowledge of their relationship with you restricted to those at the highest level. Your secret is not only keeping you in control of the Tri-State area, it's allowing you to stay alive."

"I refer to it as 'MAD,' Mr. Taylor—Mutual Assured Destruction. If it ever got out that I was feeding information about my competitors and enemies to some United States government agency, well . . ."

"The DEA has an inside view of the drug situation here in New York because of your ongoing cooperation," said Taylor. "I was briefed. Having you on the payroll is not a unique policy, although it's something the government obviously doesn't like to advertise. I've been told that Lawrence Luther Wright is in the DEA's crosshairs, and you're on the front line."

"He's one of many."

Both men were silent for a moment.

"This killer broke into my home and removed a few items that were near and dear to me," Tony D said. "He's been leaving them around—like calling cards."

Slowly shaking his head, Taylor said, "Sir, I'm not sure if I'm following you."

"M16 shells from Vietnam," Tony D said at length. "My little brother died in that fiasco, and those stupid bullets, crazy as it may sound, meant a great deal to me. There were about ten of them. And now this ghost is leaving subtle reminders of his control over me at the crime scenes. He's taunting me, Mr. Taylor, and doing a fine job at it."

"He's a dangerous and formidable enemy," Taylor said simply.

Turning his attention to a young boy skating on double runners, Tony D said, "This Steven Easter has gotten his lump of flesh, Mr. Taylor. Vincent and Johnny were the only ones at Rudy's that night. They're both dead—along with a number of my good friends."

"You're still alive."

Coughing again, Tony D grimaced, grabbed his chest, and then said, in a choked whisper, "Who really knows for how long?"

"Mr. Slattery, Mr. Walsh, and Ms. Blum want this over and done with. Quietly."

"And *you* want my cooperation?"

"Or you're on your own."

"And in return, my position in the community remains the same?" Tony D's eyebrows crept up his forehead. "Is that what you're saying?"

"That's the plan."

"Ah, so you do have a plan?"

Taylor smiled. "Came up with it all by myself."

Standing at the west end of the Rockefeller Center ice rink, Kevin Easter puzzled over the conversation taking place between Anthony DiFilippo and Gray Taylor. A young boy on double runners clung to the boards in front of both men. Two of Tony D's bodyguards stood in the background, but Hatch had yet to identify any CIA personnel, or to locate his brother. He suspected Steven wasn't here.

Hatch elected to play it safe and keep his distance.

"What are you telling him, Gray?" Hatch murmured. "Will you stick him in a safe house? For how long?"

Taylor and Tony D walked off together. Hatch looked at his watch. Ten forty-one. "C'mon, Gray," Hatch said, his breath momentarily clinging to the night air. He zipped up his coat, but didn't follow the two men. "What the hell are you doing?"

Hatch's ten-point buck suddenly came to mind. These were creatures of habit. It was time to set a trap.

CHAPTER 49
Manhattan

Another cup of cold, caffeine-laced coffee, compounded by the stress of making tonight's deadline, inflamed B. J. Butera's duodenal ulcer. It was nearly midnight, and he could almost feel the open sore bleeding in his gut.

B. J. glanced at his wristwatch again. It was 11:43 p.m., and the second hand appeared to be picking up speed as it swept around the dial. *Come on! Come on!* He shook four more Maalox tablets into his hand, tossed them in his mouth, pulverized them into a chalky paste, and continued his silent vigil in the wooden chair.

Howard Stapleton sat on the opposite side of the antique desk, hunched over the editorial copy. They were in his corner office overlooking Sixth Avenue. The glass door was closed, giving them privacy, though the large newsroom was nearly empty.

Stapleton, red pen in hand, looked over his bifocals, an irritated expression fixed about his mouth. "Do you mind? That crunching is upsetting my concentration."

B. J. swallowed the antacid and grimaced. "Sorry."

Stapleton went back to work on the story. After a few minor grammatical corrections and a written addition at the top of the first page, he removed his glasses and tossed them onto a pile of folders. He leaned back into his high-back leather chair, clasped his hands behind his head, and said, "Best piece you've ever written, B. J. The documentation supports Brian McGowan's quotes."

"Thank you, sir." B. J., with a sheepish grin, seemed to exhale the weight of the world. "I couldn't have done it without your—"

"You're sure Mr. McGowan agreed to be quoted?"

"He insists it's the right thing to do," B. J. said with a slight shrug. "The backdraft accident pretty much altered his perspective of the world."

"Tragedy is a persuasive force," said Stapleton simply. "It changes us."

"Brian said he likes being the white knight," B. J. said. "And he's an outside consultant, not an NYFD employee, so he's not breaking any laws."

"He didn't sign a confidentiality agreement?"

"No, sir. He told me there wasn't one."

"Okay," Stapleton said, letting the word draw out. "Good." He handed B. J. the lengthy article on Tony D's connection to Lawrence Luther Wright, the alleged information Katherine Montroy had passed along to the don, the subsequent murder of Matthew Philips, and the underworld war now taking place on the streets of New York—all because the Akrho Pinoy gang had attempted to flex some muscle by bringing in some outside talent with serious military backgrounds.

"Congratulations," said Stapleton. "We run your piece above the fold. Maybe we should even discuss that raise you've been hinting at."

"Yes, I'd appreciate that very much."

Stapleton glanced at the wall clock. "You have eight minutes. Why don't you bring this down to Michelle? I'll call ahead. Don't forget the photographs."

"I won't," B. J. said, springing to his feet.

"As a courtesy, I'm giving Mr. DiFilippo a call. The man deserves a chance to comment on your story, and I expect he wouldn't take a call from you."

"You have the don's phone number?" B. J. made no attempt to hide his shock.

"You might say we've been around the block more than a few times together," Stapleton said, smiling. "Believe me, he won't have anything to add. Never does."

B. J. reached for the doorknob.

"Hey," Stapleton said, "no ass-kissing commentary on my snappy headline?"

B. J. Butera, in all his excitement, hadn't bothered to look. He read the handwritten headline, turned to his boss, and laughed. "It's perfect, Chief."

After about an hour spent chatting in a Manhattan café, Gray Taylor and Anthony DiFilippo walked down Broadway, discussing the plan the senior field operative had devised earlier in the day. To an outsider, the two could have passed for father and son, deep in conversation.

Tony D hesitated for a moment, then reached into his pocket. His cell phone had begun to vibrate. Pulling it out of his coat, he looked at the LCD display and frowned. "I'm sorry, Mr. Taylor, but I should probably take this."

"No problem."

Tony D turned his back to Gray Taylor. "It's always a pleasure to hear from you, Howard." A pause. "No, no, it's never too late for an important man like yourself. I'm out taking a stroll. Yes, I have a moment." A long break, and the don began to tap his foot impatiently on the pavement. "No, sir, there's really nothing

I can do or say about it now. Didn't your deadline just pass?" He paused. "No, sir, I have no comment. Maybe my overpaid attorney will have some earth-shattering statement in the next few days, but I honestly doubt it." A pause. "Thank you, Howard. Yes. I will. I appreciate the heads-up." The don slipped the phone back into his coat pocket.

Taylor said nothing as they began to walk down Broadway again.

"Looks like Mr. Easter is going to make me more famous than I already am," Tony D said. "That was Howard Stapleton, editor in chief of *The New York Post*. I evidently made the front page of tomorrow's paper. Howard wanted my comment on their story."

Taylor came to an abrupt stop. He stared at the shorter man. "What's it about?"

"They have two disconcerting photos they intend to print. I'm in both. In the first, I'm receiving a thick envelope from Detective Katherine Montroy in a dark parking lot," he said. "The second is me and Lawrence Luther Wright chatting on a bench."

Hatch played this one beautifully. Taylor was sure this was his work. The article was intended to force Steven to move quickly, before the police questioned Anthony DiFilippo.

"This story," Tony D said, "could put me in jail, if your boy doesn't kill me first."

"We'll see about that," said Taylor.

"Who's the big white dude in the leather jacket?" Lawrence Luther asked Jamar as he slipped into the delivery truck's passenger seat.

The brown vehicle that had once been part of the UPS ground fleet was double-parked on Broadway. It had the name "BEEKEE BROTHERS MOVING AND STORAGE" stenciled on both cab doors.

Traffic was light. It was a few minutes after midnight, and the temperature had dropped considerably.

"Never seen him before tonight," Jamar said, tightly gripping the steering wheel. "But whatever he's talkin' about seems to have the old man captivated."

"How long have they been together?"

"Since about ten," said Jamar. "And the damn bodyguards ain't attempting to blend in, that's for sure." Two big men continued to trail their boss by a few paces.

Strolling leisurely down the sidewalk, Gray Taylor and Anthony DiFilippo passed the brown delivery truck parked outside an Ann Taylor Loft store. Lawrence Luther brought up his right hand and pointed the Glock semiautomatic pistol through the tinted window. His eyes darkened. "Bang, bang, Mr. Mafia man," he said. His low voice resembled a distant thunderstorm.

"All because of the note some magician left in your apartment last night?" Jamar asked, turning to look at his boss.

"'By a perversion of justice, he was taken away . . . for he was cut off from the land of the living,'" said Lawrence Luther. "Isaiah, chapter fifty-three, verse eight."

"Praise Jesus."

"Your friends in high places won't be able to save you this time, Tony." Lawrence Luther holstered his pistol, then pulled a folded piece of white paper from his inside jacket pocket. Handing it to his friend, he said, "This changes the rules of the game."

Jamar Hightower silently read the handwritten note:

Mr. Wright, your new partner—Anthony DiFilippo IV—is being run by the Drug Enforcement Agency. He monitors organizations like yours, then feeds his handlers privileged information. Why do you think the don has been bulletproof for so long? You better watch your back.

"Yeah, but anyone can make shit up," Jamar said.

"I can't tell you what surprised me more—the fucking CD, the photographs, or the fact that some guy slipped into my place, unnoticed, while I was taking a shower."

Jamar's jaw appeared to have come unhinged. "You were home?"

Lawrence Luther nodded. "And a lady friend was in my bed."

Jamar turned his attention back to Tony D and his companion. "You think DiFilippo's big friend is with the DEA?"

"My brother, he sure as hell doesn't look like an insurance salesman," said Lawrence Luther. "Makes me wonder if five Chinamen lost their lives for no good reason. Makes me wonder why Tony D didn't want his people to handle that problem personally. Makes me wonder a lot of things."

"What do you mean?"

"Maybe that Italian really did destroy my warehouse. The caller made it so obvious I'd think it was too good to be true. A little slight of hand."

"Four of Tony D's top guys are dead, Boss," said Jamar. "How do you account for that if it's not the Akrho Pinoy boys behind this?"

"At this point in time, I don't really give a shit, Jamar. The fat man's a snitch."

"So what's our move?"

"After I personally put a bullet through Mr. DiFilippo's head," said Lawrence Luther, "that's when I'll start to worry about the ghost in the machine."

CHAPTER 50

Manhattan

*C*lick.

The metallic sound interrupted Gray Taylor's sleep. Even before his eyes were open, his right hand reached for the weapon strapped to the back of the bedside table—but it was gone.

Kevin Easter sat comfortably on a wooden chair placed next to Taylor's king-sized bed. A Walther PPK .380 automatic pistol was in his hand, but not pointed at Taylor. Hatch, dressed casually in jeans and a dark blue winter jacket, turned on the lamp and said, "I put your Glock on the kitchen counter next to the cookie jar."

Rarely had Taylor been so stunned or so caught off guard. The call he'd received from Hatch while both were watching DiFilippo's neighborhood didn't come close. Even so, his tone remained flat, natural. "How did you get in?" What he really meant to ask was: *How the fuck did you get into my apartment while I was here?*

"Gray, c'mon! Where's the fun if I tell you all my secrets?"

Taylor got to his elbows and squinted at the digital clock. Four-forty-two in the morning.

"Easy." Hatch shifted his Walther, but not necessarily in a threatening manner. "Please, just so I feel better, keep your hands where I can see them. Above the comforter works for me."

"Is there a point to this?"

"Just buying myself some time."

"What are you doing? Seriously."

"Saving a life—maybe a few lives." Hatch smirked, but it came across as contrived. "God, I have to admit the way you passed Mrs. D your message was clever. And it's been awfully quiet at the DiFilippo household since you met up with the don at Rockefeller Center a few hours ago."

"I figured you'd be watching," said Taylor. "Your brother had to be close, too. Detective Katherine Montroy shot him in the ass, or that's how the story goes. He can't be feeling too chipper."

Hatch mulled this over for a moment. "Did you get DiFilippo out of Dodge?"

"You really expect me to answer that?"

"I doubt the old man will run," said Hatch. "And if he did, it would only be a temporary fix. Certain people would begin to question his courage. Hiding doesn't fit Anthony DiFilippo's profile. The old man has a funeral to attend today. Hell, I'm pretty sure you've thought this through."

Taylor's gaze was fixed on Hatch.

"Not happy to see me, Gray?"

"Let me help you."

"I work alone, remember?"

"We have the same goals," Taylor said. "Stop your brother and protect Anthony DiFilippo."

"Ah, but it also depends on your priority—your primary objective."

"What are you talking about?"

"In what order? At what cost? That's what I mean." Hatch's voice grew louder. "I'm here to get Steven out of this shitty situation in one piece, Gray. If DiFilippo happens to get killed, well, I'm sorry, but it's not really my problem. On the other hand, your mission is to protect the don and his position in the community. If somebody gets in your way—like Steven or even me—we're toast. Expendable. And yes, I know the don's a DEA mole."

"So you honestly believe Steven's behind all of this?"

Nodding, Hatch said, "It sure looks that way. And not entirely because of me and Karen, although that probably plays some part in his thought process."

"The results are the same," Taylor said. "Since you were listening in on my conversations with Jack, you realize how important DiFilippo is to this region of the country."

"Please, Gray, don't be so myopic. Administrator Blum would find a replacement before Christmas. Tony D doesn't want to lose his power, and he'll do just about anything to keep it. He'd eat his young if need be."

Taylor said nothing.

"Tony D may come across as somebody's doting grandfather," Hatch said, "but he's gotta be an evil fuck. Odds are he gave the order to murder that Tagliafero kid—his goddamned nephew, Gray. A call from some Good Samaritan to help find the body in the middle of the night, two handguns at the murder scene, ballistics reports that came together too easily. Way, way too many coincidences for this skeptic to swallow. Jack happens to be one of those skeptics. Anthony DiFilippo facilitated the death of five Chinese gang members who had nothing to do—"

"All dead because of *your* brother!" Taylor shouted.

"Chill, old man." Hatch shook his head. "If Steven gets in position to take out

DiFilippo, and you somehow get in position to kill my brother, you'll do it," he said. "I can't let that happen. I won't let that happen. Our missions are diametrically opposed."

"Have you always been this fucking delusional?" Taylor asked, exhaling audibly. "Steven stalked and executed these people, and *you* intend to just spirit him away without facing the consequences?"

"Shut up!"

"Wow," Taylor said, smiling ruefully, "did I just hit a sensitive spot or what? Maybe *you* should chill."

"I brought you something." Hatch tossed the morning edition of *The New York Post* onto Taylor's lap. "The photos and CD I dropped off to an eager-beaver investigative reporter pushed things along. From my point of view, Anthony DiFilippo and Lawrence Luther Wright have a lot of explaining to do."

The headline read, "DIS-ORGANIZED CRIME?"

On the newspaper's front page, directly below the headline, were two black and white photographs placed side by side. In the first picture, reputed Mafia boss Anthony DiFilippo IV is shaking hands with drug kingpin Lawrence Luther Wright. The two are sitting together on a park bench. The second picture has Tony D standing in a dark parking lot with Detective Katherine Montroy. Each is holding an end of a fat envelope.

"Why don't you turn a few pages?" Taylor shouted. "I'm sure you'll find more."

Hatch folded back the paper. On page two, he read the caption under the photograph of a body covered by a yellow piece of plastic, one arm hanging out for all to see. It read: "Homicide Detective Matthew Philips Murdered." Hatch didn't comment.

"You know what scares me the most, Hatch?" said Taylor, the muscles along his jaw flexing.

"Give me a second," said Hatch, snapping his fingers. "Sleeping without a nightlight?"

"You're proud of what you're doing. You're letting your brother get away with multiple murders. He's turned into a criminal, a vigilante, a felon—everything you and I work to—"

"Enough!" Hatch shot to his feet, his humor gone. The chair fell backwards onto the carpeted floor.

"Yes, Tagliafero *and* Johnny Cercone were involved in Karen's and Patricia's deaths," Taylor said, his voice rising. "Nobody else was at Rudy's Tavern that night. And now Steven is out there murdering innocent people who had nothing to do with any of—"

"Innocent people!" Hatch shouted. "Innocent! For Christ's sake, Gray, these are bad people! Dangerous people. Professional criminals. They're involved in prostitution, extortion, murder, narcotics, loan-sharking—"

"You've come to the wrong guy if you need to justify Steven's actions, which apparently you do," said Taylor. "Your brother's a cold-blooded, premeditated killer, Hatch. Say it out loud, and then tell me how you feel. He needs to be caught, tried, and imprisoned, probably for life."

"Have you looked in the mirror lately, Gray? Your description of Steven sounds a lot like you."

"I do what I do for my country. *Our* country."

"If that helps you sleep at night."

"I will get Steve one way or another," said Taylor. "And then I'm coming for you."

"How?" Hatch lifted the Walther PPK. "I have the gun."

"C'mon, what are you going to do with it? Shoot me?"

Hatch pointed the pistol at Gray Taylor's head.

"There's no way in hell I was wrong about you," Taylor said, staring fixedly at the younger man.

"Sorry, Gray."

Bronx

It was early Thursday morning when the hunter stepped into his Holiday Inn room in Secaucus, New Jersey, a copy of *The New York Post* under his left arm. His cell phone chirped as he engaged the deadbolt. Looking at the incoming call on the LCD screen, he murmured, "Damnit," then turned on the light above the double bed.

He wasn't about to answer. B. J. Butera's comprehensive article about the underworld war raging in the city was all that mattered right now.

The hunter sat down tenderly at the wooden table, four Tylenol barely taking the edge off his gunshot wound. The dressing, he suspected, needed to be changed.

His cell phone beeped twice. The caller had left a message. He listened to the familiar voice. "Hey," his brother said anxiously, "we need to talk. Like right now! Call me, man. Please! I mean it! I . . . I'm worried about you. Try this number . . ."

For the briefest of moments, the hunter felt compelled to reach out to his brother, to explain the rationale behind his own aberrant behavior. He wanted to say that getting himself killed wasn't such a bad idea *if* he eventually ended up with Patty. Then, too, the hunter wanted his brother to know just how much he loved Patricia Durante, though their relationship had been a closely guarded secret. He'd found happiness, albeit for a short time.

But that return call wouldn't be made today—or ever, probably. Contact with anyone could lead to a host of complicated legal issues—accessory to his crimes, aiding and abetting . . .

The hunter deleted his brother's message and went back to reading Butera's article. When he was finished, he glanced up at the three pink and white roses he'd purchased from a local florist—the closest he could find that resembled Cajun Moon. They stood in a tall glass of water near his elbow. "I'm sorry I was late, Patty," the hunter said. "I should have been there."

After that, it was all business. Oiling and reassembling the M40A3 sniper rifle was his first priority. The night before, he'd secretly watched Mara DiFilippo as she was hastily escorted out of her home and whisked away in a dark Buick sedan. With Mara protected twenty-four seven, as he suspected she was, Tony D was now at the top of the hit list. The gunshot wound had accelerated things, and the so-called players were now exposed because of B. J. Butera's article. As for the infamous don, the hunter knew where to locate him.

The hunter was tired of living this nightmare—tired of constantly looking over his shoulder, living on the edge. Today, one way or another, it was going to end.

But not before he penned two letters. One was written to bring closure; the other, to destroy a man's legacy.

CHAPTER 51

Manhattan

George Worthington, the Dakota's affable, rotund, British-accented doorman, dutifully ushered the elderly blue-haired woman in the mink coat to an idling taxi, wishing her a fine morning. Mrs. Albemarle smiled warmly and, with the stealth of an international spy, slipped something small into George's gloved hand.

"A little something for your daughter's college-education fund," she whispered conspiratorially. "Rumor has it she pulled a 3.8 last semester. Jesus loves a Yale gal."

George managed a chuckle. "You're truly an amazing woman, Mrs. Albemarle. Thank you kindly. Have a wonderful time shopping with the ladies, and don't you worry a freckle about that new puppy of yours. We'll check on her every hour." He closed the cab door.

Just after the taxi drove off, a red Porsche Carrera pulled up to the curb directly in front of the stately apartment building on West 72nd Street and Central Park West. Terri Taylor, dressed in sweats and sneakers, bounded out of the sports car. Her dark hair was pulled back in a ponytail, and she could have passed for twenty-five instead of a woman in her mid-thirties.

"Morning, Mrs. Taylor," George said, tipping his head. "It's a bit nippy to be running around the Apple without a coat, don't you think?"

"I'm cold-blooded in more ways than one, Georgie," Terri said, reaching for her overnight bag behind the driver's seat.

"Mr. Taylor said you weren't expected back for a while."

"Call it death by boredom," Terri said, rolling her eyes. "Chambersburg, Pennsylvania might work for my little sister, but it's no place for a city girl like me."

But that was a partial lie. The truth was, she was back to support her husband. Leaving had been a stupid mistake, a selfish act, and she was there to make things right again. Running away from the problem had not been the answer, she now understood.

"I'll have to take your word for it," George said. "Ma'am, would you like the

Porsche washed before it's returned to the garage?"

"Let me check with Gray. I'm kinda surprising him by coming back so early."
She headed for the door. "Is he home?"

"I'd have to say almost certainly yes. Your friend from Buffalo must have spent
the night."

Terri stopped, then turned on her heels. "What did you say?"

"The Indian chap who paid us a visit last summer left the Dakota as I came on
duty. We passed each other in the lobby this morning, oh . . . around five o'clock—"

"Oh, Jesus," Terri breathed. She dropped her overnight bag on the sidewalk
and bolted through the Dakota's front door.

Manhattan

Lawrence Luther Wright sat alone at his kitchen table. He sipped hot herbal
tea from a mug and stared at the front page of *The New York Post*. There was a
picture of him shaking hands with Anthony DiFilippo. He knew the photograph
had been taken at St. Mary's Park.

Deep creases formed on Lawrence Luther's forehead as he let the newspaper
slip out of his hands, fluttering to the marble floor. "'Judas, is it with a kiss that you
are betraying the Son of Man?'" he whispered in a low and angry growl. "What the
fuck is going on?!"

Manhattan

Terri Taylor switched on the kitchen's bank of fluorescent lights winked on.
Her gaze went directly to her husband's pistol lying next to the cookie jar. *He would
never, ever leave a weapon out like this,* she thought. *It's dangerous and unprofessional.*

"Gray?" Her questioning voice was very low, and had an uneasy edge to it.

Hatch had undoubtedly visited her husband. Had it been friendly? The Glock
was an ominous sign. The quiet disturbed Terri even more. She picked up the
pistol, checked to see if it was loaded—it was—and clutched the weapon with
both hands.

Instead of calling out again, she cautiously made her way from one room to the
next, stopping outside the master bedroom, dread threatening to overcome all of
her conflicted emotions. She refused to believe that Kevin Easter would harm her
husband. But Gray was right. They really didn't know this damaged young man.

Terri slowly pushed open the bedroom door, her eyes adjusting to the darkness.

Handcuffed to his bed at the wrists, nylon rope securing his legs, Gray Taylor turned his head and eyeballed the digital clock on the nightstand for about the hundredth time. It turned silently to 10:50 a.m. He'd been locked in place for almost six hours, and without some help, it was obvious he wasn't going anywhere.

Thanks to Hatch's unanticipated show of force, it felt as if a nail had been driven through his skull. Clubbed above the ear with the Walther, left with a pounding headache that closely resembled a migraine, Taylor was almost thankful the lights were off. Duct tape covered his mouth.

And even if it hadn't, the walls of the 125-year-old Dakota were legendary. Some, made of stone, cement, and plaster, were known to be eighteen inches thick. Knocking something over—even if he could manage to get near the brass lamp—wasn't going to arouse any neighbors, most of whom were extremely private to begin with.

He'd begun to think the worst: The plan he'd put together the day before was going to get Anthony DiFilippo killed. The bait—Tony D—would soon be in place, exposed and vulnerable, and Taylor and his associates would not be there to protect him.

Biasucci's showing was scheduled for noon at the Triamante Funeral Home. The funeral started at 12:30.

Frustrated, Taylor lay quietly. Expending any more energy was counterproductive and physically painful, especially to his wrists. He could hear the everyday sounds of the apartment building: hot water pumping through baseboard pipes, wind pressing up against the window, even a thump from above.

And then the door opened, light from the hall spilling into the darkness. He winced.

"Shit," Terri said softly, having a difficult time comprehending the scene in her bed. She was relieved to see her husband alive but surprised he'd been overpowered.

Just as she was trained to do at the CIA's infamous Farm, Terri swept the bedroom with her eyes before charging into a situation she didn't quite understand. She turned on two lamps and pulled a drawstring to open the curtains.

Gray's mannerisms suggested they were alone. Still, she checked all of her blind spots, including the master bath. She finally went to one knee and ripped off the duct tape covering her husband's mouth. "Baby, tell me you're okay." She lightly touched his cheek.

"In the kitchen, below the sink, get the hacksaw and a knife," Taylor said.

"Hatch did this?"

Nodding rapidly, Taylor said, "You need to hurry, Ter—this whole thing is about to unravel. DiFilippo is running out of time."

Terri looked at the handcuffs. "I have a better idea." She sprinted out of the bedroom, then returned a few moments later with a lock-picking kit—small, about the size of a pack of cigarettes—along with a carving knife she'd pulled from the butcher block in the kitchen.

"Where've you been hiding that?" Taylor said, eyeing the small leather kit.

"Shhh." Terri went to work, sticking two four-inch wires into the lock securing Taylor's left hand. She closed her eyes and manipulated the tumblers. There was a distinctive *click*, and Taylor's hand was free. Less than sixty seconds later, Terri had defeated the other handcuff and sliced the ropes affixed to her husband's ankles.

"How did Hatch do this to—"

"Why'd you come back?" Rubbing his bruised wrists, Taylor got to his feet.

Terri smiled uneasily. "Telepathy," she said. "I knew you were in trouble."

Taylor reached for the phone and punched in a restricted cell number.

"Are you calling Jack?"

Taylor raised his hand. The phone he dialed rang three times before Anthony DiFilippo picked up. "Sir, it's Gray Taylor," he said. "Where are you?"

"The Ravenite—just like we planned," Tony D said, eyeing the men at his table. "I'm about to . . . sandwich . . . few . . . associates—"

The call was breaking up.

"Look, Mr. DiFilippo, I want you to stay right where you are. Something came up, and I'm running late. Don't leave the building under any circumstances. Sir, do you understand what I'm saying?"

"Don't forget . . . Donald's service."

"I haven't."

"It's something . . . can't miss, Mr. Taylor. I'm obligated . . . be—"

"Sir, give me thirty minutes," said Taylor. "Please stay put."

Anthony DiFilippo never got Gray Taylor's last message. The connection had been severed.

Tony D pocketed his cell phone, and then turned back to the business at hand—the young man with the pockmarked face and unruly black hair, and first in line to become a *caporegime*. "What do you mean there's no record of a Steven Easter in the Marines?!" the don yelled. "I said he's retired, you idiot. *Ex*-Marine!"

"Oh," the young man said, wincing, looking as if he was expecting incoming artillery shells to rain on his chair.

Tony D pounded the round wooden table, and a glass of red wine splashed onto the linen tablecloth. "These two brothers exist! They're fucking Indians— Native American Indians, from the Seneca tribe near Buffalo," he said, cursing for the first time in years. "The Cattaraugus Indian Reservation. For those who don't own a damn map, Buffalo is at the other end of the state! They're here—in New York City. One of them was shot in the ass. I want them alive. Alive!"

Gray Taylor ran into a private study, pulled a Browning 9mm Parabellum and a box of ammunition from a wall safe, grabbed his leather bomber jacket, and headed for the door.

"You want my help?" Terri said, leaning against the wall.

"I'm good."

They stared at each other for a moment that seemed eternal.

"Whatever's going on, please be careful, Gray." Terri exhaled, then seemed to be on the verge of tears. "And . . . and I'm sorry for everything I said the other day. It was wrong."

"No need to be sorry."

"I came back because I—"

"Terri, I'm not going to kill Kevin Easter, regardless of the situation. I can't. I won't. Because you're right about me," he said. "If I did hurt him, I'm pretty sure I'd never find my way back to you. You were right to be afraid for me. For us."

Terri smiled thoughtfully. "I'll be here when you get back."

Stepping across the dimly lit study, Gray Taylor embraced his wife. He kissed Terri's forehead, then her lips. "I've never doubted that for a second."

If hell did exist, the hunter suspected the reception committee was in the process of putting out the welcome mat for his imminent arrival. Maybe then he would understand what motivated evil men—for he'd yet to consider himself evil. Even so, the hunter sensed he was very close to falling into that godforsaken abyss. All it took was one little push.

He peered through the Leupold scope attached to the M40A3 rifle and murmured, "Life isn't all about happy endings, Tony."

Lying facedown on a rooftop under a black tarpaulin, the hunter was across the street from the Ravenite Social Club. He wore a thick ski parka made of Gore-

Tex, long underwear beneath his faded jeans, insulated hiking boots, fingerless gloves, and a balaclava. A two-headed gargoyle, carved out of stone, stood directly to his left. It had an ominous presence.

Trembling from fatigue, the hunter felt himself overflowing with guilt and doubt. He just couldn't continue beyond this day, especially without something or somebody to live for. Emotionally and spiritually, his purpose on this planet was nearly over. Anthony DiFilippo's death would bring closure.

Five stories above Mulberry Street, some 150 yards from the Ravenite's front door, the hunter knew the kill shot would be almost effortless if he was given a clean line of sight—and if he could control his own tremors at the penultimate moment. The weather wasn't a factor. Tony D was inside the private club, no doubt breaking bread with some of his people. The high-tech bugs were no longer transmitting the don's conversation, but it didn't matter. Donald "Woody" Biasucci's service, scheduled to begin at noon, was the one opportunity he needed.

The hunter glanced at his wristwatch. It was 11:41 a.m. Time was running out on Mr. DiFilippo's life.

A single sentry, a bearded Italian man the hunter knew as Salvatore, stood outside the club. Although it was sunny, the big man in the designer suit and expensive sunglasses stomped his feet on the cement sidewalk every few minutes in an attempt to stay warm.

The locale was very fluid this morning. Two plainclothes policemen, both drinking from Starbucks cups, sat in their blue Pontiac sedan. At least twelve media people were camped out near the club's entrance, including the local NBC and CBS news vans. Smoking cigarettes, four teenage boys horsed around near a small group of journalists. Every time one TV reporter spoke into her mike to record a tease for her upcoming piece, a couple of the boys shouted profanities, and the rest of his buddies busted a gut. The more frustrated the correspondent became, the more the teenagers turned up the volume.

A young couple, out walking their black lab, stopped to see what all the fuss was about; others followed suit, and the diverse group of gawkers grew to at least thirty. The *Post* article had evidently elevated Tony D's profile.

Parked cars filled the tree-lined street, along with two delivery trucks, a white Cadillac Escalade, and Tony D's BMW 740L; the latter was double-parked in front of the club. The hunter rested his sound suppresser on the parapet and studied the neighborhood from his perch.

"We're almost there, Tony," he said quietly. "You and me."

CHAPTER 52

Manhattan

L awrence Luther Wright knew his pride had taken center stage, and he couldn't have cared less—not this morning. Not today. If a man, regardless of his occupation, age, race, religion, or station in life, lost his purpose, what went next? Self-respect?

As with any king whose power depended on perceptions, he needed a show of force from time to time, and that moment was fast approaching. If Lawrence Luther feared anything in this world, it was the thought of becoming ordinary. Now that he'd experienced the privileged life, it would be impossible for him to retreat to a mundane existence—or worse, prison.

The rules of the game, he recognized, had changed dramatically in the last few days. Someone very skilled had broken into his apartment and left that enlightening package. Then there was the morning edition of *The New York Post*. It was an embarrassment—and something he could not ignore.

If it ever became public that Tony D was feeding the feds sensitive information about the proliferation of illegal and stolen prescription drugs throughout the Tri-State area, would other enemies, competitors, even allies come to the conclusion that Lawrence Luther was somehow involved? Would they ever trust him again? What about those five dead Akrho Pinoy gang members? Tony D may have supplied the copied files on the Chinese gang, false or otherwise, but the shrewd old man had no blood on his hands. The don's testimony could put Lawrence Luther and his key people behind bars for life. The CD never recorded Tony D asking for these men to be murdered, although it was heavily implied. On further review, the old man had been very careful with his words.

Cliché as it might be, a picture is truly worth a thousand words. And there they were, on the front page of a New York tabloid. Two very influential underworld figures had been stupid enough to let themselves be photographed by this ghost.

Why had the don turned? And when? Now that most of the facts were out on the table, it was all so transparent. Anthony DiFilippo IV hadn't seen the inside of a courtroom in many years, all because of his unholy arrangement with the DEA. He'd been protected—untouchable.

With Lawrence Luther's help, Tony D's privileged life was about to end.

At half past eleven on a Thursday morning, traffic was uncharacteristically light as Gray Taylor threaded the Porsche around slower-moving vehicles on Broadway. Moving past steel, stone, and glass behemoths lining the four-lane street, then past Madison Square Park, he knew he was about halfway to the Ravenite Social Club. Red lights and intersections no longer concerned him, and his driving bordered on reckless. At one point, at the corner of 39th Street and Broadway, Taylor downshifted to second gear, tapped his horn, and mounted the curb to get around a crowd of slow-moving pedestrians crossing at the light. Angry people shouted, cursed, and flipped him the bird, cab drivers leaned on their own horns, and tires squealed, but none of this concerned Taylor. He was making fairly good time.

But was it good enough? Would Tony D stay in the building, knowing he'd probably be late for Woody Biasucci's service at the funeral home?

The men Jack Slattery had assigned to this bizarre vigilante case were probably of no help to Taylor. Taylor had promised to lay out his plan this morning, but Hatch's surprise visit had obviously thrown off his schedule. The agents were en route from their Bronx hotel, but probably still too far away to be of any help.

If Anthony DiFilippo was to see the day through, he needed to stay inside the Ravenite Social Club—or Gray Taylor needed to get lucky.

Pressing his right eye to the Leupold scope's eyepiece, the hunter tightened his index finger around the trigger as Salvatore opened the Ravenite's front door. Pain from the gunshot wound had all but disappeared. "See ya in hell, Tony," he said quietly, then let out a long, cleansing breath. The tremors disappeared as if by magic.

A young, dark-haired Hispanic woman dressed like a waitress gave Salvatore a stiff smile, saw the media and a mob of curiosity seekers assembled to her right, then made a hasty exit to her left. What began as a brisk walk turned into a sprint when one journalist shouted a question at her.

The hunter removed his finger from the trigger. False alarm. "You're running late, old man."

With a hard left on Bleeker, then a quick right on Mott Street, the Porsche's rear end slid along the pavement and nearly clipped a parked minivan. Taylor, his jaw set, focused on the next turn. Prince, a residential street that intersected with Mulberry, was only a block from the Ravenite.

Taylor's sports car came to a quick stop in a handicapped parking spot on Prince Street. The dashboard clock read 11:46. Out of sheer habit, Taylor patted the pistol in his shoulder rig, then grabbed his bomber jacket from the passenger seat. He got out of the Porsche and ran toward 247 Mulberry, pulled out his BlackBerry, and hit *9* and *send*. It went directly to Tony D's voice mail.

"Goddamn reception!" Taylor said through clenched teeth. He left a message: "Sir, I'm about a block away. Give your boys a little heads-up." He thumbed the *end* button. "Shit!"

Ahead, Taylor could see two satellite dishes mounted on commercial vans outside the Ravenite. More than a dozen news organizations were here to report on Biasucci's funeral and the *Post* piece implying Anthony DiFilippo had orchestrated five murders with the help of Detective Katherine Montroy. The underworld story was gaining momentum.

A few seconds after Taylor terminated his latest call to DiFilippo, his BlackBerry chirped in his hand. He looked down at the LCD screen. *Incoming Call Restricted.* Slowing to a jog, Taylor punched the *send* button and said, "Sir, I'll be there in two minutes. Please, I want you to stay in the building."

"Gray?" the male voice asked over a static-filled connection.

Puzzled, Taylor thinned his eyes. "Who is this?" His tone was harsh, impatient.

"Steven. Steven Easter. Kevin's brother."

Taylor came to an abrupt stop, yet his gaze swept the area. "Steven?" he said tentatively, then moved underneath the We Impress Drycleaners awning.

"Look, sorry to bother you, but I'm trying to reach Hatch, and I'm not exactly sure where to turn."

"O . . . k . . . a . . . y," Taylor said. He peered at some of the parked cars and trucks, then to the roofline.

"I got his message from my secretary about an hour ago, but it's a few days old. I guess he came across as a total a-hole, which isn't like him. The cell number he left went directly to voice mail," he said. "My grandfather also passed along a strange message—"

"What did Low Dog say?"

"He gave me your phone number and told me to tell you that 'fear is the mother of foresight.'"

"Sir Henry Taylor."

"Huh?"

"A dead poet," Taylor said. "He happens to be my great-great-great-grandfather."

"Gray, seriously, what the hell is going on?"

"It was my idea," Taylor said. "It tells me you talked with your grandfather."

"Enough of the spy crap," said Steven, clearly impatient now. "Is my brother in trouble or what? Did he do something stupid again? I don't care who might be listening."

Taylor, his head on a swivel, started to move toward the Ravenite again, although he turned in a complete circle every few steps. "Where are you, Steven?"

"Riyadh. In my office. I've been on the road . . . almost five solid weeks."

"Uh-huh."

"Field work. Sensitive stuff. We're way behind because . . . some . . . attacks . . ."

The connection seemed to be getting worse.

"I rarely use . . . satellite phone because nothing is really secure over here, so getting messages can be a . . . bitch," Steven said. "And security guys like me make for nice targets. I try . . . stay under the radar. I had . . . close scrape . . . year. One of my colleagues was kidnapped . . . killed earlier in the year. You know . . . my situation."

A car alarm went off, and Taylor reached for his pistol. He sighed heavily. "Steven, we have a problem here."

"Dude, c'mon! Is Kevin okay or what?" Steven said, exasperated. "*Here*? Can you be . . . more specific?"

About ninety feet from the news vans, Taylor ducked into an alley. "How do I know you're in Saudi?"

"Why would I lie?"

"Steven—"

"Look, if you think I'm full of crap," Steven Easter said, "then call . . . landline."

The connection cut out. Taylor glanced at the phone, swearing under his breath as he slipped the BlackBerry back into his coat pocket. He didn't think Steven was lying, and now he had absolutely no idea who he was dealing with, or why the murders were taking place.

He studied the media contingent and a host of other people milling around the Ravenite's front door. There had to be at least fifty. Tony D had yet to appear.

Hatch's guard will almost certainly be down, Taylor thought, if this ghost is not his brother. And so Taylor made a judgment call, one that could very well determine in the next few minutes whether Kevin Easter or Anthony DiFilippo would live or die.

CHAPTER 53

Manhattan

Kevin Easter reached for the rusted steel ladder's top wrung, pulled himself up, peered over the parapet, and stepped off the building's exterior fire escape and onto the gravel roof without making a sound. "It's over, Steven!" he shouted. Thirty feet separated him from the man underneath the black tarpaulin. "Put the rifle down."

The hunter didn't move—it was as if he were cast in stone. Instead, he kept his eye firmly on the scope, the crosshairs lined up on the Ravenite's front door.

A small entourage of grim-faced men in dark suits filed out of the building. Vehicle engines came to life, and the media and curious sightseers pressed forward, hoping for a better view. Some took photos, while video streamed to the New York City, New Jersey, and Connecticut news affiliates.

B. J. Butera, the man who'd helped initiate this circus with another front-page article, was one of many journalists waiting to get a glimpse of Anthony DiFilippo. Two policemen who'd been sitting in a blue Pontiac eating sandwiches got out of the car to help with crowd control. One cop had his hand on his billy club.

Hatch took a few cautious steps across the roof. "Steven, I said, put the rifle down! It's done."

The hunter, much of his face covered by the balaclava, slowly turned his head to look at Hatch. "I'm not Steven," he said in a low rumble filled with suppressed rage.

Hatch didn't recognize the voice, nor was he familiar with the brown eyes behind the mask, but he did understand the situation had reached a critical tipping point—his life was now in grave danger. As if in slow motion, he reached under his jacket for his Walther PPK, jerked the pistol out of the shoulder rig, and swung his right arm up and around, hoping his reaction wasn't as dulled as his decision-making.

Hatch never got off a shot.

Instead, he felt a searing pain radiate throughout his right shoulder. The hunter's slug knocked Hatch off his feet and onto his back, gravel puncturing his scalp as his head snapped backwards, and his brain, for a split second, lit up like a series of flashbulbs. Hatch's pistol slid harmlessly along the roof and came to rest against the tin bulwark. Pressing his palm against the wound, he gritted his teeth, then shouted, "Motherfucker, that . . . hurts!"

The hunter folded back the tarp. In his left hand, he held a Smith & Wesson handgun with a sound suppressor attached to the barrel. "You'll live," he said evenly. He picked up the Walther, quickly checked Hatch for another weapon, took the Buckmaster hunting knife sheathed to his leg, and returned to the high-powered sniper rifle.

Tony D had yet to appear outside the Ravenite.

Grimacing, Hatch rolled over and eyed the gunman. "Who the fuck are you?"

"Shouldn't I be asking you that question?" The hunter was back on his belly.

Hatch tried to catch his breath. "The name . . . is Kevin Easter."

And once again, the hunter took his eye off the eyepiece and glanced back over his shoulder. "Hatch?"

Hatch's jaw dropped. "Dude, hey, you're totally freaking me out here."

"You're Karen's husband." It was a statement, not a question.

"You knew my . . . my wife?" Hatch said, getting to one elbow, stunned. "What's going on here?"

"I know you two only by reputation," the hunter said, returning to the deadly business at hand. "It's funny how the world works, isn't it?"

"No offense, pal, but I don't find any of this even remotely amusing."

"No, no, that came out wrong."

"You want to try again?"

"There are probably better words to describe the situation."

"I can think of a few. None are very polite."

"*Sad* might be at the top of my list," the hunter said. "Yeah, *sad* pretty much does it for me."

"It would be nice if you stopped talking in riddles," Hatch said. "I'm kinda bleeding over here, and things are getting a little bit foggy."

"It's only a flesh wound."

"Yeah, my flesh!"

"I actually know how you feel," the hunter said. "Took one in my fat ass."

Salvatore pressed his back to the Ravenite's front door and crossed his arms over his beefy chest, as if daring anyone to make an aggressive move. Tony D hadn't come out of the club yet, though a few of his associates, including the don's personal bodyguard, Marco, had left the building, presumably getting ready to head for Donald Biasucci's funeral.

"Maybe we should compare wounds," Hatch said. "You go first."

"You want to hear about *sad*?" the hunter said, his voice taking on a miserable tone. His eye remained on the scope.

Hatch shifted his weight and was rewarded with a knifing pain to his shoulder. "Do I . . . Christ, that hurts . . . have a choice?"

"*Sad* means I was going to ask Patty Durante to marry me, Kevin, and I never had that chance," the hunter said. "*Sad* means I should have been at Rudy's Tavern on time, and if I had been, maybe I could have saved them both." He paused as if to collect himself. "But . . . but the damn florist screwed up the order, and I wanted the night to be special . . ."

Cajun Moon. The words popped into Hatch's mind. "You . . . *you* were dating Patricia?"

Nodding, the hunter said, "*Sad* means we might have been brothers-in-law, and that opportunity, among other things, died back in August."

"Holy shit."

"If not for Vincent Tagliafero, Johnny Cercone, and these lowlife hoods, you and I might have been friends, Kevin Easter. How's that for *sad*?"

The pain in Hatch's shoulder momentarily forgotten, he repeated, "Who are you?"

"My future was ripped to shreds shortly after Patty died. It's gone. All gone."

Patty loved him the way I still love you, Little Crow.

"My life is over because of people like Anthony DiFilippo," the hunter said in a voice that suddenly exploded with rage.

"Hey, Tony D didn't commit the murders," Hatch said, coming to a sitting position. "And he sure as hell didn't give the orders to have two innocent bystanders killed. Karen and Patricia were in the wrong place at the wrong time. Tagliafero and Cercone were the only ones at Rudy's that night. And they're both dead. You can't blame the whole world for *their* mistake."

"Mistake?!" the hunter hollered. His muffled voice carried through the balaclava. "Those . . . those cold-blooded little shits . . . they ruined everything when they murdered Patty. They killed *me* that night."

"So, this is all about you getting even?"

"When a dog has rabies, we put it down, right?"

"Are you fucking insane? These are people!" Hatch shouted back. "Some of them are blameless. What about that guy guarding Lawrence Luther Wright's warehouse? The one who had his face melted off in the explosion? How again did that doorman kill Patricia and my wife?"

The hunter appeared agitated for a long second, then settled back into a shooting position. "Collateral damage," he said quietly. Turning his head around to look back at Hatch, the hunter said, "Oh, now it makes a little more sense."

"Excuse me?"

"You're the one who gave the *Post* those photographs—the shots they used in today's paper. You also paid Mr. Wright a visit last night—left him an interesting package at home. Didn't you?"

"How'd you know that?"

"I bugged Wright's place, just like I did with DiFilippo. Your unexpected gift left quite the impression on Lawrence Luther. And now he has every intention of personally killing Tony D."

"That was the plan," Hatch said, exhaling. "Call it a stupid mistake. I figured if Lawrence Luther Wright killed Anthony DiFilippo, Steven would walk away."

"Steven?"

"My brother," Hatch said. "I thought he was behind all this. I thought Tony D's death would stop him. I wanted Wright to take the fall."

"But why are *you* here—on this roof?" the hunter said, shifting his weight just so.

"The plan was to flush out my brother. I figured this would be his last stop."

"And you found me instead."

"You have to admit that it worked out pretty well," Hatch said. "Almost. Biasucci's funeral seemed like the appropriate time for him—you—to strike again. And here we are."

Hatch could tell, despite his black mask, that the hunter had smiled, albeit briefly. The rage in his brown eyes even seemed to have lessened a little.

"I'm getting the feeling there's more to you than meets the eye," the hunter said. "For a freelance photographer, Kevin, you seem to know your way around."

"It's a long story."

The hunter settled the stock of the rifle against his shoulder. "I'm sorry you're here. Sorry you're involved."

"Apology accepted," Hatch said. "So why don't we pack up our stuff, call it a day, and get out of this cold. We'll drop by some hospital to plug up my hole, and then I'll buy you a beer—"

"Patty insinuated that you talked too much. She was right."

"So what's your deal?" Hatch asked. "All tricked out, blowing up shit, taking on the mob like Bobby Kennedy on PCP. You didn't learn how to buy sophisticated detonators in *Soldier of Fortune.*"

"Maybe I should be asking *you* some hard questions," said the hunter. "You figured out my intentions and then found me here. Photographing Tony D and Lawrence Luther Wright was no easy task."

"I've had lots of practice."

"Come to think of it, I saw you at the playground, taking pictures of the little kids. And were you at the Ciambella crime scene? I believe you were."

"Guilty as charged."

The hunter said nothing.

"What's with the roses?" asked Hatch, hoping to keep the dialogue going. "Those hybrids my grandfather grows? How do you even know about them?"

"Cajun Moon," the hunter said, and even managed to laugh. "Patty fell in love with them at your wedding. If I missed one of her Saturday-night performances—which wasn't too often last summer—I'd send a dozen to the theater. Patty gave them away because she didn't want anyone to know there was a man in her life, but I continued the deliveries. It became this funny private joke between the two of us." The hunter paused a moment. "God, how I miss those little things."

"I know how you feel."

"You mean pissed off? Lost? Irrelevant?"

"And a few other emotions we can discuss in group counseling," Hatch said, looking closer at his wound. It had stopped bleeding, and the pain had turned to a dull, manageable throb. "The day after Halloween, I hit an all-time low," Hatch said, momentarily pulled back into the past. "I actually couldn't stop crying. It was nuts how my emotions took control. And then my elderly grandfather got in my grill, told me to turn a cheek, to man up, to get on with my life. And you know what?"

"You did."

"Are you fucking kidding me? No way!" said Hatch. "Hey, on the food chain of life, I'm probably one step above a feral cat. I'm still screwed up."

"Welcome to the club."

"And look at me now—there's a hole in my shoulder. Thank you very much."

The hunter shifted his weight. "I said I was sorry," he said barely above a whisper.

"But the truth of the matter is," Hatch said, "you're more pathetic than me."

There was movement outside the Ravenite.

"Maybe you should zip it," said the hunter.

"At least I didn't act out." Hatch's tone had turned serious.

"This will all be over in a few minutes. I'll even call you an ambulance."

"Killing off the New York mob or starting some underworld war may sound cool," said Hatch, "but it isn't going to help bring back our ladies."

"Shut up!" the hunter snapped. "I don't care about you or anybody else."

"Don't you see? That's your biggest liability," Hatch said. "You don't give a shit. Man, you act like you're the only person on the planet who had something bad happen to them."

"I'm done listening to you."

Across Mulberry Street, Anthony DiFilippo finally appeared at the Ravenite Social Club's front door. People clapped, pointed, and shouted. A few even asked for Tony D's autograph. Smiling guardedly, the don politely declined. Cell phone cameras recorded the event. Salvatore looked anxious as the TV cameras focused on his boss. The big man pushed one teenage boy to the ground and was roundly booed and yelled at in at least three different languages.

The hunter put his eye back on the scope. His finger brushed the trigger.

"Put the gun down," Gray Taylor said, stepping onto the gravel roof from the same steel ladder Hatch had used. His pistol was drawn, pointed directly at the hunter's head.

The hunter didn't seem distracted by another intruder in his midst.

"That's not Steven you're talking to," Hatch said to Taylor.

"I know," Taylor said without glancing at his injured friend. His eyes were on the hunter. "I want you take your finger off the trigger. If you don't, I will kill you."

"Like it really matters," the hunter said, laughing quietly, lining up the crosshairs on the don's chest. "Shoot me. I don't give a fuck."

"Listen to me," Taylor said firmly. "There's a bigger picture here. The man you're about to assassinate feeds valuable information to the DEA—where the big shipments of drugs are coming from, when and how they're getting into our country, who's really in control in the northeast."

"I know," the hunter said, his voice barely above a whisper, "and I don't care."

"Because of DiFilippo, our government puts away the real bad guys—the ones poisoning Americans," Taylor said. "That has to count for something."

"It doesn't," the hunter said without the slightest hesitation.

"Easy," Hatch said. "Easy does it, guys."

"Finger off the trigger," Taylor said decisively.

"Anthony DiFilippo is still a criminal—a felon—who's done more than his fair share of terrible things. Being a DEA snitch doesn't absolve him," said the hunter. "And if you think his handlers didn't know the details about the shootings at Rudy's Tavern, then you're both idiots."

Salvatore stepped between the hunter and Tony D, temporarily delaying the shot.

"DiFilippo is a necessary evil," Taylor said. "It's business. Happens all the time. It's like the U.S. government allying with some African general because our political analysts think he has the best opportunity to stabilize a country or region."

The hunter shifted his weight again. "Not my problem."

"It's my problem," Taylor said through clenched teeth.

"Patricia would be ashamed of you," Hatch said to the hunter. "Too many people have died on her behalf, and you're gonna be next. Do you really think she'd—"

"Shut up!" the hunter yelled. "Leave Patty out of this!"

Taylor took a few steps past Hatch, the gravel crunching underneath his Nikes. "Look," Taylor said, "I'm going to do this the old-fashioned way. I'll count to five, slowly. If you don't remove your finger from the trigger and safety the weapon by the time I reach the number five, I'm putting a bullet through your brain. It's very simple."

"He's not bluffing," Hatch said, struggling to get to his feet. "He's been ordered to protect Anthony DiFilippo, and to use deadly force if necessary."

"Don't be stupid," Taylor said to the hunter. "It's over."

The hunter took in a deep cleansing breath, then slowly let it out.

"One . . . two . . ."

Before Gray Taylor got to three, a tongue of fire leapt from the sniper rifle's muzzle. There was an audible *clack* as a single .762 round exploded out of the twenty-six-inch-long barrel. A willowy puff of dirty smoke drifted languidly from the sound suppressor, and the steel-encased bullet found a target on the far side of Mulberry Street.

The hunter released his weapon, laid his head on his arms, and began to sob.

Taylor pressed his pistol to the hunter's head.

"Gray! No!" Hatch shouted. "Don't!"

Taylor hesitated for an instant, grumbled something unintelligible, then shoved his gun back into his shoulder rig. He grabbed the hunter's M40A3 semi-automatic and tossed the weapon into the middle of the roof. The Smith & Wesson handgun followed.

"What's happening down there?" Hatch said, finally managing to get to his feet.

Both Hatch and Taylor now stood at the edge of the roof, staring across the residential neighborhood. The scene remained pretty much unchanged outside the Ravenite Social Club. The media still crowded the sidewalk, plainclothes cops continued to yell at a few obnoxious pedestrians, and Anthony DiFilippo IV slipped into the BMW's backseat. Unharmed. Marco was behind the wheel, dragging his seatbelt over his thick body. B. J. Butera was engaged in a spirited conversation with an attractive NBC news reporter.

"A miss?" Hatch said in amazement, glancing over at Taylor.

Taylor pointed. "Looks like the ABC van has a flat tire. Left rear." He pulled out his BlackBerry, thumbed 9 and *send*, then walked to the far end of the building for privacy. "Sir, are you okay?"

"Only if I make Donald's service," Tony D said. "We're just about to leave the club, but the road is filled with a bunch of lunatics trying to get my picture for some ridiculous reason. I think I know how Elvis must have felt. And I hate it." A pause. "Where are you? Ten minutes ago, you were supposedly a block away."

"Sir, we got our man."

"It's over?" There was genuine relief and surprise in Tony D's voice.

While Mulberry Street remained clogged, Taylor quickly explained what had transpired on the rooftop across the street from the Ravenite. "I'll have Mrs. DiFilippo driven over to St. Andrew's for the funeral."

Marco leaned on the BMW's horn. A brown truck with the label "BEEKEE BROTHERS MOVING AND STORAGE" blocked the way.

Hand pressed to his shoulder, Hatch took a knee next to the hunter. "What's your name?"

As he gathered himself, and peeled off the balaclava, the hunter's long red hair tumbled to his shoulders. He sighed audibly and dropped his black hood onto the tarpaulin. "You were right, Kevin," he said quietly, dragging his sleeve beneath his runny nose.

"About what?"

"Patty would be ashamed of me."

Hatch didn't turn away from the hunter's grotesque scars and lumpy pink flesh—definitely the result of a fiery accident—that covered much of the man's right cheek, ear, nose, and neck. Nor did he stare. *I've seen you before.*

"I wanted your friend to kill me," the hunter said. "I want to die."

Hatch rested a reassuring hand on the man's left shoulder and said, "Are you going to tell me your name?"

Turning his head, the hunter made eye contact with Hatch. "Brian," he said. "Brian McGowan."

And then it came to Hatch—this was the fire inspector he'd seen at the Louis Ciambella crime scene. "I know exactly how you feel, Brian. I wanted to die, too."

Though his brown eyes were filled with tears, deep sadness, and regret, McGowan pinched off a smile. "We could have been friends, Hatch."

"Yeah."

McGowan had tried calling Patty that night once he'd found a suitable substitute for the Cajun Moon roses—most stores were closed by then. He was finally going to meet Karen Easter and wanted desperately to make a good first impression. And then there was traffic on the expressway. Gridlock. A cop had answered Patty's cell phone.

"I got to Rudy's Tavern around two in the morning. They'd removed the bodies by then. I watched from a distance, sitting on the curb, blaming myself. I tossed those fucking flowers in the gutter."

Hatch remained quiet.

"After the numbness wore off, I was filled with this uncontrollable anger," McGowan said, "worse than anything I'd experienced in Iraq or Afghanistan. And it was at that moment I decided I was going to get my lump of flesh—one way or another."

"I've been there," Hatch said, wiping his lips. "If my grandfather hadn't been there for me . . ." His words trailed off.

"God, I can't tell you how much I miss her." McGowan bit down on his lower lip, and his entire face began to quiver. "Patty taught me how to breathe again—after my accident and divorce . . ."

Tears ran down Hatch's cheeks and silently dropped onto his jeans.

"Hatch, I called nine-one-one," Taylor said. "They're sending an ambulance."

"Thanks."

Marco was now out of the don's BMW. Arms flailing, he yelled something in Italian at the driver of the Beekee Brothers Moving and Storage truck. A black man with long dreadlocks, wearing a leather coat that touched the top of his boots, exited the vehicle. Both drivers shouted at each other, meeting in the middle of the street, their faces only inches apart, like boxers at a pre-bout weigh-in. The media and onlookers, sensing a brawl, pressed forward for a better line of sight.

One of the teenage boys yelled, "Hit 'im, ya wimp!"

Tony D pushed open the luxury car's back door and stepped onto the street.

From the west, a distant siren wailed.

Back on the roof, Brian McGowan pointed to his own chest and said, "Patty was one of those rare individuals who looked past my disfigurement and saw me for what—"

Suddenly, a single rifle shot echoed off the buildings. People began to scream. Crouching, Kevin Easter, Gray Taylor, and McGowan looked down at the surreal scene. Onlookers who'd come to get a glimpse of Tony D ran in every direction. Some took refuge behind stopped vehicles and some huddled in doorways, while others lay prone on the sidewalk and street. Even the media scurried for cover, having forgotten their jobs. An NBC camera that had been mounted on a tripod lay in a half dozen pieces.

A second gunshot never came.

"Oh . . . shit," Hatch breathed, pointing to the rear of the green BMW.

"No," Taylor said, leaning forward.

Anthony DiFilippo IV lay crumpled in the street, unconscious, a pool of blood spreading on the pavement near his scalp.

CHAPTER 54

Brooklyn

The rented Ford Taurus came to a stop in a deserted Coney Island lot near a boarded-up concession stand about two hundred yards from Long Island Sound.

Katherine Montroy shifted the transmission into park and turned off the ignition. It was blessedly quiet inside the car—a welcome relief. This morning, the New York Police Department had officially put her on paid administrative leave. An internal investigation would take place over the next few months. Katherine's conduct near Fordham University was being questioned. Matthew Philips, her partner, had been murdered in broad daylight. A cop killer was still at large. There were murmurs of bribes taken from Anthony DiFilippo's organization. When had they begun? Who exactly was involved? Was it over now that Tony D was out of the picture?

Katherine's photograph with the infamous Mafia don, right there on the front page of *The New York Post*, could not be explained away. She'd put the NYPD in an embarrassing situation. There she was, in black and white, delivering the goddamned envelope to Tony D.

Montroy had walked through the Twenty-Eighth Precinct with a small cardboard box—personal items she'd retrieved from her desk—about an hour ago. It had been a humiliating experience. There were furtive glances, disappointed expressions, subtle shakes of the head, and hushed whispers from colleagues who had once respected and admired her. Some had been good friends. Not a single person offered support. She'd lost their trust.

Even if an internal investigation cleared her of any wrongdoing, Katherine Montroy's life as a New York City homicide detective was over. According to Montroy's lawyer, there was a strong possibility she could be charged with multiple counts of conspiracy to commit murder. No way in hell she'd drag Tracy through such a public ordeal.

Coney Island was where she had handed over copies of the classified information that had ultimately led to the murders of five Akrho Pinoy gang members. It seemed like a fitting place to stop the car. It was like returning to the scene of her crime.

Montroy stared out at the two-foot breakers. It was an unseasonably warm day for early December, and the late morning sun was high over the water. Dozens of seagulls scavenged on the deserted beach. A large black crow was perched on a utility pole, its face pressed into the salty wind.

Having made the difficult decision the night before, Katherine Montroy dropped her chin to her chest and began to cry.

Her 9mm SIG Sauer P229 sat on the passenger seat.

Manhattan

The handwritten letter explained why B. J. hadn't heard from Brian McGowan in more than a week. And if the note was legitimate—B. J. had first considered it some kind of ridiculous practical joke—there was a very strong possibility he'd never see his friend again.

A third call to Brian's cell phone went directly to voicemail.

Sitting alone in his cubicle, the noises from the newsroom muted, B. J. remembered all the revealing conversations and the sensitive information he'd received from Brian. Once it was laid out, everything made disturbing sense.

Tugging nervously on his lower lip, B. J. was again drawn to the first six sentences from McGowan's note.

I suspect this will come across as a cliché, but that's why you're the writer, B. J.

If you're reading this letter, I'm either dead, under arrest for multiple murders, or a fugitive. I'm sorry I deceived you. What you do with this confession is your decision. You deserve to know the truth about me.

By the way, you really were a great point guard.

In three more succinct paragraphs, Brian McGowan admitted to being a vigilante in New York City. He wanted to destroy Anthony DiFilippo IV. He had acted alone. The U.S. military had trained him well. Patricia Durante's murder at Rudy's Tavern back in August had been the motivation behind his revenge.

"Jesus Christ," B. J. murmured again, glancing uneasily over at Howard Stapleton's open door. "Jesus fucking Christ."

CHAPTER 55

Charlottesville

Monday morning, a week before Christmas, Charlottesville-Albemarle Airport, located about ninety miles southwest of Washington, D.C. was especially busy. Business travelers buried their faces in laptops, newspapers, or magazines. Others talked on their cell phones while parents guided their children through passengers milling about the small terminal. Some, sipping drinks from paper cups, stared at flat-screen televisions bolted to the walls in each of the departure areas. CNN was now running a piece on New York City mob boss Anthony DiFilippo, his recent throat surgery, and murmurs of a grand jury indictment.

Although Kevin Easter, waiting patiently in the departure area for his Delta Connection flight to Dulles Airport, couldn't hear the reporter on the television screen, he knew the blond woman was standing outside Manhattan's Sloan-Kettering Hospital, a world-renowned cancer research facility recognized for its cutting-edge treatments. Anthony DiFilippo had survived the attempt on his life three weeks ago thanks to Kevlar body armor, his only injury sustained when his head struck the pavement. Lawrence Luther Wright was considered a person of interest in the assassination attempt, though a number of eyewitnesses recounted that the alleged drug distributor was attending a service at Our Lady of Sorrows Church at the time of the shooting. The investigation was ongoing.

Shortly after the brazen attack outside the Ravenite Social Club, Tony D and his organization came under intense scrutiny from a far different adversary. This formidable foe was a very aggressive district attorney from Manhattan who, according to *The New York Post*, had his eyes set on the governor's mansion. Bringing down DiFilippo would go a long way toward launching the DA's campaign.

"According to a hospital spokesman," the CNN reporter said, "Anthony DiFilippo's throat surgery, to remove a benign tumor was successful. As for the alleged Mafia don's legal issues, indictments could be forthcoming."

Over the airport's public address system, a pleasant-sounding woman announced, "Mr. Kevin Easter, you have a call at the nearest courtesy phone." She repeated the message.

Hatch neatly folded his *USA Today* and checked his phone. No texts and no missed calls. Less than five people knew he was in Charlottesville, VA. Even fewer were aware of the Monday morning flight the CIA had booked to D.C. Only Gray Taylor knew why Hatch had visited central Virginia this weekend—though Hatch was beginning to wonder if that was truly the case.

Hatch got to his feet, tossed his leather jacket over the sling that helped stabilize his broken collarbone, and reached for his backpack.

A couple minutes later, Hatch picked up the orange courtesy phone next to a kiosk filled with breakfast foods, juices, coffee, and pastries. For some strange reason, he remembered the morning Jack Slattery informed him of Karen's murder.

Hatch turned toward the wall and said, "Yes, this is Kevin Easter."

"Am I interrupting anything important, Mr. Easter?" the elderly male voice asked politely. The man sounded like his mouth was filled with loose gravel.

Hatch glanced over his shoulder at the TV. CNN was running some old file footage of Tony D. Dressed in a dark suit, the handsome man with the thick white hair—who looked like a Fortune 500 CEO—was slipping into the back seat of an expensive BMW. "May I ask who this is?" he asked guardedly.

"Tony DiFilippo." He cleared his throat.

Hatch said nothing, though his left hand had tightened into a fist that was now turning a creamy white. He then forced himself to relax.

"You saved my life," Tony D said simply.

"How do you figure?"

"Three weeks ago. Outside the Ravenite. My protective vest would have been no match for Mr. McGowan's sniper's rifle."

"I guess we'll never know."

"I wanted to say thank you," said Tony D.

"Mr. Taylor deserves the credit."

Tony D chuckled. "Funny. That's what he said about you."

"I've been told you'll make a full recovery."

"The only doctor I ever trusted was Marcus Welby, and he's not real," said Tony D. "But this Dr. Brightly woman, she's not so bad." There was a pause. "They're pumping chemicals into my body as we speak, Mr. Easter. I feel like a citizen of Chernobyl. I may even lose my hair, temporarily."

A United Express official announced that Commuter Flight 606 to Cleveland was ready to board.

"Is there anything else?" Hatch asked.

"Yes," Tony D said, then cleared his throat again. "A little over a decade ago,

I started believing that life is about paying for our sins, Mr. Easter. Yin and yang, clean slate, quid pro quo. Do you understand?"

"Not really."

"This lifetime or the next, you get what you deserve," said Tony D. "The idea of burning in hell haunts me, especially as I get older. Maybe that's why I was trying to make a positive difference in my small corner of the world. Maybe I was trying to make amends for all the terrible things I've done. Vincent's murder. Katherine Montroy's suicide."

"How'd you know I was here?"

"I still have a few friends." Tony D's laugh sounded like a rough gurgle. "Imagine that."

"Yeah, imagine that." Hatch turned around, slowly. He studied most of the people shuffling through the concourse and wondered if he'd been followed these past couple of days. *What would be the point?* His gaze moved to the departure area. Flight 1101, from Charlottesville to Dulles, was scheduled to board in about thirty minutes. "Rumor has it the New York State Attorney General and the DA both want you in prison for life."

"They can get in line."

"I believe you were given an ultimatum by some of your handlers: Step down or be charged with five deaths in the Bronx, among other things. Apparently one woman in particular feels you're not worth the trouble anymore."

"Mr. Easter . . . there's something else I need to say to you—something far more important than thank you." The old man's raspy voice had taken on a somber tone. "That's really why I called. Truth is, what I'd like to tell you is long overdue."

"My flight—"

"I want you to know how deeply sorry I am for your loss," said Tony D. "I want you to understand that your wife's death was a horrible accident—the same goes for Patricia Durante." The old man paused as if to collect himself. "So young. So beautiful. Such wasted, unfulfilled lives."

Hatch opened his mouth to say something, then elected to remain quiet, sensing Tony D was not quite finished.

"My deepest regrets, apologies, and prayers are all I can really offer you now, Mr. Easter. I . . . I'm so sorry—"

"Thanks." Hatch pressed his lips together to form a thin bloodless line.

"I don't expect you to forgive me," Tony D went on a moment later. "That's not what this call is about. The loss of a wife can be devastating."

"Why are you doing this?"

"I was hoping that saying 'I'm sorry' out loud would make me feel a little better," said Tony D. "It has not."

Hatch said nothing.

"We both lost family," said Tony D, "people we love and can never replace."

Hatch let out a long sigh, then said, "I heard you and Mrs. DiFilippo have separated."

"The letter Mara received from Mr. McGowan couldn't be ignored. And lying to her, especially on such a critical matter, wasn't an option. Never again. From Mara's perspective, ordering Vincent's murder was an unforgivable offense. Trust is a very frail thing."

"Yes, it is."

"Mr. McGowan succeeded where others could not." There was an emotional hitch in Tony D's voice. "He . . . that man took Mara from me."

"You're still alive, Mr. DiFilippo. And so is your wife. Anything is possible."

"I suppose you're right," said Tony D. "What will happen to Brian McGowan?"

"What do you mean?"

"I've yet to read a single word about his capture in any of the New York papers, or hear his name on the TV news."

"He'll be punished," Hatch said, glancing at his wristwatch. "How, I don't know."

A United Express flight arriving from Philadelphia was announced over the intercom.

"Did you like the flowers, Mr. Easter?"

"I'm not sure what you're talking about."

"Oh, of course you do," Tony D said with a strained chuckle that sounded painful. "You spent Sunday afternoon with your wife. The Cajun Moon roses delivered to her grave were from me—just a very small token of my sympathy."

"They were very beautiful," Hatch said, slowly shaking his head. "I was going to give Taylor the credit."

"You two will make a great team."

"How did you . . ." Hatch caught himself. "Mr. DiFilippo, can I give you some advice?"

"I'd actually welcome it."

"Let the legal process work the way it was intended to work," Hatch said. "If you owe a debt to society, then pay it off in full. Yin and yang. Your words. You might find it easier to sleep at night. Nightmares have a way of catching up to us."

"You're a very smart man."

"And if you do end up in prison, and there's time after you get released, then maybe Mrs. DiFilippo will be waiting for you. Hope is a wonderful thing. Like trust."

"Forgiveness," Tony D said. "That's all I want now."

"Give her time. We all need time. *Dejihnyahta:se' ae.*"

"Meaning?"

"When our paths cross again." Hatch hung up the phone, found his boarding pass, smiled, and headed to his flight.

EPILOGUE

Bahamas (March)

I t was just a few minutes after midnight. Forty-seven-year-old Jeremy Silverstone, longtime fugitive from United States justice, was asleep, his dreaming in its earliest stages when the hard object pressed against his temple.

Silverstone's eyes popped open to see a black-hooded man—lean, average height—standing beside his king-sized bed. Even in the grayish moonlight, the intruder's eyes had a calm, level gaze. Silverstone suspected that how he reacted in the next few moments would determine if he lived or died.

"Get dressed," the lean man in the balaclava ordered.

A pained whisper escaped Silverstone's trembling lips as he tried to distance himself from the silenced pistol and the man holding the weapon. "I have lots of money—"

"Not for long," the lean man said, cutting him off. "We're taking a flight, Jeremy."

"Flight? Where? Where are—are you—are we going?" Silverstone stuttered, realizing now this was not a robbery.

"Back home," said a second masked man, leaning casually on the doorframe. Much bigger than his partner, this second intruder held a silenced automatic weapon in his gloved hand. Both wore brown-and-white camouflage attire, typically used by the military.

"We have a helicopter to make the trip easy on all of us," the lean man said.

"You can't do this!" Silverstone yelled.

"Sure we can," the bigger man said. "Your three bodyguards are all taking a nap, and your security system appears to have malfunctioned."

"You get what you pay for," the lean man said, chuckling.

"You have some unfinished business to attend to," the bigger man said. "Back in New York City."

"What?"

"You know how the saying goes," the lean man said. "If you can make it there, you can make it anywhere. Apparently, you hit a grand slam home run, and then you ran away with the game ball, Jeremy. That's totally uncool."

The hooded intruder standing in the doorway couldn't help but laugh quietly. "Or did you conveniently forget about all the people you screwed over?" he said. "And what about your grieving widow? That's cold."

"Hey. I think she remarried some investment banker two months after Jeremy's death," the lean man said.

"My mistake," the bigger man said. "Out of sight, out of mind, I guess."

"It was probably a rebound thing," the lean man whispered loudly.

"Jesus . . . who—who are you guys?" Silverstone asked.

"I can assure you, Jeremy," the lean man said, "our boss didn't forget about you. Neither did a few of your buddies."

"No!" Silverstone screamed, trying to scurry to the far side of the bed. "Please! Whatever they're paying, I'll give you one hundred times more. Cash. You guys can have anything. Retire. Live anywhere in the world."

"Looks like your PJs will have to do," the lean man said, grabbing hold of Jeremy Silverstone's wrist. He pulled the fugitive back across the bed, then pressed the Derma-Vac needleless injector—it was about the size and shape of a small flashlight—against the ex-financier's exposed throat. There was a brief hiss as the thiopental-ketamine-xylazine cocktail was expelled directly through Silverstone's skin and into his carotid artery. Silverstone's body went slack when the narcotics hit his bloodstream.

"Damn, that shit really works," Kevin Easter said, stripping off his balaclava and shoving it into his pants pocket. The Derma-Vac went into another pocket.

"Think you can carry the boy wonder all by yourself?" Gray Taylor asked.

"Don't be ridiculous, old man. Shit, if this partnership thing works out, I have a funny feeling I'm gonna be carrying you in more ways than one."

"Just don't go complaining about your shoulder, Little Crow," Taylor said. "Three months is plenty of time to heal from that little girly wound of yours."

"Please, can we get on with it?" Hatch said, tossing the unconscious man over his good shoulder. "I have a date tonight."

Taylor removed his own balaclava. "Excuse me?"

"Yep, I met her at physical therapy," Hatch said, pushing through the door and past his partner. "We're going out to see that Johnny Depp movie."

"What?" Taylor was a few paces behind Hatch, walkie-talkie in hand. "So, when were you going to share that information with me?"

"Maybe if you're nice, I'll tell you about her on the flight home."

Taylor spoke into the mike. "Charlie Brown, this is Linus. Do you copy?"

Both CIA field operatives stepped through Jeremy Silverstone's oceanside door, back into a warm Bahamian breeze. Hatch took in a deep cleansing breath, and then slowly let it out. "Damn, it's good to be working again."

"Roger that, Linus," said Charlie Brown, the female voice from the MD-5300 Pave Hawk helicopter. "We're approximately two miles out. Please illuminate LZ for extraction. Do you copy?"

"Roger that," Taylor said.

When they reached the beach, Taylor snapped off three flares, then stuck each into the white sand about thirty feet from each other, forming a large semicircle near the water.

Hatch gently laid Silverstone's limp body in a chaise lounge.

"We have your position, Linus," the woman in the helicopter said. "Stand by."

A quarter moon sat low in the southern sky. In the distance, Kevin Easter and Gray Taylor could see a black shape, like an airborne bug, growing larger by the second, moving stealthily over the calm water.

"You have a date?" Taylor said, spreading his hands.

"Yep."

"Does this lady friend of yours have a name?"

"Annie," Hatch said, his voice getting louder as the helicopter swept in and the rotor wash kicked up sand and debris around them. He covered his eyes and shouted, "Annie McCall!"

Taylor cupped his hand to his mouth and yelled, "Am I allowed to break the news to Terri when we get back?"

Hatch grinned. "Way ahead of you, brother. I told her last week."

"Always full of surprises," Taylor said, shaking his head. "Should make for an interesting partnership."

ACKNOWLEDGMENTS

The Samaritan benefited enormously from scores of talented people who guided me through the writing process and beyond. What initially began as a solitary endeavor quickly evolved into a team effort.

Special thanks to Harrison Demchick, a gifted editor and extraordinarily patient gentleman, who not only did most of the heavy editorial lifting but taught me to be a better writer. Thanks also to Vicki Rohl and Adam Marsh, who routinely dropped everything in their lives to read, review, and fix another updated manuscript; and Jim Lalley, Geri Moog, Peggy Quinn, Rick Ohler, Barbara Dolan, Stephen Hurtubise, George Nedeff, John Maloney, Joe and Georgette Plukas, and Amy Kimmel for reading early drafts and offering assistance, insight, and much needed direction. Thank you to Bill Thompson, former Doubleday editor, for his wisdom, continuous support, encouragement, and friendship.

Thanks to retired Congressman Jack Quinn for his view of the DEA and the United States intelligence agencies; attorney Anthony DiFilippo IV; Michael Bastine and Mad Bear, for their insight into Native American heritage, specifically the Seneca Nation of Indians; Brendan Deneen; Bob McCarthy, columnist for *The Buffalo News*; Earl "Bud" Besecker, retired parole board member at the Attica Correctional Facility; Arthur "Deke" Buchanan, retired U.S. Navy, for his view of the military in general and the CIA in particular; Euell Tritt for his expertise on weapons; Richard Plukas for clarifying the United States Constitution; and the wonderful employees at the Orchard Park Library and East Aurora Library. Thanks to Mark Palascak, Carol Jason Nigrelli, Judy Loesch Holden, Cindy Higby, and Chris Webb for marketing and promotion advice; and to Orchard Park policeman Patrick McLaughlin. Samantha Newland, Michelle Zurowski, Pete Viger, Doug Ford, Kateri Ewing, and Kevin Besecker deserve thanks for their technical support. And thanks to Bruce Bortz, who put everything together at Bancroft Press.

Finally, thanks to the International Thriller Writer's Association, ASJA, and their community of supportive writers, along with bestselling authors James Rollins, Andrew Gross, Brian Haig, Joseph Finder, Gregg Hurwitz, Brad Meltzer, Harlan Coben, James Grippando, Andy Harp, and Brad Parks, for sharing their writing and life experiences.

ABOUT THE AUTHOR

S Stephen Besecker is a graduate of Orchard Park High School (Orchard Park, NY) and St. Bonaventure University. He was born in Somersworth, NH, grew up in East Aurora, NY, and lived briefly in Palos Park, Illinois, before his family settled south of Buffalo.

Like many young boys growing up in Western New York, Steve had every intention of becoming a professional hockey player, setting his sights on the National Hockey League and the Buffalo Sabres. Nevertheless, at the ripe age of fifteen, Steve realized that his hockey talent did not measure up to his passion for the sport. The professors and Franciscan community at St. Bonaventure University open Steve's eyes to a far broader world. He received a degree in Marketing Management, while also earning the distinction of being assistant captain of St. Bonaventure's varsity hockey team.

An avid fly-fisherman, skier, hockey player, and youth soccer coach, Steve also enjoys skiing, hiking, snow shoeing, and biking.

Steve's an active member of both the International Thriller Writer's Association, Inc. and the American Society of Journalists and Authors.

Steve lives in Western New York, and is presently writing another thriller that includes Kevin "Hatch" Easter, Gray Taylor, and many of the characters from *The Samaritan*.